Infiltration

DAVID GLEDHILL

Copyright © 2017 David Gledhill

All rights reserved.

ISBN:9781520919133

CONTENTS

	Prologue .	1
1	The Wash Aerial Training Area.	6
2	RAF Coningsby, Lincolnshire.	11
3	The North Sea off Norfolk.	14
4	The Soviet Embassy, London.	20
5	Off the Western Coast of Scotland.	25
6	On an Inter City 125 Train. Approaching Carlisle.	30
7	RAF Coningsby, Echo Dispersal.	32
8	UK Air Defence Operations Centre, RAF High Wycombe, Buckinghamshire.	36
9	Low Flying Area 10 North of RAF Coningsby.	59
10	Benbecula in the Scottish Islands.	63
11	Machrihanish Airfield, The Mull of Kintyre, Scotland. The next day.	67
12	Machrihanish Airfield.	73
13	The Ugadale Hotel, Cambletown.	76
14	Two Hours Earlier, the Main Runway, RAF Machrihanish.	79
15	The Ugadale Hotel, Cambletown	89
16	Aboard the Soviet Research Ship off the West Coast of Scotland.	94
17	The Phantom Detachment, RAF Machrihanish.	100
18	The Soviet Embassy, London.	109
19	The Briefing Room, RAF Machrihanish	112
20	Aboard the Soviet Aircraft Carrier Kiev.	114

21	United States Naval Weapons Facility RAF Machrihanish.	131
22	The Aircraft Servicing Platform, RAF Leuchars, Fife.	133
23	The Flight Line, RAF Machrihanish.	139
24	UK Air Defence Operations Centre, RAF High Wycombe.	152
25	Aboard the Aircraft Carrier Kiev.	157
26	Northern Fleet Headquarters, Murmansk, the Soviet Union.	162
27	Off the Scottish Coast.	165
28	In the Iceland-Faeroes Gap.	169
29	The Air Defence Operations Centre, RAF High Wycombe.	172
30	The Soviet Task Force Off Scotland.	175
31	Off Benbecula	187
32	West of Stornoway in the Outer Hebrides.	202
33	Below the Waters of the Firth of Clyde.	220
34	The Air Defence Operations Centre, High Wycombe.	224
35	Aboard the Aircraft Carrier Kiev.	226
36	The Flight Deck aboard the Kiev	229
37	The Air Defence Operations Centre, RAF High Wycombe	233
38	Off Benbecula.	236
39	The Air Defence Operations Centre, High Wycombe.	247
40	The Soviet Embassy, London.	250
41	The Ugadale Hotel, Cambletown.	253
42	The Island Air Taxis Office, Machrihanish Airfield.	256
43	The Communications Room aboard The Kiev.	259

44	Headquarters Strike Command, RAF High Wycombe.	261
45	Holy Loch Naval Base, Faslane, two weeks later.	265
	Glossary	272
	Author's Note	276
	About the Author	279
	Other books by this Author	280

PROLOGUE

The Iceland-Faeroes Gap, 1986.

The Captain of the nuclear-powered ballistic missile submarine, HMS Renown studied the gently rippling bow wave as the black hull slipped effortlessly through the murky waters of Holy Loch, its three month patrol barely a few minutes old. At the stern, the massive screws generated barely a ripple, a feat of engineering that would mask its passage once it entered its natural environment under the waves. The merest hint of noise would cue sensitive sensors and broadcast its location to hostile listeners once it emerged into the Atlantic Ocean. Predators which lurked in the cold waters to the west might eavesdrop, eager to follow. Thankfully, the temporary disturbance would cease the moment the submarine dipped below the surface, its short transit on the surface indiscernible.

Dressed for the chill of the morning, he savoured his last breaths of fresh air, the tranquillity of the Scottish countryside etching an image he would recall more than once during the coming months. Ahead lay the challenges of a routine patrol; perhaps routine to him but unthinkable to most because aft in the weapons bay lay sixteen Polaris intercontinental ballistic missiles, dormant but primed. His relentless training over many years in the "Silent Service" coupled with his utter loyalty would ensure that he would contribute to Armageddon if called upon.

Just off the coast of Northern Ireland where the channel between the province and the Scottish mainland widened into the Atlantic Ocean, a new Soviet Sierra-class attack submarine, Karp, lay in wait its Captain hoping to latch onto the "boomer" as it made its way into the deep Atlantic waters. Too nervous to enter the confined sea lanes of the Firth of Clyde, he lay, silently, outside British territorial waters hoping for the chance detection which would earn accolades on his return to Murmansk. As with most Cold War cat-and-mouse games, he would be disappointed.

Passing the Isle of Arran, the British nuclear submarine turned southerly threading its way down the Irish Sea amongst the trawlers and car ferries. It would take longer to reach the patrol area via this route but the Captain was in no hurry. His briefing that morning had warned of the visitor, detected by the ring of sensors in the waters off the coast known as SOSUS, an acronym for sound surveillance system, a clandestine monitoring network designed to track Soviet submarines. He had no intention of conferring hero status to his opponent. Equally, he had no intention of being the first captain of a "boomer" to be tracked during its mission. Once he reached his patrol depth he was confident in his ability to remain undetected.

To the northeast another Soviet submarine was making headway. The new Akula-class nuclear-powered attack submarine, known as "Bars" or "Snow Leopard", was completing its sea trials ready for its first operational deployment later in the year. Its mission was also sensitive, to assume station in a designated box off Rockall where it would position to attack an older Foxtrot-class attack submarine whilst avoiding detection by a Tupolev Tu-142 "Bear Foxtrot" maritime patrol aircraft which was already heading into the operational area. If the Akula Captain passed this evaluation, his vessel would be declared operational and assume the mantle of monitoring the NATO nuclear submarine fleet. Already he had been harried by a Nimrod maritime patrol aircraft flying from its base at Kinloss in Morayshire. Although he had defied attempts to pin him down, it had been impossible to remain undetected once the pattern of sonar buoys had bracketed his course forcing him into shallow water where he was more predictable. He could only hope that evidence of the encounter would not get back to the ears of his military commander in Murmansk. It seemed inevitable that the acoustic signature of his new submarine had been compromised during the incident and would soon be added to the NATO database; an unpalatable reality. Giving away such vital intelligence meant that during future encounters with NATO forces the new submarine would be more easily identified. With its fuel tanks depleted and the crew elated, the Nimrod maritime surveillance aircraft had returned to base to file the post mission report. Soon, the name Akula, would be whispered in the corridors of the Old War Office on Whitehall setting in train new requests for technology upgrades.

With the start time for the exercise approaching the encounter had left the Captain little time to prepare for the real test he had been set.

*

Rounding North Cape at the northerly extremities of the Norwegian coastline, the Tupolev Tu-142 "Bear Foxtrot" had been tracked by ground based radars on the mainland, its progress monitored for the last three hours. Norwegian fighter controllers based at the Control and Reporting Centre at Magero were vectoring the F-16s at Bodø airbase to intercept the intruders. A listening post on the coast had already detected emissions from the "Wet Eye" radar identifying the Bear and hinting at its mission. If it turned south westerly into the Iceland-Faeroes Gap, the fighters could stay alongside for some time but if it pressed on westwards the controller would make an initial intercept and alert the USAF crews of the 57th Fighter Interceptor Squadron based at Keflavik in Iceland who would take over. With its limited range, the F-16s fuel tanks would quickly be exhausted and, with unpredictable weather forecast for the bases along the westerly Norwegian coastline, prudence was the order of the day.

In the event, the Soviet captain in the cockpit of the Bear made the decision easy. Hugging the coastline just outside Norwegian airspace he turned towards the Faroe Islands maintaining his altitude, his course easily visible on the radar screens in the darkened bunkers below. The turn caused a chain reaction. With the F-16 already airborne and vectoring towards the Bear, crews at the RAF fighter base at Leuchars in Eastern Scotland were called to cockpit readiness at the same time as the frustrated crews in the alert facility at Keflavik were stood down. The British Phantoms would stand ready to launch at the optimum time to shadow the Bear as it headed towards its operational area in the vast UK Air Defence Region.

*

The pilot could not fail to be impressed as he drew his F-16 alongside the

INFILTRATION

Bear, the noise from its eight contra-rotating propellers vibrating the canopy of his fighter jet. The burnished aluminium skin glinted in the morning sunlight, the red star bright on the tail fin. Positioning on the left in easy sight of the Soviet pilot he engaged the autopilot dragging a small camera from a housing on the console. Easing the stick over to check the drift towards the huge aircraft he brought the camera to his eye, the movement causing a jolt as he banged his oxygen mask. Irritated, he dropped the mask to position the camera nearer to his face and, framing the massive bulk of the Soviet airframe, he snapped off a few shots before easing in closer using a gentle pressure to override the automatics. He would capture a few details on his kneepad to keep the intelligence analysts happy before returning to a more relaxed formation position. New blisters seemed to appear on the Bear with regular monotony and his pictures would be scrutinised in great detail to establish whether extra sensors had been fitted since this airframe, door number 27, had last visited NATO airspace. The camera shutter clicked away. As he peered through the tiny eyepiece he failed to spot the imperceptible drift towards the massive aircraft alongside despite the beat of the massive turboprops vibrating the airframe. He crept indiscernibly nearer, the closure masked by the imposing image of the Bear through the camera lens. He would never know if his sixth sense saved him but, suddenly, he moved the camera away and reacted instinctively, hauling the stick over, avoiding a collision by the narrowest margin. In any other aircraft a collision would have been inevitable but the stubby wings of the F-16, even with missiles strapped to the wingtips, passed beneath the contra-rotating propellers barely clearing the screaming discs. The bulk of the Bear loomed overhead as he pushed hard to increase the separation and, suddenly, he was in clear air once again, his heart pumping frantically.

Lingering alongside, the antagonism from the Soviet cockpit was almost palpable and concerned faces watched intently from windows and blisters around the airframe. Conscious of his narrow escape, he busied himself as if to divert attention from his error. Making a few scribbled notes on his kneeboard, capturing the door number and checking his position relative to the Bodø TACAN radio beacon, he slowly relaxed, his pulse returning to normal, his task nearly over. Despite his mistake, he would stay alongside until the controller cleared him to return or his fuel gauge told him otherwise. Nevertheless, he was ready to go home. It had been too close.

Scrambled in support, the British Phantom checked in on frequency and, after a brief greeting, the F-16 pilot peeled off and pointed his nose at Bodø airfield, lying just inside the Arctic Circle, many miles to the northeast. He would eke out the fuel by staying at high level where his jet engine was more frugal. Once within 20 miles of his base he would initiate recovery through the gathering clouds to make an approach to the snow covered runway. Once again he was nervous. With few diversions in the northern extremes he had few options if the weather fell below limits. He had cheated the odds once today and had no desire to press his luck.

*

In the south western approaches off Cornwall the "boomer" slipped below the inversion layer offering even greater anonymity. With the layer of warmer water above masking its passage the crew relaxed, dropping into a well rehearsed routine, checking systems, priming weapons and stowing gear. Six months in the gloomy depths beckoned and it was best to establish order at the earliest opportunity.

They would never know that their covert departure had set events in motion that would affect many people's lives.

CHAPTER 1

The Wash Aerial Training Area.

Mark "Razor" Keene glanced down at the fuel gauge.

"Eight Two over Ten Six," he called to his navigator, John "Toppers" Topman, as he squinted at the tiny gauge through his dark visor. He was using internal fuel now and it would not be long before he reached fuel minimums.

"One more split and we'll take it home."

"Roger that," he heard in response as he transferred his attention back to the other F-4 Phantom perched in fighting wing formation alongside, the sun glinting off the canopy. Razor had been back from Germany for some time now and he was rapidly becoming one of the more senior pilots on the Squadron with over 1000 hours on the Phantom he piloted. Today he was taking a new pilot through his first look at air combat on the Squadron.

"Outwards turn for combat, Go!"

The other Phantom flashed an impressive planform as it racked into a turn, separating from its leader, steadying up on a diverging heading. Razor mentally counted off the seconds as his wingman drifted towards the limits of visual range. If either he or his navigator lost sight at this stage it was game over. That would not do for a newly qualified air combat leader. If he did, the other crew would be into a missile firing position in seconds and he would be explaining his error at the debrief. At a combined closing speed of

1,000 knots, combat splits were over quickly.

"Inwards turn, Go!" he barked momentarily pressing the transmit button on the throttles and, simultaneously, hauling the nose back towards the tiny dot in the distance. As the air combat leader he set the rules during the set up phase for the air combat profile. It was a minor advantage but once he unleashed his opponent it was every man for himself.

"Go heads-in," he called to his back-seater. "Five right, 3 miles, level."

The calls would allow the navigator to acquire the opponent on the radar and if he was sharp, he would take a radar lock in time to loose off a Skyflash missile before they infringed the minimum separation bubble; the invisible safety zone around their opponent. The margin between turn-in and closing inside the minimum range for the missile was tight and it would take some snappy work in the back to succeed.

"No lock," he heard, the frustration evident in his navigator's tone. He was not surprised at the response. Time was short and it was a one-off opportunity. Toppers was new to the game and air combat was bewildering at first. The failure was excusable.

"Come heads out," he responded. "One o'clock, range two miles. Putting him down the right."

He knew that in the back seat his navigator would be twisting his body, bracing himself against the grab bars, ready to keep sight of the opponent as the two jets merged. He peered at the rapidly expanding Phantom in the front windscreen, the familiar profile growing. The smoke plume suddenly disappeared, a sure sign that his opponent had selected afterburner and might already have a speed advantage. If he had listened to the briefings, his simulated foe, a new first tourist pilot just arrived on the Squadron, would take the fight into the vertical at the pass. A flat fight, even against another Phantom, was a quick route to defeat.

"Tally Ho," he heard from the back signalling that his navigator had regained visual contact on the "bogey". He relaxed a little. As the two jets flashed past only feet apart he pulled hard right into a climbing, arcing turn listening to the disembodied commentary from the back seat. He lost contact as he initiated the pull but that was not uncommon. Not being constrained by the need to grip the control column, his navigator would be screwed around on his ejection seat, his head at an impossible angle, trying hard to maintain sight of the opponent as it manoeuvred. It was not so easy in the front as he struggled to keep control of the heavy fighter.

"He's pulling up and turning towards. Four o'clock, range one mile. Keep the turn going," he heard in his headset. Toppers was learning fast.

Razor felt the g building and, instinctively, checked the G Meter registering the debilitating pull. It showed a steady 6 *g*. His peripheral vision narrowed and dimmed slightly. Both jets climbed rapidly, the altimeters winding up as each pilot sought to take a height advantage at the high point of the loop. It was Razor who made the first gain as his opponent passed just below, his nose beginning to pull back earthwards. With the speed reducing at the apex and the angle of attack pegged at the limit, Razor held the control column central and kicked in a boot full of rudder slewing the nose around, his eyes once again tracking his opponent's every move. At slow speed and in this regime, the Phantom could bite. The other Phantom's nose was buried. Although that made it predictable, it also meant that he had much more energy than Razor and, for that reason and for a split second, the other pilot had more options. With the nose coming down he smashed the throttles to the firewall and received a satisfying kick from the Rolls Royce Spey engines behind him as the reheats lit up. The speed increased instantly and, once again he pulled to maximum G. As his own nose came down he dragged the throttles back to idle to prevent the speed building too rapidly.

At that instant there was a massive thump from the airframe closely followed by a blaring claxon in his helmet and warning captions began to flash urgently. He looked down at the telelight panel to be greeted by an array of red and yellow warning lights. The barrage was bad news. Instinct kicked in. He jabbed the flashing "Master Caution" caption extinguishing the warning tone. The red warning light on the telelight panel glared back.

"Stop, Stop, Stop. Buzzard formation roll out west. Buzzard One has a problem, stand by."

The expletive he heard from the back presaged worse news.

"We've lost the port outer wing."

Stunned, he grappled with the implications and, more importantly, the consequences. The massive failure was not unknown and in the late 1970s a Phantom had crashed under similar circumstances. Modification programmes had, supposedly, strengthened the wing lock mechanism but, obviously, not well enough. Staring down the wing line, the familiar upwards-canted wingtip was missing, the remaining wing worryingly short. His reverie was broken by another strident alarm tone.

"The utilities have dropped to zero, carrying out the bold face drills," he called to his navigator as his hands moved swiftly, flicking switches in a pre-ordained pattern.

"Getting out the cards," he heard in response. "It looks like the flaps are damaged on that side. The leading edge flap on the main wing is missing. That's not good."

Razor could feel the effect of the catastrophic failure through the controls. The utilities powered a number of essential hydraulically powered services and the jet had become sluggish. Between them, they began the well rehearsed drill that they had practised so many times in the mission simulator. The Phantom, by now complaining as it slowed down, was responding badly. Razor allowed himself a certain amount of optimism as the reluctant airframe should still be flyable. At least it was so far. His confidence was short-lived.

"PC One is dropping. Tighten your straps."

The PC systems which drove the primary flying controls, were crucial to maintaining control. Although he had two systems this was not good. He struggled to assimilate the implications of the massive failure and its effect on his jet, sensing the frantic preparations in the back seat, all thoughts of gaining an advantage in air combat shelved. Unless they tackled this new problem life would take an unanticipated turn. They were now down to one hydraulic system powering the controls and keeping them airborne.

"I'm monitoring PC Two."

Without primary flying controls the Phantom would be uncontrollable and the advice in the flight reference cards was stark: "Confirm; if control is lost, eject."

"PC 2 is dropping, stand by to eject."

This should not be happening. Loss of an outer wing on one side should not affect the other flying control system. He racked his brain for an explanation. Both gauges dropped rapidly towards zero heralding a stiffening of the flight controls. It had been only seconds since the first warning tone. The decision was inevitable.

"Eject, eject, eject."

The aircraft flicked violently.

There was no time to adjust his own posture or to tighten his straps, still slightly loose, eased off for the air combat exercise. He grasped the seat pan handle and pulled hard, the handle coming free of its housing instantly and moving upwards towards his chest. There was a loud crack as the first of the explosive charges at the rear of the seat fired and the front canopy separated, torn free by the airflow. A sudden and violent wind blast assailed his exposed torso. The seconds passed like hours before the ejection seat began to rise up the rails and, as he felt his head forced down towards his lap under the immense g, he blacked out.

CHAPTER 2

RAF Coningsby, Lincolnshire.

"Triplex, Buzzard 2."

"Buzzard 2, Triplex, go ahead."

The transmission was distorted and chopped, the voice stressed.

"Triplex this is Buzzard 2, Buzzard 1 has ejected. I'm holding in the overhead acting as MAYDAY relay. Working Neatishead on Fighter Stud 234. SAROPS declared. Going back to tactical."

From his comfortable seat at the Squadron operations desk, the stark words jolted the Duty Authoriser into action and his hands flashed towards the minicomms panel in front of him. The key word which triggered his instinctive response was MAYDAY. His first call was to the Squadron Commander to give him the devastating news. His second was to check the tote to identify which crew was involved. At this stage he had no idea whether they were alive or dead. The warning from the wingman had been short but at least it might allow him to stay ahead of events which would escalate rapidly as news of the ejection got out. It would be impossible to contain but his first duty was to control the leaks until he could understand better what had occurred and, more importantly, whether the crew had survived. Within seconds, the Boss burst into the operations room his eyes scanning the flying programme.

"Buzzard 1; that's Razor and Toppers, confirm?"

Staccato; concerned.

"Yes Boss, They were leading a one v. one air combat sortie out in the Wash training area under Neatishead control. I don't have much to go on yet just a quick call from Buzzard 2 in the overhead."

"Did they get out?"

"I don't know Boss, I'm just about to check with the Master Controller at Neatishead."

They both experienced that feeling of dread; the cold clammy grip of nausea. It was everyone's worst nightmare. The routine sortie gone bad from which their friends might not return. Picking up the phone he dialled the Sector Operations Centre in Norfolk. It would be hectic at the other end of the line as the controller struggled to coordinate events but, as the operating authority for the stricken Phantom, the Duty Authoriser needed that vital information which, at present, only the controller could know.

"Master Controller, stand by."

The voice on the other end was gruff and harassed. The minutes after an ejection were mayhem. He tapped his fingers nervously, the static on the line hissing annoyingly in the background, the gist of a heated discussion evident in the background. The same voice came back on the line.

"Master Controller."

"Jim, it's Rick on the desk at 29 Squadron. Buzzard 2 has just called in that Buzzard 1 is down; can you confirm?"

"Affirmative. He ejected 10 miles north of Blakeney Point in the middle of an air combat split. I was just about to call. There was no warning just a routine radio call before the emergency squawk came up. We've located the position and scrambled search and rescue. A Sea King from Coltishall is on its way to the crash site now."

"Did Buzzard 2 see any sign of 'chutes?"

The call seemed harsh but it was the most important piece of information at this stage and the answer would dictate how events unfolded over the next hour. The green-clad navigator steeled himself for the response, dreading a negative answer.

An extended pause.

"Affirmative, Buzzard 2 reports two 'chutes seen. He has both in sight and he's talking to the Sea King pilot now."

"Thank God," he muttered under his breath giving the harassed Squadron Commander a thumbs up. "Roger that. I'll leave you to it. Let me know when the guys are onboard the helicopter."

He replaced the receiver wiping the beads of sweat from his forehead.

"They both ejected Boss. Two 'chutes seen. No call yet on their condition."

"OK I'll get on the phone to the Station Commander. Let me know the minute you have anything new."

CHAPTER 3

The North Sea off Norfolk.

Razor came round, the force of the ejection having stunned him briefly. His back ached and the parachute harness was digging painfully into his groin. Looking up at the multi-coloured parachute which had blossomed above him, an overwhelming sense of gratitude pervaded, thankful that he was alive. Apart from the pain in his back, the ejection seemed to have been uneventful, although the rushing wind whistled around his visor that had lowered under the enormous forces exerted during the ejection sequence. He flipped the dark visor upwards wincing at the bright sunlight that assailed his eyes. Fumbling with the oxygen mask, he ripped it clear of his face, the hose still attached to the personal equipment connector which now flailed at his side. The ejection seat which had propelled him, forcefully, from the stricken Phantom had separated and plunged into the forbidding waters of the North Sea below. He fumbled with the quick release fasteners around his backside freeing the bright yellow dinghy pack which dropped away, oscillating on the lanyard which extended some way below him. Forcing himself to run through his descent drills methodically, despite the nagging pain, already his hands clad in the thin leather flying gloves were cold and felt slightly numb. It would be much worse when he hit the sea. Pulling the knobbly black plastic handle on the stole next to his face, he inflated his life jacket ready for water entry prompting the stole to explode into life as the gas from the small cylinder surged into the chamber, inflating the collar around him. The bright dayglo buoyancy chamber emerged from the sea of green around his neck, a visible reassurance that he would float. Reaching down for another toggle, he pulled hard, setting off the personal locator beacon which nestled in one of the pockets of his life jacket. He was sure there must be something else he needed to do but his mind was already slowed by the cold. He scanned the airspace around him searching for another parachute. Please let me see him he thought, hoping that his navigator had followed him from the stricken Phantom. Nothing. He pulled hard on the parachute riser reefing the canopy around scanning the air as he turned. There it was! Off in the distance. He had no idea whether it was north, south, east or west but he could see the orange and white panels of the 'chute some way below him. Pulling again on the riser he pointed his own 'chute towards his navigator hoping to close the distance before he struck the water. As he watched there was a splash and the other canopy collapsed, falling loosely into the water. There was a flurry of splashing before a bright dayglo dinghy emerged on the surface bobbing in the angry waves. A good sign.

He became conscious of the water rushing upwards towards him and, with self preservation foremost, he closed his legs bracing for the impact. He had no desire to add a second source of pain to his problems. He vaguely remembered his parachute instructor telling him to turn into wind to slow the descent and he made a vain attempt before the waves crashed over his head and he plunged into the inky blackness. Submerged, the sea water filled every unprotected orifice and it seemed like an eternity before he broke the surface, the air in his immersion suit acting like a huge balloon, the stole of his life jacket holding his head above the water. The cold was instantly intense. Immediately grasping the lanyard he began to haul the bright yellow survival pack towards him, keen to seek refuge from the icy water. The five metre lanyard seemed to take forever to haul in and, as his grateful hands grasped the fibreglass container, he jockeyed it into position groping for the inflation handle. A quick tug and he was rewarded with an explosion of colour as the dayglo coloured dinghy emerged from its cocoon, the canopy popping upwards above the flotation chamber. He hauled it towards him, flopped over the stern and dragged himself around into a sitting position. Drawing the protective canopy around his shoulders he felt an instant protection from the biting wind and allowed himself to relax a little. The sea anchor stabilised the tiny raft and it settled into a rhythmical bobbing motion.

The second liferaft was only 100 metres away and he could see that his navigator had also boarded his raft. Feeling increasingly confident he began his housekeeping drills, anxious to make his temporary home as snug as possible.

Right!

The small antenna for the emergency beacon was persuaded through the tiny slot in the canopy and he was instantly anxious that its performance needed to be as good as possible. Its feeble, short range transmissions would be the only thing that would pick him out from the vast expanse of heaving waves. Fumbling around in the lifejacket pocket he located the emergency flares which would come in useful once the helicopter arrived on scene. housekeeping complete he settled down to wait.

Suddenly, the calm was split by the sound of jet engines as his wingman roared past only 1000 feet above the tiny dinghy. His spirits soared at the sudden end to his isolation. They were only 10 miles off the coast so the Sea King helicopter should be with them in no time and his wingman could talk the pilot on. With little else to while away the time, he struggled with the small bailer slowly emptying out the sea water which had joined him in the raft. His hands began to recover a little of their warmth and a vague sense of comfort returned. So far so good but his back hurt like hell.

*

The bright yellow Sea King crossed the coastline just east of Blakeney Point and headed out across the choppy waves. A couple walking their dog along the shoreline glanced upwards, the beat of the rotors disturbing the solitude, although they could have no inkling of the drama unfolding just a few miles north.

The pilot adjusted the needles on the small instrument in front of him, refining his approach heading as he homed in on the crash site. In his headset the incessant ping of the distress beacon transmitting on the international distress frequency urged him on. To most it was a harbinger of doom; to him it was routine. His clipped message over the intercom warned the navigator and winchman in the cabin that they had about 10 miles to run.

*

In his raft, Razor heard the throb of the helicopter long before he could see it. Pulling the liferaft canopy from around his shoulders he scanned the waters around him searching for the initial elusive contact. There, low on the horizon he caught the first glimpse of his rescuers. A rush of optimism quelled his incipient sea sickness as he fumbled for the small pack of miniflares, dragging the bright red case from its sanctuary, ripping off the small plastic lid and screwing the flare onto the firing handle. Elevating the flare gun he pulled back the trigger and the bright red distress flare arced into the sky above him following a curved trajectory before dropping back towards the sea. Even after it burned out the pyrotechnic left a trail of smoke which was visible for miles. Worried for the first time at the lack of reaction from the other dinghy which bobbed in the heaving sea a few hundred metres away, Razor returned his attention to the helicopter as it homed in on their position. Its nose reared up just short of the distant dinghy and it settled into a hover the rotors beating the wave tops into a froth.

The body of the dayglo-clad winchman emerged from the doorway and lowered, tentatively, towards the surface, his arm a constant motion urging his hidden colleague in the cabin to extend the winch cable downwards towards the sea. The ungainly pairing edged forward towards its goal and, as the winchman's body landed in the water, his legs spread out like small outriggers to stabilise his motion. There was a temporary lull as his arm became stationary and he edged ever closer to the dinghy, suspended beneath the noisy machine. A final urgent gesture dumped him, unceremoniously, into the water. Above, the cable went slack but the helicopter held its position as the winchman closed the final yards and struggled with the dormant liferaft.

Too far away to register the detail Razor was relieved to see the pair of bodies emerge from the mêlée and move upwards in a gyrating spiral towards the Sea King. He felt a momentary pang of alarm as the helicopter wheeled away before he realised it was merely setting up a new approach towards his own dinghy. He pushed the paraphernalia away from his body freeing himself from the items which, until that moment, had been instruments of survival. Suddenly, they were an encumbrance. Exposed once again to the elements, the biting wind was freezing cold but salvation was close. The ugly yet, unexpectedly, beautiful profile of the helicopter grew bigger as it closed gently on his position, the bright yellow strangely comforting. The winchman, by now back at the end of the cable, repeated the procedure. Only metres away now, Razor could see the rescue strop looped in front of his body. It seemed as if the man was walking across the water as the distance closed and, to Razor, he seemed entirely capable of emulating the Biblical miracle. Just a few metres short and with uncanny precision, he dropped into the water his arms beating the signal. There was a sudden vicious surge as his body collided with the rubber raft the forward momentum not quite checked. Strong arms grabbed the lifters on the canopy and the small craft rocked violently, propelled forward by the momentum. As he had been trained, Razor lay dormant, his arms stretched upwards to allow the strop to be dropped over his head. With the padded strap around his torso and the winchman holding him snug, another upward motion of the flailing arms prompted a lurch skywards and he was airborne once more, suspended from the cable.

Sanctuary was brief. They were unceremoniously dumped back into the water and he watched helpless as the winchman detached his shackle from the winch cable and pulled strongly through the churning waves towards the bobbing liferaft, still attached by a lifeline. A knife appeared in his hand and he stabbed at the black buoyancy chamber which until moments ago had been Razor's salvation. An attack on the bright orange canopy followed and, deprived of its air, the small craft settled low in the water where it would stay until collected by a marine launch later in the day. Returning immediately, the winchman clipped back onto the winch cable, wrapped both legs around Razor's torso, raised both arms and gestured urgently with an upward motion. The two bodies rose from the water spinning violently at the end of the winch, their feet channelling torrents of water back towards the surface.

The doorway loomed in his peripheral vision and Razor was spun around, his back to the door, the icy blast of the rotor blades freezing his body. His hands were once again numb from the cold and combined with the dull ache from his lower back, the product of his ejection, he felt utterly exhausted. The winchman's feet planted firmly on the floor of the cabin and the bedraggled Phantom pilot was forced bodily into the welcoming arms of the helicopter navigator and hauled aboard. Disentangled from the strop he followed an urgent gesture, strapping into the canvas seat at the side of the cabin. It was only then that he saw his own navigator lying on the cabin floor, immobilised on a gurney, his eyes closed, his body motionless. The helicopter crewman edged close prompting Razor to ease his flying helmet away from his ear to hear the shouted words.

"Looks like he took a bad knock during the ejection. Don't worry, we'll get him to hospital as soon as we can."

Razor accepted the proffered cup of steaming, sweet tea, gratefully, and sat back to wait. As the helicopter heeled away, the feeling of dread returned.

*

"Rick, it's Jim at Neatishead. Good news. They've picked up two survivors. They're on the Sea King as we speak, en route for Norwich Hospital. ETA in 15 minutes."

As instructed, the Duty Authoriser hit the direct line to the Boss.

CHAPTER 4

The Soviet Embassy, London.

Set in the smart suburb of Belgravia on the elegant Kensington Palace Gardens, often described as the most exclusive address in the Capital, sat the Soviet Embassy. Its imposing facade, clearly visible from the road, lay behind a walled garden. Heavy gates set into the perimeter at regular intervals, seemingly offered admission despite no prospect of a warm welcome within.

Ilya Nikishin hefted the heavy bag onto his shoulder and opened the rear door of the Embassy, striding confidently through the gate held open by the security guard. He turned along the street making his way towards the junction with Bayswater Road, sure that his MI5 secret service minder would be waiting for him as he emerged from the rear entrance. The vain hope that he may start his journey alone was tempered by the certain knowledge that if he used the striking front entrance, he would be tailed. The KGB resident had schooled him carefully and the faces of the regular secret service minders had been committed to memory. If his mission was to be successful, his tradecraft would need to be perfect if he was to board the train at Euston Station alone in two hours time. Between now and then he had plenty of time to be certain.

The Queensway and Notting Hill Gate tube stations were both nearby and he might lose himself in the throng of commuters but he needed to know first whether he had picked up a tail. Heading straight across the open ground towards the Serpentine was ill advised. He would be seen from any number of vantage points around the park and a watcher with a radio could easily position a minder. He stood a much better chance by making his way into the back streets of Bayswater. Dodging the traffic and crossing the busy road he headed up the aptly named St Petersburg Place watching the windows across the street for a reflection of the expected tail. Sure enough, a suspicious character in a trench coat - they really should try harder - hurried along in his wake, pausing occasionally yet unconvincingly to glance at a window display. Turning down the equally fitting Moscow Road he stepped up his pace. Queensway was just ahead with its abundance of restaurants and shops and he would make his first move there.

Suddenly, the opportunity presented itself. Stopping briefly as if to window shop he looked, casually, up and down the street. If he was right he had two men trailing him. One had paused further down the road following him at a respectable distance whilst the other was on the opposite side of the road and making steady progress in the same direction. He picked up his pace again heading directly for the Wimpey burger bar and ducked into the front entrance. A seething mass of humanity clustered around the counter jostling to place orders but his focus was elsewhere. Seeking out the passageway behind the service counter he passed the toilets at the rear and, without breaking stride, headed for the exit. With a glance behind as he pushed on the door, he registered one of the men making his way through the queue of customers more urgent now in his pursuit. The rear of the property backed onto a quiet street and hurriedly turning back in the direction he had come he took the first turn back towards Queensway and the safety of the hustle of pedestrians. As he rounded the corner back onto the busy street he almost collided with the second minder, the face clicking in his memory banks. It was one of the mug shots that he had seen many times during his preparation with the KGB resident and the flicker of recognition on the confused face could not hide the fact that the operative's cover had been blown. Ineffectual efforts to appear casual failed. Ilya knew that, as swiftly as the encounter was over, the man would be on his radio reporting movements so time was of the essence. Unless he was quick a new watcher would join the chase.

Crossing the stream of traffic prompting an orchestra of car horns, he flagged down a London cab, the amber caption on the roof glowing welcomingly. Giving staccato instructions for a drop off at nearby Lancaster

Gate tube station, he sat back to catch his breath. The next stage was crucial and, if executed properly, would finally throw the tail. Thumbing the tube ticket in his pocket he watched the circular underground sign approaching and hefted the strap of his bag over his shoulder. The £10 note would more than cover the short ride and the minute the cab pulled up, he would be away. The brakes squealed gently as the cabby pulled into the kerb and Ilya jumped out thrusting the note through the opening window. The generous tip would assuage the man's indignation at the hasty departure. Darting into the entrance he placed his ticket into the slot in the barrier and followed the throng, casually glancing behind as he went. There were no signs of pursuit and he could only imagine the nervous discussions being exchanged over the radio.

The moment the crowd eased, he accelerated around an elderly lady aiming down the long escalator towards the platform. As he emerged, the indicator board showed one minute until the arrival of the next tube train so he worked his way past the cluster of travellers hugging the platform edge. The train sped past his shoulder pushing the fetid air from the tunnel along the platform like a bow wave and he glanced behind to monitor the bodies emerging onto the platform watching for the elusive tail. The doors slid back and a few commuters spilled from the train before he entered the single door and deliberately blocked the access route. Checking back along the length of the carriage he watched passengers alight looking for a tell tale sight of a familiar face or for any new and unwanted attention. Nothing obvious. The doors closed and the train pulled out; just another routine stop on the Central Line. As it drew into the next station and the doors slid back once more he paused, edging towards the sill. Timing his move perfectly he squeezed through at the last moment avoiding contact with the closing doors and stepped back onto the platform. Crossing through the connecting tunnel he emerged onto the opposite line and edged his way to the far end giving an uninterrupted view of the whole platform stretching out ahead of him. The passengers emerging from the tunnel seemed unhurried and he began to hope he had finally thrown off his pursuers but he would make absolutely sure. The next train breezed into the station and he stepped aboard more confident this time. He would repeat the switch a few times more to make sure that he had succeeded before, eventually, switching from the Central Line to the Northern Line at Tottenham Court Road and heading north for Euston Station.

As the Inter City 125 train pulled out from the platform Ilya willed his pulse to slow down. The seat location was no coincidence and had been reserved to give him a clear view down the length of the carriage, his back against the bulkhead, only the engine behind him. Next to the aisle, sitting in one of a pair of airline-style seats, he hoped the presence of the bag he had so carefully clutched during his pursuit and which he had now placed visibly on the seat next to him, would deter the casual traveller. Conversation he could do without.

Born in the suburbs of St Petersburg, he had led a comfortable existence by Soviet standards. The son of an engineer he had won a bursary to study sciences but his athletic prowess had marked him out from the crowd and it came as no surprise when he had been courted by the KGB as a youth. Attending the KGB Higher School in Michurinsky Prospekt, Moscow, named after Felix Dzerzhinsky the Communist revolutionary and founder of the Cheka, he began his long preparation, politically, educationally, technically and culturally. Graduates during the 1960s right up to the 1980s were schooled in the skills needed to counter foreign intelligence services and to conduct operations across the world. With his background in the sciences, he had gone on to train in special skills in underwater warfare and served on a Lira, "Alpha-class" attack submarine with the Soviet Northern Fleet. With the British nuclear deterrent based in Holy Loch in Scotland it was natural that his duties with the Security Service had drawn him regularly to the British shores. Despite his communist upbringing, he had a secret admiration for the "Iron Lady", Margaret Thatcher who ruled the United Kingdom with an admirable firmness. The gulf in their politics would never narrow but he could admire a kindred spirit. Her determination to recover the tiny Falkland Islands off the Argentinian coastline so far from Britain was a feat of statesmanship rarely demonstrated and he was full of admiration for a principled stand. That he opposed everything that she stood for as a politician, was a quirk of nature.

He settled back in the first class seat and, confident that he had not been followed, allowed himself the luxury of a snooze. It was a long journey to Scotland and he needed to be fresh when he arrived as he had immediate business to take care of. The geography of the west coast of Scotland was firmly imprinted in his mind so, hopefully, the arrangements that he had put in place before his departure from the Embassy would work out. Nevertheless, it was an ambitious plan and there were a few aspects which were by no means guaranteed to succeed. He would need some luck in addition to meticulous planning. His hand dropped protectively to the mysterious bag at his side as his eyes closed.

CHAPTER 5

Off the Western Coast of Scotland.

Some miles west of the isolated archipelago of Saint Kilda, or Hiort to give it its Gaelic name, itself 40 miles west-northwest of North Uist in the North Atlantic Ocean, the Soviet Battle Group headed southerly, the minor vessels deployed around the capital ship "Kiev". Flagship of the Soviet Navy, Red Banner Northern Fleet based at Severomorsk and commissioned in December 1975, the ship's compliment numbered as many souls as a small city. From December 1982 to November 1984 she had undergone a major refit in the Nikolaev shipyard where she had been built and had since returned to sea. Displacing over 40,000 tons loaded, the 1600 hands occupied spaces little larger than a postage stamp and with an Air Wing embarked, the number of bodies aboard rose to nearly 2,000. Such were the cramped conditions that ghettos existed where even the officers feared to venture. With all four steam turbines at full chat the ship sliced through the water at 60 Km per hour outpacing a speedboat but, if run at more economical speeds, could travel over 25,000 kilometres without refuelling. With its sister ships Minsk and Novorossiysk it conferred a true blue water capability to the Soviet Navy, and with a fleet of oilers on call, range was not an issue its Commander worried about.

A through-deck cruiser rather than a true aircraft carrier such as those operated by the United States of America, the angled fight deck cut across the main deck giving the ship a lop-sided appearance. The red forward deck extended from the prow, past the huge superstructure towards the fantail and housed an extensive array of armaments leaving little argument as to the true purpose of the vessel. Four twin SS-N-12 Sandbox surface-to-surface missile launchers took up much of the space on the ship's prow sharing the deck with an SAN-3 Shtorm surface-to-air missile system and two RBU-6000 anti-submarine rocket launchers. Twin SAN-4 Gecko surface-to-air missile launchers had been installed to guard the lower airspace. With ten 533 mm torpedo tubes, a twin SUW-N-1 anti-submarine warfare rocket launcher able to fire nuclear-tipped rockets, in addition to an AK-630, six barrelled, 30 mm close-in weapons system and two twin 76mm anti-aircraft guns the Kiev was a formidable weapons system in its own right. That it was leading a task force of smaller vessels each one optimised for an element of naval warfare simply underlined the leap in capability which the Soviet Union had undergone.

The superstructure housed the nerve centre of the task force and naval warfare teams choreographed the entire operation in the air, on the surface and underwater once underway. Topped with an array of antennas, Kiev boasted surveillance radar systems, electronic surveillance measures, sonar, navigation radars, a combat information control system and satellite communications. Towering over the flight deck the island was dominated by the Top Sail three-dimensional air and surface surveillance radar scanning the horizon out to 150 miles. Forward and below sat the circular Headlight tracking radars for the SAN-3 system, the Pop Group tracking radar for the SAN-4 and the Owl Screech gun laying radar for the 76mm guns.

The hashed centreline of the green, angled flight deck was cut by seven white circular helicopter pads and stretched almost the full length of the ship. An embarked Air Wing comprised a total of 32 airframes. Twelve Yakolev Yak-38M fighter-bomber aircraft, known to NATO as the Forger, shared the hangars with twenty Kamov Ka-25 Hormone or, more recently, Ka-27 Helix helicopters. For this deployment, and for the first time, the Yak-38 Forger fighters would be validating short takeoff and landing procedures in contrast to the earlier practice of conducting vertical takeoff and landings. This would improve combat efficiency allowing greater payloads to be carried projecting air power over even greater ranges. In addition to the normal complement a number of specialist helicopters had embarked but speculation over the reasons for their presence was vigorously discouraged.

Admiral Vasili Gerasimek the Commander of the Battle Group peered through his binoculars focussing on the Krivak-class escort vessel, just one of the picket ships that surrounded his flagship. As the sleek destroyer cut across the bows providing an ever present screen, he switched his attention to the flight deck where six Yakovlev Yak-38 fighters were ranged across the parking area resplendent in their light blue splinter-patterned camouflage scheme. His other six fighter-bombers were unserviceable making him less than happy. Already, the Tumansky turbojet engines were proving unreliable and serviceability was pitifully poor. It would only get worse as flying operations intensified.

As he watched, technicians fussed around the airframes checking systems and priming reservoirs preparing the jets for flight. The weather had eased and the incessant squalls that had plagued him for days had moved away to the east. Behind the weather front, the relative calm and blue skies would give him the opportunity to flex his muscles. This was the first time he had been able to launch the Air Wing and he was keen to do so before the Battle Group began exercising with the submarines in earnest. So far, the deployment had gone well and the helicopters were proving typically reliable and had stayed serviceable; the Yaks were a different matter. Why did aircraft complicate naval operations? He hoped that readiness would improve because he carried only a limited spares pack and it was some time before he would dock in Tartus in Syria where he could resupply by air and regroup. Friendly port facilities between here and the Eastern Mediterranean were few and far between and, in the meantime, he had a high profile test to complete in Atlantic waters.

Despite the challenges, he felt a buzz of satisfaction as the first pilots emerged from the base of the island and made their way towards the waiting jets. Although a flyer himself, his experience was flying the Kamov Ka-25 anti-submarine helicopter and he harboured a nagging frustration at never graduating to high performance fighters. Familiarisation flights in the Forger two seater had merely scratched the itch.

Ostensibly, the next event was a rendezvous with a waiting submarine captain who already was working towards the Battle Group but he could not know of an unseen danger which would shape the deployment over the coming weeks. In reality it would prove to be far from routine. Back in

Murmansk military planners were concerned over operational capability and when the staff officers were concerned it was because their masters were asking questions and their consternation usually migrated to him. Not only were Soviet efforts to track western submarines increasingly ineffective but any operations in the Atlantic airspace were subject to ever more intensive scrutiny and analysis both in the air and under the waves. NATO, or more accurately the Americans, had established a surveillance network, the sound surveillance system, or SOSUS, a grid of underwater listening posts located around the world but with a strong focus on the area around the northwest of Scotland close to his present position. An array of hydrophones linked by miles of undersea cables straddled the choke points in the Greenland, Iceland, UK gap and it was proving superbly effective at tracking Soviet submarines as they moved from their home waters attempting to break out into the open waters of the North Atlantic. The individual sensors were strategically positioned on continental slopes and sea mountains giving long range, sub-surface acoustic reception undistorted by the undersea geography. The system was so sensitive that it could even detect the propeller noise of the Soviet maritime patrol aircraft flying overhead. Only when they emerged into open waters would the Soviet submarines become harder to track; essential if the nuclear vessels were to be able to threaten their targets on the eastern seaboard of the Continental United States. It was a conundrum.

His mission for this deployment had been made amply clear at a closed briefing at the Naval Headquarters in Murmansk before his departure. New attack submarines were being fielded which might redress the balance and offer a better chance of tailing the NATO "boomers". New sensors had been fitted in the Tupolev anti-submarine patrol aircraft which should map the undersea battle space more effectively. New tactics had been introduced to allow his own fleet to operate unhindered and unsupported in this critical area which would shape a future conflict with NATO if it should ever escalate beyond Cold War tension. His task was to evaluate these changes and to determine whether the new capabilities would tip the balance in their favour. These were not the only tasks he had been given. The fact that a submersible had been deployed with the fleet was no coincidence and a very specific and highly secretive mission was allocated to its crew.

What he knew for certain was that something had to change and the test he was commanding would establish whether the scales would tip in the favour of the Warsaw Pact or whether NATO would reinforce its technical superiority. The coming days would tell.

CHAPTER 6

On an Inter City 125 Train. Approaching Carlisle.

Ilya glanced down the carriage making sure he was not overlooked. A young man some rows away moved unconsciously, his head nodding in rhythm to the music from his Sony Walkman, his eyes closed, oblivious to his surroundings. A young couple on the opposite side of the carriage fussed, their efforts to calm their two fractious children ineffectual. That they were corralled by a table did not help.

Ilya reached into his pocket pulling out an envelope which the Resident at the Embassy had slipped into his hand before his departure. It was unmarked and seemingly innocuous but he had been assured of its importance. Tearing the envelope open he studied the single sheet of paper carefully, his photographic memory recording the contents, committing the details to mind. His eyes closed briefly as he ran over the details once more, satisfied he had understood correctly. One final check and he folded the paper into a small square and tucked it into his palm.

Rising from the seat trying to appear relaxed he made his way down the aisle, his gait matching the rhythm of the train, the small bag which had become his constant companion clutched in his spare hand. He could have used the closest toilet but his short walk gave him the chance to check out any unexpected travellers who might have slipped in unnoticed. Satisfied that he had accounted for all of his roving companions he approached the dividing door, hesitating as it slid back, the sudden wind rush from a window left open at the earlier stop assailing his senses. He pushed the errant window closed giving himself a nervous moment as the slip of paper fluttered in the draught.

Slipping into the toilet he was momentarily frustrated at the lack of a plug in the sink forcing him to stuff a paper towel into the plug hole as a temporary solution. He ran a bowl of water dropping the flimsy paper into the shallow draught and added the contents of a paper sachet. As he watched, the paper dissolved leaving just a faint discolouration in its wake. Satisfied, he relieved himself before agitating the liquid, pulling the makeshift plug clear and watching until all the water had drained from the sink. A quick wipe around the bowl and he unlatched the door and returned to his seat clutching the ever present bag. As he relaxed once more he mused over the details of the plan. Suddenly the sparse briefing he had been given before setting off from the Embassy made sense. He now had a clear idea of why the device he clutched in his hands was so important.

CHAPTER 7

RAF Coningsby, Echo Dispersal.

"Razor, come in, sit down," said the Boss gesturing towards the easy chairs in the corner of the office. "You look well and good to see you back. I've just got off the phone and it's good news about Toppers. From what I hear from the Docs he'll make a full recovery, it'll just take a bit of time. He's suffering from amnesia after the knock on the head. It was a pretty hefty whack he took."

Razor hesitated, recent memories re-emerging. The Squadron Commander pressed on sensing the still raw emotion.

"They told me his bonedome saved him. There was a severe impact on one side that broke the shell. It looks like a freak accident. The canopy separated cleanly but something hit him as he went up the rails. The best guess is that the wander light flailed as he ejected and caught him on the way out. A freak event that's all."

"Is there much improvement?" His voice cracked. "I feel that.........."

"Don't go there Razor. We all know that once we pull the handle we're on our own. There was nothing you could have done to change events. He's comfortable but he has amnesia. He can't remember anything about the sortie at all and the ejection sequence is a blank. Luckily the wind blast brought him round and he was able to get into his dinghy after he hit the water. The conditions in the North Sea are unforgiving at the best of times and even though the helicopter picked him up quickly, survival times can be short without some form of protection. The docs say his memory will slowly come back but he'll be off flying for a few months."

"I feel guilty."

"Look, you can't blame yourself. It was a massive structural failure of the wing fold mechanism. You had no choice but to eject once the PCs failed. I would have done the same. It sounds like when the leading edge flaps detached from the wing there was collateral damage, probably to the spoiler on that side. You might have got away with just a utilities failure so why it led to a double PC failure is a mystery. The Board of Inquiry has already convened and they've found the wreckage of the jet. It's in shallow water so they intend to recover it and, once it's back at Farnborough the Air Accident Investigation Team will find the reasons quickly. They've grounded the fleet temporarily except for operational tasks but we expect that to be lifted soon. Today probably if 11 Group are right."

"I guess that will give me some thinking time."

"That was what I wanted to bring up. It doesn't do to mope about these things. It's like riding a bike. You need to get straight back in the saddle. The docs tell me you have no lasting injuries, although I know it'll take a while to get the thinking straight. Your back held up remarkable well to the ejection so they expect to clear you straight away. You'll have your medical category back today once they sign off the paperwork. I want you straight back in the cockpit."

"That's pretty quick. I was expecting a longer wait. Having the docs on your case is never good."

The senior officer grimaced; the sentiment shared.

"They can move quickly when prodded and, trust me, I've been prodding. Look, I want you to get airborne straight away as soon as the jets are cleared. Just a gentle sortie. Do a practice diversion and some continuation training just to blow out the tubes. It's the only way, believe me."

"I don't know . . . . ."

"When I jumped out of a Lightning, the Boss had me back in the cockpit inside a week. I was reluctant like you but it was the best antidote. It'll seem like just a bad dream quite quickly."

Razor paused again, searching, the indecision evident. The hesitation was enough for the senior officer.

"I'll have the sortie put on the programme for first wave tomorrow. No pressure, just a gentle shakedown. If the jets are cleared today, we'll programme it immediately. Choose your navigator. Someone you're comfortable with. Any troubles I want to know right away."

Razor nodded still unsure of the wisdom but taking the path of least resistance.

"There is another thing. And you can say no if you wish."

The comment hung in the air.

"The Soviets have been doing a bit of sabre rattling. Yesterday was the busiest day for QRA for months and Leuchars suspended all training flying and armed all their aircraft. I think it's 43 Squadron holding Northern Q at present and they were up to Q7. Their remaining jets were unserviceable so 111 Squadron had four jets loaded as well. I heard they flew 12 sorties including some at night. It's all to do with the Soviet exercise off the Scottish coast and the intelligence people are struggling to understand the reason for all the activity. They think the Kiev Battle Group that's in the area has been tasked with some sort of evaluation and there are submarines as well as the usual Bears involved."

"So how do we fit in?"

"They've asked for some help. There are three distinct operational areas and the two jets on Q at Leuchars just won't be enough. For the foreseeable future the air staff at Group want more jets on state just in case it ramps up. It'll also give the Air Defence Commander up at Strike Command a bit of flexibility. Mounting sorties from here at Coningsby won't cut it though. They want us closer to the deployment area for better responsiveness. 111 Squadron will be brought up to higher readiness but the plan is to leave them at Leuchars. As the SACLANT deployable Squadron, we've been nominated to hold Q from Machrihanish on the west coast of Scotland to be closer to the action. We're planning to send five jets and a spare crew up there tomorrow so it's a decent sized detachment. I want you to deploy with the team."

For the first time that morning there was no hesitation. The response was instant.

"I'm in;" all thoughts of a furlough instantly cast aside.

"You'll need a new nav with Toppers indisposed. Any preferences?"

"I know it's unusual but any chance we could spring Flash from the OCU? I'd feel a lot more relaxed flying with someone I know well. We flew together in Germany and I'm sure he'd jump at the chance for some real flying, particularly the chance to get a few Bears on Q."

"Let me make some inquiries. I've already traded in a lot of brownie points but it may be possible. I'll have a chat with the Boss of the OCU. Meanwhile, you talk to the Detachment Commander. He has all the details so you won't have much preparation to do. As soon as you've had a familiarisation ride and got back in the saddle you'll see it a lot differently. There should be plenty of flying to go around."

The pep talk was over.

CHAPTER 8

UK Air Defence Operations Centre, RAF High Wycombe, Buckinghamshire.

The Duty Air Defence Commander stared at the backlit perspex tote, the coastlines of Europe etched out in detail, a heavy gridline superimposed on top. His eyes moved north following the outline of the Norwegian coastline around North Cape before settling on a symbol tracking slowly westwards. He picked up the phone to the Master Controller at RAF Buchan on the east coast of Scotland.

"I have a Zombie approaching 30 East. Warn off Leuchars Q and have them prepare the jets. I plan to launch them in about 45 minutes when it rounds the Cape.

"Roger that Sir," the Master Controller replied. Having watched the track on his own displays he had anticipated the call and had already spoken to the Leuchars Q shed. Unlike their southern counterparts, the FG1 Phantoms had no inertial navigation system to align but already, outside in the Q shed, external power had been applied and the crews were checking the aircraft over to make sure that there would be no delays once the scramble message was issued. Bladders had been eased, small water bottles filled and Mars bars were tucked safely in immersion suit pockets. The upcoming mission might last up to 7 hours and advanced preparation was a welcome bonus.

"I plan to launch the Victor in support and I'll give Southern Q a bit of the action too. If this turns out to be a multiple formation we'll probably have to split the assets to keep track of all of them."

He considered whether to discuss his sources with the Master Controller as he had already spoken to a clandestine intelligence cell deep in the bowels of the Headquarters and he had a good insight into the composition of the formation. That he would need more assets to monitor the progress was a given.

"Sounds good. Do you want me to initiate the scramble?"

He decided honesty was a better course of action.

"Yes. The Norwegians are planning to launch in the next few minutes. We've had a SIGINT hit that suggests there's at least one Bear Foxtrot in there and maybe a Delta. It's not the right timing for the routine Cuba run and, with Kiev operating off the coast I suspect they will be positioning to take part in an anti-submarine exercise. If so they'll turn south westerly soon after they round the Cape."

"I'll coordinate with the Norgies and make sure we pick them up before their Q goes home. I don't want them descending outside radar coverage and going dark. It's a lot of sea to cover with one Phantom."

"Sounds good. Let me know if anything out or the ordinary happens."

"Will do Sir."

The line clicked off and he punched the direct line to the Master Controller at Neatishead. The officer based at the Sector Operations Centre South controlled the airspace across the southern half of the country. For Cold War operations the majority of the air activity occurred in the northern climes and very little disturbed the ordered routines of air traffic around London. Southern QRA was relegated to a reinforcement role but for the sanity of the crews at Wattisham or Coningsby, controllers would launch the southern fighters to share a little of the action. It was a source of friction for the Leuchars based crews who saw intercepting Bears as a perk of being confined to the frozen wastes north of the border. At each base, two fighters held alert, designated Q1 and Q2. As subsequent additional aircraft were armed and brought to a higher state of readiness they would adopt sequential numbers.

"Air Defence Commander here. I have some trade for your boys Pete. Bring the tanker to cockpit readiness and launch them in slow time. Have Q1 from Wattisham follow them up and be ready to relieve the Leuchars Q1 in behind. I show a single Zombie at present but I think it will prove to be two or maybe even three Bears and I want to have assets to follow them if they split. Vector them towards a tactical towline off Stornoway. I'm guessing that the Zombies will be playing with the Kiev Battle Group and I want the tanker close by. If they should operate further north we'll leave it to Buchan and Benbecula to finesse the play."

"Will do Sir. Do you want them off at a certain time?"

"Yes. Give them warning to prepare but have them both off at minute 45. The Phantom can catch up during the transit north."

"Will do Sir."

He sat back and watched the track cross the gridline marking 30 East, its progress slow but sure.

*

Steady at its cruising altitude of 12,000 metres the four NK-12 turboprop engines with their contra-rotating propellers droned away in the background. The Captain in the left hand seat was holding a steady speed of Mach 0.9, or just below the speed of sound, which for a propeller-driven aircraft was incredibly fast. To NATO, this massive bomber known as the Bear was unique in the fact that it was the only turboprop combat aircraft ever to see service with the Soviet forces. It had an endurance of 24 hours in this configuration and, given a good wind, could strike targets on the eastern seaboard of the USA. Although not equipped with forward firing guns, the Bear was fitted with radar-laid tail guns. Four 23mm cannon guided by a small radar housed in a radome sat at the base of the fin. The Boxtail fire control radar operated only at short range but could direct the guns onto any fighter which strayed into the tail cone, the high explosive shells providing a lethal last ditch defence. Easily jammed by electronic countermeasures equipment, the UK had lagged behind in providing such protection for the Phantom and the guns could pose a serious threat at shorter missiles ranges to an unwary crew. If war broke out it would be a deadly game of who could shoot first, although it would be a slow-witted fighter crew who strayed so close.

"Captain, navigator, I have us crossing 30 East and about to send the position report to Divisional HQ."

"Roger that," the pilot of the lead Bear acknowledged. He turned up the volume on the rotary stalk on the communications panel and listened as the clipped tones of the navigator updated their controller back at Murmansk of their progress. So far the mission was routine and he had followed the same track many times in the past. Today's mission, however, was considerably more complex than normal. Somewhere in the depths of the Atlantic, a new Akula class attack boat was waiting and his task was to find it and capture as much information as possible on its movements. Part of him, secretly willed the submarine captain to succeed. It was new technology and if they were to stay on a par with the NATO fleets it had to be effective. Even so, professional pride meant that he and his crew would do everything in their power to track the new boat.

To help him, the other Bear Foxtrot would fly coordinated anti-submarine tactics and the Bear Delta would provide a surface plot of any ships in the area either friendly or hostile. As they droned west at 12,000 metres altitude he sensed a calm before the storm. The other two turboprop surveillance aircraft were maintaining a steady trail formation as briefed so many hours before.

"How long to the turning point, navigator?"

"Still 250 kilometres and the descent point is ten minutes beyond the turn," he heard in response. "All proceeding as planned. I have a good navigation fix on Nordkapp and the kit is accurate."

"Anything on the NATO chat frequencies?" he asked knowing that the air electronics operator would be scanning the regular control frequencies for the first sign of a scramble against them.

"I have been listening out on Fighter Stud 80, NATO Intercept Common Captain, and all is quiet."

He relaxed picking up the steaming cup of tea which had been passed over

INFILTRATION

by the co-pilot a few moments ago. He would stretch his legs soon because once they got into the exercise area there would be scant opportunity to leave his seat. Glancing out of the square cabin window he could see little. It was a dark night and even with the cockpit lights dimmed to their lowest setting, the red glow killed what little ambient light there was outside. There was no surprise at this height, this far north at this time of the year. When they had planned their mission, the descent to low level had been timed to coincide with the first hint of the dawn. He hoped it had been properly calculated because he did not fancy the idea of working down at 1000 metres with the two huge Tupolevs in loose formation in the darkness. The massive converted bomber had not been designed with close formation keeping in mind.

*

Preparations made, the Q1 navigator gratefully accepted the bacon sandwich and steaming cup of tea from the burly flight line mechanic. The smells had been drifting through from the tiny kitchen for some time stimulating the senses. It was one of the few pleasures of holding alert; other than pulling alongside a Bear, of course. The formalities had been completed, the systems warmed up and the cockpits ready. With only a few hours to shift changeover he could have anticipated finishing his stint inspecting the back of his eyelids but the advanced warning had changed that plan but he still had time for . . . . .

The hooter blared out, its intrusive siren unwelcome. Groaning, he dropped the plate knocking over the mug in his haste.

"Leuchars, alert QRA. Bring Q1 to cockpit readiness. . . . ."

"So much for a planned launch in 15 minutes," he muttered sprinting towards the door. Across the short distance to the jet, dashing up the steps. the crew dropped into the cockpits at full tilt, breathless with the exertion.

"Lima 01 at cockpit readiness," called the navigator in the back of the 43 Squadron Phantom, already strapping in, anticipating the call.

"Ready to copy your scramble instructions?"

"Affirmative."

"Lima 01 you are to launch at minute 40. Vector 290, climb Angels 35. When airborne contact Buchan on Fighter Stud 43, acknowledge."

"Lima 01 scrambling at minute 40, acknowledged."

A bacon sarnie was a 3 minute job. His stomach growled and he cursed the theatrics contemplating negotiating a take away delivery from the groundcrew. Already the engines were winding up with the clock showing 12 minutes to their planned launch time. The extra warning should have meant that they had had time to strap in a little more comfortably but at least the instruments were already up and running. Once the lineys had buttoned up the panels underneath, they would taxy out to the holding point and warn the Tower of their departure details. Knowing that the Local Controller would have been listening out on the telebrief, he should already be primed for their departure. Their north westerly departure should take them clear of the most congested airspace around Glasgow airport but at this early hour, the skies should be clear with most traffic passing overhead en route from North America to make an early morning touchdown at their European destinations. Both crew were happy to be going flying. They had been due to be relieved at 8.30 in any case. With a bit of luck, they would fly a quick two hour sortie and be back on the ground for an elusive breakfast in the Shed before the new crew arrived.

*

"Overhead the turn now, come left, make your heading 240 degrees."

The Captain flashed his nav lights as a signal to the trailing formation that a turn was imminent. He flicked off the autopilot and moved the control yoke to the left giving a momentary break in the tedium, the massive turboprops straining slightly at the increased demand. As the Tupolev eased into the turn, its left wing dropping he spotted the tell tale navigation lights some miles distant.

"We have company comrades," he called idly, the event completely expected.

"Affirmative, I hold an APG-66 at the 10 o'clock," called the electronics operator. "He's closing and just locked up. A Norwegian F-16."

Captain, Sonar, I'm in the blister and I see him rolling in behind. He'll be alongside soon."

"Roger, stand by."

The Captain hit the transmit switch." Okhotnik formation; leader has company. I'll call you when he hauls off. It's an F-16."

"Okhotnik 2."

"Okhotnik 3."

He was secretly pleased at his callsign. Okhotnik was Russian for hunter and quite appropriate given their mission. Within seconds the F-16 pulled alongside the cockpit, its navigation lights snapping to steady, the strip formation lights on the fuselage dimly visible in the dark night. It was some time before the pilot, more confident of his night vision now the navigation lights were steady, began to ease in gently. It was a phase the Captain disliked. Even though they were Cold War enemies, with the fighter in close formation he had to confer total trust in the other pilot's abilities.

It was still too dark for photography and there was not even enough ambient light for the fighter pilot to get a shot against the horizon so he satisfied himself with closing in underneath the belly. Had his movements been visible from the cockpit, the crew would have seen a penlight torch flash briefly to illuminate the door number under the nosewheel bay. The red beam proved useless and a brief flash of white light signalled another temporary loss of night vision for the Norwegian, albeit achieving a minor victory. The F-16 lurched downwards and away from the belly, the pilot briefly blinded. Within seconds he reappeared at a respectable distance off the wing.

"How long to the descent?"

"One zero minutes," the navigator intoned. "Getting a fix before we start the descent."

"Okhotnik 3, you are cleared to depart formation and make for your barrier position. On completion of the exercise you are clear to return to base independently, acknowledge."

"Okhotnik 3, copied and departing. Descending to 11 thousand metres and vectoring for the datum."

He had set the first challenge for the NATO controllers by splitting his force. Unless they had anticipated the split, when the F-16 broke off, which with the Bears holding a westerly course it would need to do quite soon, the anti-submarine Tupolevs would descend below radar cover and be much harder to track. The formation change elicited an immediate response and, suddenly, the anti-collision lights on the F-16 snapped back on and began a rhythmic flashing as it dropped a wing and peeled away.

""Okhotnik 2, our visitor is repositioning, confirm you are sighted?"

"Affirmative, 2 has contact."

The F-16 carried out a lazy orbit re-establishing its position on the wing of the trailing Bear some four miles behind the leader. Meanwhile Okhotnik 3 diverged and descended, separating slowly from the main group.

*

In the cockpit of the Southern QRA Phantom the conversation had been subdued after the adrenaline of the launch had worn off. Heading north at 25,000 feet they had tucked into close formation on the Victor tanker which they had quickly overhauled and switched to a quiet air-to-air chat frequency. The tanker pilot was now talking to the air traffic agencies leaving the crew free to consider their mission, or what little of the mission that they had been briefed on so far. They knew that trade had been reported passing North Cape but the pre-brief had contained little else. They could only assume that they would be given a situation report as soon as they checked in with Buchan. Used to a long haul up the east coast for QRA missions in the Outer Hebrides, today's route had been somewhat more unusual. Leaving East Anglia they had passed the reporting beacon at Pole Hill abeam Leeds and were now heading over the Lake District towards Dumfries and the Western Isles beyond. The refuelling lights on the hydraulic drogue unit had just flickered on and the tanker had streamed the centreline hose ready for them to take on fuel. As the combination of coloured lights flickered away, the tanker Captain gave permission to refuel and, with the pre-tanking checks complete and without a word exchanged, the navigator began to talk the pilot into the refuelling basket. Once they arrived in the area, with the heavy external fuel tanks under the fuselage and the wings filled to full, they would have enough fuel to prosecute their intercept.

*

"Buchan, Lima Foxtrot Delta 01 on handoff from Scottish Mil. Level at Flight Level 250. We are Delta Four, Four, Zero, Eight, Tiger Fast 60."

The Leuchars jet checked in.

"Lima Foxtrot Delta 01, Buchan loud and clear, how me?"

"Loud and clear also. Request SITREP."

"Lima 01 you have trade to the north heading inbound. I hold strength two. Presently in company with Norwegian QRA. I'll position you on a CAP at position. . . . ."

The navigator in the back scribbled furiously recording the planned CAP position and transposing it onto his map on his knee. Back plotting the position he could see that the controller was pushing them ahead of the approaching formation.

"Confirm CAP orientation."

"Look 050," he heard back from the ground. That made sense. Once they were ahead of the inbound tracks, presumably Bears, they would turn north easterly giving them the best chance to detect the huge Soviet aircraft. He felt the first inkling of the thrill of the chase.

"Check their height?"

"Last reported at Flight Level 330 but possibly descending. Mission 44 is in behind; presently working Polestar."

Polestar was the Danish Control and Reporting Post on the Faeroes. At least the controller knew the location of the formation and was still tracking it on radar. So often the intruders would descend below coverage and it became a guessing game. It could be a lottery but tonight it all looked promising.

"Buchan, Foxtrot Yankee Bravo 03, on handoff. Presently holding hands with Tansor, overhead Prestwick heading 300 at Flight Level 250. We are Delta Four, Four, Zero, Tiger Fast 60."

Southern Q had joined the party.

"Foxtrot Yankee Bravo 03, Buchan you are loud and clear, Lima Foxtrot Delta 01 is on frequency, presently 80 miles northwest of you at Flight Level 250. We have trade building to the north. Two formations splitting. One formation Zombie 01, allocated to Lima 01. The second formation, Zombie 02 allocated to you. Your target bears 340 range 150 miles, vector 320 for cut off."

The excitement in the response was palpable.

"For control contact Benbecula on Fighter Stud 45. Back to me if no contact."

"Fighter Stud 45, Foxtrot 03."

The game was on.

*

The captain of the lead Bear dragged back the throttles and began a gentle descent. He had set the heading bug from the information provided by the navigator and the entry point to their operational box was fast approaching. The briefing demanded that they be at low level by the time they entered the patrol box but, checking the altimeter, he made a rapid re-calculation realising he needed to get down quicker. Pulling the four massive turboprops back to idle he increased the rate of descent checking the speed with a blip of the huge airbrakes. The contra-rotating props grumbled and the airframe joined in the protest vibrating uncomfortably. The massive aircraft passed through 5,000 metres. He hoped his wingman was following in trail.

*

Lima 01 is Judy," the navigator called stroking the thumbwheel on the hand controller, refining the radar contact. He had just taken control of the intercept and on his radar scope the two large contacts stood out prominently.

"Come starboard 30 degrees and roll out 080," he barked, the Phantom responding instantly. Targets showing below, stand by for a range check."

The pilot stared at his own repeater display in the front, the tiny streaks in the pulse Doppler display representing two Soviet maritime patrol aircraft. It was pitch black outside the canopy and there was a total absence of any visual clues on which to orientate himself. He was flying on instruments. Only his training and the navigator's commands would position him behind the Bears. Assuming that was what they were.

"Take it down to 17,000 feet," he heard in his bonedome, "Set speed 350 knots, the target's descending."

He tweaked the controls the requested flight parameters instantly matching the commands. The jet slowly descended towards the surface of the ocean below.

"Come back port onto the reciprocal, target's heading is 230 and. . . . ." The display flickered manically and settled briefly. A full track presentation flashed momentarily before the radar broke lock again, the compulsive symbology replaced once again by the indistinct blips on the search display. Sometimes he could barely understand how the navigators could interpret the smudges.

"Target range 35 miles."

They were on opposite headings closing rapidly at a combined speed of over 800 miles per hour.

"The final turn will be to port. Level off at 8,000 feet. Target has levelled at 7,000."

He rechecked his heading and nailed it once again watching the altimeter wind down through 9,000. He checked the rate of descent ready to peg the height.

"Targets continuing the descent. Go down," he heard. "It's dark out there. Not below 1,500 feet minimum height."

"Roger, not below 1,500 copied. Passing 8,000 in the descent."

"Cross checks in the back. Regional QNH 1021 set, passing 7,500 feet. . . . . Now!"

"Cross checks."

"OK I'm switching into pulse. Let's see if I can break out these targets. OK I have them. A trail pair with the rear guy stepped slightly high. Lead contact is range 25 miles. They're in four mile trail with the rear man offset wide to the west. Hold that heading and keep it going down. Passing 5,000 feet . . . . . Now!"

The pilot knew that his back seater would be setting up a displaced approach with about five miles between their respective tracks. At low level even with the huge centreline tank hanging beneath the jet giving him a 4G limit there was sufficient turning performance to allow him to turn the corner in behind. He glanced at the blips on the display as, momentarily, they disappeared as the navigator refined the scanner position mentally calculating the height separation.

"They're still descending. Keep the descent going, call me through 3,000 feet. Any tally?"

The pilot squinted around the ironwork but the darkness was impenetrable.

"Negative. Looks like they're flying lights out. You're on your own mate. Can't help."

A frustrated sigh. The altimeter continued to wind down.

"Start your turn now, come port."

The pilot banked into a standard turn watching the instruments as he manoeuvred, sharing his scan with the blips on the radar display as the nose of the Phantom came around towards the trailing contact.

"OK if he doesn't know were coming now he's blind and deaf," called the back seater as, simultaneously, the locked up picture sprang into life. It was then that the navigator made a fundamental error. Glancing outside, hoping for a sneaky peek, he failed to notice the radar transfer lock. Although he had been setting up the intercept geometry on the trailing contact aiming to roll out at the back of the Soviet formation, a fluke of the geometry put both contacts on a similar azimuth on the radar. As the scanner settled on its demanded position the radar saw the second contact closer to the Phantom and chose it in preference. The full track display was now giving information on the leading radar contact rather than the trailer. He looked back into the cockpit. The radar contact, instead of tracking smoothly down the scope to its pre determined two mile roll out had hung up toward the left of the scope at four miles.

"Ahh Jeez, I've let it go slack," he muttered more to himself than his pilot realising that unless he acted immediately his intercept would go badly wrong. "Keep the turn coming. . . . Harder."

His commands to the pilot became more urgent but the implications of the errors in his geometry failed to register in his over-worked brain. Although he was pulling tight around the corner, because the information he was reacting to was unexpected, he was set to roll out immediately below the rear Bear. A momentary break lock to search for the leader would have highlighted his error but he stayed stubbornly locked to the contact, oblivious to the danger.

*

As the Bear Foxtrot entered the designated exercise box the crew returned to their stations anticipating the chase. The Tactical Coordinator, or Tacco, would call the play once the submarine was isolated dropping a field of sonobuoys designed to coral the submarine captain into a predictable response. The sensor operators were alert. If a periscope breached the surface, a propulsion screw cavitated or they passed overhead a submerged submarine giving them a reading on the magnetic anomaly detector, it would set in chain a new round of sonobuoy drops to tighten the noose. If that was to happen the submarine captain would have to be careless.

"Entering the patrol box, set release parameters," called the Tacco from the rear cabin as he adjusted the gain on the massive circular tactical display.

"Okhotnik 2 should be in position now, confirm?"

The co pilot craned his neck, looking across the formation at the other Bear, barely visible on the horizon. The first rays of the Sun rising in the east cast an eerie glow over the blank ocean illuminating the massive aircraft from behind.

"Tacco, Co, affirmative; he's in position as briefed."

A potential snorkel report was transmitted from the Bear Delta and he dropped a few markers onto his tactical display screen. The possible sighting was in the northern part of the box and as good a place as any to start . Running a quick bearing from the reported position towards the Task Force assuming that the Akula Captain would try to take the shortest line to his quarry, a possible plan formulated. If the submariner was predictable the course would bisect the operating area. A course correction followed and a new attack vector was calculated. He would place a line of sonobuoys down the bearing and see if he was rewarded with a ping.

"Roger, 60 seconds to first release. Sensor 3, Tacco, confirm ready?"

"Affirmative, standing by."

"Roger, release on my mark."

The intercom was quiet, every man concentrating on his own task, the culmination of a long transit imminent.

As they steadied on course he selected the payload bay doors open and primed three active buoys. Calling for a lower height he readied for the drop watching the electronic markers he had set on his tactical screen. As each marker flashed he hit the release button and a sonobuoy dropped from the belly of the huge turboprop, a small retarding parachute popping open in the airflow. Each buoy floated gently to the choppy surface of the North Atlantic, the entry to the water marked by a tight splash. Immediately the sensor operators were rewarded with a healthy ping as the buoys went active. He would soon find out if his guess had been inspired. The Bear climbed slightly as it entered a holding pattern. Nothing yet.

Switching his attention back to the broadcast from the Bear Delta, none of the other potential contacts made sense in terms of the position and intended movement of the Kiev. If the Akula was trying to breach the defensive screen it would not be heading westwards through the box. The Captain would go for the kill as soon as possible. The longer he stayed in the anti-submarine warfare area, the more chance the Tacco would have to detect him.

The wait was short.

"Sensor 3 has a contact, 270 range 5,000 metres from buoy 2."

It was the centre buoy of his stick. The cunning bastard had made good progress. He called for a closing course inbound for the centre buoy calling the other sensor operators to concentrate their searches on the new position. In the front cockpit, the pilot followed the needle on his instrument panel homing on the buoy in the water below. From the overhead the Tacco would head west to the last reported position and lay a new buoy there. It should mark the limit of the area as it would be doubtful if the Akula would try to backtrack once detected; although that tactic was not unknown. Another marker appeared on the screen denoting his drop point joining the three buoys he had already deployed appearing at the point where the sensor operator had recorded the hit. The confidence level was still low. His brain raced as he calculated further drops beyond the starting location. If he could establish a box based on the possible location it would be a good start. More markers appeared denoting the new buoys designated for deployment. A series of rapid heading changes would be needed to bracket the search area. Adrenaline kicked in.

*

"OK this guy is level at 1,500 feet but if he descends any more we don't want to be sandwiched underneath. Ease up above him for now. Make your speed 450 knots to close"

The pilot eased the throttle forward and began a gentle pull to position above the Bear. Heading corrections followed and he tweaked the needles. The wake turbulence behind one of these massive turboprop leviathans could be fierce and he had no desire to be turned upside down in the slipstream. The altimeter began to inch upwards again. Abruptly, he sensed rather than saw the confliction. Whether it was a solitary star suddenly blocked from view or a hidden sixth sense, he felt an imminent danger. Glancing upwards the lights of his own anti-collision beacon were suddenly reflected from the yawning underside of the trailing Bear. Self survival kicked in and he pushed violently on the stick, instantly arresting the fatal drift towards the other aircraft. The Phantom lurched eliciting a startled expletive from the back.

"Look up," he said, accusingly, the rebuke unsaid but implicit. The quiet in the cockpit heightened the blunder by the navigator. By locking up he had disregarded the second aircraft in the formation. His carefully planned approach on the leader had taken their flight path perilously close to the trailer and his command to climb would almost certainly have resulted in a collision but for the spatial awareness of his pilot. But for a quirk of the light they would have come together. It had been too close.

*

The tension in the control room of the Akula intensified and, despite the fact that the play was simulated, the stakes were high. Careers might be made or broken in the coming hours. In stark contrast to the frantic activity at the consoles the Captain remained stoically calm.

"Helm, come left to course 180 degrees, dive to 100 metres then make minimum revolutions."

His instructions were followed implicitly. The chase was on and the submarine was the prey but he would not give in easily. Once established on the new heading he would try to run silently for a short while hoping the diverging course would be a good compromise between prosecuting his attack and avoiding a lethal response from his pursuers. His caution was diverting him from his prey.

At the far side of the confined operations space a sensor operator gripped his headset listening to the faint ping to the east The turn would take them closer to the original sonobuoy but the Captain was gambling on the fact that the crew in the maritime patrol aircraft would centre the search around the first point of detection. Increasing the separation from that fateful first hit was vital and being predictable would be fatal.

"Buoy in the water, astern range 6,000 metres."

A pregnant pause.

"Buoy active."

The hushed response spoke volumes. The barely audible echo reverberated through the control room yet the manoeuvre had been well timed to limit further detection. Most importantly at this critical point in time, the acoustic signature reduction measures designed into the Akula hull back in the Soviet Union were about to be tested under the most pressing conditions. The ping remained elusive and distant giving faint hope. The Captain's breathing calmed slightly but it was not a moment for celebration. They were not yet clear of danger.

*

"Buoys away," the Tacco called over the intercom and, prompting the pilot in the cockpit of the Bear to climb slightly, easing back into a more comfortable holding pattern. In the darkened cabin the tactical team analysed the new information which immediately flooded the frequencies. As the latest sonobuoys began transmitting in sequence, each emission radiated outwards, feeling tentatively for their elusive underwater victim. Rapidly disseminated commands to the sensor operators primed them for what to expect, although years of training made the prompts redundant. The first part of the trap was set. He had hemmed his prey into a smaller box and depending on the reaction he would determine where to set the next line of buoys.

What would he do himself if he was trying to escape the trap? The battle of wits intensified.

*

Since the first ping all had been quiet. The Captain's next moves would be crucial. For them to be tracked, at least two active buoys had to register a hit and preferably three to give a good "cocked hat". Two bearing lines from a sonobuoy might seem to give a precise position but with inaccuracies of the technology, the apparent position could be some distance from the true position. Three hits narrowed the box, tightening the noose considerably. Right now the crew in the Tupolev needed more information and he was not about to offer it up easily. If he could hold his nerve, his ruse might work.

Minutes passed and the sounds of the electronic lasso diminished. Tactics under the sea were rarely frantic and stealth and patience would often win the battle. It was too soon to return inbound to the fleet. That would be too predictable and stunningly naive. He would bide his time. Once he was sure that the Tupolev crew had lost contact, he would track to the south of the box and try an oblique approach, hopefully avoiding the anticipated destroyer screen. He prayed that the search would concentrate to the north allowing him to slip away to the south but suspected that it would be guile rather than a higher presence that would help him out of this fix.

*

"Captain EWO, we have a fighter inbound. I hold a British Phantom, bearing 080 degrees."

"Roger EWO monitor the contact. Navigator, man the bubble and call any sightings."

"Will do. Making my way up there now. Off intercom for one."

The navigator disconnected his intercom lead leaving the massive radar display scanning in its relentless circular pattern and moved towards the sextant cupola. Climbing the stubby steps his head emerged into the light of the early dawn and he blinked involuntarily. The view that greeted him was a welcome change from the dim interior and around the aircraft scattered clouds were just visible dotting the horizon. Swivelling around he searched for the tiny fighter which he knew would be closing in. There it was, the navigation lights winking. Fumbling with the intercom lead he updated the crew reporting the position of the Phantom which crept slowly towards the lumbering turboprop from the six o'clock position, slightly high.

Reassured, the pilot returned his scan to the instruments refining the heading he had been given waiting for the interceptor to pull alongside. He hoped the fighter crew would give him plenty of leeway. The chase was not yet over and he had a submarine to find.

INFILTRATION

The Tacco watched intently as the buoys began to form a defined pattern on his display. Faint traces from the southerly pair of buoys gave a tentative fix and he called a further heading change deploying another buoy to tighten the noose. He was rewarded with an instant hit. A flashing symbol appeared as the mission system logged a position for the submarine. He had him!

Calculating an attack heading the special payload which had been covertly loaded back in Russia, was primed before he made a final check of the switches and launch parameters. There could be no screw ups at this stage. The critical moment of the sequence was approaching.

"Captain, Tacco, confirm weapons free?"

"Affirmative, clear to drop."

"Stand by."

*

On the wing, the Phantom pilot jockeyed for position, set slightly high and aft of the leading Bear. The earlier mistake had been forgotten, although in the quiet of the crewroom later, harsh words would be exchanged. The second Bear was tucked back in the four o'clock position seemingly joined by an invisible tether, the crew unaware of their close shave. The breaking dawn was casting just enough rays to consider low-light photography and conditions were improving rapidly as the navigator pulled the camera from its mounting bracket. The shutter would need to be wide open and he had taken the precaution of loading a higher speed 400 ASA film into the camera during the long transit. Dialling in 1/1000th of a second to damp out the vibration that typified life in the cramped cockpit he prepared for the shots but he still needed a big enough aperture to capture the detail. So close they could hear the drone of the Kuznetsov turboprops, he framed the cockpit in the viewfinder squeezing the small trigger on the camera body to check the exposure. The small indicator gave the bad news. The shots would be woefully under exposed. With the light still slowly improving, he compromised on 1/500th of a second and a wide f stop. Hopefully the light would improve before they broke away and he could use the higher shutter speeds.

" Whoa, keep clicking. The bomb doors just opened," the pilot announced. "Looks like we just lucked in."

Nervous energy took over as he realised he was about to be presented with the opportunity to take the photographs of the decade; the QRA equivalent of the Pulitzer Prize. The pressure to keep the camera steady had just been magnified tenfold as opportunities to capture live sonobuoy drops were few and far between. The shutter clicked.

"Drop it down so I can get a shot of the bomb bay area. We're a bit wide - ease it in. I need close ups if we can get them. No idea if there's enough light to pick out the detail," he muttered.

The Phantom responded, slotting into the new position alongside the open doors. As they watched, a sonobuoy left the sanctuary of the bomb bay and flicked into the airflow, the retard parachute deploying the minute it was clear. The shutter clicked furiously capturing the sequence as more buoys followed the first at regular intervals. As the slender cylindrical sensor reacted to the drag, it weather cocked into a vertical position and began its descent towards the surface below. The navigator twisted in his seat dragging against the resistant seat straps to capture the image of the stream of buoys descending towards the surface. Looking over his shoulder the rays of the rising sun provided a dramatic backdrop. He tweaked the exposure setting to compensate.

As he returned his attention to the Bear it climbed slightly and gently turned around onto a new heading. A series of turns followed before it dropped back down to extreme low level. The Phantom pilot struggled to hold position in close formation knowing that he had to remain below the wing line to keep the bomb bay in sight, its doors still wide open. A stream of height checks came from the back seat as he dropped slowly towards the surface of the sea below, the chop clearly visible in the early dawn.

Persistence was rewarded. After only a short time on the new heading another store dropped from the bay. The camera shutter clicked relentlessly all thoughts of monitoring the height discarded as the navigator focussed intently on the subject, his photography skills taxed to the limit. The long cylindrical object which emerged dropped into the airflow and a brightly coloured retarding parachute popped open. It lurched downwards its weight angling the trajectory into a steep dive towards the waves before it stabilised, slowed by the 'chute. The strange payload disappeared below the cockpit sill as rapidly as it had appeared.

"Yes," the navigator gloated. "I got it!"

*

"Conn, sonar, torpedo in the water!"

The call was enough to tighten every sphincter aboard the vessel. A few of the newer members of the crew prayed that this really was a drill.

"Bearing 045, range 800 metres."

The captain responded instinctively.

"Ahead flank speed, right 270 degrees, emergency dive. Launch noise maker."

There was a violent movement as the huge hull responded, the noise of the screws at the rear of the vessel suddenly dominant. Steady on the new course and unavoidably noisy, the submarine moved off at a tangent. The response was remarkably agile.

"Engines astern."

There was a pause.

"Engines stop. All quiet!"

The entire boat stilled, ears attuned to the incoming weapon, collective breathing stilled.

A hushed update.

"Torpedo is acquiring. . . . . acquisition. . . . . Homing. . . . ."

The sound of an active ping rang through the hull meaning the torpedo was at short range. . . . .

The sound of a motor passing close to the hull registered the survival of the

Akula. The noisemaker had done its job. The tension broke audibly. The drill had been uncomfortably realistic.

The exercise rules allowed the pursuing maritime patrol aircraft only one shot opportunity, no one knew why but it was just fine by the crew of the Akula. Next stop, the Kiev and woe betide the crew of the Foxtrot class submarine defending the Task Force should it decide to intervene. They were confident in their abilities in that arena.

*

Not only had they captured a sonobuoy stream but the finale had been a torpedo launch. With the roll of film exhausted the Phantom navigator was just able to capture the bomb bay doors rotating closed with his final shot. As he wound the film on he felt the tension on the lever and realised that he was done for this sortie. The film was exhausted and it was too late to load a new reel. What the crew would never know, because their security clearances were not high enough to have access, was that the markings on the torpedo were significant. Their recognition skills did not extend to identifying individual specialist weapons but as soon as the negatives were developed and the analysts in Defence Intelligence began to pore over the images, it would become apparent that this was not a routine drop. The weapon was not marked with the usual high conspicuity markings of an exercise torpedo, rather a series of barely visible Cyrillic markings. They would also be unable to tell that the weapon was not fitted with a warhead but a telemetry pack which was already transmitting vital data back to recorders onboard the Bear and, ironically, to the Akula submarine against which it was targeted. The pilot dropped the wing and the tell tale line of the underwater track of the torpedo stretched away in front of them. Their massive overtake meant they rapidly overhauled the weapon and it disappeared swiftly in the slipstream behind the Phantom.

Earlier mistakes forgotten, elation took over. Unbeknown to them they had just photographed the first launch of a new variant of the American Mark 46 lightweight torpedo from a Soviet maritime patrol aircraft.

Well to the north, the Southern QRA Phantom, its crew oblivious to the drama to the south, was completing an uneventful approach on the Bear Delta which was droning along at 20,000 feet. Their intercept would be somewhat less dramatic.

CHAPTER 9

Low Flying Area 10 North of RAF Coningsby.

Razor slotted into tight battle formation abeam the lead Phantom, the remaining pair tucked astern about two miles behind. It was good to have Flash in the back once more, the atmosphere in the cockpit relaxed and familiar. The Boss had been right. The familiarisation sortie had been essential to get straight back into the groove and, by now, the trauma of the ejection was firmly in perspective, the memories tucked away in a corner of his subconscious. A normal routine had been re-imposed.

As he watched the lead Phantom pull up to avoid a small village he corrected his own heading to maintain formation, matching the leader's speed. His own jet felt heavy and unresponsive. Not only was it full of fuel so soon after takeoff but it was carrying a full war load of four Skyflash and four AIM-9L Sidewinders on the weapons pylons. They would carry this load on every sortie once they arrived at the Scottish base but for now it was far easier to move them to Machrihanish by air than in a road convoy. The only concession from Group Headquarters had been dispensation to leave the heavy centreline fuel tanks normally carried on QRA missions behind at Coningsby. They had argued successfully that they would be flying closer to the task force and operating relatively close to the coast. With Yak-38 Forgers expected in the area, manoeuvrability had won out over endurance.

He tightened up the formation as his leader slotted back down to low level over the undulating Lincolnshire Wolds.

INFILTRATION

"Scope's clear," he heard from the back.

For now they were alone in the low flying airspace. Although he had armed the missiles and the familiar status lights glowed back at him from the jettison control panel, the Master Arm switch would stay firmly selected to "Safe" for this sortie. The only hint that he carried the weapons, other than the heavy feel of the controls, was a piece of tape plainly wrapped around the switch as a "tell tale" marking the deadly payload. With a live operation pending, normal training routines were suspended. There would be no "mixing it" with any other tactical formations they might find during this transit sortie. He shifted in closer as they approached the gliding site at Kirton-In-Lindsey. A NOTAM had warned of parachute activity at the airfield today and gently descending parachutists and fully armed Phantoms were tense bedfellows. To the right of track he could see a pair of Lightnings powering off the main runway at Binbrook heading out into the North Sea for a training mission. They would be back on the ground long before the Phantoms arrived at their destination.

"Thirty seconds to the turn," he heard from the back. To the north of the military air traffic zone at Binbrook lay the Humber river. As they turned they would slot through the crowded airspace between Doncaster International, Flash's old training base, at that time known as RAF Finningley but now a civilian airport, and Leeds/Bradford International airport. Precision navigation was vital for the next few minutes as a high speed formation of Phantoms flashing overhead the airport as the civilian airliners loaded their passengers for their charter flights to Benidorm would be less than welcome. The leader dropped a wing briefly showing his jet in planform, the signal for Razor to initiate the turn.

"Looks good," he heard from the back, a simple acceptance that they had hit the turning point accurately, no more amplification needed.

"Bogey 20 left range 20," came the call over the radio as they steadied up on their new heading. An airliner was letting down for its terminal approach, homing on the radio beacon at Leeds/Bradford. Onboard, the crew were fussing through the cabin preparing for arrival collecting empty glasses and prompting weary travellers to raise the blinds. None of the 58 passengers could know that, only thousands of feet below, they were at that very moment subject to the scrutiny of a navigator who had locked his radar to the airliner. A Skyflash missile was already receiving guidance information that, if launched, would take it unerringly to an intercept point alongside the airliner. But for a few switch selections the outcome of this chance encounter would be radically different. As it was, the armed formation threaded its way westerly allowing the captain of the airliner to return his precious cargo back to West Yorkshire after their off season holiday.

Holding the heading for only a few short minutes the leader pulled hard towards Razor setting a new heading across the Pennines towards Cumbria. Slowly, the urban conurbation thinned and the countryside turned green, the flat industrial vista replaced by rolling hills and valleys. Radars within the formation scanned the low level airspace for other fast jets whilst eyes scanned the airspace for gliders and microlights which were too slow to paint on the radar scope. The airspace was opening up and the wide expanses of Low Flying Area 13 spread out ahead of the formation. Navigation became easier and Razor widened to a mile glancing at his leader occasionally in order to hold station. When he was not looking at his leader he was scanning his instruments and the surrounding airspace. In the back Flash shared his time between the radar, the radar warning receiver and the "Six o'clock" in equal measures. They would "waggle off" any attackers but no self-respecting crew wanted an aggressor to arrive on the wing without acknowledging that they had seen the approach. To the right of track lay another trap for the unwary. Otterburn Range was active today and the Army was impressing the local populace by lobbing live shells across the pretty countryside, engaged in their latest rehearsal for World War 3. Tanks ploughed across the rough terrain whilst the live shells rained on a fictional opponent. The firing butts sat just to the north of the A66 main trunk route. Providing the Phantoms remained south of the road they were in the clear. Any drift across the divide and an irritated range safety officer would be ringing operations desks around the countryside to identify the culprits and to lodge his complaint. The lead pair skirted the range to the west giving it a wide berth while two miles behind the second element paid equal attention anxious not to register a violation and become a statistic. A radio call split the quiet of the tactical frequency as a Jet Provost training aircraft, resplendent in its high visibility red and white colour scheme, drifted towards the Phantom formation. In the cockpit, the watchful instructor monitored the gyrations of the student pilot who wrestled with the controls and his map and stopwatch, his attention divided between flying the little jet and making sure his timing along his carefully prepared track was accurate. Neither he nor the instructor saw the four massive air defence fighters as they passed within three miles of their track.

Twenty minutes into the sortie but it was another 40 minutes before they would break into the circuit at Machrihanish registering an immediate and noisy presence. There would be no distractions today. Their task was to put the Phantoms on the ground as soon as possible and deliver them to the waiting groundcrew who had driven up to the Scottish base overnight. They had a job to do and, off the coast, the Soviet Task Force would not wait for them to ready themselves.

CHAPTER 10

Benbecula in the Scottish Islands.

The UK Air Defence Ground Environment, inevitably known by an acronym UKADGE, was a complex network of radar stations working together to provide radar coverage across the whole of the UK mainland and beyond. At its heart, three Sector Operations Centres, or SOCs, controlled their own sectors with dividing lines running east-west across the country. The divisions between the sectors aligned along the 51st parallel of Latitude in the south and the 55th parallel in the north, controlled by the SOCs at Neatishead in Norfolk, Boulmer in Northumberland and Buchan in Fife. Co-located at these hubs were Control and Reporting Centres, or CRCs. Whilst the SOC provided the battle management function directing forces and controlling the airspace, the CRCs housed the fighter controllers and surveillance operators who took charge of smaller sections of the airspace. Smaller Control and Reporting Posts, or CRPs, provided a radar picture at the outer limits of coverage, manned by just a few hardy souls, often on isolated islands. For the controllers, the lifestyle during a posting to the CRP at Staxton Wold near Scarborough in Yorkshire would be radically different to a posting to the CRP at Saxa Vord in the Shetland Islands in the Outer Hebrides.

Although UK territorial waters and the airspace above extended to only 12 miles from the shore, the UK Air Defence Region stretched out well beyond, butting onto European airspace to the east, Irish airspace to the west and enclosing the airspace within a large circle centred on Iceland stretching well into Arctic waters. Known as NATO Early Warning Area

12, it covered 750,000 square miles of windswept ocean. Although international airspace, any track passing through the area without filing a flight plan or acting in a suspicious way would attract the attention of air defence commanders in Continental Europe, Norway or the UK.

Holes in coverage had, traditionally, been filled by using a mobile radar unit known as No. 1 Air Control Centre, or 1 ACC, which for most of the 1970s was based at RAF Wattisham in Suffolk. In 1979, the unit moved to RAF Portreath in Cornwall and re-equipped with a new Marconi Type 88/89 Mark 2 radar. From its new home, it was able to monitor the south west approaches where NATO expected to fight major naval battles should World War 3 ever ensue. The Unit's remaining deployable Marconi S259 radar was sent to Ascension Island in May 1982 to provide air defence early warning of the airspace around the strategic island at the outbreak of the Falklands conflict. With the loss of the mobile capability the unit was renamed RAF Portreath leaving just a fixed radar in place. Over the coming years, there would be a gap in deployable capability until new mobile radars could be funded to fill the gap. In the meantime, as part of the Improved UKADGE, or IUKADGE, new radars which were procured would be transportable, the logic being that the systems could be located to new sites should the tactical picture dictate. For much of the 1980s an extensive testing programme was conducted, often at remote locations, to validate the new systems.

The UKADGE was also fed by the radar picture from the airborne early warning Shackletons based at RAF Lossiemouth in Scotland with additional inputs from Royal Navy ships via tactical data links. RAF fighters, Bloodhound and Rapier missiles provided the teeth. At the outer reaches to the north and west and part of the Buchan Sector, RAF Saxa Vord was an isolated CRP which passed its radar picture and information, along with the picture from RAF Benbecula, to the SOC at RAF Buchan which also received information from the Danish site on the Faroe Islands. Over most of the UK landmass the system provided overlapping radar coverage down to low level but the farther away from the coastline, particularly in the northern extremes, the less comprehensive the coverage.

With the Soviet Fleet operating to the northwest, Benbecula was to become a strategic node for the next few weeks. The search radar, a Type 92 developed from the American AN/TPS-59, was located on the small island of North Uist close to the village of Balivanich, meaning "town of the monk" in the local dialect. RAF personnel stationed at the remote facility during their short tours of duty would co-exist uncomfortably with the locals whose way of life was disrupted by the temporary residents. For extended coverage out into the Atlantic Ocean, a remote radar on the tiny island of Saint Kilda, normally used by a testing range, provided vital supplementary information. Like any of the remote radar sites Benbecula could be ravaged by the extremes of the weather and serious storms brought horizontal hail generating gale force winds strong enough to blow a person over. Indeed, on one fateful day, the winds were so strong that the radome protecting the radar at Saxa Vord was blown away leaving the antenna unprotected and at the mercy of the elements for some considerable time. Such were the risks of living and operating in the isolated communities.

The islands which were linked by short causeways were inhabited by a deeply religious populace. The majority of the narrow roads were single track served by passing places making movement around the local area slow and difficult. Speaking Gaelic by choice, with a well developed sense of community, little went on in the surrounding area which did not come to the notice of at least one of the locals. The guarding routines at the RAF radar site, paranoid about the threat from Irish terrorist groups, became a source of amusement as nothing could occur in the local area without warning. Or so they believed. . . . . The theory was about to be put to the test.

Benbecula airfield was a vital link to civilisation, and many perishable items would be flown in on commuter flights. The air traffic control tower was manned by a civilian controller and operated only in good weather with British Airways and Loganair flights being the main users. Military aircraft and, particularly, Phantoms from RAF Leuchars operating with the CRP would visit occasionally providing a welcome link with the operational community for the RAF detachment but were a source of irritation to the local inhabitants disturbed by the jet noise.

Although they could have no inkling as yet, it would be this tiny joint community of military and civilians which would be most affected by events which were about to unfold as the Soviet Battle Group continued its operations just 100 miles off the coast.

CHAPTER 11

Machrihanish Airfield, The Mull of Kintyre, Scotland. The next day.

Liam Whelan winced as the door crashed closed and his sister slammed into the room. Born in Belfast at the height of the troubles, loud bangs unnerved him and his reaction was predictable if involuntary.

"Jeez Maria, you'll have that off its hinges one of these days. What's the problem now?" he muttered, in his broad Northern Irish accent.

Her blond pony tail swished as she stomped across the room and poured a cup of steaming liquid from the ever present coffee pot. She parked her perfect size 8 figure in the chair slopping the contents of the over-filled mug over the desk top accompanying the slip with another curse. Outside, the sound of a light aircraft cut the quiet calm its piston engine rattling the windows.

"It's that old busy body in the village store having a go at me again. I'll swing for that one."

"Calm down," he said, "I'm sure she only does it to wind you up. You know what they're like about newcomers around here. If you haven't lived in the village for 30 years you're an intruder. Don't let her rattle you. We have bigger things to worry about."

"That's as maybe but. . . . "

"What did you find out?" he interrupted trying to divert attention and,

INFILTRATION

desperately, attempting to calm her fiery temper.

"The word is they're expecting a detachment of military jets at the base arriving later today if the rumour is right. Brits from down south."

"To do what?"

"No idea as yet. It's just the women tattling. There's a detachment of Americans in already so the on-base accommodation will be full. They'll be staying down at the Ugadale in Cambletown. It's the only place large enough to take a big group like that. I'll go down later tonight and see if I can find out a bit more. It's not like they won't stand out from the locals is it?"

"That's true enough. This bloke who's chartered the Islander is arriving later today so I'll need to be around to welcome him. It's all very mysterious. The contract has been fixed up through the network so I don't have any details yet but we've strict instructions to be discrete and offer him anything he needs. Whoever he is, he's not working for the same team as your new arrivals. He's also very well funded. Mister Smith if you will! I don't need to take bets on the fact that that's not his name."

"So are you flying this evening then?"

"I am. I've been told he wants to be away shortly after his arrival and needs full tanks so it could be a long trip. I don't know the destination but I've not been asked to arrange a land away. Looks like an out and back but I won't land until after dark."

"All very cloak and dagger. I'll be interested to hear about it later."

Liam and Maria had moved to the remote airfield at Machrihanish some years before. Ostensibly a charter operation flying an Islander commuter plane and a Cessna 210 light single, the majority of work was legitimate. The vast majority of the jobs involved ferrying passengers around the remote Scottish islands or dropping mail and packages at inaccessible settlements that were badly served by the Royal Mail. Despite the limited revenue stream, the operation would never go under as the aircraft were financed by an untraceable funding line which led back to Belfast and the Irish Republican Army. The small operation ran quietly from a hanger on the civilian side of the RAF base and a steady stream of local customers and mundane work gave it an air of respectability. Occasionally, passengers were landed at one of the many beach runways which dotted the coastline, their journeys originating from airstrips along the Northern Irish coast. Liam had learned not to question their business too deeply and his occasional forays were well camouflaged by the legitimate activity. He turned back to his map. Until his guest arrived he could do little to prepare for the trip; the purpose, as yet, a mystery. The Islander was fuelled and serviced so as soon as he had a destination he would put in a flight notification. In the meantime he would have another coffee and a cigarette.

*

Liam watched the local taxi pull up in the lay-by outside the security barrier and the stranger climbed out. Overhead a pair of Phantoms screamed into the circuit slowing rapidly as they turned downwind. The noise abated and he watched, idly, as the undercarriage lowered on the lead jet as it prepared for its approach. Climbing from the car he made his way through the door into the cold corridor outside the Guardroom window, quickly joined by the visitor from beyond the barrier.

"Liam Whelan from Island Air Taxis, can I book this Gentleman onto base please? He's travelling with us today."

He pushed his own identity document through the small window and the Orderly Corporal glanced at it pushing the signing-in book towards him.

"Can I have some ID?" he asked Ilya and was rewarded with a British driving licence, the green paper document suitably dog-eared.

"Thanks Mister Smith," the NCO replied returning the document to the smiling Russian. The formalities were quickly completed and a temporary identification document was issued to the Soviet agent, the airman oblivious to the subterfuge. In the young corporal's defence, the document would have passed scrutiny with any Government agency and was one of many which the Soviet Embassy had acquired by various means, some more reputable than others.

Liam led his visitor through the door back into the chilly breeze and beckoned him towards the waiting car, its air charter logo emblazoned on the doors. As they settled into their seats the irony of the situation was not lost on either of the men. In Liam's case, an IRA sympathiser, he was living and working at the heart of the military establishment. His identification card and vehicle pass gave him free access to the sensitive installation on a daily basis; his aircraft conferring an air of respectability and credence. As he lifted off from the main runway every day he flew over the American US Naval Weapons Facility, home to the mysterious, elite SEAL Detachment One, a specialist special forces unit trained in anti-submarine warfare techniques. Every day he blended in amidst the tight security yet always at the beck and call of his masters in Belfast. For Ilya, a KGB operative and specialist underwater warfare expert, he had just entered the heartland of the enemy he would fight if conflict ever broke out in Europe. As they drove off towards the airfield his eyes scanned left and right taking in the details which he would record later. He yearned for a camera but that might have been pressing his luck a step too far. He made do with committing the scene to memory.

Given the secrecy which had surrounded the charter Liam had expected more conversation but the short journey to the charter office passed in silence, the mysterious visitor clutching his small bag on his knee. Alone in the office, their cups charged with strong black coffee, the atmosphere relaxed a little. Ilya had removed his coat and his casual garb further eased the tension. Unprompted the enigmatic Russian spoke up.

"I'd like to get airborne about an hour before sunset if that's possible. I understand that you have about two hours endurance on full tanks, is that correct?"

"Yes that's about right; give or take. If I climb to economical cruising height I could probably stretch that but if I stay at low level it's probably just less."

"I'll want you down at very low level tonight. I don't want to advertise our presence unnecessarily so we need to stay below the radar coverage."

"It's very patchy in this area once you get out of Prestwick's coverage. Stornoway is better placed but even they struggle keeping track of you among the islands. That is if you don't squawk and give them an identification. I don't need to file a flight plan as we can operate VFR but

I'll need to let base operations know of my plan. It would attract attention if I didn't."

"Book out for a navigation exercise unless you know of a beach strip where you could land. That would explain my absence on your return."

"That's a bit odd for an air taxi charter. Sightseeing trips at this time of the year are few and far between. So you're not coming back with me?" he queried.

"No and the reason will be obvious once we get airborne. Forgive me but for your sake, I don't want any awkwardness so I'll give you our destination once we're in the air. If they want departure details give them an outbound heading of 300."

"That takes us out to Islay."

"True. Do you know of a beach strip up that way that would be a suitable diversion?"

"Yes, there one on the western side of the island. I use it often."

"Good. Your piloting skills come highly recommended Liam. I have every confidence in your abilities and I think you'll find tonight's exercise quite interesting. In fact I'd say, very interesting."

He placed a conspiratorial arm around his shoulder. Unsettled by the sudden intimacy Liam moved off, sat down at a large planning table and began scribbling furiously on a notepad, his brow furrowed in concentration.

Ilya switched his attention to Maria moving over to the desk where she was busy making notes in a ledger. He perched on the edge of the desk. She sensed his approach and glanced up, unexpectedly meeting his piercing gaze. His eyes were disturbingly dark and his confident aura disconcerting.

"Liam tells me you have good contacts in the area."

"We've been here some time now so, yes, I know most of the locals."

"I need some information and I hope it won't be too difficult to come by,

Maria."

His use of her name was overly intimate yet menacing in equal measure and the thought of declining his request did not really occur to her as an option.

"What would that be?"

She was cautious.

"I hear a detachment of fighters arrived yesterday. I need to know how many aircraft the British are holding on readiness here at Machrihanish. Not just the ones on high alert but how many they have at lower states of readiness too. Do you think you can find out?"

"They've only just arrived but I'm sure I can. If it's the same as previous detachments they'll post their flying programme in the hotel lobby so it shouldn't be too hard to find out. I'll drop by the hotel later and take a look. When are you planning to leave?" she asked casually.

"Later this evening," he replied evasively, "but you can get the message through to Liam here. He'll pass it on."

He turned to leave

"Oh and a few names of the crews would be good if that's possible."

She racked her brains to work out why this strange visitor could possibly be interested in the identities of a few random British aircrew. No matter; she would add a generous charge to the invoice.

CHAPTER 12

Machrihanish Airfield.

Liam moved along the wing line checking the airframe for damage, a task he had completed thousands of times over the years. He stopped at the engine cowling snapping open the quick release fasteners, checking the oil level. However he tried, the viscous liquid always seemed to find its way onto his fingers. He wiped away the mess anxious to avoid clutching a sticky control yoke for the next few hours in the cockpit. Dipping under the fuselage he glanced at the nosewheel checking the strut for leaks and glancing at the tyres. All seemed normal.

Suddenly, the quiet of the coastal airfield was shattered as a pair of Phantoms broke into the circuit, the pop of the airbrakes evident as the throttles were retarded to kill the speed. He had to admit, as a pilot, he yearned to fly a high performance machine and but for his political allegiances things might have turned out differently. He watched as the undercarriage of the lead aircraft extended into the airflow as its pilot set up for the final approach. The jet disappeared from view behind the adjacent building.

He mused over the task ahead trying to decide if the risks were worth the gain. Financially, there was no doubt. It was a good contract and he would normally work for a week for similar reward. He worried that there was so much intrigue surrounding the flight. Just a simple clue as to the destination would let him prepare and, more importantly, come up with reasons for any differences to his usual flight profiles. His mysterious passenger and his odd payload worried him a little and the thought of just dumping him on a beach was alien. For most of his passengers, landing on a beach was the prelim to an overnight stay in a remote bed and breakfast. He doubted that this was the case tonight.

Climbing into the cockpit he flicked on the battery master switch and ran through a few checks. All seemed fine and he was confident that his trusty old bird would be serviceable for the flight. It was rare that it let him down. Satisfied, he flicked off the switch and the gyros began to run down, the whirring breaking the silence in the otherwise quiet cockpit. He climbed out, shut the cabin door and made his way back towards the office.

*

The inner screen of anti submarine destroyers had been troublesome and the Captain of the Akula had taken much longer to skirt around the periphery of the exercise area than he had intended. The positioning had been predictable assuming that he would take a direct line from the start point to the heart of the Soviet Battle Group. His detour around the edge of the box meant he was now approaching from due south. The sensor operators had been listening hard but it seemed that, with the exception of the close-in screen his way was clear. If the captain of the Foxtrot was following doctrine he would be positioned between his capital ship and the expected threat along the threat axis. Coming in from the south he should be able to position astern and make his attack. The chess match was reaching its conclusion and there would only be one winner.

"Captain, sensor, possible contact 045 range 2,000 metres."

The older Foxtrot class sub was noisy in comparison to the new Akula. The new plot seemed likely but maybe his luck was holding. Did he need an active sonar ping? If he did he would broadcast his position to the inner screen and escape would be much more challenging. Without it, the probability of kill of his torpedo would be much lower as he would be launching in a default mode. Sometimes big balls decisions were needed.

"On my mark, one ping."

"But Captain!"

"Stand by!" His tone overrode the caution.

"Ping."

The sound of the sonar boomed loud in the quiet control room. He was rewarded with an echo.

"Range 1,900 metres."

"Weapons check."

"Acquisition Captain."

"On my mark, launch tube 1."

There was a pause.

"Mark."

The clang of the outer door opening rang through the hull but without the ominous hiss of a torpedo leaving the tube. This firing was simulated but the recorders onboard the submarine captured every parameter for subsequent analysis.

"Left 250 degrees, ahead slow, dive 800 metres and rig for silent running."

The Akula heeled into the turn and quietly made its escape. On the surface, the undersea weapons operators were scrambling to make sense of the tactical picture as the screen lit up in response to the surprise attack.

CHAPTER 13

The Ugadale Hotel, Cambletown.

Maria walked into the main entrance of the Ugadale Hotel smiling at the receptionist as she passed. A dull murmur emanated from the bar and she homed in on the source. As she entered her suspicions were confirmed. A few couples were dotted amongst the tables around the room but a small group of men clustered towards the centre of the long bar. The smart casual trousers and V neck jumpers were almost a uniform and the English accents a sure giveaway. Spotting a free space at the far end she made her way over and perched on the bar stool. It would be ideal for what she had in mind. A discrete gap separated her from the crowd but it was close enough to be within easy earshot.

She feigned disinterest angling herself slightly away from the group but could sense the furtive glances and she pressed her advantage crossing her elegant legs, provocatively but with enough style to appear demure. The tart at the bar look was an image she did not want to portray. Glancing at her watch, a look of concern creased her features, all part of the act. The glass of wine she had ordered was cold and she took a sip, the mellow tones of the Chablis suiting her taste perfectly. For some reason she suddenly wondered what the enigmatic visitor would have ordered. For the next ten minutes she slipped an occasional look at her watch, distracted frowns playing to the crowd, or at least to anyone paying her any attention. Soon the move came and it was as predictable as she had anticipated from the moment she sat on the bar stool. A strikingly handsome man moved over and perched on the adjacent bar stool.

"Were you expecting someone?"

"Well I thought so," she replied. "My friend from the town was coming over but I guess she's been delayed. I hope I gave her the right time," she countered trying to seem distracted.

"Can I get you another drink while you wait?" he asked. "My name's Mark Keene by the way, but my mates call me Razor."

"That's an odd nickname. Oh, I see. Keene. Very droll." A little disinterest couldn't harm. As expected, he pressed on.

"I'm in the Air Force. We all have callsigns. Razor's mine. We're just up here for a short time working from Machrihanish."

"Oh are you a pilot?" she asked tweaking his vanity.

"I am as a matter of fact."

"That's exciting. What do you fly?"

"I'm on Phantoms. We're up here from Coningsby."

Razor looked for any signs of subterfuge but his attractive companion seemed genuine in her renewed interest.

"My brother's a pilot. He flies from the local airfield too but only small aeroplanes. We see the Phantoms over here from Leuchars occasionally but it'll be nice to have a bit more activity around here. It's pretty quiet most of the time."

She returned his stare during the momentary lapse in the conversation. She had to admit he was good looking but there was a hint of steel in his eyes. This one would be a challenge but she knew where she was taking this. She hoped he was good between the sheets.

A new face appeared through the crowd and a pint of beer magically materialised on the bar in front of him. He made his way over to the others in the group.

"How are the jets?" an older man asked.

"They're good Sir. We had a radio snag on Hotel but we've done a box change and it's up for a flight check tomorrow."

"Good stuff. Did the troops get away?"

"Yes Sir. They were just wrapping up the shift as I left but they should be away by now. The Flight Sergeant will see that the rest of the jets are bedded down. There's no hangar space because an American detachment is already in town but they all have cockpit covers fitted so that should keep the rain out."

"Good, thanks JENGO, well done. I'll let the Boss know."

Maria feigned interest in the young officer who was doing his best to chat her up but her ear was tuned into the other conversation. It took an unexpected turn.

"I spoke to Leuchars before I left," the newcomer announced. "It sounds like Q was airborne tonight. It was over this way apparently, just off the coast."

"Any trade?"

"They were looking for an unidentified track heading in towards the coast at low level," explained the fresh faced engineer. "They got close but it turned out its lights and they lost it. It sounds like the local commuter plane, an Islander, is overdue. They've diverted a Nimrod to look for it. It's all a bit confused at the minute"

The blood drained from Maria's face and she turned away to mask her expression. Flustered, she fussed with her handbag but her emotions threatened to win out.

"What is it Maria? You look as if you've seen a ghost," said Razor, her distress all too evident.

CHAPTER 14

Two Hours Earlier, the Main Runway, RAF Machrihanish.

Departure clearance issued, Liam turned the Islander onto the main runway and advanced the throttles to maximum power, checking the engine instruments one last time as he rolled without a pause. Accelerating into the stiff westerly breeze the twin engined aircraft was quickly airborne, its high lift wing helped by the breeze. It rose into the sky like an elevator. Already the light was fading at this northerly latitude but he was glad that at least the first half of the flight would be in daylight. As he dropped the right wing he glanced below, the hangars from which he operated clearly visible. Given the conversation with his passenger he didn't expect to see them again for a few hours. Twisting the heading bug on his compass he set 300 which was the best, and only information that he had been given so far.

"Golf X-ray Romeo, is airborne and going to en route frequency. I'll be operating VFR at low level for the next 60 minutes. I'll call you on recovery."

"Golf X-ray Romeo roger, the Belfast pressure is 1024, Portree 1025. Call me on recovery, good evening Sir."

"Golf X-ray Romeo, 1024 set and switching to en route. Good evening."

With no idea of his plan for the next hours and for want of an alternative, he left the frequency on the radio dialled to Machrihanish Tower and waited.

Twenty minutes had passed and the landscape of Islay had passed beneath and they were now over open sea, still heading north westerly. Liam ran through another routine yet redundant check of the aircraft systems, the needles still behaving impeccably. Ilya had been stubbornly silent clutching the bag on his knee which he now began to open. Unable to stifle a glance Liam watched as the bag was placed carefully on the floor, its contents still secretive. A small electronic device appeared on Ilya's knee. The inscrutable passenger played around with a few switches and random lights flashed on the small display. Used to bombs detonating in rubbish bins in Belfast streets, Liam could not suppress a feeling of alarm but his passenger seemed remarkably relaxed.

"Bring it right onto 310. That wasn't a bad guess," he said.

"Look this is killing me. There's nothing ahead other than the Atlantic Ocean and we don't have enough fuel to reach Iceland and return. When do I get to know what's going on and what the hell is that thing?"

"This Liam is a homing device and it's tuned to a beacon. If we follow this we'll land at our destination."

"But there's nothing out there but open ocean. On this heading the next stop is Canada."

"On the contrary Liam. Out there is a carrier battle group of the Soviet Northern Fleet and we will be landing on the carrier itself. The Krechyet or the Kiev as you would know it, is our destination."

There was a stunned silence.

A host of questions rattled through Liam's brain. What was the approach procedure, what frequency would he use to contact the carrier? Would a Russian speak English? There were many more. As if in reply, suddenly, a piece of paper was pushed onto his knee and most of them were answered in an instant. He was to home on the beacon and at range 10 miles climb to 2000 feet contacting "Arrivals" on 132.7. The carrier would turn into wind and he was cleared for a visual approach to the angled deck. If weather conditions were marginal his passenger would give additional guidance.

His aircraft was rugged and built to land on unprepared strips. The strong undercarriage regularly took punishment as it rode over hidden obstructions and it should cope happily with a pitching deck providing he timed his landing correctly. He would prefer to arrive on a down swell than an up swell but he suspected that might not be his choice to make. If the deck was long enough for the Yakolev fighters he knew it carried, it was long enough for an Islander.

"What happens once we're down?" he asked.

"I'll be getting out. I've arranged for you to be refuelled. They'll fill your tanks with AVGAS and then you can return to Machrihanish. Simple as that."

"Well I gotta say this is a delivery flight with a twist."

"It goes without saying that you won't breathe a word about this to anyone Liam. Will you?"

The look was menacing and the spluttered reply was out of character for the normally over confident pilot. His acquiescence seemed to mollify his passenger.

"How does the heading look," he asked, keen to divert attention from the sinister tone of the conversation.

*

The hooter sounded in the Q Shed at RAF Leuchars prompting ordered chaos. It was another day on Q and the crews were happy for some activity. Aircrew were always happy to fly but it would add more pressure on the engineers. Rushed checks complete, the fully loaded Phantom sped down the runway the afterburners reflecting from the asphalt lighting the area around the aft end of the Phantom during its brief passage. Lifting off, the undercarriage retracted into the wells and it climbed away turning west.

*

Ilya twisted the dials on the VHF radio set and listened closely to the Russian broadcast. To Liam the garbled stream was unintelligible and he hoped that by setting up on the deadside he would comply with the in flight procedures. He had scanned the surrounding area and the sky had been devoid of other navigation lights so he hoped he was alone in the circuit. The deck to his left was littered with helicopters and brightly lit. He had no idea what to expect in terms of approach lighting. It would be a revelation as he turned finals. Turning gently overhead the massive ship he made a slack turn downwind. It was obvious from the spray which slashed around the prow of the ship that it was making good headway and with his slow approach speed, he was confident he could put the Islander down in a very short space. The Russian chatter continued in his headset prompting little response from his passenger. Rattling through his downwind checks, setting the switches, he prompted his passenger to tighten his straps. Arriving on a heaving deck, being tightly strapped in was one precaution that seemed prudent. As he turned finals he set the power and dropped the flaps another notch. The landing strip was well lit and a pair of approach aids winked at him from either side of the fantail. What they were telling him was lost on him and may have been more significant to a Yak pilot but, eventually, he was rewarded with a pair of greens either side which seemed good. He played the throttle as the deck loomed closer suddenly conscious of the swell. Approaching the rear of the deck he felt it rise towards him and he flared to compensate. With full flaps deployed, he chopped the throttles and waited for the ship to do the work. The arrival was firm but it killed a few more knots and he braked firmly coming to a swift stop abeam the island. Engaging the brakes he looked around hoping for visual instructions from a deck hand. Nothing. If in doubt, sit tight.

Liam shut down the engines and waited for instructions. The Yakolev fighters were ranged down the aft deck some teetering alarmingly over the edge and with the deck heaving gently, the arc lights cast an eerie glow across the red wooden planks. With barely a backward glance, Ilya opened the cabin door and stepped out onto the deck clutching the mysterious bag and the homing device. The door slammed closed sealing the cabin once more from the elements. Outside the aircraft a Russian technician played with the refuelling cap on the top of the wing while another dragged a second, heavy refuelling hose across the deck. A third technician arrived with what seemed to be a can of oil but Liam gestured to him, lowering his thumb in the universal signal of dissent. Fuel was fine; engine oil he could do without. The technician shrugged and disappeared behind the wing line.

As he watched, his passenger opened a door at the base of the sail and stepped inside pulling it closed behind him. Still wary, Liam sat tight assuming that there would be further instructions but unsure as to how he would interpret them when they came. He could hear the fuel sloshing into the tanks above and behind his head until, eventually, the noise stopped and the metallic scrape of the hose being withdrawn rang through the airframe. The fuel cap was replaced and two of the technicians walked back towards the island. The third tightened the chin strap on his protective helmet and moved out in front of the Islander. He put on his gloves, raised his hand and rotated his wrist, indicating engine start. With still no sign of Ilya, Liam could only assume that his task was complete and he began the start sequence. From the windows at the top of the sail a green light shone down, presumably clearing him for departure. The radio was stubbornly silent.

*

Level at Flight Level 250, the 43 Squadron Phantom tickled the Mach just avoiding dropping a sonic boom on the dormant population below who by now were enjoying a nightcap. The scramble instructions had been clear but brief. Head west and contact Benbecula for control.

*

Happy with his pre takeoff checks Liam rechecked the sail confirming that the green light still shone out. It did. He increased the throttles and gingerly turned the Islander around heading back towards the stern of the Kiev the small airframe battered by the wind. The fighters ranged along the deck offered a reassuring barrier between him and the sea and his confidence returned. Assuming the ship was still steaming into wind he had more than enough deck to takeoff but, even so, he dropped the flaps to the half setting. Why take unnecessary risks? He kicked the rudder bar hard over and pirouetted around leaving a large margin to the stern but as he lined up he gazed at the unfamiliar view. The short strip was bracketed by the enormous sail with its massive radar dishes on one side and a steep drop to the ocean below on the other side. It ended over the open water ahead, a few small gun emplacements visible above the flat deck and off to the side. The red surface of the fore deck was in sharp contrast to the dull colour of the runway. The centreline marking was intersected by a series of white circles marking the landing spots for the Kamov Hormone helicopters, only one of which was visible on deck.

A tense feeling of anticipation assailed the senses as, disconcerted, he cajoled himself to pay more attention. By any standards the next few minutes would be a challenge. Pushing the throttles wide open he held the Islander on the brakes making sure the engines responded correctly. A loss of power during the takeoff roll would be fatal. All seemed fine and, almost reluctantly, he released the brakes and the small aircraft surged forward, quickly picking up speed. With the stiff breeze across the deck he felt the controls instantly become responsive and not for the first time, was grateful for the superb short field performance of the commuter plane. It positively sprang into the air, the pilot conscious of the island of the huge carrier slipping past in his peripheral vision. Almost immediately, the effect of the arc lights diminished and he was returned to darkness.

Setting heading back towards the coast, hugging the waves with his anti collision lights blinking rhythmically, reflecting from the surface below he began to calm down. There would be no one else out here and even if there was, he didn't want to advertise his presence yet. He would get back towards the coast before re-establishing contact with Machrihanish. Idle questions he could do without and he doubted the truth would play well with air traffic control. Flicking the anti collision lights off it left just the dull glow of his navigation lights shining out into the dark night.

What a bizarre episode!

*

The navigator was working hard. The radar contact fleeting as he struggled to maintain contact. The tiny blip was barely visible just clear of the Doppler notch, barely registering as the scanner moved left and right in its incessant search. He had tried to lock to the target and been rewarded with a full track display and a brief indication of the range to the target before the radar protested at the challenge and broke lock. He pattered to the pilot giving the odd heading adjustment to refine the intercept geometry as best he could but his commands lacked confidence. With the scant information his efforts were, at best, a guess. The elusive target began to drift outwards on the display, a hint that it was getting close. One thing was certain, the tiny target was at very low level given that his scanner was set well below their own height. With the area now totally dark, they had descended to their minimum cleared height of 1,500 feet but the radar still showed a small depression angle putting the target just above the waves. Both knew that on a Q scramble they would bend the rules if they needed to in order to get the elusive identification. It would be all they would get tonight because, in the pitch black, there would be no photographs.

"Can you see anything? Twenty right, no range but I reckon it's about 10 miles away."

"Looking."

The pilot peered through the windscreen, the ironwork blocking his view. Releasing his grip on the throttles he moved his head left and right peering around the intrusive canopy arch.

"Negative, nothing seen. Wait. . . . . Got it."

Instinctively, he began to turn towards the fleeting visual contact but was restrained by his back seater.

"Hold it. This guy is really slow. We'll need to lag him around the turn. He's only doing 150 knots. He's on the deck. You happy to drop down to 1,000 feet to give me a chance of tracking him in pulse?"

"Descending," he heard in acknowledgement as the altimeter wound down gently pegging at the new height.

"OK, it's drifting out. Start your turn now. Keep it gentle for starters but stand by to tighten it up. Are you still visual on the target?"

"Affirmative."

The wing dropped and the heavy jet began a gentle turn. The navigator checked the range and bearing to Leuchars running a quick calculation of the fuel they would need to return to base. With the external fuel tanks still feeding they had plenty of gas to finish the intercept but he hoped the air position indicator in his FG1 Phantom was vaguely accurate. As an ex FGR2 man he missed the inertial navigation system desperately and the confidence it gave him to work down to fuel minimums.

"OK harder, he prompted as the tiny blip threatened to skate towards the edge of the radar scope. They were committed to the turn in.

"Just lost the lights," he heard from the front cockpit and his heart sank at the very same moment that the blip disappeared from his radar scope. He flicked quickly into pulse mode and was rewarded with a flood of ground returns across the scope which made reacquisition impossible. Resisting the urge to play with the scanner; after all, the target had just been painting, he wound back the gain on the radar control panel with his left hand and the electronic mess cleared leaving a solid band of ground returns bracketing the display. He stared hard at the area just below the returns knowing that if he was to see the target again, that is where it would be. The target was hugging the deck.

"Any joy on the lights," he queried more in hope than expectation.

"Negative. Black as a proverbial witch's tit out there," came the descriptive reply.

"Keep the gentle turn coming. Looking for the target. Bring the speed back to 250 knots when you can."

He knew the pilot was working just as hard as he was. With a heavy Phantom with a full weapons load, eight missiles and a centreline tank, the aircraft was uncomfortable to manoeuvre. Add to that they were now below their minimum briefed height, it was pitch black and he was asking the pilot to reduce speed to the minimum manoeuvring limit. Nothing could go wrong. . . . .

"Still nothing seen. I reckon he saw us and he's turned his lights off."

*

In the tiny cabin, now plunged into darkness, only the instruments still glowed. Liam watched the anti-collision lights of what he assumed was a Phantom as it rolled in behind. He knew that in the darkness he was now invisible but he had no way of knowing whether the fighter crew was tracking him on radar. Although his heading was taking him back towards

Machrihanish he could not stand idly by and allow the huge jet to close. He pushed the throttles forward and pulled the tiny plane into a hard turn. As the heading began to rotate on the compass the left engine coughed and he glanced at the gauges, seemingly normal. Steadying up on his new heading he took a closer look but there was nothing to suggest anything out of the ordinary. The drone of the propellers returned to normal and he craned his head to check the reaction of the Phantom behind.

*

"Got it, range 2 miles just right of the nose. Bring it right five degrees roll out on 150," the navigator called. Hold the speed at 250 knots."

The airframe responded as the pilot tweaked the stick. The tiny blip sat just below the ground returns and he played with the radar controls to refine the contact, his head lowered over the scope, the weight of his bonedome stretching the muscles in his neck. Suddenly, the blip skated crazily away from the centreline.

"He's turning, come starboard gently."

*

Liam eased the height down but he was already worryingly close to the waves. He had no idea if there were any obstructions out here nor could he see anything. He just hoped that any ship or oil rig platform would be well lit. At 500 feet he was flying below the height of some of the bigger ones. Looking back he cursed as the Phantom had followed his turn, still doggedly in behind and closing rapidly. Surely the tiny Islander could not be painting on radar? There was only one thing for it and, yet again he pushed the throttles to the maximum setting and reefed into a hard turn. He would throw an orbit and hope it spat the Phantom out in front of him. He knew for certain there was no way the huge fighter could follow the tight turn at such a slow speed and so close to the sea. At best it would have to fly a wide orbit and, hopefully lose contact. Mind you, it was some time since he had stretched his own flying skills to these limits. As the compass rotated crazily, the Islander on the limits of its performance, there was a worrying dip in the note of the engines and amid a flurry of captions and an intrusive caution warning, the right engine stuttered. The small aircraft protested and, with the left hand engine still at full power and tightening the turn, it overbanked alarmingly with the loss of thrust. The engine died. Liam dragged the control yoke back towards central but the small commuter plane fought the correction, seemingly intent on destruction. Slowly, he overcame the inertia and the wings began to come back towards level. He was exerting a heavy pressure on the controls and, just as he thought he had recovered the situation, the left engine protested in sympathy and also died. As silence descended, the pressure he was applying on the yoke had an instant effect and the roll rate increased dramatically. Only the rushing noise of the wind past the cabin intruded into his thoughts. So close to the sea he had no options.

"What did they put in the fuel tanks?" he thought feebly, as the Islander starved of thrust and lift, flipped onto its back and nose dived, inverted, into the black waves below.

*

As the Phantom pulled up and away from the waves, the noise of the emergency transponder signal rang out over the guard frequency.

"Benbecula Kilo Lima Alpha 01, do you have that transmission on Guard?"

"Affirmative 01, stand by for instructions."

CHAPTER 15

The Ugadale Hotel, Cambletown.

They lay close, the intimacy of their lovemaking still fresh, his pulse calming, the intense ardour of a few moments ago exhausted. The noise from the bar downstairs had quietened leaving only the occasional clunk from a fire door somewhere in the building to split the tranquillity.

With her evident distress, it had not been long before Razor had coaxed her into admitting that she was worried about her Brother but her brief efforts to track his whereabouts had failed. A call to the office from the payphone in the hotel lobby had been fruitless yet it was a common problem, she revealed. He often arrived in the early hours after landing on some remote beach to drop off mail or a tardy passenger and, usually, seemed oblivious to her apprehension. Far from sympathising, the thought of landing on a deserted beach was alien to Razor and he counted himself fortunate that the Phantom needed 8,000 feet of concrete on which to land. With a few more drinks under the belt and a perfectly delivery killer chat up line, the none too subtle proposition led to a swift exit from the packed bar. She seemed to be a willing victim and they had quickly found their way to his room.

Passion spent, an edge soured her mood and it was not long before Maria began to probe.

"How long will you be here?" she began tentatively.

"I'm not sure. It depends on the exercise we're monitoring," he replied, wary of the direction the conversation might go. In the darkened room her musky scent which had up to now been an aphrodisiac was now a warning.

"It seems to be a small group you're with. Are there just the few guys you were drinking with tonight?"

"We only brought five jets with us," he responded comfortable in the fact that it was an easy detail to verify. They had just made love yet he knew he was talking to a stranger and one about whom he knew very little. He was not sure that the Station "Plod" would be so relaxed with the direction this discussion was going, particularly as her gentle Irish lilt sounded a faint warning. With his lust spent the implications of his recent actions were becoming more problematic and his head was resuming control over his baser instincts. He was keen to move the conversation onto safer ground but she persisted.

"It seems like a small group to look after five aeroplanes."

"The troops are downtown in another hotel," he replied, realising immediately that he had offered way too much information once more. How could so few words give away so much? Again he rationalised his impetuousness in the fact that the troops would already have made their presence known to the local community. He doubted that the bar at their hotel would be quite so quiet just yet.

"There are about 20 of them. The Phantom doesn't like the wet weather over here. It's a temperamental beast at the best of times. I'd be amazed if they are all serviceable in the morning so maybe I'll get a morning free? What about you? How does a young Irish lass come to be living in the Scottish Isles?"

"As I said, my brother flies from Machrihanish. He moved over here after he got his commercial pilot's licence. He's only checked out on twins so he came to where the work is. There's nothing in Northern Ireland with the troubles. No one flies around over there. It's such a small province that most of the traffic moves by road or by helicopter; at least when it's not bogged down at a check point or diverted by a road closure for another bomb blast. Most things that fly in the Province have an RAF roundel painted on the side. The work for small contractors is here in the islands."

"Did he never think of joining the RAF to fly?"

"That was never an option for a Catholic boy in Belfast. His father would have drummed him out of the house at the mere thought. No, he wanted to fly but a civilian licence was the only way he was ever going to spread his wings."

She rolled over and glanced at her watch, the dismissive gesture not lost on Razor.

"So what does tomorrow bring for you? Are you flying? What's it like to be flying with live weapons on board. It must be a blast."

His uncertainty said it all. He ducked the question but his hesitation had confirmed her thoughts. It would be easy enough to check and maybe she could catch a few pictures as a bonus.

"Not sure. We have to be at Readiness 30 at 0830 ready to respond. Luckily so far we've pulled the day shift and QRA at Leuchars is covering any night activity. We've been stood down at night since we arrived and let's hope that carries on."

"So no one is on standby at night?"

He parried the question contemplating the reason for the quizzing. She was pressing too hard.

The difficult silence hung for a few moments before she muttered an excuse and threw back the bed sheets, dressing quickly. At least that solved any difficult discussions over her staying the night. Breakfast had not been part of Razor's plan.

As she closed the door having blown a brief kiss in his direction he reflected on the conversation. The sight of her perfect figure as she had pulled on her skimpy black lingerie was fresh in his mind's eye. She was quite a catch but maybe the risks were a little too high given the circumstances. He would have to act carefully if she reappeared at the hotel. Maybe caution was the order of the day?

As Maria let herself out of the side entrance and made her way to her car, she would never know that the information she had so carefully gathered would never be used. She had pushed hard; the double entendre tickled her sense of humour. Maybe her handsome fighter pilot would have to wait a few days before she decided whether to renew their intimacy. At least she had control over events as he could never track her down unless she chose to renew their acquaintance but she knew where to find him if Ilya asked any more questions. Secretly she hoped that he would but what she did not know was that Ilya was already aboard the Kiev and his thoughts were already focussed on other matters under the waters of Holy Loch rather than the airspace off the coast.

Her mind turned back to more personal business. She could only hope that the rumours about the search and rescue operations were unfounded and that her wayward brother would reappear as he always did. A trip back to the airfield and a few more inquiries should elicit a little more information. In the meantime, she needed to work out how to pass on the information she had already gleaned.

*

Flash walked back into the hotel foyer and made his way over to the front desk. All was quiet and his half-hearted call for assistance fell on deaf ears. He glanced irritably at his watch. It was well past midnight and he had not planned to stay at the Squadron so late. He was, after all, the "guest" for this shindig. Typical that he had been roped in to run the desk on the first full day and, what was more, he had been conned into running the briefings too. With two full tours under his belt he was by far the most experienced navigator on the detachment and he knew the Detachment Commander well from his first tour of duty at Wattisham. Given that most of the other flyers had less than 500 hours on type it was natural that he had been selected. Even so, missing the first night in the bar rankled.

There was still no sign of a receptionist and his bed suddenly seemed increasingly attractive; even more than a nightcap. He slipped behind the counter and looked around for the room keys. Luckily, the long rack concealed behind the desk held a batch of fobs and he moved his finger along the row until it rested on his own room number. He slipped the key off the hook and was about to move out from behind the desk when a noise from the corridor attracted his attention. An unwarranted feeling of guilt flashed through his mind momentarily as he rehearsed his excuse for his presence behind the desk. It was quickly forgotten when an attractive woman emerged from the corridor heading quickly towards the main entrance. Odd that she was heading out at this time of night but it took few mathematical skills to piece together the plot.

Razor you old dog! He smiled. Good to see his pilot's skills with the ladies had not waned. He would catch him over breakfast and discover the sordid details.

*

As Maria checked in at the Guardroom back at Machrihanish she became aware of a flurry of activity behind the security window . Listening to the urgent phone calls she began to pick up a few disparate details but at the mention of the Islander, raw tension gripped her gut. The looks on the faces of the duty personnel told her it could not be good news. Her world was about to be thrown into turmoil.

CHAPTER 16

Aboard the Soviet Research Ship off the West Coast of Scotland.

The technician in the submersible bay aboard the research ship Akademik Mstislav Keldysh eyed the strange device warily. It had been cross-decked from the Kiev just a few moments ago and his instructions had been given by a forbidding man with piercing eyes. His very presence had been unsettling and the technician had no wish to cross him. The fact that the man would be joining the upcoming mission gave further incentive to redouble efforts to make sure the instructions that had been carefully spelled out were carried out to a tee.

The hangar deck was secure and for the last 48 hours only essential personnel had been allowed access. He had been expecting the delivery and, in preparation, the normal remote manipulation arms had been modified with a specially designed cradle to carry a unique payload. With the arrival of the box all the pieces were now in place. His instructions were to unload the device just fifteen minutes before the submersible was moved up onto the deck for launching. He hoped the fittings had been properly specified and that the complex attachment fitted properly. There would be no time for hasty modifications if not and he had no intentions of carrying out any unauthorised alterations. He would play this one by the book. Inquisitive, he briefly considered a sneak preview but the thought of crossing the visitor and incurring his wrath overrode his curiosity.

*

Back aboard the Kiev a second harassed technician carrying a portable Geiger counter pulled the operational planner aside. He should have gone straight to the Captain and his authority allowed that luxury but the junior officer had done him a favour in the past and he needed advice on this one. He also suspected that retribution might follow and it was always good to have top cover. There was a hasty exchange during which the obvious tension he was feeling bubbled to the surface. Although instinct said otherwise, the planner calmed the man with soothing words, assurances were exchanged and the technician hurried away still clutching the instrument.

The planner returned to his working space rubbing his brow nervously. The bad news from the nervous technician was that traces of radiation had been detected in a most unusual location and the readings were so high that he could think of only one potential source for the contamination. His limited mission briefing did not suggest any source even remotely likely to cause the problem so how should he tackle it? If the cause was as he surmised, indiscreet words might seal his fate. The mission was, after all, classified strictly need to know and even his immediate superior in the planning cell was not privy to all the facts. An inadvertent compromise and he would be heading back to the Gulag as soon as they docked in Syria. Some more checking would be prudent before discussing this with anyone onboard. In the meantime he would need to limit the effects just in case the measurements were accurate. If so, he had a serious cleanup operation to tackle.

*

"What do you have for me comrade?"

The air in the small cabin aboard the Kiev was rank, a mix of borscht and vodka even though the latter was supposedly banned onboard ship when it was underway. The man's foul breath suggested that more than a single shot had passed his lips this morning. The ratings, and for that matter even the officers, always found ways to bypass the dictum and elicit drinking dens peppered the bunk rooms, although visitors rarely tracked them down. The senior officers normally turned a blind eye but, occasionally, the habit surfaced more visibly. A number of ratings found themselves before the Captain when the chef had pepped up the fruit drinks served at dinner. The willing victims had gladly accepted the punishment.

The helicopter pilot watched the intelligence analyst closely gauging his condition. The information he sought might be the difference between life and death, not only for the team he was delivering to the beach but, more importantly, for him and his crew.

"I've just received some new data from Fleet Headquarters and I've put it together with our own sensor capture from the last few days," the analyst began. "The picture is quite comprehensive. Let me show you."

He scraped a few documents from the workspace and deposited them, unceremoniously, on the floor. Smoothing out a map of the west coast of Scotland he held it down with weights at each corner and stabbed a finger at a point on the coastline.

"That is the Benbecula air defence radar site and it controls the military air traffic in the airspace around here," he indicated describing a large circle over the littoral approaches. "These range rings I've drawn out in red and green show the projected detection ranges at low level and at 5,000 metres altitude. The dotted rings inside those are the estimates of actual capability and are based on information we've intercepted on the radio. The Phantom crews call their radar contacts and the ground controller verifies each detection over the frequency in use which means he must be able to see something on radar to be able to confirm the contact. Whenever we've heard those exchanges we've plotted them out and the plot you see consolidates the latest information. The rings you see are, admittedly, the best guess but based on actual sources."

"So assessed detection ranges versus observed ranges?"

"Exactly so. What that means is that as you fly in towards the coast you will be detected at longer range if you approach at higher altitude. To have the best chance of avoiding detection you will need to approach at extreme low level. At night that will not be easy and there are many high peaks along the coastline. Granite coastlines will trump a low flying helicopter every time. Will you have night vision goggles?"

"Yes, we've been issued with the latest third generation optics which are very good. They're of East German manufacture but in that field they are masters of their art and produce kit of the very highest quality. Maybe those guys are only allowed their schnapps after their shift is over," he said with a telling wink but shifting the conversation along before the analyst took umbrage. "We've done a lot of our work up sorties flying with them so I'm confident that we can work to the limits."

"Don't forget that once you're close in, you will be in their dark area, forgive the pun, but by then undetectable once more. Again, the lower you fly the better."

"How do you mean?"

"There's a height hole close to the actual radar head because the radar waves travel line-of-sight and are affected by the curvature of the Earth. It means that the further you are from the ground location the less chance you have of being detected at low level. It's like putting a ruler on a football. Unless it's curved there is a gap beneath the beams where they don't make contact. You can, literally, stay beneath the radar."

"What about civilian radars? Is the coverage any better?"

"Prestwick on the Ayrshire coast is the main international airport, although it's not as busy as it once was now that airliners have more efficient jet engines and a bigger fuel load. Glasgow Abbotsinch here," he said, indicating the large town on the western side of the country, "is busier but their radar coverage only extends out to 60 kilometres or so. It doesn't extend out over the islands. Prestwick because it's on the coast has excellent coverage over the sea approaches but the civilians rely heavily on secondary surveillance radar to track inbound flights. Obviously, you won't be transmitting an identification code as you approach so they won't see you unless they get a primary radar hit from you. Again, the lower the better if you work that far south. We think also that there is a passive surveillance site at Benbecula which can monitor electronic emissions both radio, radar and voice and can triangulate a position. Make sure you limit any transmissions that might be detected. Tell your "grunts" down the back end not to chat to their friends back on the ship over their tactical radios or it will be detected by the British. I'll assume you are smart enough not to talk within your formation."

INFILTRATION

The look was sufficient response. The analyst moved on swiftly.

"Actually, they may not be able to triangulate your position because they would need a good cross cut from another site and they may not have that capability but they would know that something is approaching."

"Are there any gaps in radar coverage?"

"Yes. This ring here to the north is the overlapping coverage from Saxa Vord air defence radar site but the topography around these islands means that you could slip through unseen through these inlets here."

He gestured at the map once more pointing out a series of inlets between the islands to the north of the target area. Immediately discounting the option as it would take him well to the north of his objective and leave him short of fuel, the pilot switched tack. He had a time on target to meet and a lengthy diversion was impractical.

"What about re-routing to the south around Prestwick?"

"You could but the gap in coverage is here and if you cut through towards the coast to exploit the gap you'd be faced with a long transit back northwards and you'd need to route overland. It might be dark and sparsely populated in that area but you'd undoubtedly be seen at some stage and maybe reported. Helicopters, particularly at night are still uncommon in this area. No certainty but it's a risk you might not want to take. Stay over the sea and you should approach unseen."

The kernel of a plan was forming. With the coverage maps committed to memory, the helicopter flight leader was mapping out a potential approach path. If he was to exploit the gaps in radar coverage he faced a long diversion and a much higher risk of being seen visually so if he was to approach the target on a direct track but avoid radar detection it was obvious that he needed jamming support. If he couldn't slip through undetected he would need to make sure that his presence was masked in another way.

Suddenly realising that he was becoming immune to the rank odours in the claustrophobic space, the pilot made his excuses and backed out of the tiny compartment. Making his way back towards the rear of the vessel he entered a section of the flight deck where a far more covert helicopter detachment was to be found. Hopefully, they could satisfy the needs of his embryonic plan at the same time as fulfilling their main role.

CHAPTER 17

The Phantom Detachment, RAF Machrihanish.

The clammy blanket of mist shrouded the airfield as Flash made his way across the dimly lit taxiway towards Squadron operations, the lights in the line hut on the opposite side glowing through the gloom as he approached. The light blue RAF Ensign hung limply on the hastily erected flag staff, the calm conditions unusual along the normally windswept coastline. A cab rank of Ford Escort estate cars interspersed with the occasional Land Rover, blended into the dismal surroundings of the bleak dispersal. Provided for the detachment by the Motor Transport Flight back at base, the drab green, matt colour scheme picked them out; instantly recognisable as service vehicles, painted to blend into the background protecting them from air attack. Perversely gaudy yellow stripes, a sop to health and safety, had been applied along the length of the vehicles making them stand out, instantly negating any tactical advantage conferred by the tone down. Doctrine had it that the conspicuity markings would be painted out on Day One of a future conflict, along with all the other last minute measures that, likely, would not be implemented immediately. Logic suggested that leaving them in a more neutral colour scheme until that eventuality presented itself might be more sensible. Fortuitously, the MT Flight had been unable to provide enough cars for the whole of the detachment's needs and the Duty Authoriser had been allocated a shiny new rental car. As the first recipient, Flash had enjoyed his drive in to work in the pristine new VW Golf. It even ran on petrol rather than the obligatory diesel that powered the Escorts and the engine was smooth and responsive rather than sounding like a sack of hammers.

Looking across the airfield he could see the Phantoms parked in a neat row on the hardstanding just a short distance away. The two quick reaction alert jets had been positioned close to the building in which the crews had already taken up a less than salubrious residence. The canopies were open and exposed to the cloying drizzle as the groundcrew who had been hard at work for some hours already checked them over. The aircrew who were about to take over the duty were engrossed in the cockpits setting switches and positioning straps ready for an anticipated scramble. He checked his watch. They were due to declare on state in about fifteen minutes. Please let there be no delay on the first morning or the phones would be hot and he would be the butt of any criticism. The three remaining jets were closer on the flightline still cocooned in the rubberised cockpit covers to protect them from the elements. The protective shields reminded him of giant condoms. He put that thought aside.

Flash had been upset to pull the first stint as Duty Authoriser but, having just spoken to the "Met. Man", it might be that his luck was in. A nasty little weather front was working its way through the area from west to east and it was, presently, sitting right overhead the Soviet Battle Group so the chances of launching off the deck were somewhere between slim and zero. He guessed that if the intelligence assessments were to be believed, with limited instrument ratings the Soviet pilots would not be flying for some hours yet. The front was slow-moving and not expected to pass through Machrihanish until late morning and his first directive had been to warn the engineers to keep the canopy covers fitted on the training jets until the heavy rain passed through. As the front pushed in, it would stir up the fog and it would lift into low stratus clouds but it would be low enough to ground the Phantoms for the morning. The two jets on Q would be held on a "Mandatory" state and would only launch in dire operational need but for the next few hours training flying was out of the question. The last thing he needed was for the jets to divert to another base with the risk of being declared unserviceable during the landaway. Trying to send engineering support to somewhere like Prestwick did not bear thinking about, although he could imagine that the groundcrew would be happy with yet another change of scenery. Conditions were expected to improve once the front had blown through so he would give the hotel a call and let the crews have a leisurely breakfast. A little sop to individual comforts never hurt. The intelligence briefing scheduled for the afternoon could be brought forward and, at least they would do something productive to start the day.

Pushing into the darkened Nissen hut he flicked on the lights and the fluorescent tubes flickered into life, reluctantly at first. The old wartime sheds with their rounded tin roofs were dotted around the airfield, a legacy of the rapid expansion during the Second World War. The more substantial brick-built infill at the end of the hut held a rickety door and two equally suspect window frames barely adequate to seal the temporary quarters from the hostile Scottish climate. Double glazing had not yet reached this Scottish outpost. This would be their home for the duration of the deployment so the onus was on them to make the most of the austerity. Stoking up the fire would be a good start.

Making his way through the makeshift crewroom, the easy chairs arranged around the walls in regimented fashion, he entered the hastily configured operations room with its raised desk backed by Perspex covered boards ready to spring into action as the flying programme got underway. The rudimentary operations desk boasted only two telephones in the way of technology and the chinagraph markers which would be used to annotate the flying programme were more World War 2 than Star Wars. As the harsh fluorescent lights illuminated the scene the planned flying programme seemed instantly optimistic. The two QRA aircraft were prominently marked at the top of the board with their nominated crews who had just declared on state at first light. The telebrief box in the corner of the room reverberated with radio checks adding a reassuring familiarity to the unfamiliar location. Unlike their compatriots at Leuchars, they had not been tasked to mount Q overnight, filling only the daylight commitment; a rare luxury. With the alert crews now on state in the adjacent, equally palatial Nissen hut, he would drop in and say good morning as soon as he had rearranged the programme. Perhaps he would coincide with the delivery of breakfast from the Officers' Mess across the airfield.

With five jets available they had optimistically planned three waves of two Phantoms. All the jets were armed so he could use any of them for QRA duties if the need arose including when they were airborne. Providing the QRA aircraft had sufficient fuel for a supersonic intercept they could remain on state but, as soon as their fuel reserves ran below that magic figure they would be recalled and refuelled before going back on alert. It had been tempting to plan the three remaining jets on the first wave but prudence had suggested keeping the last jet as a spare for QRA. Falling down on the commitment would generate phone calls from an assortment of unwelcome desks at the Headquarters and the Boss had already diplomatically suggested that the Air Officer Commanding No. 11 Group was taking a personal interest. A call from his outer office would be a fun start to a dank day. He drew a swift chinagraph mark through the first pair cancelling the sortie, pencilling in the intelligence briefing for 1000. That meant that the mid day wave could brief at 1100 and launch at 1200 when, hopefully, the poor weather would have cleared through.

Lossiemouth on the Moray Firth was ahead of the weather front and was still wide open blue with fair skies. He would be able to use that as a diversion for QRA until its weather deteriorated as the front passed through. Hopefully by then, the worst would have cleared the west coast and Prestwick should have improved to give him a local diversion behind the weather front and the chance to lower the recovery fuel. He made a quick call and booked the airfields as diversions before the rest of the flying units caught on and submitted block bookings. Another quick call to the hotel to alert Squadron Leader Silversmith, the intelligence officer, to bring his briefing forward sorted out the hastily arranged running order. He had already booked a met briefing for the crews when he had dropped into the Met Office so that just left him to boil the kettle for his second cup of coffee of the day. I love it when a plan comes together he thought, contentedly. Now how do I get myself on the flying programme?

He stoked the coals in the archaic metal stove in the centre of the room coaxing the embers back into life. The heart of the fire glowed promisingly and he added a few nuggets of coke prompting a welcoming bank of flames. Warmth radiated from the stove and his morale instantly picked up as the kettle grumbled on the coffee bar, its contents slowly stirring to life.

The door pushed open.

"Afternoon, Mike," he remonstrated. "Nice of you to pop in."

"Sorry Sir," the ops clerk mumbled, "My alarm didn't go off. I had to hitch a lift in with the lineys."

"Detachment rules apply. The transport leaves on time and if you're not there, it goes without you. We'll call that your joker but don't be late again. This is an operational detachment. You're lucky there's no flying this morning or I might not have been quite so relaxed!"

"Sorry Sir," he repeated sensing a lucky escape. "Let me sort out the coffees. Yours is standard NATO isn't it?"

"It is. I'll be in the ops room."

Flash held his best irritable look until he was beyond the connecting door. The young airman fussed around the makeshift coffee bar, dragging together the ingredients for the drinks, giving the milk a hesitant sniff test before adding it to the large mugs. He breathed another sigh of relief at avoiding "jankers" realising that his other morning task had been to drop into the NAAFI on the way by to collect the milk. Another bullet dodged.

*

The chatter quietened as the overhead projector flickered on, the bright light illuminating the confined space. The small briefing room was crowded and a few bodies that had been late to arrive were propped against the side walls filling every available space.

"Morning Gents," Flash began, "We'll start with the met forecast."

The forecaster stepped up and placed his first slide on the projector, the spider lines of the synoptic chart filling the white wall that acted as a temporary screen. His lilting Scottish brogue suggested he was at home on the secluded coastline of the Western Isles.

"A deep low pressure over Iceland is heading east at about 30 knots. A warm front passed through Machrihanish at 0600 Zulu and is now affecting Abbotsinch airport to the east. The occluded front which is following is just to the west of us now and will pass through at about 1000 Zulu so expect a clearance shortly afterwards. Its progress is brisk so I would expect blue conditions by 1200 Zulu. Conditions behind the front are good. Machrihanish is presently red in fog with 400 metres visibility and a 100 foot cloudbase. The surface wind is calm but will pick up to westerly at 10 knots as the front approaches. Kinloss and Lossiemouth are presently blue but I expect the conditions to deteriorate as the warm from passes through. Prestwick is also red, tempo amber in fog and will pick up about the same time as we do. Leuchars is blue and will not go down until well into the afternoon. If they experience the same poor conditions as we have now you can expect QRA to be mandatory for a few hours. You may be the first line of defence against the Soviet hordes for a while," he smiled. "Behind the front conditions are good and I expect good flying conditions for the next two days before further depressions begin to work in from the Atlantic. Any questions gentlemen?"

"How about conditions in the low flying areas?" called a voice from the back of the room.

"Unusable at present but once the front goes through you're looking at 10 kilometres plus on the visibility and scattered clouds at about 3000 feet. You may see some clouds on the hilltops but few and far between. If you head east you'll chase the front down and rapidly run into this stuff he said pointing to the front on his charts."

"Good conditions tonight?" asked a green-suited body on the front row knowing well that he was immune as his crew duty hours would be all but exhausted by then. His interest was more attuned to pale ale and scotch than practice intercepts.

"Yes indeed. You can expect blue conditions all night although a wee breeze may step up at dusk. There's nothing that should give you any crosswind problems though."

Flash thanked the genial forecaster as he rustled his slides together and passed on a printed copy of his forecast before leaving.

Flash took over.

"Gents, we have four jets serviceable but Papa needs rectification for a radar snag. The engineers are just about to work on it once the rain eases and it should be up in about an hour, well before the weather clearance. X-Ray and Lima are Q1 and Q2. Uniform and Oscar are available for the training sortie but all the jets are fully armed and carrying a gun so watch your weapon safety checks during any intercepts. Base is using Runway 28 with all the aids serviceable with the exception of the TACAN which is on maintenance. They estimate it will be back online at 1000 Zulu before we start flying. There's no flying state yet but expect a No.1 diversion of Leuchars and a No. 2 diversion of Prestwick. Leuchars fuel is 4800 lbs on the ground and Prestwick is 2800. Once the front is through I hope we'll have visual recoveries with Prestwick fuel on the ground. Expect the No.1 diversion to change as the front goes through Kinloss but check before you brief for the sortie. The West Freugh and Luce Bay weapons ranges are live today with air-to-ground firing so avoid those unless you want a bit of frag. damage. There's a Royal Flight heading up the Ambers passing Polehill reporting point at 1330 Zulu and then heading north easterly and landing at Aberdeen. The Queen is heading for Balmoral so make sure you don't provide an armed escort! Any questions on ops? Sir. . . . . " he said deferring to the Detachment Commander."Would you give us an update on 11 Group's orders and the rules of engagement."

The Detachment Commander took over the podium.

"Our task is to monitor the exercise activity but with a particular emphasis on the Forgers. The Nimrods will take care of the submarine activity and they've been shadowing the fleet since it entered our waters. We're reasonably happy with the Hormones and how they operate but if you see anything of interest make sure it goes in the ADMISREP and take pictures. It's not often we get chance to observe them so closely so don't pass up on an opportunity. Leuchars Q will take most of the trade to the north coming through the Iceland-Faeroes Gap and they can expect a bit of help from the US fighter squadron at Keflavik in Iceland. Once it comes down into the area expect it to be our problem. You'll be flying live armed jets on every sortie so be absolutely fastidious over your weapons safety checks."

There was a murmur amongst the aircrew. The Phantom was configured to replicate flying with an armed load of weapons for every training sortie and the indications on the weapons panels and the audio warnings in the headset were similar whether it was carrying a drill Sidewinder or the real thing. Apart from the feel through the controls caused by the weight of the increased weapons load, there would be no difference in the cockpit that would alert the crews to their deadly payload. The piece of duct tape around the master arm switch, somehow, seemed barely adequate as a warning of the implications of selecting "Arm".

"The rules of engagement. . . . . There is no change to normal peacetime rules."

There was a groan.

"You have the sovereign right of self defence and the right to use equivalent force as always. Other than that you are "weapons tight". Make sure you are scrupulous with your safety calls. If you're working Benbecula or with the Shackleton you'll receive calls for safety checks at 10 miles. If you're autonomous make sure you cross check within the formation. No exceptions. Normal visual identification signals apply if you intercept a "Zombie". Recheck the procedures from the flight information handbook and carry them with you. There's additional guidance in the classified "noddy guides". Remember, the Soviets are operating in international waters so they have as much right to be there as we do. Think those things through carefully and discuss it as a crew. Don't wait until you're alongside before you think about your response to a bit of aggression. Screw up and over react and I'm afraid you won't find too many allies at Group Headquarters. Careers will be made during this exercise so expect their "Airships" to demand perfection. It's easier in an office to second guess an inappropriate response than it is to get it right in the first place. Unless there's an increase in the Counter Surprise state it's still a case of fire only if fired upon."

There was a murmur of discontent in the audience. It was to be expected given the obvious aggression of recent days from the Soviets but disturbing nonetheless. He pressed on.

"Flash has a copy of the Operation Order on the ops desk. Take a look and make sure you're familiar with its content. The RoE are summarised in there and you'll all carry "noddy guides" with a summary of the key facts. Flash."

"Thanks Sir. OK let's move on to the intelligence. Squadron Leader Silversmith."

The grey haired intelligence officer stood up and moved to the dais. He flipped a slide onto the projector and a full screen shot of a sleek ship flashed onto the wall.

"The Battle Group Flagship, the Kiev," he announced pausing for effect.

CHAPTER 18

The Soviet Embassy, London.

The thick-set man slumped into a richly ornate sofa and lit a foul smelling cigarette. His companion relaxed opposite sipping sweet Russian tea, the tranquil ambience at odds with the substance of the discussion.

"Did the Karp pick up the British boomer on departure?"

"No. It wasn't even in the right spot. I think the Brits had advanced warning of our screen. The wily old bastard in the submarine headed south through the Irish Sea and out into the Southwest Approaches and is, by now, deep in the Mariana Trench. He's already gone silent."

"This can't go on. The Politburo is paranoid about the risks from NATO and our continued failure to track the nuclear boats is making it worse. Since the Americans deployed SOSUS the whole situation is now dangerously one-sided. The problem is that the Brit boats have free rein yet our own submarines are invariably detected by the sensors. They're just too noisy. We have someone on the inside at Brawdy from where the SOSUS is controlled and his reports of its effectiveness are acutely worrying. It seems to have almost a 100% success rate over the recent weeks and, unless the new Akula proves its worth during the present trials we have a severe imbalance."

"That's hardly our problem here in London though Comrade. There's no way we can infiltrate Faslane. It's sealed up tighter than a drum. Any progress will be down to the efforts of the Banner Fleet."

"Of course that's true. We can only support the operation that's planned and Murmansk has the lead on that. All the tasking will, and must, go through formal channels but we need to be responsive."

"Is our man aboard the flagship?"

"He is. The insertion was perfectly executed. Your arrangements were flawless so congratulations."

"Perhaps, but I assume you heard the news? We lost the pilot I'd been cultivating. The details are hard to come by but it sounds like an unfortunate accident. The flight out to the Kiev was at night but the plane didn't return to Machrihanish. Search and rescue operations were initiated but, so far, there is no sign of any wreckage. The newspapers report that contact was lost with the plane somewhere just off the coast."

"Unfortunate. Do you have a replacement?"

"Not directly and finding a new pilot as capable as him will be difficult. Mind you, the Scots are a canny race and they are always willing to take a fast profit. I just have to make sure they cannot link any future operations back to us here. They may be fond of a fast deal but most of them are fiercely patriotic. Any hint of foreign involvement and they will close ranks. Now the Irish are a different proposition with the troubles in the Province. That may be an easier solution. I'll follow it up with our friends in Belfast. I'm sure they must have more than one pilot on the books."

"Does it affect the current operation?"

"No I don't think so. All the pieces are in place already. I do have one other option if I need local support but the agent is not a flyer. I'll try not to exercise it if I can avoid doing so."

"Very cryptic. I won't delve."

"Perhaps better not."

There was an easy silence.

"What of our man aboard the Kiev once the operation is complete?"

"There is a complication I must admit and I need to play my hand carefully. Leave that detail to me. I'll make the arrangements for his repatriation. I'm under instructions direct from Moscow on that one."

"So what is our role now?"

"We sit tight and wait for further guidance. It's gone to plan so far but you know what they always say about plans. They never survive first contact with the enemy."

CHAPTER 19

The Briefing Room, RAF Machrihanish.

"Gentlemen, this is presently the most potent ship in the Soviet fleet and, right now, she's sitting just a few hundred miles off the Scottish coast," announced John Silversmith stabbing his pencil at the reflected image of the Kiev. "Your task is to monitor the exercise activity but let me update you on the intelligence background so that you can put it in context. I'll start with the composition of the fleet and the supporting forces, then give you some politics, outline their mission, and finish with the Task Force Commander's intentions as we understand them. A health warning; don't ask me about sources because I'm not at liberty to discuss them. Then again, I'm sure you don't care where the information comes from do you?"

The carefully primed stove in the next room groaned audibly, on cue, somewhat spoiling the contrived drama.

"Kiev is the flagship for Admiral Vasili Gerasimek the Commander of the Battle Group. It's a powerful warship in its own right armed with four twin SS-N-12 Sandbox surface-to-surface missile launchers with a total of eight missiles. Add to that, ten 533 mm torpedo tubes and a twin SUW-N-1 anti-submarine rocket launcher with nuclear rounds and two RBU-6000 anti-submarine rocket launchers. It looks impressive but there's more. For self defence it has two twin SAN-3 Shtorm anti-aircraft systems, two twin SAN-4s, the equivalent of the land-based SA-8 Gecko, two twin 76mm guns and eight AK-630 close-in-weapons systems. It normally carries a compliment of 12 Yak-38 Forger fighter bombers and 20 Kamov Ka-25 Hormone anti-submarine helicopters. For this cruise it has its full complement of both types aboard. It's capable of 32 knots at full chat which would see off most speedboats but you'll probably keep up in your Phantoms. Stay with me, there'll be a test at the end."

He glanced around and, remarkably, there was no sign of hangover-induced lethargy. The gravity of events had seen most of the aircrew in bed at a sensible hour the previous evening, unlike many previous training detachments. It was an unusual precedent and there was an air of determination pervading the room.

"The supporting vessels include two Kashin class destroyers with an anti-air warfare capability, three Krivak II anti-submarine frigates, two SAM Kotlin air defence picket ships and the Moskva helicopter carrier. Finally there are three fleet resupply tankers, an ocean-going tug and two Ropuchka class landing ships. One vessel is a surprise addition. We've identified the research ship Akademik Mstislav Keldysh but quite why a research vessel should be accompanying the group is a mystery. We've tasked the Nimrod crews to keep close tabs on her movements in case she slips away from the fleet. She carries a submersible that could cause mischief if allowed to roam unchecked in these waters but if she attempts to launch it there should be plenty of warning. It's normally quite a protracted operation to get it into the water. The group is supported by Bear Charlies, Deltas and Foxtrots operating from Mother Russia routing into the area via the normal flight path around North Cape. They are working with two submarines in the area. One is thought to be supporting the task force, a Sierra class hunter/killer, the Karp, whereas the other is a new Akula class attack submarine which we think is undergoing sea trials prior to operational declaration. The Nimrod boys are tracking their movements daily."

He moved on to a topic more close to the hearts of his audience.

"We're particularly interested in the Forgers and if you should come across one, particularly if it reacts, make sure you take copious notes and file a full report. This is the Soviet answer to the Harrier and it's the first time we've seen them in the forward area. They've built over 200 of them including a two seat trainer variant that is fully operational. The main Tumansky turbojet engine develops about 16,000 lbs thrust giving it a theoretical maximum speed of about 700 knots at low level although we all know the limitations of big fan engines given that the Harrier hits a barn door at 500 knots. Its service ceiling is about 36,000 feet but, unlike the Harrier it relies on two Rybinsk lift engines to give it its vertical takeoff and landing capability. The intake is set in the upper fuselage and a door opens into the airflow at slow speed diverting air into the lift fans. There's some movement on the aft thrust nozzles but it's not the full range such as you'd see on the Harrier. The up side is that the lift engines are powerful and it has reasonable manoeuvrability in the hover. The down side is they carry that dead weight at all times and that gives operational limitations. There are a couple of interesting features. Approach and landing to the carrier is fully automatic. They obviously don't trust their pilots that much so the automatics do it for him. If you have the chance to observe this phase, pay close attention and have the camera ready. If the lift fan fails, the seat automatically fires and ejects the pilot. Let's hope they have that function working correctly or you may get some dramatic shots. It carries rocket pods, gun pods and air-to-air missiles on four external hard points but it doesn't have an internal gun. This is where the limitations come in. Because of payload restrictions it can only carry about 4,500 lbs of ordnance. The rockets are all dumb, line-of-sight weapons with no guidance; just ballistic. You might see it fitted with two air-to-surface, AS-7 Kerry missiles if it's operating in the anti-shipping role. That also needs a targeting pod which takes up an additional pylon and we'd like some pictures of that if you get close enough. We're not sure if it can take an air-to-air missile on the spare pylon in this fit so, again, keep an eye out. For self defence it can carry up to four AA-8 Aphid infra-red guided missiles both the Alpha and Bravo variants. The latter has infra-red counter-countermeasures so let's hope our flare designers are on top of that problem, although with those RoE you might not have the opportunity to find out. The guns are standard Gsh-23 23 mm cannons similar to those carried by the Mig-23 Flogger Bravo. It's a good gun and very reliable; a high rate of fire and very few jams from what we've observed on the training ranges in East Germany."

As he made each point, a picture showing various weapons fits flashed up, the origins of which were extremely questionable prompting a good deal of interest from the crews. The sharp images were a refreshing change from the usual grainy pictures in the vault back on the Squadron.

"If you have any chance to carry out a performance comparison of the

Forger against the Phantom, take it. Any parameters are of interest to us such as straight line speed, top end speed, acceleration, turn performance and climb rates but anything you can assess at all is of value. Analysts can predict all day long but real world comparisons are invaluable."

A slide of a bulbous looking submarine replaced the shot of the Soviet cannon breaking the mood as the efficacy, or otherwise, of the underwater design was lost on the air defence crews. With their lack of an air-to-ground capability, other than the SUU-23 gun, submarines were someone else's problem.

"Make no mistake, this is the most powerful task force the Soviets have ever formed and they are making a statement, so why? Two years ago we ran an exercise in the West called "Able Archer". It's now recognised that we came as close to provoking a Soviet nuclear response as it is possible to come without actually releasing nuclear weapons. It was as close as the Cuban Missile Crisis of the 1960s A paranoid Soviet leadership saw the exercise play as being so realistic that it believed the preparations were underway for a pre-emptive nuclear attack on the Soviet Union. It seems that getting the Prime Minister involved was not as useful as it might otherwise have seemed to the exercise planners. Thankfully, disaster was averted and a lot of effort has gone into calming Soviet nerves in the meantime. The consequences, however, are that the current Soviet leadership has strengthened its conventional forces and is intent on projecting Soviet influence. Its first step is to match the efforts of the US Sixth Fleet in the Mediterranean but more of that in a moment. What you are witnessing here is the first Soviet demonstration of naval power in our own back yard."

He switched slides, a map of the operational area appearing on the wall behind him.

"This is the exercise area. It's quite a large piece of airspace because of the submarine play. The submarine captains need a broad front in order to approach the fleet unseen. We know the Akula is in the north of the area and working roughly in a southerly direction towards the task force. Expect heavy Nimrod activity in the vicinity of Rockall, here," he said pointing out the small rocky outcrop at the top end of the slide. "We expect daily activity from the Bears setting anti-submarine screens to prevent its passage south.

INFILTRATION

If you keep a daily plot of where the Bears and Nimrods are operating you'll get a feel for how the underwater exercise is unfolding. We think the Akula is tasked to take out a Foxtrot class submarine supporting the Kiev and is acting alone. The Sierra is tasked to take it out but it has the entire anti-submarine forces of the Battle Group to assist. That's a formidable defence. If the Akula succeeds there will be some worried staff officers in Moscow. If it fails, there will also be some worried staff officers in Moscow but, under those circumstances, more from within the project team. The Akula has been touted as the saviour of the Northern Fleet and is rumoured to be quiet enough to track a "boomer". If so, the Naval HQ at Northwood is going to be having some sleepless nights over the coming months."

The last slide flicked off.

"Let's finish up with intentions. I mentioned that the Sovs want to challenge the US naval presence in the Med. Once the Battle Group concludes its exercise manoeuvres it will head down the west coast of Ireland, through the Straits of Gibraltar and into the Mediterranean. We expect it to conduct more flying operations off the North coast of Africa working with the Libyan Air Force before sailing east and docking at Tartus in Syria for a port visit. We think it's all to do with sustainability as well as flag waving. They have to satisfy themselves that the Forger is supportable for an extended cruise. We already have our doubts and will be monitoring how many jets they manage to launch on each flying event. The PR9 photo reconnaissance Canberras will detach from Wyton to Sigonella air base in Sicily to monitor that phase along with a Nimrod flying from Gibraltar. Don't discount a Phantom detachment to Gibraltar in support if the Libyans show any tendency towards sabre rattling."

Spirits rose instantly at the thought of a sojourn to Gibraltar rather than the bleak Scottish coast. At that moment to door to the briefing room opened and a face peered in, instantly self conscious as every head in the room turned to face the interloper.

"Sir," the ops clerk called hesitantly, attracting Flash's attention. "You have a call from 11 Group. It's Air Defence Fighters on the line. Sorry to interrupt but he says it's urgent."

Flash moved swiftly towards the door mumbling his apologies. What now, they hadn't even started flying yet! Behind him he heard the Detachment Commander wrap up the briefing which broke up noisily. The ops clerk handed him the phone and he subconsciously, took in the detail from the weather tote anticipating a rebuke over their inaction. Taking in the colour states of the local airfields and analysing instantly the meteorological situation, he was ready to respond. The front was nearly through and the airfields to the west were showing much improved conditions. The excuse had been rehearsed before even hearing the accusation. As it was the conversation was immensely more promising. His summary of the operational situation confirming that they would have flyable weather within the hour was almost dismissed without challenge and the news was positive. He acquiesced without complaint returning to the briefing room to impart the good news to his pilot. He had been given a solution to his earlier challenge as to how he might insert himself onto the flying programme.

"Razor, they want us airborne as soon as we can fire up a jet. They're happy for us to launch with a risk of diversion if the front slows so I figured that as I was just handing over the running of the operations desk and that we were next in line, that we'd take the trip."

It was all the prompting his pilot needed. A trip was a trip after all.

CHAPTER 20

Aboard the Soviet Aircraft Carrier Kiev.

The group of pilots sat around the briefing table shuffling pens and sipping mugs of hot tea, the presence of the steaming samovar in the corner of the briefing room giving a cursory semblance of normality despite the clinical metal clad surroundings. The rattles and groans of a working military vessel left no doubt that life was far from normal.

At the head of the table, the tactical air controller brought the proceedings to order, the Political Officer on his right immobile, his gaze inscrutable.

"Comrades, this is our first full-up tactical mission in NATO waters and we aim to demonstrate our presence and exercise our rights of navigation. Firstly our Political Commissar will introduce the strategy."

The Politico began to speak, his face serious, his oratory formal.

"Thank you Comrade. Today we will show that we can project air power into the very heart of NATO waters; airspace that NATO has dominated for far too long. We have already been followed by NATO warships shadowing us, albeit at a respectable distance and they continue to track our progress. That is fine and to be expected. We have drawn their attention and, dare I say it, their respect in displaying our new capabilities. The air forces have been less accommodating but today we will show our hand. We plan to demonstrate that our tactics are equal to theirs and that, no longer can they operate with immunity in the rear areas."

The audience was respectfully attentive yet perplexed. Unlike the party man they had been flying from the deck and had watched events from first hand.

The tactical air controller took over bringing matter back to Earth after the Politico's carefully prepared speech.

"Today's mission is to execute a set piece tactical scenario optimised against the British and American Phantoms carrying the AIM-7E Sparrow or Skyflash missiles. Operating from their bases in Scotland and Iceland they patrol these waters and, in wartime, have the endurance and firepower to operate well beyond their coastline. If this deployment was an operational mission we would be well within the range of these weapons in our current position."

He glanced at the Politico who nodded sagely, clearly unaware of the differences between a Sparrow and an Atoll missile.

"Your callsigns will be Molotok for the attack force and Serp for the formation simulating the Phantoms. Translated into English these callsigns mean Hammer and Sickle so I hope the honour of adopting them is not lost on you. You will receive vectors to your nominated start points from your respective controllers and your briefing sheet has the coordinates for those positions. Our technology for computing the coordinates from a moving vessel is in its infancy so your controller's instructions will override any radio information. If they reposition you must pay close attention to your instructions. The new datalink will be tested again today and, if possible, all instructions will be relayed via the link reducing our vulnerability to monitoring and, more importantly, to hostile jamming. Once at the start point, Serp will be vectored inbound and will fly a formation similar to the profiles known to be flown by the Phantoms, known to them as battle formation or combat spread. Molotok will begin at its own start point and the first section will be flying in loose combat formation vectoring towards Serp. The second section will orbit in a left hand pattern and pick up a trail formation in behind but will also fly in loose combat formation. The spacing between the formations must be exactly 12 kilometres and precision is critical if the tactic is to be effective. It represents the maximum range of the Sparrow missile at the heights you will be flying. I want your radars in standby mode to allow me to set up a passive attack. You may operate your infra red missiles normally but it is unlikely that you will detect Serp until much closer and, probably, only when you are in a firing position. You may, however, detect the lead formation from within the trail formation so it might give you situation awareness. Hold loose combat formation until you receive the instruction "Widen". At that point open out to 3 kilometres between aircraft and follow the vectors I pass to you. Under no circumstances should you activate your radars until called as it is vital not to warn the defenders. At the "Execute" command, you should turn through 90 degrees in the direction called. The direction of turn will depend on the intercept geometry at the time so pay close attention. This will drag Serp into a tailchase behind the lead formation allowing the second section to position in behind and take a missile shot. Wait for the call of "Activate" before you turn on your radar ranging sets."

He was concerned at the lack of attention and not a single note was being taken. Either their recall was impeccable or they were planning to rely implicitly on the directions from the ground. They might be operating over NATO waters for the first time but flexibility was a feature that would take time to develop, heaven forbid that it should be encouraged.

"Any questions so far? We will also demonstrate a second scenario allowing Serp to attack the trailing formation. When the attack occurs, the leaders must turn through 270 degrees and position in-behind to press home a follow-on attack. In both circumstances, once you have locked on the missile seeker heads I will give authority to engage if I am satisfied with your parameters. We will practice both scenarios today."

The aircrew remained silent used to receiving instructions rather than being asked for opinions. Free thought was wasted and the presence of the Politico guaranteed their subservience. They would hold their thoughts until the privacy of the flight briefing.

"Very well comrades. We can split now for your own domestics briefing and be ready to launch at the slot times on your briefing guide."

The small group broke up and the pilots left the room obediently.

*

Senior Lieutenant Artyom Kedrov walked across the deck towards his

Yakolev fighter. His forename meant follower but, far from emulating this trait, he was strong willed and his dogged persistence bordered on belligerence. It had often earned him rebukes from the political commissars and he was unlikely to repent. Today was his first mission in NATO airspace and he was looking forward to it. For too many years the Soviet forces had massed behind the Iron Curtain, as they called the fortifications in the core of East Germany, but with its new carrier air wing, the Kiev was able to project a significant force right into the West's back yard and the time for vacillation was over. Before the mission could begin they had to assemble at the start point some kilometres distant. Once airborne they would make their way to the marshalling point remaining at low level before popping up into radar coverage. The Ship's Captain had no desire to signpost the Fleet's position by allowing them to pop up in the overhead although the constant stream of maritime patrol aircraft that had flown past had made it abundantly clear that their presence was an open secret. NATO satellites made hiding in open waters almost impossible nowadays. Even so, today was their chance to respond. If he came across a Nimrod during the sortie he would make sure that they were given a demonstration of Soviet air power despite his rigid orders. Tasked to lead the second element he had been allocated the trainer bird and he would be carrying a new squadron pilot in the back to give the youngster some experience. To be honest, they were all learning rapidly as none of the pilots had operated in open waters before. This detachment was a far cry from the shake-down sorties in the quieter northern waters off Murmansk. If he was honest though, he had little appetite to train the youngster. His own upbringing had been harsh. Stick, search and report and woe betide any young pilot who failed to do so. Why should the new breed be any different?

A Kamov anti-submarine helicopter lifted off, its contra rotating rotor blades whipping the turbulent air over the deck still further. Kedrov shielded his eyes from the debris being flung into the air as the "cab", as helicopters were impolitely known, clattered off into the lee of the ship. After a brief walkround he climbed up the access ladder and dropped into his cockpit glancing down the line of jets ranged towards the stern. Behind him, the groundcrew fussed with the youngster strapping him in diligently the progress evident in his mirrors which flanked the canopy arch. His wingman sat at the opposite end of the line of fighters their positions carefully choreographed to aid the line up and departure. Flicking on the power he watched as the cockpit sprang to life, instruments shuddering like manic marionettes as they aligned themselves with the horizon. A slight shifting in the artificial horizon was evident as the bow of the huge vessel rose and fell. He dropped into the familiar routine setting the switches ready for start before, with a thumbs up from the flight line mechanic below he fired up the Tumansky R-28 V-300 turbojet engine following almost immediately with the Rybinsk RD-38 turbojet lift engines which would power him off the deck. The fans gave him a unique capability in Soviet naval aviation allowing the Yak to operate from the impossibly short flight deck of the cruiser.

Last to taxy, he watched Serp formation power off down the deck followed by the lead element of his own formation. His barked command over the operations frequency prompted instant movement from the wingman before he eased forward onto the marked strip and lined up with the bow. The carrier had turned to increase the air over the deck yet further and the ship was already making 30 knots against the wind as he felt the airframe being buffeted during line-up. Ahead, the circles marked out for helicopter operations showed stark against the red deck but were irrelevant to him. The centreline which would guide him stretched out ahead and would be his only reference as he powered off the deck assisted into the air by the downward blast of the lift fans. With a final clearance from the dispatcher he rolled, the wings quickly taking the weight of the Yak and catapulting it airborne. As he cleaned up the gear and flaps and turned downwind his wingman followed at a respectable distance. Within minutes they dropped to low level in fighting wing formation and set heading for the marshalling point. In the back the young pilot was silent.

*

"Alpha Lima Foxtrot 45, pop up contact bearing 290 range 80, strength two."

The controller rolled his track ball across the circular display placing the cursor over the fuzzy blip refining the bearing. In the back cockpit of the Phantom Flash adjusted the thumb wheel on his hand controller setting the scanner in the nose of the Phantom. Both men zeroed in on the elusive contacts.

"45, check target's heading?"

"Going away," came the perfunctory response.

A pop up contact meant that whatever the controller was tracking had pulled up from low level. At that range and with the target opening, there was no way that Flash could detect the contacts in pulse Doppler mode. For him to have any chance of seeing them they would have to turn towards. For now, the controller's calls were all he had to go on and, for the moment, he would have to be satisfied with forming a mental air picture. Unbidden, Razor eased the jet around and the compass settled on 290 as the speed eased upwards and the distance between the two formations began to close. They would vector towards the group and allow proceedings to unfold, although the targets were dictating events. At this ponderously slow rate of closure it would be a long wait.

"45, instructions?"

"45 Benbecula, interrogate and shadow."

"45, copied, vectoring 290 to close."

More hope than intention.

Suddenly an indistinct blip appeared on the display.

"Benbecula 45 holds contacts bearing 280, no range." Flash eased the thumbwheel downwards registering the position of his elevation markers. Showing below, it confirmed his assumption that they were climbing up from low level.

"Targets are climbing now heading towards."

"45, Benbecula confirmed."

Flash watched the contacts intently. There was little point in locking-on at this stage as the blips on his radar scope faded intermittently, still at the limits of the detection capability of the radar. For now he would watch and wait enjoying the familiar tickle of anticipation. The range between the formations wound down.

*

"Serp formation this is Director, I hold you contact. Orbit in your present position. Molotok formation is pulling up, stand by for instructions."

The formation leader acknowledged the command beginning a gentle left hand turn glancing down at the data link panel, recycling the errant device hoping to clear the apparent fault. The equipment cycled through its built-in test sequence flashing up a series of error codes as it failed to synchronise with the master station onboard the distant carrier. The panel which by now should be displaying steering commands from the controller stayed stubbornly blank.

"Link still down," he called to his wingman. "Check your status?"

"Link inoperative," he heard in response. If both receivers were inoperative, maybe the fault was onboard the Kiev? Whatever the problem he could not influence matters from the cockpit. Adjusting a switch setting and initiating a third recycle he made absolutely certain that he could not be accused of a switchery error. The fighter formation checked in on frequency and his attention switched to more pressing issues. The instructions followed; staccato.

"Molotok formation, I read you strength five, set heading 090, climb to 10,000 metres and set speed 450 Km per hour."

The four Yaks climbed slowly conserving fuel for the upcoming exercise. Already established in trail formation, the second element sat precisely at the pre-briefed range behind the leader.

"Molotok check your link status," questioned the controller more in hope than anticipation.

"Link down." The reply perfunctory. Yet again the onboard data link system was proving unreliable and questions would be asked of the technicians after the sortie. In its absence the formations would communicate over the insecure frequency passing vital intelligence across the ether, which would be gratefully received by the listening Brits.

"Molotok, this is Director, call me when parameters are set."

Kedrov in the second element of Molotok formation adjusted his speed.

"On parameters," he heard from his leader.

*

"I'm going to have a quick check of the range," said Flash as he moved the acquisition markers over one of the fuzzy blips on his radar scope. Squeezing the trigger the radar hesitated over the target before bursting into life, the full lock display appearing bright on the screen. The range marker ran out before settling at 48 miles near the top of the scope. He immediately broke lock to avoid alerting the opponent's radar warning receiver.

"Did you get a delta H?" he asked.

The small instrument in the front cockpit showed the relative height separation between the formations, a vital piece of information in the three-dimensional puzzle.

"Affirmative, they're showing the same height. Looks like they're climbing, passing through our level."

"Affirmative, they're now showing above," the navigator grunted as he wound the scanner gently upwards to keep painting the targets. "Looks like multiples but I can't break out a formation yet. Still at long range, all he could see was a fuzzy response and it would be some time before he could guess at the formation. He would switch to pulse mode when they were closer in to break out the formation positions.

"Medium speed," he intoned. "Let's start a gentle climb. It would be better if we could stay above them if we want a good look at what they get up to."

"Depends on what height they go for," replied Razor. "If they go much above 30 thousand I won't have any spare performance without using burner. We won't be around here for long if I have to do that."

"OK, we'll stay below for this first one."

They both knew the Phantom's limitations in the upper air.

*

"Serp this is Director, vector inbound heading 270, climb to 9,000 metres and set speed 400. Confirm you are in the briefed formation."

"Serp affirmative. Parameters set. In formation."

Many miles distant Molotok began to close on Serp and Kedrov rehearsed the briefed manoeuvre once again in his mind. The engagement would be heavily choreographed by the controller aboard the ship but, despite his innate confidence, he would avoid any mistakes which might attract adverse attention at the subsequent debrief. He would chose which battles to fight.

The youngster in the back cockpit had said little since they had popped up from low level but now that they were inbound it was a blessing in disguise. Kedrov concentrated trying to assimilate the tactical information and building a mental plot of the disposition of the other formation. If the other pilots were in position they would be flying an elongated card formation. As the range between Serp and Molotok wound down he absorbed the scant information frustrated at the arrogance of the ground controllers. Information was power and, without a capable air-to-air radar, he was relying on the limited commentary leading to a chance visual detection. Not that his radar would help much even when he was instructed to turn it on. A simple range-only device, it was more suited to the ground attack role and gave very limited information in the air-to-air role. It certainly had no chance of detecting an inbound fighter. It was in this crucial aspect that the rhetoric in the briefing diverged from the reality in the air. The Soviet Union had a large technology gap to close. Nevertheless, once visual, the four AA-8 Aphid air-to-air missiles he carried under the wings would come into play with their exceptional off-boresight capability. He would be reliant on the controller to put him in the right piece of airspace to engage but with the right calls he would launch his weapons.

"Range 20," he registered in his subconscious, his fingers twitching to make the switches live. He stared through the front windscreen at the spot where he expected the targets to appear.

"Execute!"

That was the signal for the leader to turn. He moved his head slightly looking for the tell-tale flash of a planform to register in his peripheral vision. There, just below the canopy arch. He should have warned the youngster in the back of the manoeuvre to come but his concentration was intense and losing sight now might prove terminal. He moved the stick hard over to shift the tiny dot into the clear area of the canopy. There was a grunt in the back.

Established in the turn, the leading element of Serp formation moved rapidly round onto the beam dragging to the left. Had the attackers been Phantoms equipped with air-to-air radars, the manoeuvre would have been detected prompting a reaction. The evasive turn would pull the attackers around onto the beam in front of the trailing formation. For this heavily scripted event the outcome was a foregone conclusion and the attackers obliged without question. Serp formation crossed Kedrov's flight path following the lead pair willingly. He drew the gunsight onto the tiny dot in the distance, easing the stick over to track the target waiting for the acquisition tone. Glancing in his mirrors his wingman held fighting wing formation following his manoeuvre, the head in the cockpit glued to the formation references. As he arced the turn the range closed rapidly and he waited for the call from the ground.

"Activate."

He snapped on the ranging radar gratified that the shot was in the heart of the envelope. The parameters were sweetening all the time as he closed from the rear quarter unseen by the pilots ahead.

"Shoot."

The harsh command from the controller loud in his ears prompting him to squeeze the trigger. The incessant warbling of the acquisition tone filling his headset as the infra-red seeker registered the heat of the targets engines, its guidance head transmitting positioning information to the missile's onboard autopilot. He glanced down at the master armament switch that had prevented the missile leaving the rails. As it was it would never be released to close on its hapless quarry but the R-60 missile would have had a trouble free passage to its target.

*

Razor watched the set piece manoeuvre unfolding above him. In the back, Flash scribbled down a sequence of notes amplifying the diagrams he had sketched on his knee board. The "decoy" tactic was one which the Mig-23 Flogger pilots of the Group of Soviet Forces Germany had employed during his days back at Wildenrath and was easily recognisable. Optimised against the Sparrow missile it was often rehearsed in East Germany but, clearly, the Soviet Navy had been comparing notes with their Army Aviation brethren.

"No reaction at all from the attackers," he observed, "or from the radar warners in the defenders if they have them fitted."

"That looks like a straight forward scripted run to me," replied Razor. "It'll be interesting to see whether they ramp it up for the next one. Looks like the trail pair of the 4-ship are the shooters. How about we try to shadow the targets for the next split?"

"Sounds good. I'm not comfortable down here though. We'll come in from above on the next run and try to get a better look. They must know were here. This is all being run by the fighter controllers on the ship and we have to be registering on radar. It's almost as if they are doing it for our benefit."

As the Forgers separated, Razor latched on to the independent pair and followed them outbound. He wished silently that he could monitor their frequency, although with his lack of any Russian language skills it would probably be futile.

*

The subsequent run was also nicely choreographed with Serp formation acting out the submissive role perfectly. It was there, however, that the roles were switched and the attackers turned back towards the trailing formation in order to threaten. Close to the merge, Kedrov strained to catch sight of the pair when his eyes were drawn to a smoke plume slightly above the canopy arch. A distinctive shape slowly emerged at the head of the smoke trail, its vector directly towards him. Uneasy, he shifted the stick over to reposition the contact in the canopy where he would have a clearer view, checking behind once again to make sure his wingman had followed. The manoeuvre broke the collision but the approaching trail bore down on him unerringly. Why was the jet smoking so badly he questioned. The Tumansky turbojet that powered the Yakolev was almost smoke free. It was not long before he had his answer. As the detail formed, the functional features of a combat jet became evident and, far from seeing a Yakolev pass abeam, he recognised the unmistakable planform of a Phantom. As the jet flashed past close aboard and slightly above, the wing dipped.

Kedrov struggled to recall the words of his tutor during his brief training as a Sniper pilot back in the Soviet Union. The smoke was telling him something. Its presence meant that the opposing pilot had not engaged afterburner before the pass so he would be short of energy, particularly if forced to turn hard in the upper air. That meant that Kedrov should be able to disengage easily providing he did not bleed off too much speed during his turn. He looked back over his shoulder grateful for once that he was flying the trainer variant as the massive canopy gave a much better view of the surrounding airspace. The Phantom had begun a gentle turn at the merge but rather than hold level, it had over-banked, screwing rapidly downwards and using gravity to accelerate. Disappearing temporarily from view, it reappeared in his eight o'clock already having made angles on him. It was a simple tactic. The "low yo-yo" was designed to trade height for speed and the three dimensional manoeuvre had been perfectly executed. Within seconds the Phantom had turned through 180 degrees and was already closing in on his tail and he was unable to respond with anything more than a 3 g flat turn. The briefing had been specific. He had a height to hold. He could imagine the rapid switchery in the Phantom cockpit as the pilot selected his infra-red missiles and took a simulated shot. Suddenly, fear knotted his stomach. Surely it would be simulated? He had been unable to see whether the Phantom was armed as it flashed past. His hand dropped to the countermeasures control panel which was his only defence. He doubted he could out turn the Phantom at this height, particularly with his wingman tucked in tight. He was a hostage to fortune. The pilot in the back had been blissfully unaware of events and he doubted that he had even noticed the presence of the other aircraft. Soviet pilots were taught to concentrate on ground instructions and to select weaponry when called, not to try to visualise the world outside the cockpit. The youngster was following his training to a tee. His controller on the ground, however, was well aware of the threat and babbled incessantly adding to the confusion. As the Phantom closed Kedrov armed the defensive system and selected infra-red decoys.

He hit the dispense button and a sequence of flares emerged into the air rising above the fuselage and falling back down through the jet wake. The flares bloomed brightly in the mirrors. It was a tense wait but, after a few moments he breathed a sigh of relief as the Phantom pulled nose high and broke away. The barked instructions from the controller finally penetrated his consciousness, control reasserted.

"Molotok, Serp formations, return to Mat."

For once, Kedrov was happy to comply.

"Let's take it back," he muttered to the torpid pilot in the back seat.

*

At a secluded console towards the rear of the operations room at the Control and Reporting Centre at Benbecula, an RAF surveillance operator watched the engagement play out. His presence was not always acknowledged, particularly when the myriad of visitors passed through. His language skills were even less publicised and his chain of command stretched back through the intelligence community rather than the fighter control community which provided most of the other operatives with whom he shared the space. A skilled Russian language speaker he listened intently to the radio calls listening closely for key words that would give an indication of what was underway in the air off the coast. The unexpected windfall was extremely welcome given that his usual source of information was a snatched transmission from a Bear or a stream of barely intelligible transmissions over the high frequency networks. Normally only snippets of voice transmissions were captured and his bread and butter was deciphering strings of data link traffic that had to be untangled to give a vague inkling of air defence tactics. Here he was listening in clear to Soviet pilots exercising their procedures just off the coast. The reception was crystal clear. Behind him, tape recorders whirred away and the recorded content would be analysed carefully later, if not by him, by other highly trained analysts at the Government Communications Headquarters in Gloucestershire.

His eyes lit up as he jotted down yet another unusual codeword glancing at the radar screen to link it with events in the air. That was without doubt from the fighters. Gold dust.

CHAPTER 21

United States Naval Weapons Facility RAF Machrihanish.

Despite its isolated location, Machrihanish was a strategic NATO installation where the US Navy had established the Naval Aviation Weapons Facility to support operations in the eastern Atlantic Ocean. Apparently harmless to the casual observer, the armoury on the remote southern side of the airfield housed nuclear depth charges and torpedoes in the special weapons facility. As naval operations ramped up towards a cataclysmic Third World War, the weapons would be distributed to US, British and NATO naval forces ranged across the disputed waters conducting anti-submarine warfare. With Detachment One of the elite US Navy SEALS permanently based at the airfield, the outwardly quiet Station hid an awesome but apocalyptic capability.

Eerie Port, on the northwest shore of the Great Cumbrae in the Firth of Clyde, housed a listening post which recorded underwater sounds in the approaches to the Firth. Vessels, and particularly submarines, attempting to penetrate the Cloch Boom, the sea lane between Dunoon and Cloch Point, would be detected acoustically and their presence fed into SOSUS. Nothing could move in these carefully monitored waters without being detected and tracked by the ever present sentinels.

The Scottish facilities worked with another installation known as NAVFAC Brawdy, located on the RAF base in Wales of the same name. The base also housed the main SOSUS station. It was hard to camouflage the huge trench which had been excavated down the valley into the sea close to the airfield and local scuttlebutt had it that the trench contained cables laid to connect to the system of underwater listening devices set up around the coast. In the control room US personnel became adept at interpreting the odd responses recorded by the sensors and could distinguish between the sounds of normal waves, whales, ships and submarines. Supplemented by airborne search aircraft such as the Nimrod MR2, a final component was perhaps the most secretive. In an effort to track the communications signals from Soviet submarines dispatched in short burst transmissions from the surface, a network of listening posts was set up codenamed "Project Sambo". Working together, the complex system was remarkably effective at keeping tabs on the activities of the Soviet submarine fleet.

Over the coming hours, signals detected by these secret organisations would build a comprehensive picture which would astonish even the most hardened intelligence operatives in Whitehall.

CHAPTER 22

The Aircraft Servicing Platform, RAF Leuchars, Fife.

The armourer trudged towards the Phantom his waterproof jacket cinched tightly around his face protecting him from the stiff wind blowing off the sea. The sodium lights bathed the aircraft servicing platform in a yellow glow but deep shadows stretched out from under the brooding jet. This was his third load of the day and he wondered briefly why the Russians were suddenly so busy off the Scottish coast. Night shifts were generally demanding but with seven jets loaded for QRA there would be no rest on this shift. As he approached, a Land Rover towing a missile trolley pulled up alongside, the Skyflash and Sidewinder missiles stacked onboard ready to be fitted to the fighter jet. He walked over to the K loader rubbing his hands to ward off the cold. He started the small engine ready to begin the missile upload.

The Spey engines rose in pitch briefly as the jet left the runway and eased onto the loop taxiway. It canted off at an angle, the thrust from the nozzles increasing briefly causing the brake parachute to billow before being released by the pilot. It flopped, unceremoniously, onto the grass at the side of the taxiway slowly deflating and sinking to the ground. Bodies emerged from a waiting Land Rover and gathered the discarded canvas and webbing hoisting it into the back of the waiting vehicle. As the jet emerged into the light cast over the dispersal, the missile load was clearly visible, the fins of the Skyflash missiles protruding from the underside of the fuselage. The engines dropped to idle before increasing noisily as the jet swung around in front of the empty bay in the QRA hangar lining up on the white centreline marking. The noise died as the crew shut down and the engines wound to a halt. A boarding ladder was hoisted over the intake ramp and the crew disentangled themselves from the ejection seat straps making their way down onto the concrete apron. The lights in the tiny annex alongside beckoned. As soon as Q1 was pushed back into the shed the turnround would begin and the aircraft and crew would be called back on state as soon as possible.

Across the apron, the blue ballast missile was downloaded from the front station and eased gently across the tarmac to the waiting trolley. Parked alongside its aggressive playmate the inert round seemed boringly benign. The white Skyflash which replaced it on the cradle was strapped into place for its short journey across to the Phantom where it was raised gently into place in the empty front launcher housing. As it was locked into place the remaining guidance fins were slotted into the housings on the missile body and it took on an air of purpose. The yellow bands denoted a live weapon and coupled with the mighty AN/AWG 11 radar in the nose radome it was a formidable combination. Armourers scurried underneath preparing each semi-conformal launcher individually as all four Skyflash missiles were loaded in turn. Efforts turned to the Sidewinders which were manhandled individually onto the LAU-7 launchers fitted under the wings. Slotted into place, retaining clips prevented the missiles from inadvertently riding forward unless persuaded by a rocket motor. With all eight missiles loaded a technician patiently checked the system for stray voltages before the loading team retreated to the sanctuary of the crewroom to defrost.

*

Back at Machrihanish, as the technicians settled down in the crewroom with a brew the Junior Engineering Officer pored over the Phantom Air Publication, known as the AP to those in the know. He was in his element because it was rare to be allowed to delve into the inner workings of the Phantom weapons system and the challenge he had been set was a challenge indeed. Gathered around him, the group of visitors watched his progress. They were an interesting bunch but he had been warned against speculating about the identity of one of their number by John Silversmith, the intelligence officer from Strike Command, who seemed to be spending most of his time with the detachment at present. He had been joined by a trials officer from the Central Tactics and Trials Organisation who was a past visitor to the Squadron at Coningsby when he had evaluated a weapon system update. To the engineer, he seemed like a knowledgeable character; for a pilot! The second visitor was none other than the engineering authority for the Phantom who had arrived at no notice from Group Headquarters; an unusual event in itself. If he gave the go ahead, the box which had arrived along with the group would be installed later in the morning and the paperwork to authorise it to fly would mysteriously appear. How the box could be tested was altogether a more complicated problem. The final visitor was a real enigma. Dressed in an American flying suit, his accent was definitely not from downtown Manhattan, and with a name like Yuri Andrenev, his origins lay somewhat further east than west. He mused on the name. He was sure he'd heard it somewhere before maybe from one of the aircrew. Andrenev . . . . .

The piece of equipment which he had brought with him was a revelation. The Cyrillic script on the cover left little to the imagination concerning its country of origin and its presence might explain the mysterious stranger. Its function had been described in some detail by Silversmith who, clearly, had more knowledge of its origins than might have been expected. The engineer could see how it would be a real boon if he was able to find a way to integrate the "black box" onto the Phantom. Designed to interrogate the Russian "Odd Rod" identification system, the box could provide an indication to the aircrew if the target aircraft was transmitting a Soviet identification code. It worked in a similar way to the NATO Mode 3 interrogator system that was to be fitted to the Tornado Air Defence Variant that was just entering service. By selecting the code on a small cockpit panel and hitting the interrogate button, the crew would have an indication whether the target on the radar was hostile; or was that friendly given that it was speaking electronic Russian? Knowing whether the other jet was a hostile might give that critical edge during an intercept and allow better tactics to be employed. The speculation was the limit of the engineer's tactical prowess and his job was to see if he could get it to work. He would leave the tactical stuff to the aircrew.

The trials officer wanted a link to the main radar so that, if a positive identification was made, it could be displayed on the radar scope in the back cockpit. There was no way he could do that in the short time he had available without modifying processing boards in the radar pack. To help with the installation, Silversmith had translated the interface control document that accompanied the black box and he could see a way that he could trigger the device if he could simply identify a wire that ran from where the box was to be installed in the missile launcher and onwards into the cockpit. He would need to fit the small display in a suitable location both to allow the navigator to set the code and to show whether a "friendly" response was received. That just left him to decide on a location for the small transmit/receive antenna that was winking at him from the desk. Thankfully, the device was powered from a 115 volt supply so it was compatible with the Phantom electric supplies. Now where to put it? He went back to the wiring diagrams searching for the elusive solution.

*

Ilya pushed the heavy metal door against the brisk wind and stepped over the raised lip onto the red coloured flight deck of the Kiev. The wind took the door from his grasp and it clanged shut despite his efforts to slow its passage. He moved into the lee of the huge island shielding himself from the wind over the deck and, despite the chill, it was good to escape the oppressive claustrophobic atmosphere of the planning room. Being outside prompted the urge for a cigarette even though it was months since he had given up. Despite the predictable impulse, even if he had thought to scrounge a cigarette he would have been unable to indulge as the smell of aviation fuel permeated the air around him, carried on the stiff breeze.

He was glad to be back onboard ship. It was good to get back to his roots and memories of training as a youngster flooded back. The ship was making good headway in the moderate seas and it should be a decent flying day. Towards the stern, the Yak-38 fighters were ranged along the deck with their tails overhanging the edge leaving a forbidding drop to the churning waves below. Technicians fussed around each airframe opening panels and plugging in services as they prepared the jets for flight. He watched, curious, as the elevator from the hangar deck rose into view carrying another Yak upwards onto the flight deck. The huge platform clanged into place prompting another flurry of activity as the technicians swarmed around. Within seconds a towing arm was slotted into place on the nose wheel and a squat tractor pulled the jet across the deck towards the fantail.

The exact manoeuvring so close to the precipice seemed truly daunting as the jet was pushed into place alongside the others taking its place in line.

The planning meeting had been relatively uncontroversial given the complexity of the task ahead and he had been surprised at the lack of questions but it had been clear to everyone present that the key would be in achieving precise timing. With three concurrent operations and the need to coordinate precisely between them to achieve the desired effect, it would not be easy. His mind worked through the sequence of events slowly and logically and he set each objective into context. The targets lay up to 300 kilometres apart and the latitude in timing was mere seconds. If they were opposed at any stage, particularly by the Phantoms based at Machrihanish or for him the ever present Nimrods, he could not guarantee the result. The most disturbing thought was that, with the exception of the coordinator, he was the only one in the room who had clearance to see every aspect of the plan. Some had even been asked to leave once their own individual briefing was complete. "Need to know" was paramount on this one and most onboard did not have either a need to know or sufficient clearances to gain access to the detail. It would all come down to unquestioning adherence to the operational plan and absolute precision.

The aspect which worried him most was the time that it would take to launch the submersible. The crew was capable enough and seemed up to the task but they would need to position close enough to the target to cut down on the transit time once submerged. Too far away and they risked detection in transit. If he was forced outside the tiny craft into the cold water he would freeze within minutes. Once he was done, they could make an escape into deeper waters where the tender would wait. Further offshore it should not attract as much attention if it was tracked by the coastal radars but it was still a risk. The outward appearance of the research vessel with its sprouting antennas and aerial masts might make it seem like one of the intelligence gathering vessels which routinely took up station around these waters listening to the Navy radio traffic and monitoring activity at the naval communications bases at Prestwick and Machrihanish. He did not relish the extended time underwater, particularly with the need to dive to the sea bed and the return to the surface would need to be carefully timed to avoid the risk of the bends. He expected to be submerged for up to an hour. At least the hip flask containing his favourite malt whiskey would be waiting for him in his kit once he was back aboard. One thing was certain, if the Royal Navy was active in Holy Loch tomorrow night his task would be considerably more testing.

A look of concern creased his features as yet another detail intruded on his thoughts. He was over thinking the problem. Leave the detail to the individuals. He moved back towards the access door wrestling with the hatch once more. As the door clanged shut extinguishing the lights outside, his heart sank. The harsh fluorescent light re-exerted its pallid glow causing a disconcerting feeling of malaise. It was not long to wait until he was transferred to the tender.

CHAPTER 23

The Flight Line, RAF Machrihanish.

Razor and Flash walked across the short stretch of concrete towards the line hut, a low, squat, green-painted hut sitting alongside the aircraft servicing platform. The three Phantoms were parked close by in a neat line facing inwards. Beyond them the two Q jets immobile, silver weather protectors refitted, draped garishly over the canopy area. Tapes had been carefully secured, positioned for rapid removal in the event of a scramble. The third Phantom was a hive of activity, its radome drawn back and the radar pack extended on a long pole giving access to the black boxes slotted in along its length. A technician in the back cockpit was barely visible his head down concentrating on the display in front of him, running the built in test. A group of bodies was clustered around the missile pylon deep in discussion and Razor recognised the trials officer from the Central Tactics and Trials Organisation who was speaking to the junior engineering officer. John Silversmith detached himself from the group and headed back towards the engineering hut, his head down clearly distracted. There were rumours about a magic box of tricks being fitted to one of the jets but, if that was what was going on, progress seemed slow.

Despite the appalling weather, the set up at the remote Scottish base had gone well and already the detachment was settling into an established routine. Familiarisation with the job in hand and years of training had taken over and, despite the presence of the Soviet Battle Group sitting just off the coast everything seemed almost normal.

"What time did you get back last night?" Razor asked as they emerged from the Nissen hut which had been hastily converted into a flying clothing locker room.

"Way too late," replied Flash, "The bar was already closed and I didn't even get a beer before I hit the sack. How is the hotel? I've barely had chance to look around so far."

"Pretty good. The rooms are not half bad."

There was a cute lady leaving as I got to reception. Quite a looker. Nothing to do with you by any chance?"

The smile said it all.

"Good to see some things never change," smiled Flash resignedly. "Who is she?"

"The sister of the local air taxi pilot. I met her in the bar earlier in the evening but I thought she'd taken offence at my chat up lines. She left the bar like a hairy bear but luckily she came back later."

So you moved in on her then?"

"A real Irish vixen!"

"Irish? You want to be careful Razor. Loose lips sink ships and all that. Where does she live?"

"Local now. They moved over from Belfast to follow the air taxi work. Not much going on the province apparently."

"Watch out old son. Make sure you know what you're getting yourself into. You can't be too careful. If the Det. Co. finds out you're telling stories out of school he'll have your balls on a platter."

For once, Razor had the decency to look slightly abashed. The discussion quickly forgotten, they walked into the bustling Line Hut greeting the Chief who was controlling the see-offs as he bawled out a group of flight line mechanics who, reluctantly, emerged from the small crewroom and headed out towards the waiting jets. Steaming mugs of coffee would cool before the owners returned. The two navigators leafed quickly through the avionics diaries before heading out of the door just behind the mechanics, the noise of an external power set already firing up signalling their arrival at the nearest Phantom. The Form 700s had been arranged neatly on the countertop and each pilot flicked through his own nominated jet's paperwork carefully checking each section, cross-checking the figures for the servicing which had been carried out. Some problems were being carried and the green and red pages in the flight limitations log would identify any which might be of significance for the coming mission. With a quick signature responsibility for the multi million pound warplanes transferred ownership.

At the jets the canopies were already raised and the two navigators were crawling between the cockpits checking switches before connecting the external power. Signals were exchanged with the liney before the external lights flashed bright bringing the aircraft to life. Back in his own cockpit Flash began the sequence of button presses which would start the alignment sequence for the inertial navigation system, or INAS, before turning his attention to his Martin Baker ejection seat. The first piece of equipment he hoped would assist him throughout the mission, the second piece of equipment he hoped he would never have to use. The fact that he was taking part in this detachment and that his friend "Toppers" would be some time before he sat on a bang seat again was not lost on him. His attention snapped back to the task in hand as Razor's head appeared above the canopy rail and climbed into the front cockpit his walkround complete.

"Clear to cycle power?" Razor asked receiving a grunted approval from the back.

"Affirmative," Flash responded checking the flashing red light on the INAS control panel. It would be some time before the sequence was finished and he hoped the transitory power spike didn't throw the alignment out of kilter. There was a brief shudder as the generators attached to the spooling Spey jet engines took up the load but the electronic box of tricks took the disruption in its stride. Flash returned to the radar, his left hand flicking the power switch into standby simultaneously pressing the small black button to fire up the display. After a few moments the time base glowed green on the scope and began to cycle left and right rhythmically with muffled thumps from the radome in front registering the scanner's protest as it hit the end stops. He glanced at his watch. It was still 5 minutes before the nominated taxi time so he would run through a quick self test of the radar and missile to make sure there were no hidden snags waiting to catch him out. Hopefully, he would not find a fault because he wanted to go flying so, if he did, he was tempted to ignore it and see how the system performed in the air. The tiny box at his right elbow was temperamental. Sometimes it flagged up imaginary faults which were not evident after takeoff. Sometimes when the technicians tried to identify a problem after the sortie it would stubbornly refuse to cooperate and the technician would log a "no fault found" until the fault reoccurred during the next sortie. It was a little more of a risk with a live weapons load aboard but the urge to go flying would probably win over any caution.

Up to now the radio had stayed quiet but the peace was broken by the navigator in the second jet.

"Falcon Lead from 2 we've got an INAS problem. Realigning but we'll be another 15 minutes."

"Two copied, wait."

"What do you reckon Flash?" Razor asked.

"We're serviceable. Why don't we head out into the area and set up for the first run. We need to fly anyway because they want a position for the Soviet fleet and we need to carry out a loose article check."

"Good point. Break."

"Falcon 2 from Lead, we'll launch and set up for the first intercept as target. Follow us out and we'll meet you on the pre-briefed frequency."

"Roger, wilco. See you in the area."

Buzzard Ops, Falcon Lead do you read?"

"Falcon, Buzzard go ahead."

"Did you copy my last? Falcon 2 has an INAS snag and will be another 15 minutes. We'll head out into the area and set up for the first run. Can you advise Benbecula of the delay."

"Roger copied, will do."

"Falcon Lead to Stud 1."

The canopies travelled and Flash switched to Tower frequency as the Phantom eased forward off the chocks. Ten minutes later and the Phantom was heading west at 15,000 feet. The radio was once again quiet after the usual flurry as they exchanged tactical information on first contact.

"I guess we'd better get this loose article check out of the way, me old mate."

There was a groan from the back seat. The previous evening during the after flight inspection a technician had dropped a screw into the bowels of the cockpit and had been unable to recover it. Loose objects and flight control runs were unhappy bedfellows and it was important to recover the errant item before it lodged in some inaccessible cranny. The easiest and often quickest way to do so was to fly a sortie and turn the jet upside down, hopefully dislodging the offending article. The down side was that this involved pushing negative G, one of the more uncomfortable experiences in the cockpit. The backseater's lack of enthusiasm was tangible and as the jet rolled onto its back, the deep blue sky replacing the dark blue sea in the canopy the world became inverted. As the negative g came on, a small cloud of detritus rose from the floor, some lodging itself behind Flash's visor despite having drawn it down to protect from the onslaught. Two or three larger items rose into the canopy arch trapping themselves at the apex of the transparent dome. Both crew grunted at the exertion, the straps from the ejection seats rising in sympathy and flapping around manically in response to the negative G. Flash reached up and grabbed at the closest item which looked nothing like a screw. Something else had passed in his peripheral vision and he screwed around in his seat, assisted by his weightlessness, cranking his head over his shoulder. He could just make out a dark shape immediately behind the headbox and flicked the seat raising switch, moving the seat to the top of its travel. He reached out again clutching at the elusive item just managing to close his fingers around it.

"Got it," he called over the intercom and was rewarded by a lurch as the world returned upright and his body thumped back onto the hard seat pan cushion with a painful thud. He glanced down at the small screw clutched in his white flying glove, thankful that the unpleasant manoeuvre would not have to be repeated. He tucked it safely away to be returned to the Line Chief after landing.

"Falcon Lead, Benbecula, your playmate has cancelled, check intentions."

There would be no practice interceptions today.

"Roger Benbecula, copied. We'll continue as briefed. We'll be descending to low level once contact with our objective and call you pulling up for recovery."

The message was deliberately cryptic. Flash knew that eavesdroppers aboard the Soviet vessels in the task force would be monitoring the frequency and he was not about to broadcast the plan in advance. It would be hard enough to find the ships in the vast ocean as it was. He had already inserted a destination into the inertial navigation system; the predicted position for the centre of the task force based on the last contact by a Nimrod surveillance aircraft the previous evening. The needles instantly slewed around giving a range and bearing to the predicted position and Flash gave Razor a snap vector towards the point where hopefully, the Soviet flagship was steaming along at the centre of its Battle Group.

Dropping his hand to the radar control panel he switched into mapping mode and the familiar "B scope" with its elongated baseline morphed into the more traditional "cheese wedge" map display. He rolled the scanner down a couple of degrees and was rewarded with a series of blips on the scope, tiny responses from the fleet of fishing boats which plied the coastal waters. A cluster of contacts about 30 miles away were almost certainly fishing vessels and way too close to be a group of warships. The inshore waters gave no protection from prying electronic sensors and the Admiral who was doing a respectable job of masking his presence was unlikely to stray this close to the coastline.

Flash glanced at the map on his knee estimating the range and bearing from the needles and marked a small cross at the point where he expected to see the fleet. He transferred back to the radar mentally comparing the point on the map with a position on the extended centreline around 150 miles ahead.

"Once we find them," he briefed, "We'll reverse the heading to make it seem that we've lost interest and then do a Tirpitz to low level before turning back outbound."

"Copied that," replied Razor, instantly attuned to the plan. A Tirpitz was a rapid descent to low level and would be difficult for the radars aboard the ships to track. Aiming back towards the coast Razor would roll the Phantom onto its back, pull hard down through the vertical and descend rapidly to low level before resuming the chase. Although they would be visible to the surveillance radars on the ships at medium level, once at low level they would be able to close to maybe 25 miles before being detected once more leaving the ships no opportunity to evade the approach. That said, the chance of a ship evading the attention of a determined fast jet was somewhere between slim and zero.

Flash tweaked the scanner position again centring his search on the point indicated by the needles on his compass. Although the scope was stubbornly blank there was another small return at about 130 miles which was not too far away from the expected spot. He marked another position on his map and made a quick calculation of the offset from the original.

"I think I've got them," he announced making a final check of his mental assessment. "OK let's take it down."

The Phantom rolled over and plummeted seawards, the altimeter unwinding rapidly, it's needles registering the drop.

"5,000."

"3,000."

He felt the angle of descent flatten and the horizon rose in his peripheral view.

"1,000 for 250," he warned receiving a brief acknowledgement from the front. The Phantom bottomed out a scant few feet above the waves having descended in mere seconds now heading back towards what Flash hoped was the Battle Group.

"Radalt bugged at 150 feet," he heard from the front. If the audio sounded that would mean they had dropped below their authorised height and should prompt a climb. Should. . . . . On this occasion, low was good. He switched back to pulse Doppler mode as it would be some time before he detected the ships which by now were below the radar horizon and invisible. If there were other jets down here with them he wanted advanced warning. Equally, their own emissions should not be detected for some time until they were closer to the predicted position for the fleet. It was a game of cat and mouse of who would be detected first.

The radar continued its lazy search, the scope now predictably blank in the open waters as they extended the range from the coast. A blip suddenly appeared close to the nose.

"Contact 260, no range," he called alerting his pilot to the unexpected presence.

"Looks to be on the deck with us, showing level," he intoned. "Come starboard five degrees to centre him up."

He began a snap assessment of the heading watching for the blip to drift across the tube but it remained doggedly fixed on the nose. The contact was heading directly for them.

"OK I make his heading 080 degrees, I'm going to take a quick lock for range," he called. Placing his acquisition markers over the target he squeezed the trigger and the radar entered its acquisition mode searching for the distant contact. Its brief electronic verification complete the symbology changed and a full track display burst onto the screen, the range marker settling at 30 miles. He immediately broke lock, hoping that the brief interrogation had not registered on the other aircraft's radar warning receiver. It was obviously fast jet traffic as its speed was a steady 400 knots. A glance at the additional information briefly displayed had verified his assessment. The contact was heading directly for them and it was travelling at a similar speed to themselves. He looked down at his own radar warning receiver checking that the switches were correctly set and that he was listening to the correct electronic frequency range. Satisfied, and with the instrument reassuringly blank he looked back at the blip.

"Which side do you want it on Razor?"

The pilot looked outside to check on the weather conditions and the position of the sun having been monitoring his navigators activity on the radar repeater.

"The sun's to the south," he called. "Put him on the right and we'll try to come at him out of the sun".

Low on the horizon, the winter sun was bright and reflecting from the waves. It might indeed provide some cover as they made their final attack turn shielding their approach from an unwary opponent. He responded to the corrections noting the new heading on his compass. The navigator chatted away making more small corrections as they closed in range finessing the approach. Razor checked his speed and adjusted to 420 knots which gave him the best cornering velocity should he need to manoeuvre. The angle of bank began to increase as the navigator sensed the target nearing. They were beginning the final turn in behind whatever target they had latched onto. Just at that moment there was a muttered expletive.

"The target's turned. His velocity just rolled off and I've lost him. Keep that gentle turn coming and look in your two o'clock. No range but I estimate about 10 miles. Can you see anything?"

Was the turn luck or deliberate? Had something alerted the opponent of their presence or was the turn an unlucky fluke? The navigator had little information on which to base the rest of the intercept and his carefully planned geometry had been negated by the evasion turn. The target had simply disappeared. He had only his mental air picture on which to work.

Razor stared hard through the front quarter light jinking his head left and right to stare around the canopy arch which obscured his view.

"Got it. It's in a left hand turn range about 5 miles turning across our nose. No ident yet."

Flash breathed a sigh of relief. A peep was worth a thousand sweeps. Up ahead the small fighter showed its belly to the Phantom crew its pilot oblivious to the threat.

"Bloody hell mate, you're not going to believe this but it's a Forger. In a left hand turn and it's rolling out on our heading."

Flash had already returned his attention to the radar and flicked through into pulse mode, the scope now flooded with the electronic noise from the sea returns. He rolled the scanner a few degrees and was rewarded with a solid radar contact at about 4 miles ahead.

"Contact," he called. "I'd say this guy will do our job for us. I reckon if we tuck in behind he'll lead us right back to the Kiev!"

"You read my mind old son."

The Yak-38 Forger had climbed slightly and was framed against the horizon at 1,000 feet, well above the Phantom which trailed in its wake hidden in the Soviet pilot's blind cone. As it jinked left and right making minor correcting turns the Razor shadowed patiently, watching and waiting.

"If you're happy I'm switching the radar to standby Razor. No point in advertising our position if this guy is giving us a tow in towards the fleet."

"No trouble. I've got him tally."

They trailed the fighter closely maintaining their position low and behind for some miles before the Soviet pilot began a lazy, climbing turn.

"Tally, two o'clock, 10 miles," called Flash from the back, both their eyes fixing on the distinct shape of the square island which emerged on the horizon marking the position of the carrier. At that very moment they flashed overhead a Krivak class destroyer which, in their keenness to keep track of the Forger, they had missed. Seemingly, the Soviet crew had also been caught napping because the moment they flashed overhead, the radar warning receiver began an urgent bleeping as the SAN-4 surface-to-air missile system radar aboard the Krivak entered its acquisition cycle. A solid I band vector flashed its warning as they tucked in behind the tiny Soviet fighter using the Forger's presence as cover. They hoped the aggressive behaviour was posturing but even a gung ho Soviet missile team might think twice about firing missiles in the vicinity of the task force. Keeping a respectable distance Razor followed the Forger into the pattern. If the pilot was about to begin an approach they had no wish to cramp his style. He might be one of the opposition but they had no intention of forcing him into an error which might jeopardise the safety of his aircraft. Whatever the intent, the Soviet missile system continued to follow their movements around the pattern, the threat vector tracking their progress relentlessly.

As the Forger positioned itself on short finals the large intake door on the spine popped into the airflow and it began to transition to the hover making a slow approach to the stern of the huge Soviet aircraft carrier. Razor eased the Phantom out onto the dead side of the traffic pattern slowing down to match the rapidly slowing fast jet as best he could. With its lift fans powering away the speed slowed quickly and Razor struggled to formate. Dropping down to the same level as the island Flash snapped away in the back cockpit the lens of the camera capturing the approach in detail. As the Forger passed over the broad fantail of the Kiev Razor eased his Phantom upwards and opened the throttles, the speed slowly building back up through 300 knots. The Phantom once more felt alive.

As they overshot, Flash quickly wound on the film and clicked open the back of the camera juggling to insert a new film canister, his flying gloves making the operation difficult. Slotting the film leader over the take-up spool he wound it on and closed the camera back raising it once more to his eye as they turned downwind. Making one last pass he clicked off a few more shots of the Forgers on deck. There were five airframes ranged along the side of the ship towards the stern, angled forward into wind. The jet which had just landed had pulled well forward and was manoeuvring gently around the deck under its own power next to the island. Resisting the urge for a final flypast, they pulled up and headed back towards the shore. The radar warner gave a final menacing rattle and fell silent. The radio stayed silent as they were well outside the range of the land-based radar site but whether the lines were hot between the Soviet Embassy and the MOD would become clear after landing. In the meantime they had a time-sensitive cargo.

"I think that should do nicely. I've got that all on film," Flash announced with a degree of satisfaction. "Let's take this back to base"

*

The technician delved inside the LAU-7 launcher and connected up a lead to its main power supplies. The strange electronics package was unlike anything he had ever worked on at Coningsby but with the "oracle" standing next to him, he had all the top cover he needed. The man represented the Engineering Authority so whatever he said was gospel.

The installation was natty if he said so himself. The small space just behind the nose fairing of the weapons pylon was now tightly packed with electronics and the wiring loom snaked off into the centre of the pylon before making its way alongside the trigger firing circuit up into the cockpit area through the bowels of the aircraft. The radar technician in the back cockpit was completing a built in test on the missile control system and, once proven, he could fit the control panel into the cockpit.

The modified pylon fairing was neat and Station Workshops had done an amazing job. The angled leading edge had been modified to accept the small antenna and the dielectric panel looked as if it belonged there. It may not be rated to Mach 2 but it would certainly stand up to the Mach 1.1 speed limit that the aircrew had demanded of the modification. In any event, it could easily be removed if they decided it didn't work. A dozen fasteners and a new fairing could be reinstalled in as much time as it took to turn the jet after a sortie.

He double checked the connections, confirmed that the power light was illuminated, refitted the access panel in the side of the launcher and stepped back. A pair of size 9 service shoes preceded the wearer as the MCS technician arrived on terra firma, offering a thumbs up and beckoning for him to head up the boarding ladder into the back cockpit. He mounted the steps clutching the tiny control panel.

As he settled onto the hard pad of the ejection seat he could see the brand new connector protruding from the space between the grab bars, immediately in front of his face. He slotted two small brackets into place and secured them with fasteners to the metallic structure. The connector twisted into place easily, as did two more fasteners on each side of the small panel and, without fuss, the new control box was staring back at him from its new home. There would be no extensive testing because there was no time to mount an extensive evaluation. Running the wires alongside the missile firing circuits was somewhat of a gamble but the spare circuit he had used really was the only one available between the launcher to the cockpit.

It was that or nothing. That the jet was live armed only added to his anxiety as he reached forward and moved the power switch to on. He closed his eyes involuntarily, the whine of the auxiliary power set loud in his ears. He was relieved not to hear the whoosh of a Sidewinder missile leaving the rails in response to his actions and he relaxed, embarrassed by the bead of sweat that had formed on his brow.

The panel was simplicity itself. A four digit window allowed a code to be set. A button marked "Int" allowed the navigator to send out the electronic question to a distant Soviet aircraft and two simple lights, one green one red, indicated the reply. He pushed the button and the lights remained blank for a moment before the red light winked on. In the absence of a "friendly code" from a cooperating Soviet aircraft that was to be expected. It was now down to the aircrew to make use of his handiwork.

CHAPTER 24

UK Air Defence Operations Centre, RAF High Wycombe, Buckinghamshire.

John Silversmith ambled over to the main dais set above and behind the banks of control consoles in the darkened operations room. The Duty Air Defence Commander, Wing Commander Phil Boyd seemed distracted as he scanned the huge totes set along the front wall.

"How's it looking Sir?" he inquired of the grey haired pilot.

"You got back from Machrihanish quickly John," the Air Defence Commander replied.

"I got a lift back courtesy of the Devon communications squadron Sir. They even choppered me over to the helipad here. Quite a service. I must have friends in high places."

The older officer smiled, distracted.

"Maybe the AOC-in-C had a word for you? It's all quiet at the minute John but if yesterday is anything to go by, it won't last for long. We haven't had an exercise like this in my time and I've seen quite a few."

A former air defence pilot, he had plenty of experience to draw from. With many hours flying the Lightning filling his log book, he was well versed in the patterns of Soviet air activity in the Eastern Atlantic. His professional upbringing had been in the Q Shed at RAF Leuchars scrambling to meet intruders, short of fuel the moment his undercarriage retracted into the wheel wells. Since his medical grounding and subsequent remustering to the Fighter Control Branch of the RAF, he now evaluated the patterns from the bridge of the Air Defence Operations Centre rather than from the cockpit of a fighter. At times he wondered which was more challenging.

"How did the fit go?"

"Good Sir. They were just finalising the test installation as I left. We only have the one box so it will be fitted to a single jet. I've got markers out in case the Americans have any spare sets of the kit but it might take some time to get our hands on them even if they have. If there's one to spare I'll get them straight up to the Detachment."

"I need to bear that in mind if this situation heats up. I'm not use to Phantoms having an identification capability. It's a bit of a game changer. We'll have navigators taking decisions if I'm not careful!"

The intelligence officer was glad not to be the butt of the senior officers banter for a change.

"I thought you might like to see the daily intelligence summary before it hits the streets Sir. There are a few snippets from other sources in there that you may not have picked up from yesterday's activity. Defence Intelligence has included an interesting piece on a planned Soviet exercise in the Med. It looks like the Kiev will be heading south once she's finished in Scottish waters."

"Any indication on the target for the sonobuoy drops yet?"

"Looks like it may have been the new Akula attack submarine which was involved. Early days yet because whatever we detected doesn't fit our signature library. We're coordinating sources but the Nimrod crew picked up some interesting stuff which is being analysed as we speak. That will take time but we'll have them brief you as soon as they have identified it. We can set up a secondary tote so you can see the undersea plot if it will help. The sources are classified but I'm sure you don't care where they come from providing you have the information."

He winked conspiratorially. The older officer nodded, the subterfuge washing over him. The endless game played by the intelligence world frustrated him no end. In the nonstop bid to protect sources, information vital in the tactical battle often was withheld to avoid compromise of its origin. Despite his impeccable security clearances, others would decide whether he would have access to the high grade intelligence. All he cared was that he had the tools to fight the tactical battle to the best of his ability. Sometimes he wondered whose side the faceless analysts were on. That the Americans had an underwater network monitoring submarine activity was an open secret in military circles. He could do without the drama.

"Thank you John." he replied conspiratorially. "What else have you got?"

"We'll need a full analysis but initial assessments suggest that the Bear dropped a copy of the new American Mark 46 lightweight torpedo."

The intelligence officer paused to let the fact sink in.

"Holy shit!" the senior officer replied. "That'll get them running around in the Old War Office. What the hell is a Bear doing launching an American weapon?"

"Good point. We have no idea where they might have acquired it from. Even the Americans have not completed all their operational testing yet so it's a major leak. If they are prepared to compromise such an important acquisition it can only mean that this is a full blown operational test of the new submarine. If they are happy to let us capture the test data, including the acoustic signature of this weapon, it means it's significant enough to make it worth running the test in the operational area. Much of this work is normally done back in the Arctic testing grounds where we have little access and can't collect against them. They must have known that we would monitor the activity so it's important all right. The big question for the analysts is how they got hold of the design so early in the cycle. We have no reports of a weapon being lost so questions will be asked as to how they were able to copy it and how representative it is. Maybe they got hold of design blueprints but I'm speculating now. If they can field an equivalent weapon it changes the game for the submarine chaps."

It came as no surprise to the veteran air defender. The Soviets had been copying western technology for years in a bid to redress the technical imbalance. The AA-2 Atoll infra red guided missile was a clone of the AIM-

9B Sidewinder. The design had been copied after an example had fallen into Soviet hands in the Far East. It had been deployed rapidly on the Mig-21 Fishbed giving it a quantum improvement in capability, light years ahead of the beam-riding technology of the earlier AA-1 Alkali missile. That the espionage efforts continued today came as no surprise.

"What about the air activity?"

"We've had reports that the Bears at Murmansk are active already this morning. There's a lot of chatter on their engineering networks so it sounds like they are preparing for a sortie. No flight plans have been filed, as usual, so we won't know for sure until the Norwegian air defence radars pick them up coming around North Cape but I'd say you can bet on it."

"What's your best guess on timing?"

"Hard to say but after yesterday I'd say it would be a good idea to warn off Leuchars to have Q3 and Q4 loaded tonight and a few crews on readiness 60. The Kiev has been flying around the clock including at night so don't discount anything."

"Night flying? That's new for them isn't it?"

"They fly at night back at base but it's the first time we've seen deck ops at night in open water. We had a crew fly past yesterday and caught some interesting pictures on the Q camera."

"Don't tell me; they're still being analysed. . . . ."

Silversmith smiled.

"I'll give Leuchars a call and warn off OC Ops. Don't want the crews having too many beers in the bar if there's work to be done do we? What about the Machrihanish Detachment? I'm of a mind to ask them to have jets on readiness tonight too. They've had it easy so far with only day flying."

"Your call Sir but I wouldn't be surprised if the Sovs don't plan another set piece event. There's no sign of them heading out of the box they've established off Benbecula just yet. They've held within a tight area since they arrived off the coast."

"Thanks John. I'll make those calls. Looks like we're in for a busy day and maybe an even busier night."

CHAPTER 25

Aboard the Aircraft Carrier Kiev.

The small planning cum briefing room was warm and the incessant hum of the air conditioning in the background strangely soporific. Ilya looked at the faces around the table, most engaged in intense conversation, the Russian words comforting after his diet of English. Most wore the working uniform of the Northern Fleet but others stood out in their blue and white striped t-shirts typical of the Soviet Spetznaz special forces. Around the room battle dress jackets had been discarded to cope with the rising temperature in the confined space as it filled with bodies. A large map of Scotland covered the centre of the table.

"OK let's run through this quickly, it's getting hot in here. You've all finished your Stage One planning. I want to run through the broad strategy to check for flaws and then each of you will have a chance to put your own thoughts. I want ideas or suggestions for changes."

The mission leader to Ilya's left made eye contact with each of the key players who would play their part in each element of the intricate mission.

"The overview. We run tomorrow night. Timing is critical and each component must hit the time-on-task precisely. R Hour will be 0100 Zulu and there's a good reason for choosing that time; more of that later. Make no mistake comrades, if this mission succeeds it will represent the biggest improvement in operational capability since the Great Patriotic War. As many of you might know, presently, we are unable to monitor the movements of the British nuclear ballistic missile submarines as they leave their base at Holy Loch in the Firth of Clyde. Following the standoff during Exercise Able Archer in 1983, the Supreme Soviet has become paranoid about the risk of a nuclear first strike by NATO. If we can track the British deterrent as it leaves harbour that risk factor is reduced. Knowing where they are holding will allow us to respond neutralising their deterrent. Our new Akula class submarines have the potential to tail the boomers unseen but, to do so, our crews need to make contact in shallower water. You have no need to understand the precise detail of what we plan tonight but, if we achieve the aim, our efforts will allow us to do that. Most of what will occur tonight is strictly need to know and the rest of your teams don't need to know. We don't want to or need to compromise the real reason for this operation. If your teams press for detail, the line that you should follow is that we are shaping the battlespace to give the Carrier Battle Group free rein as we transit south. That story should deter casual interest."

The eyes around the table remained blank and he wondered if they realised the implications of their plan. It was a bold initiative in peacetime.

"If any one of you should be detained we have a diplomatic cover story for each operational objective. As it's the Group's first deployment, we must avoid surveillance at all cost and many of the objectives are installations that would track our operations. We'll use a force of Kamovs to act as a decoy to cover the force to the north. As our main targets are the air defence radar stations we'll try to achieve our aims without resorting to kinetics. If we can disable them in more subtle ways we will. The southerly team would be easily detected if we insert by air so, for that reason I've gone for a seaborne approach using a submarine and inflatables for that insertion. That leaves the biggest risk from the Nimrod anti submarine aircraft based at Kinloss on the Moray Firth. With its Searchwater radar it's easily capable of picking up even the tiny radar signature of the RIBs. It's been on station every night for the last week providing coverage of our movements. We need to make sure it's prevented from moving in too close once the operation starts," he said pointing to a pilot called Kedrov towards the far end of the table. "That will be your task."

The man nodded and scribbled a few notes.

"Timing; the Carrier Group will move in to the start position to be in place at 0010 Zulu. The mini subs will launch at 0030 carrying Team One and will aim for the insertion points to be ready to hit the beaches at R Hour. The Yak-38s will be on alert ready to attack the Nimrod if it should appear on task. As the landing craft emerge we will be at our most vulnerable and will need to keep its crew busy until the teams are ashore. The objectives for the two teams are to neutralise the radar heads at Stornoway here, and Benbecula here, for the duration of the operation," he said indicating the locations on the chart. "You each know the means at your disposal to do that. Benbecula feeds its picture back to the Sector Operations Centre on the east coast of Scotland, here at Buchan. The group manning the site comprise a small staff of controllers plus a maintenance team. They are principally technicians not fighting troops so should not give you too much resistance if they are alerted to your presence. Stornoway is more of a challenge as No. 1 Air Control Centre, callsign "Crowbar", has been deployed to the site from RAF Portreath in Cornwall, we think to monitor our activity. It's a mobile control facility and, because they are on exercise, we expect them to be more alert but there's no suggestion they will be active tonight. They have guards from the RAF Regiment, a specialist team well versed in airfield protection, and they will be more of a challenge. Expect stiff opposition if they realise that this is a real operation. There is also a detachment of Rapier surface-to-air missiles carrying out a secondary exercise also manned by the regiment gunners. Store that fact away as it may be significant as they may be testing a new version of the Blindfire surveillance radar. The insertion will be conducted under cover of electronic warfare support according to standard doctrine. The Kamovs are carrying jamming equipment targeted against the NATO radars and jamming will commence simultaneously with the launch of the inflatables. That should make the approach more covert, albeit at the expense of surprise."

"Are we allowed to use force if we are discovered," a stern looking officer wearing the striped rig of a Spetznaz captain asked, pointedly.

"Good timing. Rules of Engagement. This is not intended to be a shooting war. If you can avoid contact with the enemy that is good. If we can get in and get out without drawing attention to the insertion force, all well and good. We need not cause any more damage than that required to achieve the identified objectives; that should be the aim."

"With respect, that didn't answer the question Comrade."

"You always have the sovereign right of self defence even on their territory but I don't want overt use of force where it can be avoided. For the crews in the air it's a bit more complicated as you'll be flying in international waters. The Brits are in a peacetime posture so the only armed aircraft you should meet should be the QRA Phantoms from Leuchars and the Phantom detachment operating from Machrihanish on the west coast here," he said stabbing the map once more. "I hope to have more local intelligence on that score soon."

"How do they request authority to engage?"

"A critical fact. They will have difficulty getting clearance because there has been no elevation of the alert states so they are operating to peacetime rules of engagement. Providing we don't provoke them too much there should be no reason for them to respond with force. They have to use voice channels to request clearance which then has to be relayed from the Sector Operations Centre to the Air Defence Command Centre in England. That will take time. The frequencies are also susceptible to the jammers carried aboard the helicopters. If the Duty Commander is brave and takes on the responsibility himself it might take minutes but if he consults his political masters it will take much longer."

"Will we have written orders for the mission?"

"Of course Comrade, you would expect nothing less," he replied catching the eye of the political commissar. "Just remember that you may have to think on your feet."

The commissar joined the ranks of the scribblers, undoubtedly recording the conversation to make sure his own position was covered in the event of a mistake. Flexibility was not a welcome addition to the plan in his highly scripted world.

"The main reason we are all here is to deliver an underwater payload and that is where our friend comes in," he announced beckoning to Ilya. "You don't need any detail other than to know that this is the whole reason why you are providing the covering forces. This part of the plan will be mounted from the research vessel which joined the task force specifically for the task.

Its precise operational location is classified but suffice to say it will be operating close to the Firth of Clyde. The biggest threat to its success are sensors on the sea bed but the fleet planners will tackle that problem and it need not concern any of us in this room. Our job is to shape the battlespace so that others can do their part. Let's just say that for the plan to succeed, timing is absolutely critical."

The implication was clear.

"You may all have noticed that our plan is not without risk. Jamming the NATO radars could be construed as a hostile act under NATO rules of engagement. As I suggested, our advantage is that the British are operating in a peacetime posture and that they will be reluctant to respond with force. They are not as paranoid about their territory as we in the Soviet Union, despite their recent history. We can apologise profusely via diplomatic channels and blame over enthusiastic exercise play but if live weapons are traded it would be difficult to explain away as merely over exuberance. Just be aware of that fact should you come into direct contact, particularly with the alert Phantoms which will be armed. Restraint is the key comrades."

His enthusiasm of moderation was clearly not shared. The mood was pensive but he knew that discipline would prevail.

"OK, more questions? Let's go around the room."

CHAPTER 26

Northern Fleet Headquarters, Murmansk, the Soviet Union.

"Sir, I've had word from Moscow. The Libyans want the plan for the exercise to be brought forward to allow time for a port visit for some diplomatic hosting. Moscow wants the task group to head to the Mediterranean at the earliest opportunity; as in straight away."

The fleet planner stroked his brow, his irritation close to surfacing, a nervous tic the only visible clue to the state of his ragged nerves. He sometimes wondered whether the idiots in the Kremlin spoke to each other. Then again, the answer to that question was abundantly clear virtually every day. Of course not. With the SOSUS operation scheduled for tonight there could be no way to bring forward the onward passage which was already scheduled for later the following day.

"Signal them back and tell them that is impossible. Events for the next 24 hours have been carefully scripted and it is impossible to amend them at this late stage."

"I'm afraid I've already tried that line Sir. The aide asked that you contact the General personally to confirm his wishes."

The planner grumbled quietly as he picked up the telephone and dialled the familiar number. Arranging the backdrop for cocktail parties using expensive Soviet warships was a feature of his life that he detested. Surely if communism was to have any virtues, avoiding such frippery should be top of any list of things to ban.

He exchanged brief pleasantries with the aide feeling the usual mixture of regret at the man's plight and relief at his own fortune in avoiding the blighted existence the poor chap suffered. The line became noisier as he turned the key to secure the line, the confidence light blinking on. The aide's voice became instantly distorted as the cryptographic protection kicked in. He waited patiently.

Eventually, the cantankerous patrician picked up the handset. His life centred around the diplomatic cocktail party circuit and, most days, it was possible to pacify his outrageous demands through careful forward planning. Occasionally though, immoderate proposals were dropped in the in-tray at short notice and the planner suspected the General did it on purpose just to underline his perceived importance.

Opening platitudes were dismissed without acknowledgement and the planner listened warily, testing the mood. The man might be a pain but he was a pain with influence. The stream of invectives left little to interpret and his caution heightened.

"Yes Comrade General, I understand the significance of the diplomatic ties with Libya but I'm afraid the fleet exercise has been carefully scheduled. There is no way I could have the Kiev leave British waters immediately. The testing is reaching a critical stage and is not due to conclude until the early hours of the morning our time. A number of key objectives have yet to be met," he explained patiently avoiding reference to the main event. The underwater insertion was known only to a few key personnel and he certainly did not want it broadcast around the cocktail party circuit.

The tirade from the other end of the line radiated impressively from the handset despite the cryptographic interference and he realised an unconventional approach would be needed to mitigate his intransigence. It could do no harm to at least try to mollify the indignant senior officer.

"You will be aware, Comrade General that the task force is planned to arrive in Syrian waters next week after the Libyan exercise," he explained patronisingly. "With the current tension in Israel our masters intend to exercise a show of solidarity with our Arab brothers. They have only a short stay planned on the Cyprus buoy before docking in Tartus which may give some leeway. Perhaps you could adjust your timings to take advantage?"

The torrent of abuse signified his failure. His head nodded imperceptibly.

"I'm sure the Secretary has good reasons for wanting to host Comrade Gaddafi aboard the vessel Comrade General but please be assured it's impossible for me to arrange such a departure from schedule at my level. Perhaps I could have one of the support vessels detach from the fleet to fulfil the task? I'm sure that not all the ships are fully committed."

The stream of invectives signalled that yet another ploy had failed.

"Yes I can see how that might be misconstrued in Tripoli but we have some extremely impressive vessels in the task force which may suit your needs. Regrettably, as I say, I'm unable to dispatch the Kiev on my own authority, or indeed yours," he said instantly regretting his lack of caution. "Can I suggest you speak to General Stepanov in the Politburo Secretariat? He has been briefed frequently on the current operation in Scotland and is aware of the implications. The plans were coordinated with the Operational Requirements Division and the Exercise Coordination Cell to ensure that everyone's needs were taken into consideration. I'm sure you could reach an accommodation."

He stared blankly at the now dormant handset, the connection summarily terminated. That was unusual even for that old goat.

CHAPTER 27

Off the Scottish Coast.

The Akula lay silently beneath the surface, rigged for silent running. Around him the faces of the crew were tense, the strains of the pursuit beginning to tell. He had been forced inwards towards the coastline and the submarine was now lying in water shallower than ideal, hemmed in by the task force to the south west. By his estimates he should be within striking distance soon but could not risk using his active sonar for fear of detection. After evading the earlier attack his approach had been more cautious but the outer screen had been troublesome and he had been left with few options but to lie up and wait. To make matters worse, his morning sitrep had indicated that a British Oberon attack submarine was moving into the area and would probably become problematic if his goal was not reached soon. Time was running out. Fleet orders terminated the exercise at 2200 Zulu before the Battle Group moved on to a new task in the Mediterranean. Termination without engaging Kiev would represent a huge blow to his reputation and it was a failure he was not prepared to countenance. Even so, in this game inactivity was sometimes the best gambit and he resisted the urge to press his luck. Detection and simulated destruction of his own boat was an even less attractive option.

"Contacts closing."

The call was unforeseen.

"Two contacts," breathed the passive operator.

"Any identification?" he responded conscious that any stray noise from within the hull would be radiated.

"Negative. One minor and one major vessel."

"Roger, monitor."

The exchange was deliberately clipped for fear of compromise. With the vessel once more silent he strained to detect the noise of the approaching vessels, rewarded by a faint thrum transmitted through the water.

"Shows a constant bearing. Heading directly towards."

He could hardly believe his luck. Rather than having to penetrate the troublesome destroyer screen it appeared that the carrier might be doing his work for him. If this was the Kiev his luck, surely, was in but timing would be critical. One ping was all he could allow himself in order to confirm his target was within range. If he could engineer a shot he could separate into deeper water. Too soon and the underwater team aboard the carrier would be alerted. Too late and the ship would pass by before he had the chance to refine his shot. He would have one fleeting opportunity for glory and he was too experienced to allow it to pass.

The noise of heavy screws driving through the water was now unmistakable.

"Contact confirmed. The larger contact is the Kiev, bearing 210."

"Weapons, man your stations."

The command prompted a flurry of activity.

"Helm, ahead slow, steer 210."

"Prime tube three. Practice weapon only. This is a drill, repeat this is a drill."

The silence was broken and the familiar noises returned as the submarine eased around to face the incoming warship.

"On my mark, one ping."

The presence of the approaching vessel was unmistakeable, the noise deafening through the water. If it passed close by, not only would they hear it but they would feel it too. He was almost tempted to take the shot in autonomous mode and allow the torpedo to do the work. Only his desire to log indisputable proof overrode his caution.

"One ping," he called, the noise of the active sonar splitting the air instantly.

"Range 1000 metres and closing."

"Fire three. . . . Ahead flank speed, right 260 degrees, emergency dive. Launch noise maker."

He could not suppress the grim smile as the Akula responded to his directions. The shot was a certainty and, for an exercise firing, it would be assumed that the guidance and fusing would operate correctly. There would be hell to pay at the debrief and he was glad he would not be on the receiving end. Now, if he could avoid the attention of the Krivak escort he could look forward to some relaxed running and give the crew a well deserved break.

*

Ilya lay on his bunk wedged tight into the confined space of the tiny cabin many decks below the flight deck of the Kiev unaware of the drama unfolding beneath the water. Alert klaxons had been blaring for the last fifteen minutes and, occasionally, the ship heeled over in sympathy. They were a necessary evil of life aboard and he was secretly glad he was not caught up in the trivia of the exercise. There were a few minutes to kill before being cross-decked to the research ship and he had been reassured that the exercise would be terminated before the operation began. In the background a turbine whined as a Kamov anti-submarine helicopter lifted off, presumably tasked to hunt down the Akula which was, probably the cause of the raucous warnings.

Planning was complete, everyone briefed and, by now, the crews would be making final preparations readying their aircraft for departure. It would be his turn soon. He should be feeling relaxed and content. Everything thus far had been perfect. His arrival, the preparation of the device and the mission briefing had all gone virtually to plan. So why was he so concerned?

INFILTRATION

A nagging doubt persisted in the back of his mind yet he could not explain his apprehension. One thing was for certain; he was a good judge of character and someone was not being as honest as it appeared. The operational planner seemed genuine and Ilya was reasonably confident in the man's abilities so who was the object of his unease? Perhaps it could be explained by the fact that he had been required to rely on untested assets? He was accustomed to planning his operations using resources from within his close knit intelligence community. This time he had been obliged to trust the Embassy staff in London and the Irish pilot and his sister. He would need to trust others again before the night was out. Why did he sense a deep rooted feeling of betrayal?

The problem was sidelined, unresolved. At least the next part of the plan was relatively uncontentious. The cross decking onto the research ship would be brief and, once aboard the submersible and below the waves, there were only two men who could directly affect the outcome of the mission. He was one and the other was the pilot of the small undersea craft, an old compatriot in whom he had every confidence.

There was a rap on the frame outside his space breaking his train of thought.

"Comrade, the pilot's compliments but they are ready to board as soon as you join them on deck."

He rose from the bunk pulling on his cold, rubber-soled shoes, all negative thoughts banished for the time being. Perhaps he was simply being over cautious.

CHAPTER 28

In the Iceland-Faeroes Gap.

The first formations to enter the operational area had launched from their bases in Mother Russia many hours earlier and were already well into their sorties. Rounding North Cape they had been picked up by Norwegian QRA and monitored as they turned southerly around the icebound coastline. Closing in on the massive bombers had been easy but confirming their identity had been far more challenging for the F-16 pilots who had resorted to torchlight to confirm the door numbers. Up to that point it had been a familiar routine.

Embedded within the formation one identification caused consternation: Bear Charlies, a standoff bomber equipped with the massive AS-3 "Kangaroo" missile. The forerunner of today's cruise missiles, the Kangaroo looked like a small aircraft and was thought to be derived from the Su7 Fitter fighter-bomber. Mounted in a semi-recessed housing in the belly of the Tupolev it was able to strike targets at ranges of up to 200 miles and could be equipped with a nuclear warhead. The missile, nearly 50 feet long from nose to tail weighed-in at 10 tons; enough to do serious damage to even a hardened target and, certainly to a radar facility against which it would be trained today. Not particularly accurate, it relied on brute force to do its job. After launch it would climb to a cruising altitude of almost 60,000 feet at a speed of Mach 1.6. Initially, the missile would be guided by a command link from the mother radar in the Bear but after receiving a mid-course correction, it would begin its terminal dive from a range of over 100 miles from its target. By the time it struck home it would be travelling at Mach 1.8 and just the kinetic energy alone would cause massive destruction. The follow-on nuclear blast would decimate the target area.

The Bear Charlie was fitted with sophisticated and capable electronic jammers. Electronic countermeasures pods mounted to the left and right of the tail gun in prominent fairings provided coverage to the rear with additional fairings to each side of the weather radar at the nose. An innovative terrain bounce jammer was fitted to seduce approaching radar-guided missiles, deflecting them towards the ground. By reflecting a jamming signal downwards from antennas on the underside of the nose and under the rear fuselage, active and semi-active missiles would see a false target some distance away from the huge bomber and impact harmlessly in the sea. It was an ingenious design uncommon in the West. To complete the suite, radar warning receiver antennas were mounted on the fin and on both sides of the front fuselage with chaff and flare decoy dispensers fitted to the landing gear doors. With such comprehensive protection, downing a Bear was by no means guaranteed even if a Phantom could close inside missile parameters.

Leading the formation by some significant distance was a pair of Bear Delta variants equipped for maritime patrol. Theirs was a far less sinister role and they were would work with the Battle Group to continue the hunt for the Akula which had gone silent since its successful attack on the Kiev. For the maritime patrol forces the results thus far during the exercise were less than spectacular and the much vaunted new technology was proving immature and unreliable. After early gains the Bear crews were on the defensive and anxious to redress the imbalance in their favour.

Completing the formation, two Badger Juliet specialist electronic warfare support aircraft had already fanned out into a broad frontage. Positioning on the flanks, their moves had been choreographed precisely and their positions relative to the bombers would become vital as the mission progressed. The presence of the Badgers, a less common sight, had raised interest amongst the air defence pilots but the presence of the armed Charlies had been a revelation and had generated a flurry of urgent reporting up the NATO command chain from cockpit to command bunkers. It was rare to see a composite package and even rarer to see Bear Charlies armed with their deadly payload.

At the designated "vul. time" the onboard jammers in the Juliets would begin to emit a series of carefully designed electronic sequences which would jam the ground based radars at Saxa Vord. An electronic receiver onboard the specialist platforms was dedicated to monitoring "India Band", the part of the electronic spectrum inhabited by the air intercept radars aboard the Phantoms and the F-16s. At the first sniff of interest, jammers would be tuned in and a barrage of noise jamming would make life in the Phantom cockpits even more difficult. The remaining Bears would press in towards their targets, the Charlies remaining at medium level relying on the electronic mayhem for cover, the Deltas descending to low level and diverging towards the Battle Group. Today, the Charlies would only carry out a training run but decision makers on the ground could not yet know that and their presence had raised the stakes considerably. Planners in Moscow were playing a dangerous game and had not anticipated the effect that the presence of the nuclear weapons carriers would have and how much it would upset the normally reserved defensive posture. In isolation, their presence might have caused concern. When coupled with the other events about to unfold, it would paint an altogether more sinister picture. It would not be a normal day for the UK air defence forces.

CHAPTER 29

The Air Defence Operations Centre, RAF High Wycombe.

"What do we have Julie"? Phil Boyd snapped irritably as he dragged on the headset.

It had been only 30 minutes since he had retired to the small bedroom in the back of the operations complex. Hoping to catch a few hours sleep to ward off the inevitable fatigue during the wee small hours, he was to be denied any rest tonight. The fighter controller was efficient as she ran through her situation report.

"We had advanced warning as they rounded the Cape Sir. Two Bear Deltas followed the Badgers towards the exercise area and they are now at low level to the north of the Kiev's last reported position. The Leuchars Q1 jet has stayed alongside the Badger that positioned to the west of Benbecula. He's still up at height and is in contact with the controllers."

"Confirm it's a Juliet?"

"Yes Sir. Identified as a Juliet by the Phantom crew. Not much ambiguity there with that big jamming radome. It's the first time we've seen one here for over a year so, certainly, unusual."

"Have we seen any jamming?"

"Not yet Sir."

"What's that off Trondheim?" he asked gesturing at a single track well down the Norwegian coastline.

"A Coot Alpha Sir, nothing to do with the package in the area and it seems like his presence is a coincidence."

"I'm not treating anything as a coincidence tonight Julie. Is Oerland holding Q?"

"No, The F-16s at Bodø are holding primary alert at present. The GCI site at Grakallen is active but it's only a remote head. The controllers are at the CRC at Sorreisa."

"What's his role, do we know?"

"The Coot Alpha is a military version of the IL-18 passenger airplane. It has electronic surveillance equipment onboard and is often used by the Soviet Air Force as an airborne command post."

"So why would he sit off the Norwegian coast with the exercise running off the west coast of Scotland? He's too far back to act as a radio relay for VHF or UHF channels. He has the range to work closer to the Fleet doesn't he? Am I missing something?"

"Not that I can see Sir. He certainly could make it across to the west coast if he chose. His presence is always unusual any time he comes around the Cape so maybe the Soviets are just goading us into splitting our effort. Maybe he's acting as a comms relay for the Bear Charlies? His presence is certainly unusual and has sparked interest."

"Are the Norwegians alongside?"

"Not yet Sir but they've launched and are headed south."

"Does that leave us exposed at Bodø?"

"Yes, once the F-16 recovers it will be about 30 minutes before they can turn him and get him airborne again. That's assuming they can replace the pilot. The Norwegians have trade unions and it's always a lottery whether the union rules and crew duty time will allow the pilot to remain on state. Add to that, the forecast for Bodø for later in the flying period is poor."

The older officer shook his head making his views on unions evidently clear but his concerns for short-range single seat fighters flying from snow packed runways, at night, was genuine.

"Have Leuchars brought to cockpit readiness. I want to be able to get one airborne straight away if I need to."

"Will do Sir."

She flipped the headset back into place and spoke urgently into the microphone. A light on the tote responded instantly showing the status for the Leuchars Q jets change from "RS10" to "Cpt" almost instantly. Boyd could visualise the mayhem he had just instigated as crews rushed from the Q shed towards the waiting Phantoms. He paused to assess.

"I want some airborne coverage over the maritime force if the Soviets decide to jam Benbecula. Where is the Shackleton?"

"He's on the ground on Readiness 30 Sir."

"Bring him up to cockpit readiness and get him airborne. Hand him off to Benbecula. Give them tactical control but ask them to hold him to the northeast to act as a gap filler just in case."

The fighter controller rattled off more instructions and the tote flickered once more.

What the hell were the Soviets up to Boyd wondered.

CHAPTER 30

The Soviet Task Force Off Scotland.

At the designated time, the research ship Akademik Mstislav Keldysh detached from the safety of the Carrier Battle Group and headed southerly towards the coastline. To the stern, the red flag fluttered in the breeze, the Hammer and Sickle prominent, picked out by the arc lights that bathed the scene in a suffused glow. The small yellow submersible sat immobile on the foredeck, its robotic arms extended at the front of the vessel covered in tarpaulin screening its payload from prying eyes.

The research vessel owned by the Shirshov Institute of Oceanology of the Russian Academy of Sciences in Moscow had been operating since 1980. The 6240 ton vessel with its crew of 45 was supplemented by 20 submersible pilots, engineers and technicians and up to 12 scientists and could carry 12 passengers. Its civilian credentials were of little consequence to the military leadership who had been hard pressed to find a suitable vessel for the task in mind. From its home port in Kaliningrad on the Baltic Sea its Captain had received orders to join the Battle Group as it sailed from Arctic waters. Scheduled to receive the new Mir submersible shortly, a temporary military vessel had been added to the ships compliment before departure, specially adapted for the mission. Few of the regular crew were privy to its capabilities and the pilot for tonight's mission had not been trained at the Institute. Normally, speculation would be rife but with political commissars forming the majority of the passenger complement, it had been easy to ignore the urge to speculate. They would resume their more familiar habits when the ship departed for the less controversial waters off Greenland once the exercise was complete.

Ilya, on the bridge of the vessel, felt protected from the savage elements as he watched the waves break over the prow but could not suppress a slight feeling of nervousness at the approaching challenge. Hopefully, the conditions would be calmer in the launch area, shielded from the power of the Atlantic swell by the surrounding terrain. He could do no more. The pieces of the plan were in place and elements of the force were converging on the start positions. Timing was everything but it was the one aspect that he had no control over. He was reliant on others to fulfil their contracts.

The sailor stationed by the brightly lit hatch beckoned and Ilya descended the spiral stairway to the deck access hatch. He moved quickly across the slippery deck and stepped over the lip into the submersible. The entrance way was also wet and slippery, a function of the howling wind that blew around the superstructure, whipping up a spray. Once inside, he discarded his bulky over garment and passed it back to the waiting rating outside the hatch. He slid forward to take his seat behind the pilot. The twin seats were staggered slightly, affording him a free view forward and an unobstructed sightline over the pilot's station. His controls, which would only come into play later, were set in front of his crew station and the lights glowed welcomingly. He had run through his checks many times in the trainer but it was the first and only time that he had sat in the real submersible yet he was instantly comfortable. The robotic arms stretching out in front of the craft were still shrouded in tarpaulin, the crew having strict instructions to reveal the payload only at the last minute. Outside, final preparations were underway and the technicians moved with a purpose. Behind him, the hatch clanged closed sealing the cabin from the inclement weather, the change in pressure instantly obvious as the cabin conditioning units of the life support system fired up. He felt the familiar strain on his eardrums as the overpressure built up within the confined space. Within minutes, amid calm and reassuring gestures from the pilot, the vessel lifted gently from the deck and hung in the air suspended below the crane arm. It lurched to the side and, suddenly, they were suspended over a hostile looking ocean, swinging gently in the wind.

As the submersible lowered smoothly, a sudden swell caught the skids underneath the tiny craft acting like a windsock setting up a violent oscillation. Outside, urgent shouts from the crew competed with the wind noise warning the winch operator of the impending disaster. Alerted by the frantic gestures, he reacted instantly; the submersible lurching to a halt only metres above the surface. The oscillations slowly dampened down and the descent began again, the skids breaking the swell cleanly easing the strain on the suspension harness. Free of its restraint the small craft bobbed violently in the swell the perspex cabin windows dipping in and out of the waves. A diver surfaced alongside and quickly unhitched the cradle leaving the tiny vessel free. The harness lurched upwards, the strop flailing as it rose. With his job done, the diver disappeared yet again beneath the surface.

The lights in the cockpit shone out as the ballast tanks blew and the submersible entered its element disappearing beneath the waves. At this stage, given the increasing swell and stiffening breeze, whether the craft could be recovered back on deck after the mission was anyone's guess.

*

It was time to begin phase one of the plan. For most of the voyage the mysterious helicopter had been tucked in the corner of the Kiev's hangar deck shrouded by tarpaulins. A few hours earlier it had been prepared for flight by its Air Force servicing team and its crew had prepared the complex equipment for action. They would have preferred a shakedown sortie but such luxury had been denied them given the covert preparations. The first time the equipment was called upon in anger would be to support the unfolding operation.

The helicopter was a specially modified Mil Mi-8 Hip Hotel variant normally based in East Germany with the Group of Soviet Forces Germany. Its rear cabin housed racks of electronic jammers able to target systems as diverse as the large air defence surveillance radars on the mainland to the air intercept radars in the Phantoms to simple man-portable radios and to do so over a large frequency range with enormous power.

With the pre-flight checks complete, it lumbered across the hangar floor manhandled towards the cavernous elevator which would lift it up to the flight deck. Even though darkness had fallen, its time up top would be short to ensure that unnecessary speculation on its presence onboard the

INFILTRATION

Kiev was avoided. Once at deck level it was pushed quickly onto the fantail where its crew finalised the preparations, started the main engine before it lifted noisily, heading south easterly into the darkening night. Its target tonight was somewhat controversial and if the British fighter controllers had known that it would be jamming the civilian air traffic control radars at Prestwick within the hour they might have already have been contacting their political masters for guidance. Unbeknown to the operational planners the crew had also agreed to a carry out a secondary mission to help out the flight leader of the helicopter carrying the insertion team. If the rotary community could not help each other out with a favour it was a sad day.

*

On the dispersal at RAF Lossiemouth, the crew of the aging Shackleton airborne early warning aircraft, some members nearly as old as the venerable aircraft itself piled out of the decrepit crew bus and formed an orderly queue at the door at the rear of the converted maritime patrol aircraft. A scramble was a much more gentlemanly procedure for the Shackleton crew operating from Readiness 30 when compared to their fighter brethren! The "Shack" as it was affectionately known, had been rapidly pushed into service as a stopgap surveillance aircraft awaiting the development of the Nimrod airborne early warning platform which was still a number of years away from entering service. In the meantime, the Shackleton would have to last out for a while longer.

The aged Griffon engines, developments of the wartime Merlin engine immortalised as the power plant for the legendary Spitfire, fired up belching plumes of smoke into the air. The aircraft's lineage dating back to the Lancaster bomber, was readily apparent to bystanders and it seemed more suited to a Second World War mission than a Cold War operation. The choking fumes cleared slowly as the engines clattered and roared into life but it would be at least 15 minutes before the old warhorse reached the runway for takeoff.

As the Shackleton finally trundled off down the runway, the engines piercing the still calm of the Scottish countryside, the tail wheel slowly lifted and the aircraft cocked slightly into wind as it reached takeoff speed. Lumbering into the air it turned slowly onto a westerly heading and set course for its operational station or barrier. It struggled to gain height and would never climb much above 10,000 feet limiting yet further its maximum radar range which was already poor. In the cabin down the back end, following a well rehearsed tradition, the air electronics officer, or AEO, unstrapped and made his way to the galley to start brewing the first cup of tea of the day. As priorities went this was up there at the top of the list. Even though it was only a few hours since their pre-flight meal, firing up the boiler was an essential part of the pre takeoff checks and by now it was bubbling nicely. Having a cup of hot tea in the Captain's hands by top of climb bolstered by a few chocolate biscuits should improve the chances of a smooth flight. With the austere conditions down the back end of the Shack the rear crew were grateful for small mercies.

*

Kedrov watched the stocky figure battle the freshening winds over the deck as he made his way towards the Yak fighter, picked out in the floodlights. Plugging the headset into the receptacle beneath the cockpit the normally quiet intercom system crackled into life and the throaty Russian accent broke the stillness.

"Comrade, you have a scramble instruction but the Air Commander wishes you to remain in radio silence. You have two targets closing on the task force and the Admiral wants you to warn them off."

"What type of targets?" he snapped back. "It's pitch black out there."

"The first is a Nimrod maritime patrol aircraft which is working in towards the defensive screen. Sonobuoys have been dropped to pin down the submarines taking part in the operational test and if the Nimrod presses too hard he may disrupt the test objectives. The Admiral wants him pushed back outside the screen."

"And how should I do that? Am I authorised to shoot him down if necessary?"

"Not quite comrade but the Admiral has approved the use of warning fire."

The implications sunk in. Warning fire meant guns not missiles and it was as dark as a witch's tit out there.

"How can I verify that?" he asked, his self preservation instincts kicking in. So far without instructions transmitted over the radio and with no authorisation other than this entirely deniable briefing, he was out on a limb.

"The Admiral was very specific. He said to relay the word "Zheltovsky". He said you will understand."

Kedrov understood only too well. The codeword was, indeed, significant and had been nominated specifically at one of the first briefing sessions as they had sailed from port. It was to be used only in extremis and not to be questioned. There could be no debate; he instantly acquiesced.

"And what of the secondary target?"

"A Shackleton airborne early warning aircraft working further to the northeast. He is positioned to extend the British radar coverage out into our area. The Admiral would prefer if he was also persuaded to withdraw to a safer distance."

"You know we don't have enough fuel to interdict both targets so you are asking me to split my forces and send my wingman alone against one of these aircraft? He has scarcely 300 hours on the Yakolev and even less night hours. He can barely think for himself in the air and you want me to send him out alone at night?"

"I can only relay the Admiral's wishes comrade."

It was a dereliction.

"Give me those positions."

He copied the coordinates quickly onto his map on his knee pad. The Nimrod was relatively close but if it came closer would be a threat to the test. The Shackleton was well to the northeast and at the limits of his range from deck alert. Luckily, the track to the Shackleton took him within 15 miles of the plotted position of the Nimrod. With luck they could leave as a pair and he could make the first intercept and drop his wingman off en route to persuade the Nimrod to desist. He would then press on to try a similar tactic against the venerable snooper.

"Relay to flying control we want a radio silent departure and an outbound vector of 030 degrees. I'll get airborne and make one orbit to collect my wingman after he launches then we depart. Brief my wingman so I don't have to transmit."

"Comrade!"

The man disconnected and moved along the flightline reluctantly. He would have preferred to withdraw to the comfort of the island given the weather. Kedrov looked across towards his wingman, disturbed. A face-to-face briefing would have been preferable but the youngster was trained to stick, search and report and he hoped he had the skills to do so as they headed towards their prey. He also hoped he would be sharp enough to remember not to transmit on the radio. One slip and their covert approach would be blown. The lack of any further radio messages should be a clue. As the technician climbed down from the cockpit he gave the wind-up signal and his engine sprang into life. Gesturing prominently he hoped the wingman would take the hint.

Taxying onto the strip he looked up towards Fly Co. A green lamp stared back and he immediately advanced the throttle bringing the main engine up to full power. With the RPM stabilised he advanced the lift engines and rolled. With the assistance of the cushion beneath, the Forger lifted almost instantly helped by the stiff breeze across the deck. Fortunately, he carried only two AA-8 Aphid air-to-air missiles for this mission but he would have preferred some external fuel tanks to extend his range. Airborne with gear retracted and flaps up he reefed around and ran tight downwind watching for his wingman to follow his lead. The kid was doing well. The other Yakolev rolled and, as he turned over the ship they matched speeds in line abreast formation before he broke over the top of the other jet and rolled out on a north easterly heading. Looking back over his shoulder the other jet dropped into a loose fighting wing formation and stuck tight the navigation lights winking in the dark night.

*

Without an air intercept radar he was reliant on the ground position he had been given before leaving the deck. He had to make a night visual intercept against a manoeuvring target which might not be pleased to see him. At least it couldn't fight back, he thought grimly. His navigation at night was rudimentary and that was putting it mildly. He had marked the map and drawn a track from the carrier's position to the symbol. His outbound heading had been his best guess. A quick mental calculation and he glanced at his watch. Eleven minutes to go. At least his wingman was holding position. The kid must be petrified. His first operational deployment and not only was he night flying but he would have some serious work to do when they got there.

A plan formed in his mind. If they could harass the Nimrod enough to persuade the pilot to back off and then feint towards the Shackleton, maybe it would be enough to solve both problems. With what he had in mind, hopefully the Nimrod pilot would make enough noise on the tactical frequency to solve his dilemma. He eased the throttle back and the speed trickled down to 420 kilometres per hour. Eight minutes to run.

*

Kedrov was fast approaching the target's last known position and without the benefit of radar, he had little choice but to scan the dark horizon looking for a chance detection. The moon occasionally broke through the scattered clouds giving him enough references to orientate himself. It had been a long time since he had worked so hard; in fact he had never flown on such a dark night so far from land but he was enjoying the challenge. There would be none of the usual scripted scenarios tonight. Holding a steady height 1,000 metres above the waves he checked his watch yet again. The realisation that there was nothing he could do without a fighter controller to talk him on magnified his feeling of isolation. He was almost at the estimated position. Nothing. . . . .

Suddenly he spotted a brief movement in his peripheral vision. Red navigation lights flashing rhythmically through a gap in the scudding low clouds emerged dimly from the darkness. He pulled hard towards, checking that his wingman was following. Good. Up to now, they had avoided transmitting on the radio so their approach should have been unannounced. The trap was about to be sprung.

The target was flying on a high crossing angle and drifted rapidly in towards his nose, crossing ahead and solving his intercept geometry. Losing it temporarily behind a small cloud bank he held his nerve, willing the fleeting contact to reappear. There it was. The geometry looked perfect and he began a gentle turn in behind slipping into the rear quarter. He began to pick out brighter lights from the cabin windows ranged down the fuselage, the shape of the Nimrod now clear in the moonlight, the flashing navigation lights a beacon in the gloom.

The large jet was straight and level and some way below his height so he eased down towards the sea, tentatively, his eyes dropping regularly to his altimeter. His wingman had repositioned on his left, the steady nav lights marking his position. As the formation closed on its prey, he flicked his radio to the International Distress Frequency, 243.0 or "Guard", and hit the transmit button.

The two Yak-38s pulled alongside.

"Aircraft approaching the Soviet task force heading 240 degrees, this is Wolf Leader, come up on 243.0."

His accent was harsh on the radio frequency. He waited patiently. No response.

"Aircraft in the vicinity of Soviet task force state your identity."

Still nothing. . . . .

"Aircraft in the vicinity of Soviet task force you are disrupting operations and are a threat to safety. I am authorised to use force. Make your heading 030 to clear the area."

He suspected his instructions were worthless without the intent to enforce and the transmission which followed confirmed his fears.

"Wolf Leader this is Kilo Echo Zulu 45 on Guard. I am a British aircraft in international waters conducting routine operations. Maintaining heading."

Hesitation was pointless. He switched back to the tactical frequency and barked a command to his wingman who immediately backed off and pulled up and above the formation. With the other Yak well clear he dropped back. The next manoeuvre would be demanding even in daylight. At night it was bordering on the suicidal. He flicked his weapons switches methodically and was rewarded with gun symbology glowing menacingly in his gunsight. From a perch position in the eight o'clock he steeled himself for the pass. Yanking the stick to the right he pulled the sight on before reversing the turn and checked the Nimrod's movement across the gunsight. He tracked the huge airframe, momentarily aiming at the cockpit before pulling harder and shifting his aiming point well ahead. The target loomed quickly, surprising him with its bulk and he squeezed off a short burst before rolling off the bank and pulling up and away from the Nimrod's flight path. The tracer interspersed among the high explosive incendiary rounds arced away from his jet lighting up the dark sky, the short burst quickly extinguished as they fell towards the sea, gravity taking its toll.

His heart pounding, he steadied up on the left wing of the maritime patrol aircraft and watched his quarry for a reaction. He could see heads moving in the cockpit and could only imagine the discussions going on between the pilot and his controller on the ground. Anxious faces appeared at the cabin windows. Without further preamble the Nimrod began a lazy turn away to the north, the crew persuaded that further discussion was pointless and, indeed detrimental to survival.

Satisfied, he switched back to tactical and checked on his wingman's fuel state. The response was unexpected. Where the hell had the lad's fuel gone? No matter. Recriminations were wasted at this moment and he ordered him to return to the Kiev. He would dig deeper at the debrief but, in the meantime, the mere challenge of landing on was sufficient for the youngster. Pulling up, he kept sight of the Nimrod now well below and watched as it crossed his flight path heading back towards the coast. It would continue to monitor as it withdrew but he had fulfilled his part of the contract.

With his wingman returning to the ship and now well clear above the surface of the sea he relaxed a little. Flicking through the notes on his kneeboard he checked a list of frequencies he had been given before taking over alert duties. His torch picked out the six frequencies which the intelligence officer thought the British Phantom fighters might be using. Methodically switching the dials on his radio he ran through each frequency, dwelling briefly, listening for activity. When he finally selected the correct one there could be no mistake. An urgent exchange between the Nimrod and the controller virtually blocked the channel. It was a struggle to follow the exchange with his limited English but a few key words left nothing to interpret. "Hostile" and "fire" stood out amid the other garbled transmissions.

"Roger Kilo Echo Zulu 45, Q1 is airborne. Break, break, Anyface, retrograde," he heard distinctly.

Anyface was the callsign of the Shackleton and the cryptic codeword was his order to withdraw. With his aggressive interrogation of the Nimrod, Kedrov had achieved his objective without even needing to threaten the lumbering veteran. He was secretly relieved. The thought of barrelling around the aging piston engined aircraft at low level, at night, at slow speed had filled him with dread.

With a final check of his fuel gauge he hauled the Yakolev around and headed back towards the carrier battle group. If anything, he had allowed the fuel to go below the normal sensible reserve but with only two jets airborne he remained confident that all would be well. Switching to the recovery frequency he listened out simultaneously dialling the homer into the correct frequency and watching the needles swing around, pointing at his objective. He adjusted his heading the distance beginning to wind down. Still some kilometres to go, a few broken transmissions crackled through the static on the frequency. It should have been the first warning.

"Mat this is Wolf Leader, on recovery," he called.

"Wolf Leader Mat, standby."

Mat, or Mother, seemed tense. He waited patiently.

"Wolf Leader, Mat, Wolf 2 has crashed on deck. We are presently unable to accept recoveries."

The vital facts took time to register.

"Roger Mat, I'm happy to make a vertical landing. I'll take instructions when I'm closer in."

"Negative Wolf Leader, your wingman hit two helicopters. We have fires on deck and a massive fuel spillage. Unable to accept recoveries at this time. Head inbound for point Romeo and await further instructions."

His fuel gauge now became the most important instrument in the cockpit. Already on minimums he had planned a rolling landing. A vertical landing would cost another 150 Kg which he could barely spare. He throttled back to endurance speed and waited the altitude increasing as he climbed to eke out his scant reserves.

The fuel gauge slowly sank below any recognised level he had ever seen in the Yak cockpit. His sense of unease was rapidly becoming one of alarm.

"Mat, Wolf Leader I am on fuel minimums, request immediate recovery or I will flame out. I estimate five minutes to tanks dry."

"Wolf Leader, Mat, I'm sorry comrade but recovery is impossible. The deck is carnage."

"Roger I'll be ejecting in five minutes. Launch the SAR helicopter."

"Negative Wolf, the SAR chopper was one of the helicopters he took out. We'll launch a recovery craft. Best of luck."

The realisation struck home and a survival instinct set in as his mind raced identifying options which would give him the best chances of survival. Checking the lanyard attaching him to his emergency dinghy more than once, he tightened his straps and, flicking the canopy release handle, the heavy perspex cover flipped backwards into the airflow, disappearing rapidly. It suddenly became very noisy and cold in the cockpit. He waited for the inevitable.

The fuel gauge flickered one final time and, as the engine wound down, he pulled the ejection seat handle and tensed. . . . .

CHAPTER 31

Off Benbecula.

The surface of the waves parted in a roiling foam, the stumpy conning tower of the midget submarine rising above the breakers. As the circular hatch of the Triton 2 opened, black-clad bodies emerged onto the deck, preparations for disembarking immediately underway. Subordinate to the Intelligence Directorate of the GRU, the five man Naval Spetznaz team had been handpicked for the insertion and, despite the raging wind and the waves which drove against the now stationary hull they were utterly silent as they assembled their gear on deck. Watertight packs were clipped to lanyards which were, unceremoniously, dumped into the sea. Masks and snorkels were donned and flippers fitted before the slick bodies followed the bobbing packs into the water. At this latitude the night was pitch black and had been for some hours and, although the beach lay only a few hundred metres away, the sandy cove which was their target, was invisible to the frogmen. In order to dispense with the need for the more familiar IDA-71 rebreathers the midget submarine had moved in close to the coastline. In more populated waters they would not have had the luxury but here in the isolated islands the presence of the clandestine craft would not be noticed. The SOSUS network was searching for more predatory targets. As the commandos kicked for the shore, the submarine pilot filled the ballast tanks and it slipped once more into the shallow depths. It would wait there until the nominated exfiltration time.

It took only minutes for the men to cover the short distance to shore. The small island of North Uist was sparsely populated and little occurred in the tight communities without someone noticing and commenting but even the hardy fisherman would be tucked up in bed at this late hour, only manning their boats as dawn broke. The Spetznaz team emerged from the surf discarding their swimming gear alongside a rocky outcrop, pulling weapons and equipment from the dripping packs and readying to break out.

The beach they had chosen was broad and flanked by a low cliff line fringed by dunes. Their passage up the beach to the north disturbed a colony of fulmars nesting in the low cliffs and the unruly flock made its displeasure known in a raucous rejoinder. As the shadowy figures turned to track up the stream bed, a corncrake, disturbed from its nest in a tussock, let go a strident call which would have alerted any guard worth his salt who might have been within earshot. Luckily, with no one around at this ungodly hour their passage went undetected other than by the birds. They had no intention of being on the island by the time the locals stirred.

To the northern end, a small river cut the low escarpment allowed an easy route out towards the main road, the A865, which followed a circuitous route around the coastline. Not surprisingly, the radar head which was their target was located on higher ground at the centre of the narrow coastal strip near the settlement of South Clettraval some way to the east. The main island road formed an almost perfect circle around the remote radar site but, fortuitously for them, a small track led from the main trunk road in a straight line across the undulating terrain and up the hillside. In order to make good time they would be forced to use the road at least for part of their approach. If the intelligence was correct, there were no sensors or cameras along the way so they should be able to arrive unseen. Electronic surveillance was an impossible luxury in the islands. The first obstacle, the village of Baleloch lay in their path and for the initial part of their hike forcing them to avoid the roads to limit a chance encounter.

Skirting the settlements giving the village of Hosta a wide berth, they covered the flat ground quickly before encountering the narrow access road flanked along its route by a single, remote farmhouse. As they approached, despite the rubber soled shoes they wore, a dog sensed their presence and a bark rang out. Dropping to the ground they held still for a few moments but its defiant warning continued to sound. A light snapped on in a bedroom in the farmhouse and a disgruntled voice urged the insistent dog to be still. Despite the solitude, a torch fanned out over the approaches to the cottage, weak but intrusive, searching for the source of the disturbance. The owner was more inclined to blame a marauding animal than the sinister figures who grubbed lower into the peat. Hidden by the low grass bordering the road they waited until the dog lost interest.

With everything once again quiet progress resumed, the group skirting the smallholding to avoid further scrutiny. The inhabitants were unlikely to have observed their passing but they would give it a wide berth on their return trying hard to comply with the instructions to avoid contact. Target preparation had shown that the access road skirted the hill on the southerly slope and entered the guarded site from the east but they had no intention of arriving at the Main Gate. As the isolated outpost loomed above them, its position marked by the gently flashing red obstruction light on the radar head, they began their final climb up the hillside towards the perimeter fence.

The security lights shone across the concrete hardstandings illuminating the area around the main radar head. Bathed in the glow of a number of strategically placed sodium lights, less determined visitors might have been discouraged, although why anyone would target such a remote installation, present company excepted, was a mystery. The leader was undeterred as his area of interest lay a short distance away out of the omnipresent glare. Two of the team began to scrape away the earth beneath the security fence and within a few minutes, a gap big enough to crawl underneath had opened up. With the earth replaced after their departure, it was unlikely that anyone would spot their entry point. Once through the breach the team split with the first section making its way to the main power supply room housed in the makeshift administrative building, grandly known as Station Headquarters, and the second group moving swiftly towards the standby generators housed behind a low brick wall.

The door to SHQ yielded quickly and three men entered quietly. A corridor led towards the rear of the building and, with luck, that would be where they would find the main power room. As they moved silently past the vacant, darkened offices a glow bled from beneath a single door, the sound of a boiling kettle breaking the silence. Beckoning for the others to halt, the leader silently directed them to flank the doorway. The security guards should have been holed up in the guardroom at the Main Gate at this hour and the unexpected presence in the headquarters building was a setback, albeit one which they had anticipated. Dropping into a pre-arranged routine, two of the team positioned to one side of the door with the remaining commando retreating down the corridor. A further gesture and a door opened and closed, the perpetrator stepping inside, the sound reverberating around the quiet building. The noise elicited an instant and, perhaps guilty response.

"Who's that?" the nervous airman called; sounds of movement. "Is that you Ken?" the man asked again. Further sounds from the kitchen preceded a head which popped, hesitantly, around the door frame, its owner making his way towards the source of the unexpected noise. With his back to the silent commandos he did not expect the chloroform-soaked gag which clamped around his mouth before a hood cut off his view. He was lifted forcibly off his feet and dumped like a sack of potatoes onto the linoleum covered floor. Snap restraints quickly bound his wrists and ankles and he was bundled, struggling and grunting back into the kitchen. Without preamble a syringe appeared from a backpack and a hastily administered cocktail of drugs would ensure that even if he managed to concoct a cover story, he would have no recollection of the real events. The mixture of scopolamine and Percocet had been used for some years as a palliative for pregnant mothers in labour but when he revived it would guarantee at least temporary amnesia. His efforts became increasingly feeble and within a few minutes ended completely. The leader pulled a small flask of local scotch whiskey from his backpack and tipping his head back to open the airman's gullet, applied a generous dose to the victim's lips. When he woke, the after effects of the drug would be masked by the potency of the malt.

"When he's discovered, if he can even remember us, which is debateable, they won't believe him," the leader muttered softly. "I'd say he'll be on a charge once he's found, particularly with the plans we have in mind for this place."

They would remove the restraints before departing leaving the unfortunate guard to his fate. With the unexpected threat neutralised the three men moved quickly towards the power distribution panel and, as expected, the supply cabinet was located just inside the doorway. The designers had been wonderfully naive and when the buildings had been erected in the 50s, the main power supply from the local grid which served the whole site had been routed through a single conduit. Although the massive radar heads which operated on a much higher voltage would continue to turn, everything else such as lighting and communications was dependent on this single domestic voltage power line. Once severed, the unit would be isolated and unable to communicate with the air defence network for some time to come.

The denial plan was essentially simple. An innocent looking portable apparatus was hooked up to the power supply and the expressionless Russian watched intently as the device sprung to life, lights flashing, gauges registering the current. The contraption hummed quietly as he waited for the "ready" light to illuminate. After a final time check and a nod from the team leader he hit the button prompting a bright flash, and sparks lit the room as the power supply arced dramatically. The panel fell dormant instantly. In the control room across the site the lights dimmed and the emergency lighting kicked in as the air conditioners fell silent. Within seconds the standby power automatically fired up bringing systems back on line amid a chatter of reluctant electronics. What the RAF technicians could not know at this point was that with the introduction of an additive to the diesel tanks by the second team the generators would run for only a short time before becoming utterly fouled. The strip down and clean up would take many hours closing down Benbecula as a viable air defence site.

Their work done, the team withdrew from the still silent building locking doors as they went. The short distance to the breach in the fence was muddy but they covered their tracks as best as they could, pulling the wire of the security fence back into place before retracing their tracks. Deniability! After making a rendezvous with the remaining Spetznaz troops they made their escape down the slope towards the road. Remarkably, all had gone to plan and the operation had been undetected save for the unfortunate guard. The jog down the hillside was somewhat easier than their arrival.

Back at the main door to SHQ, the Orderly Corporal fumbled with the bundle of keys before finally identifying the correct one. He pushed open the heavy door which creaked in protest. Although the corridor was dark, light streamed through a crack at the far end as, guided by his torch beam, he followed the source pushing into the Kitchen. The bundled form on the floor was immobile but after checking the dormant body for signs of life he breathed a sigh of relief at the strong pulse.

"Oh bloody hell mate, you've done it this time," he muttered smelling the reek of alcohol, slapping the face of the dozing airman in a futile attempt to revive him. "They'll have your bloody arse in a sling for this one you stupid bugger."

The contrived fate of his friend had achieved its aim, diverting attention away from the real reason for the power failure. It would be some time before the charred mess in the supply room was discovered and the duty electrician could be called out to take stock of the mayhem.

In the operations room on the radar site, the duty fighter controller had more pressing worries as the standby power finally failed. Once again the room was plunged into darkness and this time there would be no respite. He hit the comms panel attempting to check the status of the radar heads but was rewarded with a dead line. Picking up the external phone line, again he heard only silence. Benbecula Control and Reporting Centre was, effectively, neutralised.

*

Kedrov spluttered as the heavy seas rose and fell around him. After pulling the lanyard connecting him to the liferaft and wrestling with the handle on the hard container, the inflation bottle spluttered ineffectually and the survival pack remained stubbornly inert. He felt the first pangs of nervousness. The last message had made it clear that the search and rescue chopper had been damaged and was not going to be searching for him any time soon. He hoped that the inflatable boats that had been promised really had been launched and were on the way because, already, his hands were losing feeling in the cold Atlantic waters. He reckoned he had mere minutes before they would be useless and with a loss of dexterity came the real risk of succumbing to the cold water. With no prospect of protection from the inflatable dinghy he fumbled with his personal locator beacon, snapping it into place on the stole of his lifejacket teasing the antenna erect. He could vaguely hear the ping from the electronic device knowing that it was his one hope of rescue. With such a sea swell there would be no chance of a visual sighting from the distant fleet. He would be all but invisible amongst the heaving surge. At least he had ejected near to the task group so the search area was confined to the near vicinity but with his feet now numb and his hands totally seized and useless, it had taken only minutes to reduce him to this helpless state. Bizarrely, he was hoping that the Brits had not launched their own SAR helicopter or he may find himself as an unwelcome visitor aboard a British boat, probably not a good outcome after his intervention with the Nimrod. He had after all, opened fire on one of their mates and they may take umbrage at his actions.

A wave subsided and he caught a welcome glance of a small craft bearing down on his position. Reaching beneath the heaving waves, he scrabbled with his pack of flares, his hands almost reduced to clubs. Luckily the gnarled cap rotated easily in his grip and he dropped the redundant plastic into the water. A small lanyard unfolded and he tried to grasp the ring which popped out but it flopped uselessly into the sea. Another glance through a gap in the waves revealed the small boat flashing quickly past. Time was critical. This may be his only chance of rescue. He tried again, finally wrapping the errant string around his glove and gave a hefty pull. The pyrotechnic burst into life and a bright orange plume lit the surrounding area between the wave tops, prompting an enormous sigh of relief as the note of the inflatable's engine changed and grew, rapidly, louder. They must have seen the reflections. Please don't run me down he thought flippantly.

*

As the Spetznaz team donned their wet suits and snorkelling gear there was silent satisfaction amongst the commandos. It would be a short time before their extraction and the timing seemed perfect. There would be no need to bring it forward if that was even possible. In the wrap-around blackness on the beach they were confident that nothing could now go wrong, although the strident calls of the fulmars would have seemed out of the ordinary to a local had anyone been within earshot. They sheltered in the lee of the rocky outcrop awaiting their rendezvous with the Triton 2.

High tide would erase any evidence of their brief presence.

INFILTRATION

*

The inflatable hove-to alongside and Kedrov was hauled over the black rubberised buoyancy chamber and dragged bodily into the small heaving boat. The AK-47 assault rifles clutched by some of the small crew seemed over the top but he was grateful that their smiles were friendly. He took the proffered blanket gratefully pleased to feel his teeth chattering as his temperature began to recover. It was a good sign. The small hip flask was even more welcome and he slugged the shot gratefully. The engine picked up again as the small craft crested the waves aiming back towards the bright lights of Kiev's flight deck. He began to recover his spirits, although the loss of a Yak-38 would not go down well with the Air Commander. At least he was blameless on that score, although the same could not be said for the young pilot who had rearranged the flight deck. Approach and landing was an automatic function. How the hell had he screwed up so badly?

*

The Hip "Hotel" helicopter turned onto an easterly heading popping up from low altitude, establishing its pre-planned racetrack. Up to now it had approached below the radar coverage, the insertion unobserved. The onboard jammers targeted via racks of oddly shaped antennas on the side of the cabin were extremely directional and at least one helicopter would need to be facing towards the target throughout the allotted time if the jamming was to be effective. The Soviet Navy Hormones which had been dispatched as part of the package did not have the same jamming suite but could target some of the emitters of interest. The key was whether the planner who had been tasked to produce the electronic attack plan had done his homework properly. In the darkened cabins the electronic combat officers huddled over the screens making last minute adjustments hoping he had.

*

"Speedbird Golf November Alpha, come right onto 280, closing heading. Contact Prestwick Radar on 119 decimal 45."

"To Radar on 119 decimal 45, Speedbird November Alpha."

The young trainee first officer in the right hand seat switched channels and paused, listening for activity on the new frequency. Satisfied he hit the transmit switch.

"Prestwick Radar, Speedbird November Alpha is with you, localiser established."

"Roger Speedbird November Alpha, Runway 31 in use, the QFE is 1014."

"1014 set, Speedbird November Alpha."

The veteran 100 series Boeing 747 Jumbo Jet, one of the first to enter service with British Overseas Airways Corporation, the forerunner to British Airways, headed back towards the distant coastal airport, the two pilots locked in concentration on the small instrument landing system dial, the centre of their universe for the next ten minutes. Already they had pounded the radar pattern for an hour, the tally of instrument approaches slowly rising moving the two trainees aboard the jet closer to their goal. Once qualified, they would progress to their inaugural passenger carrying flights. The vertical needle began its predicted drift inwards towards the centre of the dial as the airliner closed towards the extended centreline, the trainee pilot correcting the heading to slow its progress. The horizontal glide path bar stayed stubbornly fixed towards the bottom of the dial.

"Speedbird November Alpha, outer marker."

Electronic beeps marked the passage over the marker beacon.

"Speedbird November Alpha continue, call me glide path descending."

Normally a fully automatic procedure, even with the obsolescent technology aboard the veteran 100 series Boeing, today's exercise demanded manual approaches from the crew, insurance against the day when the technology failed. Isolated in the darkened cockpit, bathed in the red floodlights, the crew could not know that others had designs on making sure that the surveillance radar and the landing aids would not be quite so reliable this evening. The Boeing would be the unfortunate victim of collateral electronic fratricide.

At the designated time the electronic combat officers in the helicopters eased the gang bar forward and the massive jammers sprang into life. Brute force and ignorance, otherwise known as a Megawatt of electronic power flooded from the antennas blotting out the frequencies over a very specific bandwidth. Targeted mainly at the surveillance radar a strobe immediately blotted out the azimuth along which the helicopters lay. Radial spokes appeared in sympathy turning the normally placid screen in the radar control room into electronic mayhem. On the ground, the talkdown controller issued a series of Anglo-Saxon expletives assuming the local RAF detachment at Machrihanish was the culprit and cast doubt on their heritage. One of the unintentional casualties was the instrument landing system.

"Bloody Air Force exercises," the controller muttered.

"Is that the Master Controller?" he queried stabbing the direct line to Buchan Sector Operations Centre. "Can you call off your hounds. My radar looks like the opening manoeuvres on D Day down here. British Airways are not going to be happy if the training flight is grounded. Who have you got in the air?"

The response from the controller at Buchan was quizzical. A check revealed that apart from the Leuchars Q bird all his jets were on the ground. The Canberra squadron had gone home many hours earlier.

In the cockpit of the Jumbo, the Captain glanced at the trainee who pressed on with his approach, oblivious to the unfolding drama.

"Speedbird November Alpha, glide path descending."

Unsurprisingly, the vertical needle was locked to the centre of the dial and its horizontal twin had joined it. But for the vivid "off flags" on the face of the dial it would have been a classic ILS approach and would have delivered the Jumbo precisely to the touchdown point. Unlike a military cockpit there were no indications that the incipient failure was due to anything other than a malfunction nor could the young trainee be aware that the failure was due to electronic mischief but the Captain sensed an opportunity for a training exercise. Glancing through the side window, he saw the cloud scudding past, the jet still enveloped in the cloying mist but they were still 1,500 feet above touchdown elevation. The easterly approach onto the main runway at Prestwick was over open sea with the threshold set just the other side of the coastal road. It was an ideal opportunity to demonstrate a vital lesson to the tyro. The captain waited for signs of a revelation as the huge jet began its ponderous descent. Surely no one could miss those off flags?

In the Talkdown control room mayhem reigned. Assurances from the air defence operations centre at Buchan that the jamming was nothing to do with RAF operations met with resistance and even disbelief. In fairness, it was not the first time that the radar screens had been disrupted by wayward electronic warfare signals from electronic warfare training aircraft in the shape of Canberras from RAF Wyton but the lack of any airborne activity which normally presaged the disruption was curious.

Back in the cockpit of the 747 the crew eased the jet slowly towards the runway threshold.

"Notice anything unusual?" the Captain queried as the jet continued through the thick blanket of cloud.

"It all seems to be going well," the hesitant voice responded from the right hand seat knowing with increasing dread that he had missed something vital. Such questions were never casual.

"Speedbird November Alpha, are you visual with the ground?"

"Speedbird November Alpha, negative."

"Speedbird November Alpha carry out a missed approach and contact Prestwick Radar on 129 decimal 45."

The voice over the ether belied the chaos below. The Captain glanced again out of the side windows, looking down and registering the first glimpses of choppy, white wave tops below. Looking ahead, the windscreen suddenly cleared and the runway lights appeared bright in the near distance. They were well below the glide slope but as the descent had effectively been uncontrolled it was no surprise.

"Speedbird November Alpha, runway in sight. Change of intentions, request clearance to land."

"Speedbird November Alpha, roger, take over visually. Clear to land, surface wind is westerly at 15 knots."

"Clear to land, Speedbird November Alpha ."

The crisis passed as quickly as it had appeared.

The Captain paused. "Look at the flags on the ILS."

The damning realisation struck home. Had it been for real, the trainee may have delivered his passengers into the ground at an uncontrolled rate of descent. It was a pilot's worst nightmare and he had been incompetent in the extreme. So close to success too after his earlier approaches.

"I have control."

The words no student pilot wants to hear from his instructor.

"You have control," he responded meekly.

The descent checked instantly and the jet drifted rapidly back towards the centreline urged away from its random aiming point some way off the piano keys.

"We'll talk about it on the ground." Another pause.

"Speedbird November Alpha to Tower."

"Roger to Tower on 118 decimal 5 goodnight."

The Captain clicked the dials and adjusted his approach.

"Prestwick Tower, Speedbird November Alpha, short finals to land."

"Speedbird November Alpha, clear to land, surface wind westerly at 15 gusting 20 knots."

He rolled the wings level bringing the nose back onto the centreline, adjusting the heading to compensate for the drift. As he steadied up, a gust picked up the right wing and he jockeyed for better control. The combination of low, slow and off the centreline conspired causing an over-compensation. As he crossed the piano keys the left wing rose in complaint and the heavy multi bogey undercarriage units on the right side struck the runway first. Had they all arrived in concert he may have got away with it but the aft bogeys arrived marginally before the front before making a supreme effort to run up to speed in the fraction of a second demanded. Despite the low fuel state the demand proved too great and the tyres screeched in protest, emitting clouds of dense, acrid smoke. The arrival was firm and inelegant as the huge jet settled onto the long runway yet all might have been recoverable but for a further over-enthusiastic application of brake. Suddenly persuaded to reverse their instruction to spin up, the tyres spurned his efforts and, in unison, burst. The Jumbo lumbered to a halt in a cloud of smoke, the first inkling of a brake fire as the wheels came to a sudden stop.

"Speedbird November Alpha, hold your position, emergency crews on the way."

The Captain groaned.

"Prestwick Tower, Cargolux 347 short finals, confirm the runway is blocked?"

"Cargolux 347 affirmative, carry out a Grade One diversion to Glasgow Abbotsinch. Follow a missed approach and contact Prestwick Radar on 129 decimal 45."

The Captain groaned even louder as the Douglas DC8 freighter passed overhead already climbing out and heading for the nearby international airport outside the Scottish city. It would be some hours before its cargo returned to the distribution sheds at the busy hub. Discussions would be intense between harassed operations officers.

In the Radar Room the jamming had caused the perfect storm and operations would be disrupted for hours to come.

*

The Badger Juliet, a specialist electronic warfare variant was an unusual visitor to the UK Air Defence Region. As normal, its presence as it passed 30 East was flashed up to the NATO air defence network and its progress monitored by Norwegian F16s as it headed west at medium level. Tracking north of Iceland, F-4Es from the 57th Fighter Interceptor Squadron based

INFILTRATION

at Keflavik had scrambled to meet it and tracked its flight path across the cold Arctic waters. As it turned southerly, QRA from RAF Leuchars was scrambled and the Badger crew had little time to become lonely before the lone British Phantom hove alongside. Cursing the fact that the darkness would make photography of this unusual visitor almost impossible at these northerly latitudes, the crew had made best efforts to capture the profile against a dark horizon.

The circuitous route was intentional. Although its target was the radar installation at Saxa Vord, the long looping approach from the west would ensure that it approached on a carefully planned vector providing cover jamming for a force which, as it began its inbound track, was leaving the deck of the Moskva helicopter carrier which had detached from the Soviet task force.

The Phantom crew had settled into a familiar routine plotting, as much as their antiquated air position indicator - the navigation equipment - in the F-4K allowed, the course of the Badger as it headed south. Assuming it would target the Soviet fleet there was brief discussion on its intentions as it turned back to the north east headed directly for the northern tip of the island of Unst. Sitting in close formation attempting to capture close up shots of the canoe shaped radome slung beneath the converted bomber, the navigator had placed his AN/AWG11 radar in "standby" mode deactivating the radar transmitter. In its dormant state the radar was not emitting so was unable to display other targets in the area but the receiver still held a passive vigil. As the electronic combat officers in the cabin activated the electronic jammers, the screens in both cockpits registered the sudden burst of electronic energy and a barrage of jamming strobes flooded the displays. At long range, the navigator could field an array of anti-jamming techniques to prosecute an attack. Here, alongside the Badger there was little need as the pilot's "Mark One Eyeballs" held them in position.

Under the rules of engagement with which the British crews had hurriedly been issued, the Soviet crew had just committed a suspected hostile act. Had the vector been towards the Soviet fleet it might have been justifiable but on the north easterly course there could be only one target for the electronic mischief. The attack generated a flurry of activity over the radio.

A harassed ground control intercept officer in the radar room at Saxa Vord announced the jamming of his own surveillance radars across a band of frequencies. The Phantom navigator confirmed the electronic attack prompting further discussions with the Air Defence Commander in the bunker at High Wycombe. Unheard by the Phantom crew, the senior officer was far from calm.

As the air defence forces reacted to the attack, a small force of helicopters approached the westerly coastline of the island of Unst unseen amid the electronic confusion.

There had, however, been a major miscalculation by the Soviet planners. The jamming activity could easily have been put down to collateral effects from the exercises against the Soviet Task Force. The presence of two Bear Charlie missile carriers which were rounding North Cape as the electronic attack began, however, was less easy to explain and was guaranteed to set nerves in the UK Air Defence Operations Centre on edge. Within minutes the Air Defence Commander made his decision and more hurried scramble instructions were issued, this time to the Phantom detachment at Machrihanish.

CHAPTER 32

West of Stornoway in the Outer Hebrides.

As the three Kamov Ka-24 Hormone helicopters rattled towards the landing zone on the island of Stornoway the section leader rehearsed the scenario in his mind, drifting back to the briefing which seemed like days ago.

The huge fixed radar head on the northern tip of Unst, a Type 96 air defence surveillance radar and its associated HF200 height finder, had been lighting up the radar warning equipment aboard the helicopter during the run-in. It was the task of the standoff jammers in the Badgers to target this sensor electronically to mask their insertion and he hoped that the incessant audio warnings did not signify that they were already being tracked and reported. Once on the landing zone they would shut down and wait for the Spetznaz special forces teams huddled in the rear cabins to do their job. He was not looking forward to the enforced idleness knowing the helicopters would be vulnerable during the wait.

The temporary resident on the island, No. 1 Air Control Centre, callsign "Crowbar", has been deployed to the exercise location from RAF Portreath in Cornwall and the intelligence officer aboard Kiev had speculated that the unit had been inserted to monitor the maritime activity off the coast. A mobile control facility, 1 ACC regularly plugged gaps in the air defence coverage around the British coastline but it seemed more likely that the deployment, so close to the larger air defence unit on the island, might be there to conduct research and development. Of more concern to their mission was a detachment of the RAF Regiment, a specialist organisation well versed in airfield protection, which was providing not only a section of Rapier surface-to-air missiles but a specialist guard force. The Rapiers were carrying out a secondary exercise firing training missiles over the sea. In combination it was an added complication for the small force. How much of a complication would soon be seen.

As they approached the shoreline, light signals flashed between the cockpits and the helicopters fanned out. The beach was bathed in moonlight and they approached on a broad frontage picking out individual landing zones. It was a tight fit but they alighted almost simultaneously and the rotors rapidly slowed, braked to a halt before the engines shut down. Doors drew back and teams of black clad figures streamed onto the hard packed sand and made their way swiftly up the beach.

The mission had been hastily planned. Although the electronic combat officers aboard the Badgers would neutralise the main radar on Unst for the duration of the main operation, the intelligence officers aboard the flagship had spotted an opportunity for a windfall. Back in Mother Russia, the new Almaz S-300 surface-to-air missile system, known to NATO as the SA-10 Grumble, had been deployed around Moscow but the performance of the early operational systems was suffering from a lack of computing power. The processors which had been designed in the Ukraine were not able to cope with the millions of processes needed to track and engage multiple targets. Efforts to redesign the bulky circuit boards had so far failed and it had been decided that espionage offered a faster route to success. The Brits had made rapid advances in the field of military electronics and their research establishments were known to be world class. The deployable radar which was being evaluated on the remote island was fitted with a revolutionary new central processor and if the team could gain access to, or even better acquire a working processor, the development of the new strategic SAM would be advanced immeasurably.

The Team covered the ground between the landing zone and their target rapidly not really needing the night vision goggles as there was enough ambient light to offer easy progress through the scrub. Their advance was silent and it was not long before they came across the first signs of a temporary camp. The speedily installed radar head was shielded from the elements by a protective, rubber radome which stood out pale against the darker background. Alongside, a smaller control cabin hooked into the structure via thick umbilicals, a separate power generator linked in parallel to each portable building. Adorned with garish commercial logos, a Portakabin proudly pronounced the corporate presence of Plessey Avionics, the developer of the new radar system. Other hastily erected cabins stood a little way distant providing temporary workshops for the contractors attached to the team. The site was deserted. A soft target, the leader forced the door lock and eased silently inside, working methodically through the benches and equipment racks. Their target, the computer controller, was obviously a key component of the system and would be found in the main engineering section of the control cabin if the assessments were correct. However, there may be examples here in the support cabin that might prove easier to exploit and avoid the need to strip down the main radar.

Individuals had been carefully briefed and began inspecting electronic boxes hooked up to the portable test equipment. Serial numbers and descriptions were checked and some items discarded, although some checks took longer than others. It was some time before one of the men gestured to the leader beckoning him over. After a whispered discussion a "black box" was disconnected from its support harness and tucked into a backpack before, with a wind up motion, the team withdrew to the door. It had been a massive stroke of luck but the elusive control unit was in their possession. In the absence of any activity there was little to be gained from remaining on site. The electronic combat officers in the distant Badgers could fulfil the rest of the mission.

Not wishing to press their good fortune the leader took an alternative path back to the beach skirting around the edge of the test site. The scrub suddenly gave way to a concrete dispersal and there, laid out on the hardstanding, stood a Rapier Field Standard B missile fire unit. Although it had been covered in tarpaulin, the launcher rails protruded distinctively and there could be no doubt as to its identity. This might be an intelligence coup if they could exploit the system as they waited. The team without further recourse pulled back the covers and a camera appeared from a backpack ready to capture vital images. The leader could sense the congratulatory debrief already. He took the camera from the trooper and framed the image in the viewfinder eager to make the most of the opportunity. He hoped the high speed film and the low light lens would be up to the task. Using a flash might be pushing their luck too far.

The muted noise of the camera shutter proved instantly inadvisable as a warning broke the stillness.

"Halt, RAF armed guard. Stay still and raise your hands."

The Spetznaz Leader cursed silently. Around him his Team had dropped to the ground, the scrub providing limited cover. Although the defensive position occupied by the guard was off the main path he had a commanding view of the track back to the beach and it would be impossible to detour outside his arcs of fire. The Leader flipped his night vision goggles down over his eyes and the green glow bathed the scene. The Guard had emerged from a sangar that had been well dug-in and carefully camouflaged. There would have been little chance of seeing it and it had only been good fortune that their route to the radar site on the way in had bypassed it. The Guard was becoming more confident and, clutching his self-loading rifle, he edged forward towards the path. The Leader could see that he was in the dark; literally. Without goggles he was relying on ambient light of which there was very little as the clouds had by now gathered over the moon.

"Armed guard, identify yourself," the man shouted hesitantly.

Events were escalating rapidly and the Leader saw no easy options if the mission was to remain covert. A dash for the beach was unlikely to succeed without alerting other guards who may have been deployed around the Rapier site. They would have to try to keep this one man quiet and hope that he was alone. On a signal to a trooper lying close by they began to ease forward, hugging the ground. The Guard was showing increasing signs of agitation and his movements became rapid as he scanned the surrounding scrubland nervously, his rifle describing wide arcs as he moved forward. The technique was amateurish. The Spetznaz Team closed to within 10 metres when finally alerted to their presence the Guard pointed his rifle directly at the Leader.

"Halt or I fire." The rifle moved towards a trooper in the scrub. Two shots

INFILTRATION

rang out.

The Team Leader winced.

"OK, exercise, exercise, exercise, you're dead. Stand up and show yourself."

The rapid-fire English words meant nothing to the Russian so he responded instinctively in the only way he knew how. Assuming the shots had been in anger he trained his weapon on the man he fired a double tap. The body crumpled and lay still. Cursing he stood up and moved quickly towards the prone figure which was clad in a NATO chemical warfare suit. Peering through the goggles at the lifeless body the look of surprise on the man's face was evident. Blood pooled on his chest darkening the charcoal impregnated fabric even more. Checking the rifle that had fallen to the ground he cursed even more forcibly because attached to the end of the barrel was a yellow fitting designed for firing blank rounds. The reasons the shots had not caused injury was readily apparent. This had been an exercise and they had been mistaken for exercise intruders. The rounds were blanks.

He quickly ran through his options. He could not leave the man here and better that he disappeared rather than risk his discovery, gunshot wounds and all. Sounds from the area beyond the sangar made the task more urgent. Lights snapped on and the outline of two tents suddenly became visible about 100 metres away. Voices were raised and bodies were moving around, obviously dressing and collecting weapons.

Urgent hand signals and the body was hoisted onto the shoulders of a burly trooper before the Team set off in double time down the path. It was still some way to the beach but it would, hopefully, take some time for the guard's absence to be noticed.

*

After such a heavy day and two long sorties, Razor and Flash were glad to be able to relax in front of the television as the mindless dirge flickered away on the small screen. Someone had been resourceful and had purloined the two TV sets and video recorders from the local SSAFA office on base. Without them, life on Q could be brutally boring. The Land Rover carrying the "hotlocks" containing the evening meal had just arrived and the first sounds of satisfaction were drifting through from the groundcrew crewroom beyond. Shortly, the main pleasure of the day beckoned as the foil trays were placed in the oven to reheat the meals they had ordered earlier. Dinner would be served in ten minutes.

The Soviets had been busy today Razor mused, although Leuchars had taken the lion's share of the activity as usual. A seemingly endless stream of Bears had poured into the exercise area which seemed to be confined to a box about 100 miles square, well to the west of Tiree. The Norwegians had picked up each formation as they rounded North Cape and Leuchars Q had shadowed the formations down through the Iceland-Faeroes Gap before the Machrihanish detachment had replaced them to monitor the flight profiles as they manoeuvred against the hidden submarines beneath the dark waters. Razor and Flash had already flown twice before coming on Q for the evening. They were gambling on the activity quietening down and the Soviets maritime patrol aircraft heading back to their distant bases. The Q2 jet had launched to cover the intense activity topping up the numbers in support of Leuchars, the harassed Air Defence Commander opting for singleton scrambles to extend the on-task time of the Phantoms and to stretch his assets further. The Phantoms were not the only ones who were busy and a Nimrod had been positioned close to the Task Force to monitor activity beneath the water.

The smell from the kitchen was tantalising. Hopefully, they were done for the Day and they could look forward to a quiet evening. Hopefully. . . . .

The blaring noise of the hooter broke the reverie and, with thoughts of dinner shelved, a tumble of bodies shoved through the doors sprinting the short distance across the concrete to the waiting Phantoms. The aircrew raced up the ladders as external power sets revved up. Navigation lights flashed on and the dormant airframes, the air-to-air missiles slung menacingly beneath the fuselage, sprang into life. With the flight line mechanics still helping with the ejection seat straps, the right engines wound up, seat pins were stowed and heads lowered in the cockpit monitoring a myriad of actions as the Phantom was rapidly prepared for flight. Within minutes, the jet taxied off the chocks, the groundcrew watching with satisfaction, pleased at their swift response. After a short taxy to the runway, and without pause, the afterburners lit the night sky, illuminating the runway threshold as the Phantom began its take off roll.

INFILTRATION

Within six minutes of the hooter sounding, the wheels were travelling as the crew powered off into the blackness of the Irish Sea.

"Saxa, Romeo Foxtrot Echo 43 is on frequency, Charlie 4, 4, plus, tiger fast 60."

"Romeo Foxtrot Echo 43 loud and clear, how me?"

"Loud and clear also, sitrep."

The Crew were anxious to understand why they were once again converting Avtur into fumes. The response would be justification enough.

*

Listening to the commentary from the Leuchars Phantom as it closed on its target Razor and Flash assimilated the tactical picture.

"Romeo 43, Saxa, Experiencing "music". Hooter" bears from me, 240 degrees. Triangulating."

To a layman the message was unintelligible. To the crew it meant that the jammer was transmitting electronic countermeasures which were showing on the screens of the huge air defence radars on the remote island, the jamming strobes shielding the position of the culprits. By comparing the relative bearings from Saxa Vord with signals from other air defence radars it might be possible for the controller to plot a position for the jammer. If he could do so, he could vector fighters inbound to make an intercept. Flash looked at his blank radar screen thankful for small mercies. At least his own scope was unaffected; so far.

"Romeo 43 vector 300 for cut off. I'll turn you onto heading shortly. Report any contacts".

The Controller was on the ball but he was missing vital information. His plan was to position the Phantom along the bearing of one of the jamming strobes and to fly down the line, hopefully choreographing a chance encounter. Assuming the jammer maintained its interest in the ground radars and not the air intercept radar in the Phantom it might be possible to pinpoint the source of the interference. Unfortunately, the Jammer was already many miles ahead of the Phantom and heading home towards Mother Russia, its job done. It would be a long tailchase.

*

The helicopters lifted in unison from the flat beach and crept forward at a walking pace, the leader's nose dipping as he accelerated. With the disc of the rotor blade angled rearwards a billowing cloud of sand was thrown into the air inducing a choking loss of visibility in its wake, reducing the view from the cockpits of the trailing helicopters to almost zero. The number two pilot veered rapidly to the right safely clearing the choking blanket, popping out into the clear night once again but the number three was less fortunate. Unsure of the position of the two helicopters ahead and shackled by radio silence he transferred to instruments, groping through the clag. The transition was fraught with risk so close to the ground and in such close proximity to the other helicopters and his optimism in engineering a safe outcome was short lived.

The tip of the leading rotor struck the ground as he attempted to pick up forward momentum causing instant chaos. Steel blades shattered destroying the symmetry on which the machine relied to remain airborne. Shards of torn metal disgorged at a tangent embedding themselves in the surrounding sand marginally in advance of the helicopter as it crashed back onto to the beach. The cockpit of the Kamov struck first, collapsing the bulbous radome, shattering the Plexiglas and distorting the frame. The tail boom, denied forward velocity, slammed back to earth breaking off, piles of metal coming to rest. The cabin rolled onto its side and slewed around at right angles to the trajectory, fortunately coming to rest at the top of the tangled wreckage. Almost before the mass of debris had settled, a gap emerged, the door heaved aside allowing the Spetznaz team who had been strapped inside to exit, dazed but alive.

There had been no time for the pilot to put out any sort of emergency call, and given his orders to operate in radio silence, would he have been permitted to do so. As he followed the ground troops from the wreck he listened intently orientating himself to his surroundings. With hopes rising, he registered the sound of his leader circling back around and, although the lights on the wreck had extinguished, there was enough ambient light to make out the bulk of one of the remaining Kamovs edging its way back towards the landing zone. The bulky airframe crept back over the breaking waves and set down 50 metres from where the group huddled. Rotors still turning, the cabin door slid back and urgent gestures from the crewman prompted the surviving members of the insertion team to run towards their salvation, heads bowed, intimidated by the whirling rotor blades. At the rear of the group of survivors, the pilot helped an injured man who limped his way painfully down the beach the only apparent victim of the carnage. Safely inside the cabin, already full with other members of the Spetznaz team, the newcomers strapped into the few spare parachute seats along the sides of the enclosed space. With no obvious alternative, those without a seat arranged themselves along the centreline and huddled down. Within seconds the door slid closed and the helicopter lifted again, the Kamov creeping forward to begin yet another turn back out to sea.

The Formation Leader broke away as his number 2, by now at fighting speed, closed in from his rear quadrant. Normally fitted with depth charges for anti-submarine duties, the hastily adapted S-5 55mm rocket pods had been misappropriated from the Air Force Hip helicopters aboard the Moskva but had been a prudent forethought. A brief gout of flames announced the departure of a salvo of unguided rockets from the pods mounted on stub pylons beneath the helicopter. Tracking unerringly towards the shattered hulk on the ground the projectiles struck the wreckage through the open door. Doused in aviation fuel, the mangled remains of the hulk ignited instantly and a fierce but short-lived fire burned out the remains, the framework distorting quickly becoming unrecognisable. It was a poor substitute but it would, hopefully, slow down an investigation until the Task Force had left the area. Others would need to plan the cover story to satisfy the British authorities.

The remaining helicopters set course for the recovery point many miles to the southwest. Unbeknown to the pilots, in the absence of the stand-off jamming which should have masked their exfiltration, the departure was now easily visible on the air defence radars on Unst. With the Badgers already heading back towards North Cape, telephone calls were made to the Air Defence Commander adding to the confusion and speculation as to the identity of the intruders had begun.

With the jammers withdrawing, the Phantom crew had been ordered to recover and were already making their approach to RAF Leuchars. It was a small mercy for the Soviets but at least the helicopters would be unmolested during their return to the Moskva. Perhaps the enforced disengagement would put a lid back on the tinderbox and prevent further risk of escalation. Back in the wreckage the unexplained body of an RAF guard would be much harder to rationalise.

*

Phil Boyd scratched a few notes as he watched the plots on the tote trying to understand the mindset of the Soviet planner. Things had escalated rapidly and he had yet to digest the implications of the attack on the Nimrod. He could not delay any longer before reporting this up the chain. If he failed to bring this to the attention of the senior leadership he was leaving himself wide open to become the scapegoat.

"Sir, we've lost contact with Benbecula. The landlines seem to have gone down but we've also lost their feed into the recognised air picture. That leaves us a big gap in coverage in the operational area."

More good news.

"Any indications why?" he barked at the nervous junior officer who looked as if she was about to burst into tears. He tempered his aggression. There was little point in reducing his limited staff to a state of jitters.

"No Sir. We have the comms technicians working on it now but it seems as if it's a power failure. The new exchanges are normally quite efficient but we've had some problems at Pitreavie Castle recently. They're tracing it through and, hopefully, we can get them reconnected soon."

She did not look any happier in being the bearer of the news.

Boyd looked again at the plot. He could ill afford gaps in coverage. It was bad enough off the Western Isles at the best of times. The Shackleton he had scrambled earlier was moving to its fallback barrier position, safely removed from the immediate vicinity of the task force and outside the range of a roving Forger. The pop-up contact had once again disappeared but there could be little doubt that it had been a Forger from the Soviet carrier. If shots really had been fired, and he had no evidence to doubt the frantic reports, the Soviets were playing a provocative game. It was one thing to bring down unarmed airliners in Soviet airspace but it was an entirely different game to engage a Nimrod in his own back yard, particularly when armed Phantoms were in the vicinity. Such provocation was way beyond the recent norms for the Cold War and reminiscent of the dark days of tension during the Berlin Corridor operations.

The Bears had split and two distinct groups had formed. The southerly group containing the Bear Deltas was heading for the fleet exercise area and showing all the characteristics of an anti submarine formation. The northerly group was of far more concern. The reports of jamming from the Leuchars crew meant that he had now watched two suspected hostile acts committed in the space of 15 minutes. The events were too structured to be coincidental yet the presence of the Bear Charlies was his biggest worry. He needed Phantoms in amongst them in case things deteriorated further. There would be no time to cover events from ground alert and with reports of missiles aboard he needed defence in depth. If, God forbid, missiles were launched, they had to be intercepted as soon as possible after launch.

The young fighter controller interrupted his thoughts again.

"Sir, message from the Norwegian air Defence Commander, the weather at Bodø is forecast to deteriorate. They're expecting heavy snow and he's placing QRA on "Mandatory". They will only launch for an emergency or if ordered by the NATO CAOC. We still have the Norwegian radar picture but they can't scramble fighters."

The tote showed Leuchars generating the additional Q birds he had asked for and they were already prepping Q6. He thought he might need them before the night was out and he thanked the gods that he had held Machrihanish on alert tonight. He still had Southern Q to reinforce if necessary even if it did take time to get them up into the area.

His time for vacillating was rapidly diminishing. It was nearly time for political decisions to take over from military decisions. He ordered another Leuchars Phantom into the air. Another Victor tanker from Marham followed a few minutes later; its training task on Towline 5 over the North Sea could wait.

The phone rang and he grabbed it irritably.

"Sir, Mike Phillips, Master Controller at Buchan. I've just been speaking to the Senior Controller at Prestwick. It seems that their radar and ILS went down briefly causing problems with a British Airways training flight. They accused us of jamming their frequencies until I explained that there are no Canberras airborne tonight. We're looking at it now but it looks like something from the Task Force that we've yet to identify was responsible. Prestwick is black after an incident. It sounds like the same training flight landed heavily, although it's not clear whether the two incidents were related. He's pretty wound up and threatening to report the incident formally."

Normally such a revelation would have given him a welcome distraction easing the boredom of a night shift. As he pondered the latest twist it made his decision easy.

"Tell him to report it immediately. I have no idea what's caused this escalation but there's mischief afoot. Have Leuchars prepare every serviceable jet they have. Call a generation exercise. I want them all armed and manned soonest."

*

The pilot eased the Phantom around the final turn, the heavy centreline tank limiting the g available to him. He had expected to be in the Bar by now but here we was over the Western Isles instead, the night outside the cockpit as dark as any he had seen recently. He had not even been scheduled to sit Q today. The navigator watched the blip track down the radar tube perfectly on track for a tight roll out. As he squeezed the acquisition trigger his radar display unexpectedly lit up with heavy noise jamming and the radar reverted to search mode.

"Saxa Romeo Foxtrot Echo 44, I have music, request instructions."

With the Badgers withdrawing the electronic interference was unexpected. Jamming the Phantom's radar was a coarse tactic and under more aggressive rules of engagement might be seen as a hostile act. It was the first in a series of escalations which would tax the crew to the limit. The navigator reached down to the control panel by his left knee and selected

"J", the anti-jamming mode, returning his attention to the electronic spoke which flooded his tube. A few corrections to the switch settings and the narrow band of noise which now obscured his target became more distinct and tightly defined. He moved the marker around the jamming strobe and squeezed the acquisition trigger again.

"Are you visual?" he asked.

"Affirmative," from the front.

He relaxed. Eyeballs on the target and a visual range were far simpler than the complex series of manoeuvres he would need to undertake to confirm the range in the back.

"Range one mile," he heard just as the radar warning receiver intruded on the conversation. The tail warning radar had been activated and the Boxtail radar in the small radome at the rear of the target was scanning away, the antennas on the fin cap of the Phantom picking up the emissions and displaying a flashing warning strobe on the small screen in the back cockpit. That confirmed its identity without question as a Bear. It was a noise he had heard many times as they had rolled in behind similar Bears in the Iceland-Faeroes Gap.

"Can you make out the mark yet?" the navigator queried.

"I see a radome under the fuselage so it's a Delta or a Foxtrot," replied the pilot. It's not a bomber. The navigator could see the reflections of the pilot's head in the canopy as moved rapidly from side to side peering past the heavy ironwork around the gunsight, highlighted by the red glow of the cockpit lights. So far it was a familiar plot.

"Jesus," he heard suddenly. It was not an expletive that was welcome or expected.

"He just fired the tail guns. They're still raised in the parked position so the rounds went high but that's not very friendly," he said sardonically. "I'm backing off outside guns range."

The throttles retarded and the heavy jet responded instantly, the range between the Phantom and the Bear opening slowly. The slow scan of the tail warning radar paused, replaced immediately by a rattling crescendo as the system locked on. Only seconds passed before high explosive rounds thumped into the airframe and a barrage of warning lights illuminated on the telelight panel. An acrid smell filled the cockpit and the crew snapped their mask toggles down, simultaneously flicking selectors on their chest-mounted oxygen regulators. With 100% oxygen selected they were sealed from the cabin air and the smell dissipated. Instinct kicked in.

"Mayday, Mayday, Mayday, Romeo 44 is under attack, position 290 range 100 from Benbecula and has taken damage. Request instructions."

The silence was deafening.

"Bloody hell mate, what the hell do we do now?"

The navigator paused.

"We've been attacked. We have the right to respond but is that the right thing to do?"

"The bastard fired first."

"I know that but that wasn't my question!"

The radio remained quiet. The decision was made.

"Romeo 44 is under fire. Engaging!"

The pilot ran rapidly through the weapons checks. The coolant was already on increasing the sensitivity of the Sidewinder missile seeker head, ensuring that the massive turboprops stood out against the cool background of the upper air. He flicked the master arm switch to "Arm" and reached down with a gloved hand flipping the weapons selector to "SW" selecting Sidewinder. Expecting the aural tone instantly to fill the earphones, he was greeted with a flat monotone. A silent curse. The jet had only just been put onto Q this morning and the weapons should have been checked before it was accepted. It was a duff Sidewinder. His hand went back to the missile selector and he hit "Sidewinder Reject" cycling away from the bad missile, taking the next one in turn. The symbol on the weapons panel switched to the starboard outer missile and the tiny SW light illuminated on the weapons panel. The insistent growl of the infra-red missile suddenly dominated the intercom as he pulled the reticule onto the massive bomber that now filled the gunsight, the tone instantly responding as the tiny seeker registered the heat from the exhausts. Tracking the inboard engine on the starboard side of the Bear the growl changed from the flat background tone to a strident growl. He pulled the trigger.

Within seconds the starboard outer missile left the launcher rail with a bright flash from the rocket motor and sped away in a cloud of smoke. Unseen to the crew, following a corkscrew path it looped towards its prey. From the firing position only a mile behind, it was less than eight seconds before the missile, still boosting under power from the rocket motor, passed a point just above the two massive turboprops. Living up to its name as a missile, it had tracked to a centroid between the engines when its electronic brain was prompted into action. As the fuse sensed the passage of the huge boots which contained the undercarriage it triggered a pulse initiating the warhead. A central explosive payload expanded outwards forcing the rings of the expanding rod warhead through the thin missile body and into the airflow. Moving at supersonic speeds they ripped into the heavy skin of the maritime patrol aircraft shredding the structure and peppering the fuel tanks. A massive section of the trailing edge flap detached from the airframe and fell away leaving a heavy plume of escaping fuel bursting into the airflow.

Behind, the Phantom navigator turned off the KD-41 radar camera which had captured the attack and the Phantom rolled, rapidly, to port, descending quickly, the incessant rattling of the radar warner quietening as they dropped into the lower air. Once clear, the crew began to work methodically through the range of warning lights which had announced the implications of the strikes from the 23 mm cannons in the tail of the Bear. The wounded Phantom would not be recovering to Leuchars and the navigator swiftly worked out the range to Machrihanish where the Phantom detachment could help them repair the damage.

High above them, the crew of the Bear wrestled with their own problems. Why they had opened fire would be the subject of a heavy debrief if they made it back to their base. Engaging a Phantom had not been an objective for their mission and they had, unwittingly, ramped up the tension to breaking point.

*

Admiral Vasili Gerasimek was not a man to take risks lightly. Years of mind wrestling within the Soviet command structure had taught him many lessons, not least of which was to review his options carefully. His entire career had been built on a foundation of weighing up the advantages and disadvantages of any course of action and determining the most advantageous outcome; normally to his own benefit. Although he had finessed the military art of decision making, he was not naive in the ways of politics but, on this occasion his decision would be analysed across the two spheres. There would be no cosy chats with mentors in the Kremlin to gauge political opinion first. The burden of command weighed heavily at this moment and he faced an unfamiliar quandary.

The flight watch channel on the HF network was alive with chatter. The regular status reports from the crippled Tupolev were increasingly edgy. The crew would be lucky to nurse it home to Engels in Mother Russia. It was a long and hazardous journey home. He had a range of options that he could deploy. The Yakolev fighters sat patiently on deck, the pilots awaiting his call to scramble yet they were ill equipped for the challenge. Lacking an effective air-to-air radar and poorly trained for night combat the pilots would respond to the best of their abilities but he might be placing them in jeopardy. Using them now against the vastly superior Phantom crews courted further disaster. Should he lose an aircraft to hostile fire, not only would questions be asked in Moscow but he would have little choice but to escalate his response. He hoped the crew of the Tupolev would not give him that unenviable dilemma.

His other main option was to engage one of the Phantoms using surface-to-air missiles and here he was much better placed. The range of weapons arrayed on the foredeck of Kiev, not to mention the SAN-4s fitted to his air defence picket screen, were more than a match. Without electronic countermeasures and flying at medium level, the Phantom crews would have little defence other than to withdraw outside the missile engagement zones.

He had the SS-N-12 Sandbox standoff missiles aboard the Kiev and he could consider a retaliatory attack against a coastal installation. There was a range of appropriate targets within the air defence network and they had, after all, been directing the Phantom when it made its attack. A secondary retaliation not aimed at the perpetrator, however, was a significant upping of the ante. It sent a powerful message to the British commanders but it was a message his masters in Moscow were not intending to send at this juncture, nor had they expressed such an intent at his pre-deployment briefings.

Unusually in this case the list finished with do nothing; normally an opening option but one which was increasingly attractive.

His analysis would be incomplete without considering the reaction of his British counterpart sitting in his underground bunker at High Wycombe. What would he expect and how would he respond. Would he consider the exchange to be an unfortunate error or was he likely to think deeper? In many ways he was better placed than Gerasimek. He had his quick reaction alert assets on permanent call and had already demonstrated his flexibility when threatened. The surge generation which his signals intelligence analysts had just reported had produced ten aircraft within hours and, presumably, that was only using one squadron. If called, the second squadron would also generate. The British demonstrated this capability regularly in response to no-notice call-outs during NATO exercises. There was also the matter of the detachment at Machrihanish with its five jets and they lay even closer to his operating area. He should not discount the squadrons of Buccaneer bombers based at RAF Lossiemouth in the Moray Firth. He had seen their abilities first hand when they had carried out a mock attack against the Fleet as he had approached the northern Scottish shores. Equipped with the TV tracked Martel missile their approach had been stealthy and their arrival unannounced. The warhead the missile carried had the potential to cause havoc.

He stared out of the armoured window at the sailors as they scrubbed at the blackened decks, scarred when the Yakolev had struck the helicopter. That incident in itself was an embarrassment and he knew some who would gloat at his misfortune. Explaining away a chance engagement between a Tupolev and a Phantom was one thing. Explaining away the loss of one of his destroyer screen was altogether a different matter. The skirmish had the potential to escalate to a full scale exchange in what might be considered disputed waters. His very presence here with his Fleet was already provocative. No; he would err on the side of caution. The last thing he needed at this stage was additional unwelcome scrutiny from Moscow. Sometimes diplomacy was a safer route than aggression and this might be one of those moments.

"Stand down the alert 5 jets," he announced resignedly. He would make a satellite call to the Fleet Headquarters and have the diplomats take up the matter in their fancy London clubs. There were matters below the water which demanded caution not confrontation.

CHAPTER 33

Below the Waters of the Firth of Clyde.

The red light from the searchlight mounted on the submersible cut a tight swathe across the sea bed, the unnatural glow eerie in the dark surrounding waters. It was already warm inside the enclosed perspex bubble and Ilya struggled to concentrate, the incessant buzz of the batteries and the noise of the scrubbers soporific. The skids touched the floor gently bringing him alert, arresting the gentle movement.

Momentarily, the cabin was plunged into darkness and the motors fell silent causing Ilya to tense involuntarily.

"Now we wait," he heard from his companion hidden in the all-enveloping blackness, the cabin now lit by only a few discrete instruments as the pilot conserved the batteries.

Sitting in the dark, the noise of spinning gyros the only sounds cutting the silence, a distant thrum grew slowly louder. From a barely imperceptible hum it amplified to an overpowering beat, the resonance intruding physically on their motionless bodies. They had slipped into the confined waters of the Firth of Clyde and were positioned almost centre channel but the ethereal noise which assailed their senses was not from a surface vessel plying its way along the shipping lane. Barely 100 metres above them the vast bulk of a Resolution class nuclear submarine slipped by. Had there been any light from above it would have been extinguished by the bulk of the vessel. As it was, their other senses recorded its passage. As the thrum began to wane another noise dominated with the sudden reverberation of a battery of ballast tanks blowing off. As water was replaced by air the submarine lifted towards the surface, its six month patrol over. The sequencing of their arrival had not been a coincidence.

"It's time."

This guy was some conversationalist.

The red lights flicked back on and Ilya blinked involuntarily as his eyes adjusted once more. The impulse motors spun up and he registered a slight tilt of the dive vanes as the small craft lifted off the sea bed amidst a flurry of silt. Moving forward gently in a crabbing motion the tiny craft followed an underwater ridgeline, the pilot intent on a small gauge on the console. Ilya knew well of its significance as he had piloted such a craft himself. The seconds passed and the sharp contour of the ridge flattened, the course of the submersible following the feature precisely, offset by a few metres. The pilot throttled back, the hum of the propulsion abating as he adjusted his position in relation to the ridge. Edging forward slowly he closed on the small feature dabbing the controls lightly, refining the approach. White lights snapped on bathing the surrounding sea bed. Night turned to day destroying their carefully nurtured night vision. Cables snaked in from Ilya's peripheral vision zeroing in on a small underwater plateau. At the confluence was a small round disc, domed on top. But for the cables it would have been invisible in the surrounding silt but, as it was, it stood out clearly on its perch. A SOSUS sensor. Now it was his turn. He had been a long time working towards this moment and the sudden onset of nerves was not unexpected.

The submersible pilot had put him within metres of his quarry. The bright white lights illuminated the area around his target and he willed himself to relax as the critical moment approached. The device which Ilya intended to plant was clutched in the robotic grip of the submersible's arms hovering a short distance above the SOSUS sensor, secure in the metal fingers outside the cockpit. Before releasing the payload, he had to ensure that it was correctly aligned. Once free, it would sink into position and magnetic couplings would clamp around the periphery of the SOSUS sensor and hold it in position but to achieve that, the alignment had to be perfect.

Both arms extended a fraction and Ilya congratulated himself recognising that the approach had been almost perfect. The pilot had left him little to do. Satisfied with the placement, he thumbed the release button and the robotic fingers snapped apart, the device beginning to sink towards its quarry, tentatively at first, the pressure of the water slowing its progress. Imperceptibly, an oscillating motion built up and the disc began to gyrate downwards, the light reflecting back from the shiny surface. All might yet have been fine if the oscillations had matched at the point of impact but he watched in morbid fascination as the disc closed on the sensor. With only centimetres to go, the edge of the disc struck the body of the sensor and flopped to the side, hopelessly askew. He cursed silently.

Steeling himself and readjusting his grip on the controls of the robotic arms he set up for another attempt. Unless he could reposition the small device properly he would be forced to resort to Plan B, leaving the safety of his temporary cocoon wearing a diving suit which did not appeal to him just now. His skills in the water were the reason that he had been selected for the job, otherwise the pilot alongside him could have completed the task alone but he was keen to avoid the need to demonstrate his prowess. The tiny submersible had only a primitive air lock which was designed only to offer an emergency escape route. It was not intended to be used routinely even though they were still at depths accessible by divers. Suiting up in the confined space would be a nightmare and, although not unplanned, would not be easy. He had no wish to exercise his skills tonight and redoubled his efforts.

The sweat on his fingers made the controls slick as he stroked them gently. Luckily for him, the disc had settled upright and was easily accessible. A few deft movements repositioned the arms alongside, bracketing the device once more. A final tweak and the mechanical fingers clamped shut collaring the errant disc tightly. Easing the arms upwards he repositioned above the sensor for a second attempt, a little closer this time.

Had his fingers not been wrapped tight around the controls he would have crossed them as he released the device for another try. This time the passage was cleaner and the disk sank vertically the final few centimetres onto its intended target. As it settled into place, the magnetic clamps operated crisply and he could see the tell tales retract indicating that the device had aligned correctly. It was in position. He could not disguise the sigh of relief as he slumped back in his seat.

There was nothing more to do down here. Others onboard the support ships and the aircraft carrier would check the operation of the device from here on. He gave a thumbs up to the pilot and the motors once more spooled up as the small craft backed slowly away, the plateau receding into the gloom. With nothing to see, the white lights snapped off and they were plunged back into near total darkness.

It was only a short ride back to the surface. The carefully orchestrated yet complicated sub-surface manoeuvres of the past hour had been for a single purpose and that had been achieved. Ilya's mind had already switched to his next challenge and for that he needed to be back ashore.

CHAPTER 34

The Air Defence Operations Centre, High Wycombe.

Wing Commander Phil Boyd considered his alternatives thoughtfully, trying hard to remain detached. Emotional indecision would not help. Why had this happened on his watch? He had thought his grounding from operational flying would herald a quieter life and yet he had been plunged into the centre of a developing international crisis.

The maritime patrol aircraft had pressed on into the operational area and the Badgers had withdrawn but the bombers were still pressing southerly. If he could have seen the electronic mayhem on the radar screens at Buchan just a short while ago he might have been even more worried. As it was, his tote showed the individual formations in stark relief. It was a classic set piece attack; if of course the intention was to neutralise the radar site at Saxa Vord. He had analysed similar scenarios during his Air Warfare course at RAF Cranwell. If the intent was to take down the radar it all fitted perfectly and he might have positioned the forces in this way himself. What did not make sense was the uncharacteristically aggressive response from the Soviets way more aggressive than usual. It was as if they were goading him to respond. Unfortunately, the outcome was not as predictable as the staff solution at Cranwell and he would not be the arbiter.

His biggest concern was the formation of missile carriers to the north. What was their intention? One thing was for sure, without the appropriate rules of engagement he had no options other than to respond defensively.

He punched the number for the secure, direct line to the Commander in

Chief's residence. Even the C-in-C got to spend time at home but his slumber was about to be disrupted. This call was one of the few made at High Wycombe that could bypass the normal protocol of routing through the outer office or through his Personal Staff Officer. The groggy response signalled that the Commander had been asleep.

"Sir, we have a situation developing. I think we may be under attack. I recommend we raise the Counter Surprise State to Orange. I need to brief you urgently."

He hoped that the big man was in a decisive mood.

CHAPTER 35

Aboard the Aircraft Carrier Kiev.

"Congratulations on the insertion Ilya. A copybook operation if I might say. I assume there were no problems? I've checked with the sensor operators and the device is up and transmitting. We've had the monitors checking its performance since it was put in place and all is well."

The operational planner seemed content yet hesitant.

"Thank you. There was one minor glitch but only to be expected."

Understated, Ilya was not about to describe the few moments of near panic as the device took on a mind of its own.

"Are your plans still unchanged? I have a jet on readiness to get you back ashore so you can leave when you wish. We've been ordered to move the Battle Group at maximum headway into the Mediterranean. We're already underway and heading south. Gerasimek is under new orders now you're complete."

"A jet? I'd assumed you would drop me back by helicopter. Why the express transport?"

"I think you may want to leave quite quickly. . . . ."

The man hesitated. The atmosphere was suddenly leaden.

"Look there's no way I can sugar-coat this. You've been shafted comrade."

"How so?"

Realisation at the nagging doubts.

The device you planted was hot, and by hot, I mean glowing. What did they tell you about it?"

"Only that it was a clone of the SOSUS sensor and that it would provide tracking data on the British submarines. What more did I need? You know it was all conducted on a limited access basis."

"Did they also say that it would provide the data probably for a hundred years? The damned thing is nuclear powered and let's just say that the shielding in the transit case left a lot to be desired. If you were carrying that thing around with you for any length of time you've taken on a lifetime dose of radiation. You need some specialist medical checks and, I'd say, pretty quickly."

Ilya's emotions surged; the inscrutable facade slipped if only briefly before discipline re-exerted its hold. The revelation was stunning in its cynicism. His mind flashed back to the first time he had seen the device. The heavy case in which it had been stored. The indecent haste as the Embassy staffer had relieved himself of the damned thing. A few more disparate facts aligned and the conclusion was inevitable. The planner continued but his low tone was barely registering in Ilya's subconscious any more. A steely determination exerted a hold. He had, indeed, been compromised and in the most contemptuous way. His concentration returned. A plan of action formed. His mind refocused on the conversation.

"I've had a decontamination team working on your cabin since shortly after you transferred to the submersible. One of the routine monitors picked up a hot spot and it was traced to your space. As you'd guess, nuclear leaks are a hot topic on these ships, if you'll excuse the pun. The trail of contamination mirrored your movements of last night perfectly so it didn't take long to work out the source of the problem. From the levels of residual contamination the team is picking up, I'd say you've had a heavy dose Ilya."

"How wide has this gone? Who knows?"

"It's contained in more ways than one. The team are used to minor issues onboard and they've been warned not to speculate. The political commissar has already put the fear of death into them. They won't be discussing it with anyone outside their immediate workmates. I'll need to work on a story for the submersible. Luckily, it may be as easy as a routine change of the robotic arms as they were the only points of contact with the device. If you'd carried it onboard the craft it would have been different. Maybe we can arrange for the errant items to be lost overboard? You may have to make arrangements to cover up your means of arrival. That light aircraft will announce its presence if it goes within a kilometre of a Geiger counter. You might guess that the Admiral's not impressed. I'm sorry, that's a little insensitive. It must be a shock for you and I'll help where I can."

Ilya muttered a few words of concurrence little knowing of the fate of the unfortunate Irish pilot. Unbeknown to him it would be one detail which would not need wrapping up. Even so, his carefully laid plans were unravelling. How could he trust the Embassy to arrange a medical check? If the staff were complicit he was hardly likely to be given an impartial examination. In any event, the symptoms of nuclear radiation were a ticking detonator. It was unlikely that the dose was enough to cause his early demise. More likely it would lead to leukaemia or some equally pleasant end in the years to come. How could they not have warned him of the risk? He could have mitigated the effects had he known. Either way, for once, he would look after himself first. This was a watershed. His options flashed rapidly through his mind. There was one man who might help but he had to get back to London and time might be more critical than he could know.

"I'll take that offer of the fast transport thanks. When can I leave?"

CHAPTER 36

The Flight Deck aboard the Kiev.

As the single seat Forger rolled, lifting off the deck, the two-seater increased thrust and manoeuvred onto the departure slot. Pausing briefly for last chance checks the engine spooled up to maximum thrust and it powered off down the take off strip, the lift engines propelling it skywards before it even passed the end of the deck. It was Kedrov's first flight since his ejection and he had been keen to accept the challenging mission. The other jet would act as a diversion. Cleaning up he pulled the Yak around in a lazy arc setting heading for the beach. In the back seat Ilya settled down for the short flight his mind racing with details. He was quickly returned to the present as the aircraft descended to low level skimming the waves. Above them, the single seater set up a decoy run at medium level its course diverging rapidly from their own. If the Phantoms were waiting, the air defence surveillance radars would already be calling the medium level track. Ilya listened idly to the British voices on the radio as his pilot monitored the air defence frequencies for any sign that they had been detected. It was only a short flight to the coastline.

*

The door covering the heavy lift engines snapped open as the jet fighter transitioned to the hover, its speed slowing rapidly as the engines took the strain of supporting its forward flight. The elongated canopy of the twin-seater, extended to take the second seat, gave the aircraft an ungainly hump-backed appearance and, had the beach not been deserted, the image of a praying mantis may have crossed the mind of a casual onlooker. In the fading light the beach looked markedly different from the grainy satellite images Kedrov had seen at the short brief for the mission. Even so, there was enough light remaining to identify the lead-in features on the shoreline that the pilot had chosen and he guided the lumbering jet ever closer, the downwards thrust of the engines whipping up a heavy spray from the wave crests. The next few moments were critical and he hoped the heavy jet, lightened of its fuel load for this very reason, would not sink into the hard packed sand too deeply.

The Forger dropped into its final approach.

The noise from the main jet engine still screamed its siren call. Thankfully, the lift engines had been shut down and the gently rotating blades clattered in the gaping intake just behind the cockpit, deprived of their momentum. The massive door, hinged at the rear, towered over the cavernous pit, slowly lowering as it was deprived of the hydraulic pressure holding it up. Ilya wriggled out of the life jacket depositing it on the ejection seat as he had been briefed, the bonedome following. Tucking ear plugs into his ears, the racket from the auxiliary power unit barely abated and he quickly secured the seat straps around the flight gear anxious to escape the painful noise. Satisfied with his efforts, he edged his way rearwards cautiously grasping the huge aerodynamic strake which extended behind the cockpit, balancing precariously, his feet groping for the leading edge of the canted wing some distance behind. The airframe vibrated beneath him and he could only imagine the forces contained by the light blue fuselage as the air rushed through the combustion chamber just inches from his head. His feet made contact and he edged slowly onto the slick surface twisting as he went. Deprived of the temporary handhold he began to slide down the wing slowing his descent, aided by the tactile flying gloves. He caught the wingtip arresting his fall before pivoting over the edge and dropping unceremoniously to the sand below. More luck than judgement, his arrival on terra firma was reasonably gentle, albeit ungainly.

Ilya watched the Forger lift off; a final salute from the pilot. Stones thrown up by the lift engines which had once more screamed into action, ricocheted off rocks strewn around the periphery of the enclosed bay. Discretion won over curiosity and he hunkered down behind a large rock to shelter from the debris cloud protecting himself from injury. As the jet pivoted on its axis and receded into the gathering dusk he brushed himself down and made his way towards the cliff face.

Orientating himself, he made for a prominent crevice in the coarse rock face. Hidden from view, tightly packed nylon ropes were concealed from all but the most inquisitive of visitors. His back up team had done well and they were exactly where he had been briefed to expect them. Stripping off his flying suit and tucking it into a recess in the rocks, his black clothes blended perfectly with the shadows. Unclipping a harness from the shackle he wriggled into the contraption, tightened the straps and reattached himself. Tugging firmly on the rope, he took the strain and, thankfully, it held tight. Given the earlier revelations he could not be entirely confident that the support team had his welfare at heart. Not for the first time he began to wish that he had taken the extra time to make these preparations personally but it was too late to doubt the plan.

He hooked the jumar onto the rope and stepped back to take in the contours of the rock face. An overhang blocked the obvious path which explained the slightly odd route the ropes seemed to take up the cliff. He began the slow climb searching methodically for footholds in the deep shadows. Progress was slow but he gradually worked his way up the wide rift in the rock. Above his head the crevice was narrowing and it angled across the cliff face disappearing into a shallow fissure. Somewhere ahead he expected to transfer to another rope line for the final climb to the top and, sure enough, the rope looped over a carabiner attached to the face and returned downwards. He groped around feeling for the next rope and his hand fell across its rough surface hidden in the gloom. Unhitching and reattaching himself to the new run, he crabbed his way across the crag and the rope settled into a new cleft which stretched towards the summit above him. With a healthy shot of adrenaline helping his efforts, he surged upwards. The crevice narrowed imperceptibly and he became conscious of the oppressive sides of the ever-tightening chimney. He pressed upwards kicking out from the face but the rope dragged him inexorably back into the confines of the gap. With increasing nervousness he pressed on, the rocks slowly pressing in on both sides, the gulley deep enough now that he could no longer push out from its stifling embrace. Suddenly, he heard the distinct noise of metal on rock and his progress was arrested. He shook the errant rope trying to free it off but there was absolutely no play, his weight preventing any further movement. It would neither feed out nor could he advance. Reaching upwards he felt for the carabiner. It was hardly ideal to be clipping-off at this height but he had few options and his hands were becoming increasingly cold. His fingers closed over the metal ring feeling for the spring-loaded gate but the metal loop was solid. He would not be extracting the rope from this "carabiner" any time soon. Far from a normal carabiner it was a closed ring with no way to release the rope. Questions formed as the harsh reality set in. It had been one final betrayal and he regretted not going with his gut instincts and resorting to crack climbing, unaided. Yet again, relying on others was proving to be his undoing. He had no choice but to cut himself free. His hand fell to his pocket feeling for his clasp knife.

The flap was open and the knife was gone.

Abruptly aware of the oppressive pressure from the surrounding rocks against his shoulders, he recognised that he was wedged tight. Utter fear, an emotion entirely alien to Ilya, exerted its grip. Panic replaced calm.

The noise of the dawn chorus began, slowly at first. As the sun rose, the ever more strident calls of the sea birds in their feeding frenzy increased to a crescendo drowning out his ever weakening calls for help.

No one who had any thoughts of rescue would ever hear them.

CHAPTER 37

Air Defence Operations Centre, RAF High Wycombe.

The discussion had been short and predictable and the C-In-C had been inevitably grumpy being awoken from his beauty sleep, his legendary caution evident from the outset. Far from giving blanket authority he was on his way down to the bunker and a tense briefing was sure to follow.

Boyd had to make sense of the operational scenario before the senior officer arrived. What was he missing? What would he say when asked why the Soviets had opened fire? More importantly, how could he explain the presence of the Bear Charlies? Was it a training run or did he have indicators that this was for real? The fate of Saxa Vord might depend on his answer.

He sensed rather than saw the imposing presence of the Commander in Chief as he entered the operations room. The briefing was as tense as Boyd had anticipated.

"So let me be sure. Was the Nimrod damaged?"

"We don't know yet Sir, he's not landed. I'll get a full report from the mission report post flight. I'll get it to you as soon as I have it."

"But he didn't give a damage report on frequency?"

"No Sir but . . . . "

"And the Phantom. Was it damaged?"

INFILTRATION

"We don't know that either Sir. He lost his radio but we don't know if that was as a direct result of Soviet fire or not. Again, we'll know when the crew submit their ADMISREP."

"And the jamming. Any damage to our assets other than the 747 involved in the Prestwick incident?"

"No Sir."

"And the jammers have pulled back?"

"Yes they've withdrawn and the music has stopped."

"Any news from Benbecula?"

The questions were rapid fire.

"Not yet Sir. The lines are still down and their feed has still not been restored. I'm using the Shackleton to fill the gap in radar coverage for the time being."

"It's all inconclusive Phil. You must be able to see my reservations?"

Or lack of evidence of any testosterone-fuelled equipment thought Boyd irreverently.

"Sir, my biggest concern is the track closing on Saxa Vord. I've had reports from the Norwegians that the Bear is carrying an AS-3. You're familiar with the capabilities of the stand-off missile?"

He instantly regretted the barb. The sour look said everything.

"Is the profile normal for a Bear Charlie?"

"No Sir, far from it. They normally route direct from the Cape and simulate launch at about 100 miles before heading back. This one has come much further south west and is tracking back north easterly already. I've seen nothing so far that suggests a weapons run but I can see no other reason that a missile carrying platform would venture that far south."

"So there's no indicator that he has hostile intent?"

"No Sir, not at this moment but it's highly unusual given the other incidents."

The senior officer stroked his cheek nervously.

"Then I have no reason to elevate the alert state. Keep the Phantoms at a prudent distance where you can. Try not to provoke any further incidents. I need to make a call."

Boyd blanched. This felt completely wrong. Too much had happened for this to be a coincidence. These incidents were linked and, to him, the significance was blindingly obvious. Was he being set up as the scapegoat here?

What he did not know was that his had not been the only call the C-in-C had taken this evening.

CHAPTER 38

Off Benbecula.

Razor glanced across at his wingman who had been scrambled to join him on CAP, boredom rather than tactical foresight shaping his routine. The pair of Phantoms droned around their combat air patrol, their navigation lights marking their presence. At such a distance from the coast only pilots in passing airliners starting or ending their transatlantic journey were aware of their presence.

The navigators in the back cockpits scanned the airspace out to 60 miles ahead. Somewhere well to the west the Kiev Battle Group was manoeuvring, unseen on the pulse Doppler radars and probably outside the detection range. The occasional flick into mapping mode failed to show any sign of the ships at their reported location.

He was frustrated that they had not seen the Badger jammers before they had withdrawn. It would have been quite a sight to see the unusual visitors set against the dark horizon. Since the Soviet aircraft had returned north easterly it had been desperately quiet and boredom had well and truly set in. Dinner seemed like a distant, tantalising memory.

On top of his bonedome Razor adjusted the weight of the heavy night vision goggles which he had drawn back into a more comfortable raised position. He had no real need for them at this stage of the sortie and, if lowered back into position in front of his eyes, there would be an even greater strain on his neck, particularly with any momentum under G. He had briefed his wingman to keep his navigation lights on for the time being limiting the strain on his long suffering neck muscles. If they found a contact they could kill the lights and, hopefully, make the approach to the target unseen. As he stared into the black wastes, the prospect of finding anything out here at this godforsaken hour seemed unlikely.

"Not a thing," muttered Flash from the back seat. "Mind you, I hadn't expected to see anything tonight. Can't imagine the Sovs are flying Forgers in this airspace in the dark. They have their heads screwed on the right way. Not like us."

The grumbling was to be expected and the fractious navigator's complaint mirrored his own thoughts. They were oblivious to the drama which had unfolded earlier or they might have been less dismissive. Air defence exercises were notoriously boring at night and the isolation of the Scottish Islands reinforced what to them was an inevitable conclusion.

Razor blipped the transmission button twice and his wingman reacted instantly, pulling towards him into a turn. Razor held his height knowing that the other Phantom would avoid him and watched the black shape descend below his level passing scant feet underneath in the turn. As they pointed back towards the coastline, the radar repeater scope in front of him flicked into pulse mode briefly and the coastline painted at 90 miles before the display returned to the familiar pulse Doppler mode. The apparently pointless search resumed.

"Eight two over thirteen one, wing tanks transferring, weapon switches still made, Skyflash selected."

It was the fourth time he had run through the weapons checks and nothing had changed other than the slowly reducing fuel load. His wing tanks were empty and he flicked the fuel selector over, selecting internal fuel. The fuel transfer was remarkably normal.

"Roger, base bears 080 range 100," he heard in response from the back, the housekeeping checks routine and uninspiring. "We're tiger fast 45," Flash calculated meaning they had enough fuel for another 45 minutes on station but could still conduct a supersonic intercept if called upon. There seemed little prospect of that.

"Anyface, Romeo Alpha Mike 23, sitrep," Flash prompted over the radio, more in hope than expectation.

"Clara," he heard in response from the intercept controller aboard the Shackleton some miles distant, the radar screen in the back of the aging aircraft equally devoid of activity. The Phantom crew had no idea as no one had thought fit to update them on their arrival that the Shackleton crew had headed out of the area as fast as was humanly possible in response to the presence of the Forgers and now sat well to the rear. It would be a minor miracle if they detected anything of significance from their remote position. Even a "stranger" penetrating the area might have been an excuse for a more animated dialogue

"Deep joy."

The scanner flipped left and right and it was all Flash could do to avoid staring directly at the time base, mesmerised as it moved rhythmically across the scope, the green glow reflecting in the darkened canopy above him. He experienced an unwarranted sense of anticipation despite being conditioned by the usual inactivity of a night-time air defence exercise. The wait was short. Suddenly a familiar smudge appeared much to his astonishment setting in train a flurry of activity. Things switched from turpitude to an adrenaline high within seconds.

"Anyface, Romeo Alpha Mike 23, contact 090, no range, slow speed," he called to his controller, alerting his wingman simultaneously, receiving two clicks in acknowledgement. Probably a helicopter on the islands run, he thought, but anything was of interest. Anything to break the monotony.

" Romeo 23, Anyface, nothing seen. Investigate and report."

"Roger, Anyface, Romeo 23 is investigating. Break, break, vector 090."

The heading shifted imperceptibly as his pilot took up the new vector. Simultaneously, in the front cockpits of both Phantoms, night vision goggles snapped down into position, the navigation lights snapped off and the cockpit lighting was ratcheted down a notch. For the pilots the world took on the eerie green hue of low light operations. In the back, both navigators hunched down over their radar scopes instantly attentive.

"Contact shows low level, taking it down to 5,000 feet."

"Romeo 24, no joy."

The wingman had yet to make radar contact and, so for the time being, Flash was calling the shots. As the Phantoms began to descend, the speed of the contact slowly increased.

"Target now showing 400 knots."

It had to be a fighter but why the speed variations and why was it operating so close to the coast? He had almost forgotten the new device which the engineers had installed even though the power light flickered, annoyingly, in front of his eyes. The pinprick of bright red light was a distraction but, if it did the job he had been promised, it was distraction he could accept. Shining his wander light onto his kneeboard he memorised the four figure code and flicked the tiny rotary wheels until the numbers stared back at him.

"Anyface, is Leuchars Q airborne?"

"Negative, no other fast jet traffic reported in your area. Investigate and report."

"Investigate, 23."

"Passing 10,000 feet in the descent," he heard from the front, cross checking his own altimeter making sure he had set the correct regional pressure setting so that the instrument would give him a height above sea level. It would be a critical reference as they descended in the gloom.

"Radalt set at 1,500 feet."

If they went below that height, an audio warning would sound. Equipped with night vision goggles it would depend on conditions at low level as to how close to the water they chose to go. That would be a decision saved for later. The Phantoms descended tentatively towards the cold Atlantic Ocean below.

*

In the cockpit of the Yak-38, Kedrov checked his RSBN navigation display, the instrument rotating slowly, not yet locked on. His Odd Rod identification system was active and the status light showed steady, signalling his identity back to the Kiev. As yet unconcerned, he knew that the task force was now moving slowly southerly away from the ever persistent Nimrod maritime patrol aircraft which had constantly tracked their movements. So close to the shore there would be little chance of avoiding scrutiny until they headed further south later in the day skirting west of Ireland and giving a little breathing space. He cross checked his heading and pushed his speed up to 500 kilometres per hour, adjusting his height to 1,000 metres. Having dropped the uncommunicative agent on the beach it should be a short and uneventful hop back to the ship and he could finally unwind. In the meantime he had one final challenge for the night, namely landing back on deck in the dark. He had little experience of night operations at sea, although his experience was rapidly increasing but the short landing strip was rather too short for his liking. The marked out area on the runway back at Murmansk which represented the flight deck of the Kiev and where he had practised relentlessly, suddenly seemed more inviting than the real thing. He glanced at the Sirena 3 radar warning receiver but flicked his eyes immediately back to the instruments in disgust. Even for this critical mission there had been insufficient spares to get it working. So early in the cruise, who knew what state the jets would be in when they finally arrived at Tartus?

*

Flash moved the acquisition markers around the target and squeezed the trigger watching the symbology stutter on the display. As the full track lock stabilised he glanced at the range and immediately tightened the pressure a second time breaking the lock. The display reverted to the familiar pulse Doppler search mode. The brief lock had been enough. The target was at 45 miles. He hit the interrogate button on the magic box of tricks more in hope than in anticipation. Untested, he doubted that it would do any good but within seconds, the small green light flickered on. Bloody magic he breathed. He had a hit.

"Delta H, 5,000 below," he heard from the front. Razor was on the ball. As Flash had locked up he had been watching a tiny gauge in the front cockpit which gave relative height separation from the target. The brief lock had been enough for him to get a reading confirming that the target was flying close to the surface. A look at the altimeter and Flash had a height and a range giving instant air picture. Other symbology that he had taken in at a glance gave him enough clues to adjust the approach geometry and refine his attack. If he displaced the target off to one side of his track he could roll in behind and take a closer look at the mysterious contact.

"Target showing hostile," he announced to his startled front-seater. "But don't get too excited yet. The rules of engagement still mean we need a second indicator before we can fire. Check switches safe."

"Switches safe," he heard in response but was that disappointment he could sense?

*

In the Yak-38 Kedrov continued on his westerly heading the surrounding skies now clear. It was a dark night and without any visual references he concentrated solely on the instruments, particularly his attitude indicator and his radio altimeter. In the far distance the barely visible navigation lights of a ship marked the horizon. He could not quite understand why but a feeling of disquiet tickled his nerves. Perhaps it was the thought of the night landing?

*

They were a mere 2,000 feet above the target and Flash had displaced the radar contact to the right. His wingman had already confirmed that he was now in radar contact and the two Phantoms pressed inexorably towards the intercept point. The blip began to drift towards the side of the radar scope, a sure sign that they were closing the range increasing the adrenaline buzz. Even though there was no suggestion of engaging the target yet; their instructions were to investigate, he felt something more than the routine thrill of the chase. Calling for Razor to increase the angle of bank, he started to pull the contact back towards the nose knowing that, in the front, his pilot would be straining for a brief glimpse of the elusive contact. His commentary in the back increased in pace directing his pilot's eyes along the bearing, urging him to locate whatever lurked in the blackness. The lack of response from the front could only mean that the target was also flying without navigation lights. Very odd. He blipped the transmit switch twice knowing that the wingman would look towards him and recognise that they were now in a hard turn towards the target. He wanted him to follow their turn in loose trail. It was imperative at this stage that they stayed within visual sight and the target could only be a few miles away by now but it was still stubbornly quiet in the front cockpit. Suddenly a voice over the radio broke the silence.

"Tally Ho, right 2 o'clock, range 3 miles, closing."

It was Razor's voice from his own jet.

"I see him. I'm tightening it up," Flash heard as the pilot, now with visual contact, became more aggressive in positioning the Phantom. Flash dropped his own night vision goggles into place and stared through the quarter light shifting his head left and right to peer around the grab bars that obscured his line of vision. He was rewarded with a flash of a profile of a fighter aircraft that looked remarkably similar to a Harrier.

"Anyface, Romeo 23 identifies one Forger," he heard simultaneously not recognising who in the formation had made the initial identification. In front, Razor had an advantage in that, for the whole of the descent, his night vision had adjusted to the lower light levels through the goggles and he had a better view of the surrounding seascape. Even with his restricted view from the back cockpit, there could be no mistaking the sleek shape of the distinctive Soviet fighter standing out over the green-tinged wave crests.

"Anyface, Romeo 23, instructions." he prompted aggressively, pressurising the tactical coordinator in the Shackleton.

"Romeo 23, Anyface, stand by."

"Great," he muttered, knowing that the minicomms station at the intercept controllers console in the Control and Reporting Centre would be hot as the successive layers of command and control sought "top cover" before committing to a potentially aggressive act. Within minutes, the Duty Air Defence Commander at Strike Command would have been consulted by wary subordinates.

"23, 24 Flight, go lights on," Razor called, all pretence of a stealthy approach discarded. Secrecy was unnecessary now with the intruder caught in the act and, although the Forger had left British territorial waters and was once again in international airspace, there could be no dispute about the origins of his track. First contact had come inside the crucial 12 mile limit.

*

Kedrov felt an overriding sense of disquiet and dropped his right wing making a gentle turn towards the lowered wingtip. As the Yak-38 drifted into the turn he was startled by the navigation lights of a fast moving aircraft which flashed rhythmically in his peripheral vision dropping into his 6 o'clock. Increasing the turn rate, straining for a better view, he dropped worrying close to the wave tops, correcting at the last minute, his control over the height restored. He craned his head over his shoulder to reacquire the aircraft which had dropped back out of sight working at the limits of his capacity. Sensing a further presence, his sixth sense heightened, a further set of navigation lights flicked on, near to his nose at close range. It was obvious from the way the lights held position that it was another fighter and it was flying at a similar speed. The red and green wingtip lights flared brightly, marking the extremities of the airframe and their relative positions meant that he was looking at the jet in planform. Although indistinct, it began to drift away from the centreline. It had to be a British Phantom posing a dilemma. His orders were clear. He was to complete this mission unobserved and a positive identification would be undeniable. He needed some type of diversion before he was compromised. Little did he know he was already too late and that messages had passed between his opponents. Reflexes kicked in and as he pulled his gunsight onto the lights and the head up display rattled into life, he flicked to guns. The opportunity would be fleeting.

*

Razor felt the added weight of the goggles on his neck muscles as he pulled hard around in a tight turn but was still grateful for the technology which had turned night into day; well almost. Manoeuvring hard in the green goldfish bowl he could still see the unforeseen antagonist over his shoulder and it was, undoubtedly, a Forger. Flash's commentary shaped his response as he played the turn and, slowly began to pull the Soviet aircraft down the canopy back towards the front sector. This was as near to air combat at night as it got and way beyond the bounds of routine training over the

North Sea. Comfortable again, he called "Tally" silencing the chat from the back cockpit. One word was all that would be needed and it would resume should he lose contact again. It was at that moment that he realised that the tactical picture was not developing as he anticipated. His wingman should have been well around the circle following him around in his 4 o'clock but he had appeared ahead of the Forger and, more disturbingly, the darkened shape of the Soviet fighter was making angles. This was not how the intelligence analysts had predicted the fight should go. This Soviet pilot was good.

"Are you still Tally?" he asked over the radio, prompting his wingman to acknowledge the deteriorating situation. It was a prompt which should have been unnecessary but the other Phantom pilot had been caught napping.

"Affirmative, I'm stretched."

Stretched was an understatement. The only way the Forger could have made such progress was if the wingman had dropped back out of position prior to the merge. The inept pilot had allowed it to develop and was now under threat. Swearing, Razor pulled harder, monitoring the G meter as he tickled the airframe limits willing the nose to respond. Drawing his gunsight towards the receding pair he lined up a shot hoping he was able to acquire before the Soviet pilot pressed his advantage. It was marginal who would succeed first.

*

Kedrov had one fleeting opportunity. He lined up his gunsight on the centre of mass; or where he thought it should be, adjusting his angle of bank to stop the pipper sliding and squeezed the trigger. A long burst of gunfire, armour piercing rounds interspersed with tracer, split the darkness, arcing towards the target. He tracked for a few more seconds before rolling off the bank and diving for the sea watching the altimeter unwind rapidly. His RSBN equipment had miraculously locked to the beacon aboard Kiev showing the range of 60 kilometres. He turned towards the carrier, the Yak bucking as he hit the airframe limiting speed in an instant. Unloading the controls he levelled the wings and pushed towards the surface monitoring the height loss as he disengaged.

*

"Anyface, Romeo Alpha Mike 23 and 24 are engaged, position 290, 54 miles from Machrihanish, target is declared hostile. Shots fired!" Razor shouted, stunned by the swift retribution. There could be no doubt, Tracer fire was unmistakeable and the target had been his wingman. The expletives from the back merely confirmed his analysis and, without prompting, the radar sprang back into life, a target reappearing on his repeater scope, locked up at two miles and slightly off the nose. He pushed the stick forward and followed the descending "hostile". Altimeter checks rattled at him from the back seat as the height wound off. He would need to press in to a mile to be in the heart of the Sidewinder envelope. He selected the infra-red missile, the background tone dominating the intercom. The noise in the cockpit competed with the weapons tone magnified as the speed built up. He chased the elusive Forger down.

"Locked on, clear to fire," he finally heard after what seemed like an age. There was no questioning the evident hostility or any confusion over the Soviet pilot's intent but it would be his call whether he pulled the trigger. A glance showed the target well inside firing parameters and the Sidewinder growled aggressively in his ears, its seeker head locked onto the infra-red emissions from the egressing Soviet fighter, adding to the urgency.

"24, are you hit?" he queried over the radio. No reply. A feeling of dread spread. With his wingman worryingly silent, the controller aboard the Shackleton interrupted the flow. He sensed the worst.

"Aircraft squawking emergency off Benbecula say your callsign." The radio remained quiet.

"Aircraft squawking emergency, if you are Romeo Alpha Mike 24, squawk ident."

There was a pause. Romeo Alpha Mike 24 was his wingman.

""I see your squawk. Do you have a further emergency other than a radio failure? If not cancel emergency squawk and squawk 7600."

A further pause.

"Roger, I see your acknowledgement and understand no further emergency. Vector 110 degrees for recovery to Machrihanish and I'll advise your operators of your problem. Your playmate is engaged."

Relief passed between Razor and Flash, unsaid but palpable. It was a simple radio failure, presumably brought on by the swift bout of gunfire but, hopefully, no worse. Getting the Phantom back on the ground before any further complications seemed prudent but Razor and Flash still had a job to do. Switching attention back to the aggressor their own height had dropped off rapidly and Razor re bugged the radio altimeter as they drifted below 500 feet beginning to level off. The target was still running fast on west and their own speed had picked up to 500 knots, the Soviet jet's speed easily matched by the powerful Speys of the Phantom. The strident tone of the radio altimeter sounded a warning as they breached 240 feet way too low in the darkened airspace, only the night vision goggles allowing them to fly so low. There could be no way a Forger could out run them with its massive fan engine and that they would close further was inevitable yet the controller in the Shackleton was eerily quiet despite their aggressive prompting. Razor steadied the gunsight over the fleeing target which was now slightly above and much easier to track. The Sidewinder continued its grumbling dialogue as Razor held the sight off unwilling to descend lower. The Forger pilot had committed a hostile act in opening fire. He was perfectly justified in taking the shot. His Sidewinder was locked on the tiny head tracking the Forger's every move. The aim dot bounced animatedly around the aiming circle. The growl was strident in his ears and the radar was locked solid. . . . .

This was pointless. He snapped the master arm to "Safe".

"Let's take this home."

The disbelief from the back seat was plain.

CHAPTER 39

The Air Defence Operations Centre, RAF High Wycombe.

Boyd stared at the tote struggling to make sense of the tactical situation. None of this yet made any sense. If this was the opening moves of World War 3 why were there no other indicators? Why were Soviet forces not massing on the Inner German Border? Surely they would have chosen a comprehensive suite of targets and the air defence radar sites would be smoking ruins by now? There were three sector operations centres ranged along the length of the country, ports, airfields, military headquarters. Why would they make a precision attack on a lonely outpost at the northern tip of the country?

His assets were in place. All it would take was one simple clearance but did he have the authority to issue it. The phone rang. The Master Controller sounded just as nervous as Boyd.

"Sir, I estimate the Bear Charlie is approaching launch range. The Kangaroo missile climbs to extreme height and accelerates after launch and will be almost impossible to engage. If we don't engage now it will be too late. What are your instructions Sir?"

He suddenly felt just as cautious as the C-in-C.

"Standby."

He knew he was being indecisive but this was not a decision to be taken lightly. The consequences were massive. He glanced back at the senior officer. The C-in-C watched from the back of the dais but his lack of action was disconcerting. If his call had been so important why no further direction? Boyd was now sure that he would not be the one to order the first moves which would turn the Cold War hot, and he was not about to leave himself exposed. One word might signal the start of a conflict that would lead to mutually assured destruction. The apocalyptic strategy on which he had cut his military teeth, which had been discussed endlessly during staff college lectures over the years, was playing out before him. He was not prepared to make the call that his superior officer was avoiding. The Commander in Chief was present and it would be his call or nothing.

"Haul him off. Order the Phantom back to CAP and declare weapons tight. Repeat, weapons tight."

The sweat trickled down his back as he waited for his order to be countermanded but the room was hushed. The Bear Charlie moved inexorably towards the tiny island of Unst. Prayers seemed utterly inadequate and no higher power would intervene if he had made the wrong call.

*

The Navigator in the cold cabin of the Tupolev bomber watched as the coordinates of the target drifted onto the outer extremes of his radar display. He marked the dull smudge on the tiny peninsular at the north of the remote group of islands. Having studied the target folders on many occasions, he knew just what the radar picture should look like. The predictions had been remarkably accurate and it was almost like the radar mapping strips which were locked in the target vault back at his airbase in Mother Russia. He would update the precise aiming point on his return.

" Launch in 5, 4, 3, 2, 1, mark."

As he squeezed the commit button the tell tale wink of the indicator light flickered as it switched from "ready" to "launch" and he felt the pilot pull the massive bomber into the turn to begin its descent to 25,000 feet on its return back North. He felt the sweet sensation of anticipation as he imagined the AS-3 missile mounted in the belly of the bomber, streaking away on its deadly mission. Despite the descent, frozen in a moment of time, the target glowed bright on the radar scope as the weapons officer made his final designation of the precise coordinates of the Saxa Vord radar site. The command link in the belly of the bomber passed the deadly update message to its simulated projectile as the bomber turned slowly onto its recovery heading. It had been a drill, albeit entirely realistic up to the point at which the cruise missile should have left the belly housing.

"Nav give me a heading for home," the pilot called.

It had been a mission rehearsal in precise detail in all but the final weapon release.

CHAPTER 40

The Soviet Embassy, London.

The muted chatter in the communications room came more from the bored clerks at the control desk than from the callers. Individual screened booths, mostly unoccupied at this early hour, surrounded the windowless room. With the time difference between London and Moscow, they would fill up later as harassed staffers in the Soviet capital reacted to their master's wishes firing random tasks at the Embassy staff. The bureaucrats in Moscow would expect them to be completed as the pen pushers retired to the bars for well deserved vodka shots and be ready for their return to work in the morning.

The man chose a booth and pulled the door closed behind him, the atmosphere instantly more claustrophobic. As he inserted the cryptographic key into the telephone the device sprang into life and a series of lights illuminated on the handset. Glancing at his watch he settled back into the chair and waited for the phone to ring.

The muffled ringtone shook him out of his reverie and, as he acknowledged the instruction to go secure from the distant caller, the sound of the remote voice took on an ethereal tone in the confined, insulated environment. The light on the handset winked rhythmically confirming that a secure line had been established, the electronic devices having completed a "handshake". The distorted voice sounded as if it emanated from the Moon.

"We have an issue comrade."

"Good morning. How is it in our wonderful capital city this morning? And why is that always so?" he responded wearily.

"The operation went well overall and the device is in place but we have a few issues. The Brits are not happy."

The encryption made the voice hard to understand, burbling and distorted, the volume rising and falling.

"We can hardly expect them to congratulate us on our operational efficiency. We are, after all, operating in their back yard."

"It seems that a Phantom took fire from our maritime patrol aircraft and is permanently out of commission. It will not fly again. They have made a formal complaint about our aggressive behaviour. We've prepared a defensive briefing for the Ambassador but it is inevitable that he will be called to see the British Foreign Secretary later. Can you make sure he receives the briefing as soon as it arrives? We need a tight line on this one. But that's not the worst of our problems. We lost a helicopter during the operation. The loss was unfortunate and might otherwise have been deniable but there is a complication. It seems the infiltration team was surprised by the local guard force. After an exchange of fire a guard was shot and killed. The Team Leader decided that by taking him back to the Ship his disappearance might have become an unexplained mystery. Unfortunately, his appearance in the wreckage of a helicopter on a beach in the Scottish islands is less easy to explain away."

The agent stroked his brow nervously. Life in London was never dull.

"And what were you planning to do to cover that little bombshell comrade?"

"I was hoping you could offer us a way out comrade. Given that the operation has been briefed to the Politburo this morning, we seem to be expected to save face in some way."

"If, as you say, the wreckage has already been discovered it's too late to send in a cleanup team. We'll need something more subtle."

"Can I assume that you will tie up the other loose ends as planned?"

"Everything is in hand. The details of the operation were only known to a few key personnel and those individuals will be sworn to secrecy. I can assure you that the risk of compromise of the real reason for our activity is minimal. I'll give the other matter some thought and we'll get back to you."

The line went dead.

CHAPTER 41

The Ugadale Hotel, Cambletown.

"So what did you make of that me old mate?"

Razor and Flash had just returned to the hotel bar after holding an intelligence debrief with the much travelled Group intelligence officer. The first pint was slipping down nicely.

"It sounds like Squadron Leader Silversmith has been busy this week going back and forth from here to Strike Command. If the Comms. Squadron issued air miles he would have racked up enough points to travel to an exotic beach for a few weeks."

Flash's response was typically blunt.

"I'd say we were just fed the proverbial crock of shit."

The debrief had been short and perfunctory. Silversmith had summarised the air activity describing the maritime exercise almost as if it had been an extract from an exercise intelligence scenario. The fact that the Air Defence Commander had almost allowed Leuchars QRA to engage a Bear Charlie during its training profile had been conveniently sidelined and the fate of the Bear which had fired was still a mystery. Their question about why the Forger had been operating within territorial waters was almost ignored. The barely credible explanation that the Soviets had apologised for navigational errors was laughable. After all, both of them had used the excuse many times in the past and it was rarely true. It had seemed like a very deliberate cover up.

"So why didn't you pull the trigger? We had clearance to engage and the shot was heart of the envelope. It was a guaranteed kill."

Razor swilled his beer around the glass, his mood reflective.

"What would it have achieved? The guy is probably just like us. He spends time at sea but probably goes home to a wife and kids in downtown Murmansk. He was just an aviator doing his job. How would a Sidewinder have changed the world?"

"You've heard the rumours that a helo is down on Unst and it might not be one of ours? If it's true the Sovs have been involved in more than just a routine maritime exercise."

"Silversmith didn't give any inkling of activity onshore. All we've been told about are the usual Bear and Badger intrusions around North Cape. All of that can be explained by the anti-submarine exercise, particularly if there's a new submarine involved."

"I guess Ivan is flexing his muscles. He's got a new toy and he wants us to know that we're not as safe in our backyard as we thought we were. From what we saw up there today, the Forger isn't going to change the balance but if the descriptions of the new RAM-K and RAM-L fighters are correct then we'll have a fighter threat over the North Sea within a few years."

"Not much we can do about that but our masters have it all in hand. The new Tornado ADV will sort them out."

Flash looked across at his pilot, the glint of amusement giving away the lie. Neither of them believed that statement.

"So how is Toppers, have you heard from him?"

"He's good. He's been given a few more weeks off to recover and then we'll be getting airborne again to finish his operational work up. He's a good lad. Lots of potential."

"How's your back holding up?"

"Not bad. I get a few twinges pulling g but it'll be OK. I'm sure as hell not going anywhere near the docs or they'll find some reason why I shouldn't be flying. A couple of pills here and there and it'll be fine. I bet I'm an inch shorter when they measure me at my next annual medical."

There was an easy silence between the two flyers.

"So it's back to Coningsby then," the young pilot said, the reluctance conspicuous. "It was good to work together again Flash. You looking forward to getting back to "Basic Radar One" on the OCU?"

The question went unanswered. The Detachment Commander walked in, the termination signal which had just been received clutched in his hand. The brief message announced that the Soviet Task Force was now steaming towards the Mediterranean at maximum speed. The Phantoms would be withdrawn to their Lincolnshire base and await further tasking, possibly flying onwards to Gibraltar. Leuchars would be able to cope with QRA with normal levels of activity resumed. The news generated a buzz amongst the assembled flyers.

"Can't wait mate. Way more fun than this operational stuff," Flash muttered inaudibly.

"Mushroom syndrome" had prevailed. The crew would never be privy to the real events of the last few days.

CHAPTER 42

The Island Air Taxis Office, Machrihanish Airfield.

The Duty Corporal had been sickeningly cheerful as Maria signed in at the Guardroom. Dawn was breaking as she let herself into the small office at the air taxi firm and she looked around, despondently. With Liam gone, the operation would have to be wound up as she had no intention of taking on the mantle. The aircraft would be collected by the same anonymous pilot who had made the original delivery flights. The office space was only leased from the MOD and could be handed back quickly and she had little desire to spend more time in the remote community than was necessary. There was a small working balance in the Company accounts which would help her move on. It was luck, or should she believe good fortune, that the task she had just completed should provide the funds for her new enterprise. The feeling of isolation, however, was strong. Her brother had been ever present in her life and she missed him.

Picking up the 'phone the dial tone jarred as she hit the numbered buttons on the trimphone handset.

"Soviet Embassy."

She was taking a big risk making this call from here. What if communications from the base were being monitored? Too late but the staffer should have been more discrete. No matter. An identity change was called for and she had friends in Belfast who arranged such things routinely. She gave a pre-arranged codeword.

"One moment please," replied the operator followed by an audible click as her call was transferred.

"Yes?"

There was no preamble, nor did she expect any.

"It's done. The consignment is secured and there's no means of escape," she said cryptically. Even if the call was intercepted nothing could be gleaned from the exchange. She assumed that the "consignment" was the enigmatic man who had visited the office yesterday. Who else would need to climb a rock face on a remote beach? Speculation over his identity and his role had been fruitless. That she suspected that he may have, somehow, been responsible for Liam's disappearance merely sweetened the bitter pill.

"Excellent. Your reimbursement will be deposited immediately."

The line went dead followed by the return of the dial tone. She replaced the handset and smiled.

Her mind drifted back to the cliff top. The pitiful cries had been, somehow, disturbing. When she had rigged the climbing ropes she had been unable to rid herself of the feeling of claustrophobia knowing that whoever used the tackle would be working their way into an inevitable trap. The carabiners had been set carefully to ensure there could be no escape. Even wielding a knife in the confined space would have been impossible. The strident calls of the gulls and the fulmars would have been a natural backdrop to an inopportune end. She shuddered at the thought.

The young pilot had not been her only conquest recently. The attractive young sailor she had bedded had been an unexpected pleasure. Why her mysterious contact had insisted she ask the sailor to take a keepsake to sea with him was a question never posed. Curious, she mused. The photograph frame was strangely weighty. She had been proud of her picture but wondered if its presence in the frame might come back to haunt her. Maybe a simpler rural Scottish scene might have been a smarter move?

By making the call she had, unwittingly, saved herself from an untimely end. The funds would, indeed, be deposited in her account later that day yet her survival had never been part of the original plan. Maria Whelan had, without knowing, guaranteed her future rather than her demise. By the time the next visitor made his way to the air taxi office, it would be closed and she would be on the ferry back to Belfast and anonymity.

CHAPTER 43

The Communications Room aboard The Kiev.

The teleprinter chattered and began to emit a roll of punched tape into a basket. The print out was unintelligible at this juncture so the technician allowed the machine to run its course. As it finally returned to silence he loaded the tape into a decryption device and it began chattering away deciphering the coded message.

As the signal emerged, by now recognisable as the Captains weekly orders, the clerk folded the long print out carefully and placed it in an envelope. Looking around the enclosed space he checked for any other ratings secreted in a nook or cranny. Curiosity was getting the better of him but, more importantly aboard ship, information was power. It could also act as hard currency and he knew of a few individuals who may be persuaded to part with a few roubles for the contents. Seeing that he was alone he smoothed down the print out and started to read.

The opening paragraphs summarised the exercise and the success or failure of each of the participants. The Akula captain, far from being exalted as a Hero of the Soviet Union would be lucky to keep his command. Although he had made a successful attack on the task force he had allowed his new submarine to be detected by the NATO planes. Intercepts suggested that his new ship's acoustic signature had been compromised. That guaranteed an interesting debrief on his homecoming.

The summary of the air operations in the British waters was an eye-opener and he marvelled at the fact that all this had been going on from the decks above and yet he had been oblivious. Reading on, the subsequent paragraphs were of more parochial interest. The Kiev was to proceed immediately past Ireland and through the Straits of Gibraltar into the Mediterranean. As the task group broke out into open water they would exercise with the Migs and Sukhois of the Libyan Air Force in the Gulf of Tripoli. It would be a full scale exercise with the Libyans mounting simulated air attacks against the fleet. He looked for any suggestion of an extra port visit to Tripoli but was disappointed and his spirits dropped. That would mean they would be locked down for at least three days at battle stations rather than let loose in the flesh pots of Tripoli but there was even gloomier news. The arrival in Tartus was delayed a week and the task force was to hold on the Cyprus Buoy for the final days. Far from additional shore leave they would wallow in the Eastern Mediterranean tied up to a buoy for another week. And joy of joys, an additional replenishment at sea had been arranged before arrival. They would refuel and resupply from a support group sent out from the Black Sea ports as they sailed past Crete. That would mean a shortened port stay.

He would need to be careful how he used this information. Too much detail and it would be traced back to him. The recipient would need to be carefully chosen and briefed but he could already feel the Roubles that the information would unlock.

CHAPTER 44

Headquarters Strike Command, RAF High Wycombe.

Wing Commander Phil Boyd drew stiffly to attention and snapped off a crisp salute before the Commander in Chief's desk, his dog-eared Service Dress hat firmly in place. He listened intently to the stern words delivered forcefully, clearly unscripted. He had been around long enough to know when to speak but, more relevant when not to respond. This was a lost cause. Pondering the sequence of events many times in his mind over the last hours, he could not see where that he might have reacted differently but, even so, the vociferous tirade from the "Four Star" left him in no doubt that the senior officer did not share his conclusions.

"Anything to say Boyd?"

"No Sir!"

The tense air softened slightly.

"OK that's the formal bit over but don't be under any illusions Phil; I'm not happy. You've been around as long as me and I know these split second decisions are never simple but when events are briefed at Number Ten it becomes my concern. Take a seat over there," he said gesturing at the group of chairs in the corner of the office. "Let me hear the story again and we'll see how we recover this mess. Take that stupid hat off and relax."

Boyd bit his tongue, walked wearily across to the chairs and relaxed into the soft cushions. He knew the Commander-in-Chief of old and the man had

INFILTRATION

changed noticeably from the stress-free Flying Officer who had shared a crewroom at Wattisham in the late Sixties on a Lightning squadron. His political ambition was legendary and any failure which impacted on his reputation or more importantly, his chance of becoming Chief of the Air Staff, was taken as a direct challenge. His progress up the slippery pole would not be interrupted. Attention from Whitehall and, particularly from the present Chief of the Air Staff's office, was attention he was not prepared to countenance. That the PM was involved sealed Boyd's fate. A scapegoat would be found and it would not be the C-in-C.

The tray of coffee that appeared from the outer office hinted that there may be a compromise.

"I've been called to MOD later to discuss a formal response to the Soviets if it becomes necessary. I need facts not speculation so why not go through the sequence of events again so that I understand fully."

Boyd hunkered down and began to recount his recollection of events in precise detail yet again. It took some time.

"That's the situation as I saw it Sir."

"Hmm. I need to make sense of this "air attack" and whether there was intent. An exchange of weapons, even though everyone seems to have exercised their legal rights should never happen in peacetime and certainly not by accident. If this helicopter crash on Unst proves to be one of theirs, then there can be no doubt that there was mischief afoot. The events have to be linked."

"What we can't explain, Sir, is the body found in the wreckage. We're having DNA tests done now but it seems likely that it will prove to be that of the missing RAF Regiment guard. If so, how did he find himself aboard a Soviet helicopter? He's the most unlikely candidate for a spy. None of our own cabs are missing so it seems like a foregone conclusion that there were Soviet intruders ashore. According to the Special Investigation Branch investigators who have taken a first look, he was about as unlikely a Soviet spy as is humanly possible. Just a regular lad from Oldham. My best guess at this stage is he was abducted; but why?"

"It leaves me in a quandary in taking this forward. The CAA have the lead on the investigation into the loss of the Islander commuter aeroplane and rightly so. There doesn't seem to be any military involvement other than that the pilot was operating from an RAF base. There's still no sign of any wreckage yet and I think that the investigation team leader has called a recess until they can finish a search in the area. If we're lucky, something will wash ashore. They examined the tapes from the ATC agencies and, from what I hear, that was inconclusive. The departure from Machrihanish seemed undramatic although it's not clear whether he planned to land elsewhere. There seems to be confusion over whether he intended to drop his mysterious passenger off at a beach strip. No one has heard whether the passenger has reappeared yet. He signed onto base but never signed out. Maybe I could have the civilian team take a trip over to look at the crash site. I would normally convene a military Board of Inquiry with a Wing Commander President but, as it's not our aircraft, that would be quite inappropriate under the circumstances. If another Nation's military aircraft comes down on our soil we offer assistance to the Nation in question to help conduct an Inquiry. As the Soviets have not even announced that they have lost an aircraft, that's another option that seems to be out of the window. Has the crash site been secured?"

"The Station Commander at Saxa Vord has closed access to the site Sir. He's mounted a 24 hour piquet and the whole area has been closed off by the local Police. No one will be poking their nose in without your clearance."

"This is not your problem Phil. It's for the chaps in Flight Safety to run down but I think I need to brief the Chief of Defence Intelligence that all may not be as it seems. So what have the Soviets been up to?" the senior officer mused. "There's something we don't understand going on here and I think I'm going to need answers from Defence Intelligence to unravel it. Keep digging this afternoon and update me before I go in to see the Chief. Look into the SIGINT and see if we intercepted anything that might give a clue as to what this whole operation was covering. It was too well orchestrated to be a simple anti-submarine exercise. The First Sea Lord wants a pre-meeting which doesn't make sense if this was mostly air activity. Maybe that Akula submarine is the key? Anyway, speculation is wasted energy, I need to work on facts."

INFILTRATION

The meeting ended quickly; Boyd's coffee unfinished.

CHAPTER 45

Holy Loch Naval Base, Faslane, two weeks later.

The submersible jockeyed for position alongside the jetty at the naval base at the head of Gare Loch, the occasional whirring from its electric motors breaking the beat of the waves against the pilings. Above the cabin two davits hung ready to lift the small craft as soon as the pilot completed the delicate manoeuvre. A diver splashed into the water, disappearing briefly before resurfacing and clambering aboard, hauling himself up using barely visible grab handles. As it lowered within reach he grasped the swinging chain and pulled it downwards, clipping the shackle firmly in place. Encumbered by his scuba gear he shuffled towards the rear, ungainly out of his element before repeating the operation on the rear shackle. Signalling to an unseen operator he launched clear of the manacled vessel landing with a noisy splash alongside and disappeared from sight.

As the submersible rose from the water closer inspection would have revealed a device resembling a large hockey puck, clutched in the claws of the robotic arm at the front of the small vessel. Water cascaded from hidden nooks and crannies tumbling back into the sea below leaving the bright yellow hull glistening in the moonlight. Progress slow, the craft edged over the ramp where a dolly waited. Lowering slowly onto the cradle a team of technicians attached tie-down straps anchoring the swinging bulk in place. A motor revved and a small tractor pulled the yellow craft gently through the gaping doors of a darkened hangar moving swiftly out of sight of inquisitive eyes. Scant minutes had passed since it broke the surface and only an eagle-eyed intelligence analyst would have spotted its brief journey

INFILTRATION

on terra firma.

Safely inside with the doors secured, arc lights snapped on, casting a harsh light over the small space. A technician fussed around the hull completing a familiar post dive routine whilst another clambered up and released the outer entrance hatch. Two bodies emerged and made their way down the metal gantry which had been pulled into place to aid their exit. The casual dress worn by the crew was in total contrast to that of the single figure standing close to the base of the gantry, the silver colour of his hazmat suit reflecting the arc lights. After a brief exchange, responsibility for the craft passed to the handling crew. A technician who had released the hatch appeared inside the bubble canopy of the submersible poised to assist in the yet undefined task. The suited body approached the robotic arm tentatively, giving the device clutched in the claw a respectably wide berth. After a short inspection and a few urgent gestures, the lights of the craft blinked on and the hum of electrics cut the quiet, the arm beginning to move, rotating the small device level and extending out and away from the nose.

The two men who had emerged from the submersible disappeared through a door in the hangar, their gait rapid. Whatever had occurred during the short mission clearly demanded immediate discussion, their part in the recovery over.

The suited figure made a lowering gesture, the technician in the cockpit manipulating the levers letting the arm sink downwards towards a smaller trolley, the agricultural green-painted metalwork in sharp contrast to the high tech surroundings. As the hockey puck settled tentatively onto the flat bed, the claw released and the device settled into its new cradle. Freed from the load, the arms lifted clear and the man moved forward and waved a small sensor over the metal fingers. He raised his arm, the lowered thumb clearly visible to the technician in the cockpit despite the bulky hazmat gloves. Whatever the meaning, the lights of the craft snapped off and without fanfare, the face disappeared from view. Securing the mysterious electronics box back into a pouch in his suit he moved to the front of the trolley, picked up the stubby handle and the device began its journey through the hangar to its final destination.

Unheard, a message flashed to the control room activating a well rehearsed routine which would be intimately familiar to the staff at the nuclear submarine base. A red overhead strobe light flashed on, the beams reflecting from the stark concrete walls, accompanied by a strident warning message ringing out over the tannoy. A renewed urgency became apparent as the alert triggered an immediate response amongst the staff.

Ensconced in a warm briefing room the two men, recently emerged from the submersible had been joined by a third.

"How did it go?" the new arrival asked.

"Very smooth, in fact, no problems at all. The SOSUS sensor site is easily accessible and our new submersible performed flawlessly. We took about twenty minutes to replace the Soviet device with our own clone."

"Do we know exactly what the Sovs were up to? When did we spot the intrusion?"

"I think they underestimate how sensitive SOSUS really is. They probably thought the signature from the submersible was small enough to go undetected but it's not. I must admit though, it was good piece of work by our sensor operator who picked up the activity. They were clever in trying to hide the movements by timing the drop just as HMS Resolution recovered up the Loch. It could easily have gone unnoticed."

"Have we had any trouble with the Americans given that we are messing with their system?"

"No they're fully involved and were really quite helpful and briefed us on the design and functionality. It would have been impossible without their cooperation."

"Why did the Soviets attach the "bug", if I can call it that, to the sensor?"

"They had no choice really. The positioning of the sensor is no coincidence. It's down to simple underwater geography. There's a good reason why the Americans chose that location. It's a natural choke point for traffic in and out of the Loch. They see our movements even though we always notify them when a submarine is in transit. Departures are always coordinated with satellite overpass times so that we don't advertise activity, particularly during that critical phase. The boomers regularly transit either side of Great

Cumbrae and then submerge once in the deeper water in the Firth. More importantly, we need to know if there are any other, shall we say, less than friendly watchers in the area during a departure in case anyone should try to latch onto the departing submarine in shallow water."

"So what is this device that it was so important to penetrate our territorial waters?"

"It has two functions. The first is as a detector. It sends out warning signals during the passage of a boomer. The signals are random and only triggered during a passage. It seems to have a simple sensor that can recognise the acoustic signal of a ship or a trawler and compare it with that of a submarine and then categorise the response. There may be some specific circuitry to refine the fact that it has detected a boomer but we need to work on that. Once it has the identification it sends out a time-stamped burst pulse as an event. It's very selective."

"And the second?"

"The second is more sinister. It can communicate with the SOSUS sensor and effectively join the network. Although it's not live data, any time the Soviets can put an intelligence gatherer close enough to establish line of sight, they can stimulate the device to pass vital data about not just that sensor but others in the network. There's an AGI, a Soviet spy trawler that sits off Malin Head almost constantly. If they move that into range they can harvest data at will. I think we can expect to see a new pattern of operations developing over the coming months."

"I can see why they would want movements data but how come it's so important for the Soviets to know when a sub is leaving?"

"With a precise time at the neck of the Loch they can predict when it might emerge. If it takes the Northern Route that timing will be quite accurate, although they can't be quite as precise for a southerly departure. Even so, any help they can get means that they have a much greater chance of getting an attack sub into place to pick the boat up as it breaks out into open water. Otherwise, they are working on a chance sighting during a satellite pass and we make it as hard as possible for them to succeed on that one."

"So what have we replaced it with?"

"We substituted a new device which is configured to emulate the signals we had seen from the original. We'd collected a few hits on our sensors and wrote a program to match what we'd seen. The original device pushed out two signals. There's a routine health check which goes out about once a week, telling the Sovs that the device is working. The only other signal we've seen is the warning burst if it detects a vessel. As it seems smart enough to differentiate between a surface ship and a submarine, we ran a few ships past it before we removed it and the take showed a range of signals. There must be another data signal that we've not yet seen. We need to work on that. The clone we've installed can push out identical signals on command providing we can emulate the original signals. There's scope to push out some disinformation as we get smarter."

"How long do you think our new device will fool the Soviets?

"Who knows? The biggest risk is that there is something that the original device might be able to push out that we haven't yet detected. We'll need to evaluate the electronics and try to make sure we have everything programmed correctly. This is new technology and we're emulating Soviet electronics. There are still risks involved. If we get it wrong they'll be onto us in a flash."

"I can see that. Are we sure it's worth trying to exploit this device. Why not just make it clear to the Soviets that we found it?"

"If we decide we want to terminate the programme we can simply trawl it up in a fishing net or send the submersible out again to recover it. Granted, the location is prominent and it would take a pretty inept fisherman to do that but we can work on a contingency plan to make it seem convincing if it ever comes to that. In the meantime, we can play a few games with them. They're already paranoid about our ability to operate undetected. It's always good to keep them guessing."

"Worth knowing. Anything else I need to know?"

"The first thing is to make the original safe. It's powered by a long life power plant based on a nuclear fuel pellet. That thing is hot and the Geiger counter on the submersible went crazy when we snagged it. If it had sat there for any length of time we'd have been trawling up luminescent prawns before long. It would have lit up the local sea lanes with its fallout. That was an error on the part of the Soviets because it would, eventually, have alerted us to its presence."

"At least we're in the right place to make it safe. We have some of the best nuclear technicians in the world here."

"True. Once it's cleaner, and I don't mean clean because it's going to be contaminated forever, we can start a quick evaluation. We'll have to limit exposure times for anyone working on it but we can do most of the testing in the sealed contamination chamber. We have the procedures in place."

"Good. I'll get a briefing prepared. I've been called down to the Old War Office tomorrow to deliver the briefing personally. The First Sea Lord has been warned off and is showing a personal interest. They don't want to risk compromise. This Project is about to go into a security compartment with a special access caveat. Only a few key people will even know about it. Security will be even tighter than the norm and it's normally tight as it is."

The submersible pilot stretched and yawned, suddenly weary.

"I think I might sleep tonight."

"I think you might. You deserve a wee dram before you turn in. How about we swing by the Wardroom on the way out and I'll buy you a drink?"

"That's the best offer of the year. Sounds like a sound plan to me. See you there."

*

The British boomer descended deeper into the Gully, a familiar feature in the underwater geography of the Atlantic Ocean, its search for anonymity constant. Onboard, the crew went about their routines oblivious to the omni-present threat.

Some way behind, the Karp maintained its vigil, its presence registering nothing on the sensitive sensors aboard its prey. The Captain glanced once more at the new instrument that had been installed shortly before departure marvelling at its simplicity. He had little interest in the technology that drove the gadget, only that it worked. The symbol marking the British nuclear submarine glowed brightly up ahead. Safe in the knowledge that he could hold his position covertly, he had no need to close to a range where his presence might be detected. Whatever had been planted by whoever was immaterial but his ability to track his prey was transformed. It was now simpler to achieve the impossible. He wondered whether, if he could detect the signal, the sensors aboard the British submarine may also pick it up. Discovery was an ever present risk but for the time being at least, his job was immeasurably more straightforward.

The balance in the deadly game of nuclear brinkmanship had shifted decidedly in favour of the Soviet Union and, for now, the weight of British influence at the Security Council table had been compromised. Moves were being formulated in the corridors of the Kremlin and subtle hints would be dropped in diplomatic circles. Never again would the members of the Politburo be caught unawares. In one bold operation an arm of the Western nuclear deterrent had been, effectively, neutralised. Whether this advantage was permanent was moot but, achieved once, it could be done again.

The consequences of Exercise Able Archer, literally, ran deep.

###

GLOSSARY

ADMISREP. Air Defence Mission Report.

ADV. Air Defence Variant. The fighter version of the Tornado.

ADOC. Air Defence Operations Centre.

CAA. Civil Aviation Authority.

CAOC. Combined Air Operations Centre.

CRC. Control and Reporting Centre.

CRP. Control and Reporting Post.

Delta 4, 4 Zero, Eight, Tiger Fast 60. The code signified the Phantom armament state to the controller. The first letter showed the external fuel tank fit with Delta meaning it carried a centreline tank. Alpha was clean, bravo a single centreline, charlie two external wing tanks. The first number was the number of Sparrow of Skyflash missiles, the second the number of Sidewinders, the plus signified a gun whereas zero meant no gun and the final number was the number of forward hemisphere capable weapons. This became relevant once AIM-9L was fielded as it had a head on capability.

DF. Direction finding.

"Eight Two over Ten Six". A fuel check typical of the Phantom. There was only a single fuel gauge in the front cockpit which led to significant "nagging" from navigators particularly as the fuel contents reduced. The fuel in the external fuel tanks was not gauged. The first figure was known as the "tape" and the second the "counter" describing the appearance of the fuel gauge. The tape registered the fuel in the fuselage fuel tanks and the counter the total fuel in both the fuselage and internal wing tanks. As the internal wing tanks emptied the two values matched.

ETA. Estimated Time of Arrival.

EWO. Electronic Warfare Officer. Responsible for operating the electronic surveillance, protection and attack systems.

Going dark. To descend below radar coverage.

GRU. Soviet military intelligence.

INAS. Inertial Navigation Attack System fitted to the Phantom FGR2 only. The FG1 had a much less effective air position indicator.

IUKADGE. Improved UK Air Defence Ground Environment. Replacement transportable ground based radars which were procured in the 1980s to modernise the defence infrastructure. A replacement for the Bloodhound surface-to-air missile was envisaged but never funded.

JENGO. Junior Engineering Officer.

"Mushroom syndrome". To be kept in the dark and fed on "fertiliser".

Odd Rod. Soviet electronic identification system fitted to Warsaw Pact aircraft during the Cold War.

PC, A hydraulic system which powered the main or primary flying controls on the Phantom.

"Q". The abbreviation for Quick Reaction Alert.

QRA. Quick Reaction Alert.

Retrograde. An instruction to withdraw from an operational area.

RIB. Rigid inflatable boat.

RoE. Rules of Engagement. Detailed instructions of when a crew was allowed to open fire.

RSBN. The Soviet radio navigation system similar to TACAN.

SACLANT. Supreme Allied Command Atlantic. A NATO command headquarters located in Norfolk, Virginia. The NATO Commander is responsible for NATO Atlantic waters.

SAROPS. Search and rescue operations.

SHQ. Station Headquarters. Administrative Wing.

SIGINT. Signals intelligence.

SOC. Sector Operations Centre. The organisation responsible for battle management in an air defence sector in UK.

SSAFA. Soldiers, Sailors and Airmen's Families Association. A services welfare charity supporting the troops.

Stranger. An unidentified track.

Squawk ident. To transmit an identification code to a controller using the Identification Friend or Foe system.

Tansor. A codename for the QRA tanker operation.

TACAN. Tactical navigation system. A radio aid giving range and bearing to ground based radio beacons. It also provided a range between cooperating TACAN boxes in an airborne mode known as air-to-air TACAN.

Take. Intelligence jargon for signals detected by collection sensors.

Tally. Short for "Tally Ho", a codeword signifying that a pilot or navigator has visual contact on a hostile aircraft.

Tansor. The operational nickname for the QRA air-to-air refuelling tanker.

Trade. Nickname for opposing targets either hostile or friendly.

UKADGE. The UK Air Defence Ground Environment. The network of air defence radars, ground based missiles and fighter bases which formed the air defence infrastructure.

Utilities. A secondary hydraulic system which powered services on the Phantom.

Visual. A codeword signifying that a pilot or navigator has visual contact on a friendly aircraft.

Vul. Time. The notional start time for a combined air operation.

Zombie. A suspect air track conforming to air traffic rules or following a recognised traffic pattern.

AUTHOR'S NOTE

Writing a book, although solitary, is never a solo effort and my thanks go to Phil Keeble and Andy Lister-Tomlinson for helping me edit the draft, Mandy Skayman for specialist advice on rock climbing techniques and to Jane Mullen for describing the topography around the radar site at Benbecula. In particular, thank you to Dean Crawford for another superb cover design.

Many of the scenarios in "Infiltration" are based on real events. Quick Reaction Alert duties were the maid duty for an air defence squadron in peacetime. The procedures I describe are as accurate as I can make them. No. 29 Squadron was indeed the NATO deployable British Phantom squadron during the Cold War and would have been moved to a forward operating base to be closer to the operational area had the tactical situation demanded. If live operations had ensued, both Machrihanish in Scotland and St Mawgan in Cornwall might have seen detachments of Phantoms arriving to give air defence cover for maritime operations in the South West Approaches and off Scotland. Indeed the airfield in Cornwall was equipped with hardened aircraft shelters specifically to host visiting fighters.

The Soviet aircraft carrier Kiev which features in the novel was one of three vessels in the class named after Soviet cities. It was laid down at the Soviet Shipyard No. 444 at Mykolaiv on 21 July 1970, was launched on 26 December 1972 and commissioned into service on 28 December 1975. After a relatively short time in service for a capital ship it was sold on the commercial market in 1996. Its sister ships the Minsk and Novorossiysk were constructed in short order. The Minsk was also sold but the

Novorossiysk was broken up at Pohang, South Korea in 1997.

When it emerged on an operational deployment in the mid 1970s Kiev caused great consternation in NATO circles. With its complement of Yak-38 Forgers, the Soviet Union was, for the first time, able to project air power well beyond its borders. In reality it was a token gesture. The Forger proved unreliable and many compromises had been made in order to achieve the vertical takeoff and landing capability, particularly in weapons capability and radar performance. It was quickly discounted as a serious threat as it was out performed by most of its western peers including the Phantom. Even so, in a show of force during its maiden deployment, a Carrier Battle Group led by Kiev steamed through the English Channel en route to the Mediterranean making a clear statement of intent. The invulnerability of the NATO rear areas was being challenged by a resurgent Soviet Navy.

The involvement of the research ship Akademik Mstislav Keldysh is obviously fictional although the vessel supported the Soviet military at various times, particularly in the search for a Soviet submarine, the Komsomolets, which sank off the north eastern coast of Norway in 1989. The ship is perhaps better known for its voyages to investigate two famous wrecks, the liner Titanic and the battleship Bismarck. Film maker James Cameron led three of the expeditions diving on the Titanic twice in 1995 and again in 2001. The ship actually featured in the modern days scenes of the movie "Titanic".

The events recounted in Infiltration are clearly fictional but such activity was real and QRA missions into the Iceland-Faeroes Gap occurred every week at the height of the Cold War. Arming the whole of the complement of Phantoms from the Leuchars Wing was not uncommon, particularly during maritime exercises such as the one described. Happily, events never became so tense that shots were fired but devious tactics, particularly at night, were commonplace. Crews lived on their wits in uncompromising scenarios and the cold, dark airspace off the Scottish coast could be an unforgiving environment.

As always, I have tried to make the descriptions of air defence operations, the action in the cockpits and of the locations in the story as accurate as possible. I hope my friends and colleagues in the worlds of submarines and anti-submarine warfare will forgive my less than comprehensive knowledge.

ABOUT THE AUTHOR

David Gledhill joined the Royal Air Force as a Navigator in 1973. After training, he flew the F4 Phantom on squadrons in the UK and West Germany. He was one of the first aircrew to fly the F2 and F3 Air Defence Variant of the Tornado on its acceptance into service and served for many years as an instructor on the Operational Conversion Units of both the Phantom and the Tornado. He commanded the Tornado Fighter Flight in the Falkland Islands and has worked extensively with the Armed Forces of most NATO nations. He has published a number of factual books on aviation topics and novels in the Phantom Air Combat series set during the Cold War.

OTHER BOOKS BY THIS AUTHOR

Have you ever wondered what it was like to fly the Phantom? This is not a potted history of an aeroplane, nor is it Hollywood glamour as captured in Top Gun. This is the story of life on the frontline during the Cold War told in the words of a navigator who flew the iconic jet. Unique pictures, many captured from the cockpit, show the Phantom in its true environment and show why for many years the Phantom was the envy of NATO. It also tells the inside story of some of the problems which plagued the Phantom in its early days, how the aircraft developed, or was neglected, and reveals events which shaped the aircraft's history and contributed to its demise. Anecdotes capture the deep affection felt by the crews who were fortunate enough to cross paths with the Phantom during their flying careers. The nicknames the aircraft earned were not complimentary and included the 'Rhino', 'The Spook', 'Double Ugly', the 'Flying Brick' and the 'Lead Sled'. Whichever way you looked at it, you could love or hate the Phantom, but you could never ignore it.

"The Phantom in Focus: A Navigator's Eye on Britain's Cold War Warrior" - ISBN 978-178155-048-9 (print) and ASIN B00GUNIM0Q (e-book) published by Fonthill Media.

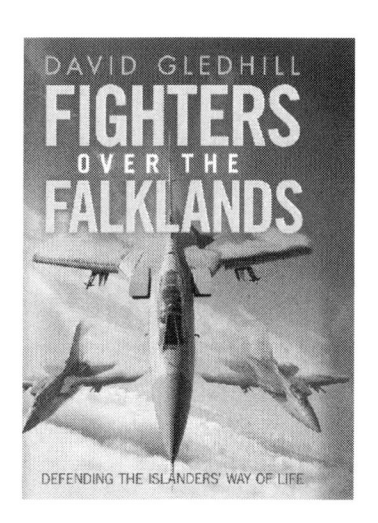

Fighters Over The Falklands: Defending the Islanders' Way of Life captures daily life using pictures taken during the author's tours of duty in the Falkland Islands. From the first detachments of Phantoms and Rapiers operating from a rapidly upgraded RAF Stanley airfield to life at RAF Mount Pleasant, see life from the author's perspective as the Commander of the Tornado F3 Flight defending the islands' airspace. Frontline fighter crews provided Quick Reaction Alert (QRA) during day to day flying operations working with the Royal Navy, Army and other air force units to defend a remote and sometimes forgotten theatre of operations. The book also examines how the islanders interacted with the forces based at Mount Pleasant and contrast high technology military operations with the lives of the original inhabitants, namely the wildlife.

"Fighters Over The Falklands – Defending the islanders Way of Life" - ISBN 978-17155-222-3 (print) and ASIN: B00H87Q7MS (e book) published by Fonthill Media.

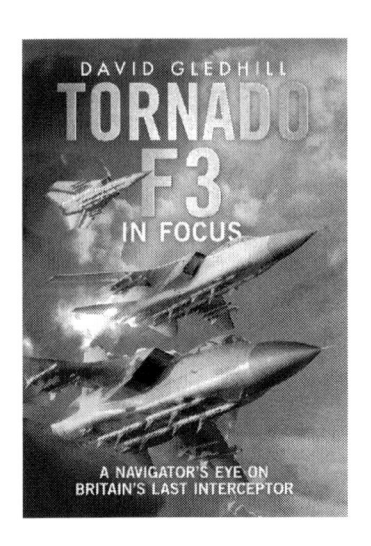

The Tornado F2 had a troubled introduction to service. Unwanted by its crews and procured as a political imperative, it was blighted by failures in the acquisition system. Adapted from a multi-national design and planned by committee, it was developed to counter a threat which disappeared. Modified rapidly before it could be sent to war, the Tornado F3 eventually matured into a capable weapons system but despite datalinks and new air to air weapons, its poor reputation sealed its fate. The author, a former Tornado F3 navigator, tells the story from an insider's perspective from the early days as one of the first instructors on the Operational Conversion Unit, through its development and operational testing, to its demise. He reflects on its capabilities and deficiencies and analyses why the aircraft was mostly under-estimated by opponents. Although many books have already described the Tornado F3, the author's involvement in its development will provide a unique insight into this complex and misunderstood aircraft programme and dispel some of the myths. This is the author's 3rd book and, like the others, captures the story in pictures taken in the cockpit and around the squadron.

"Tornado F3 In Focus – A Navigator's Eye on Britain's Last Interceptor" - ISBN 978-178155-307-7 (print) and ASIN B00TM7A80E (e book) published by Fonthill Media.

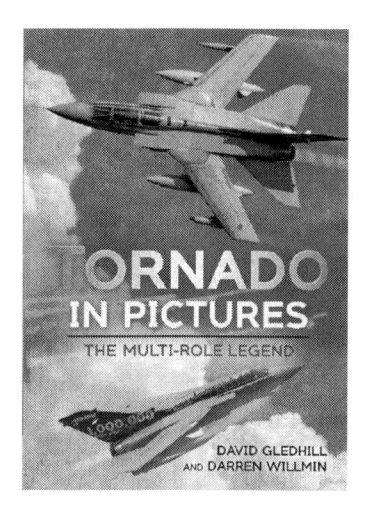

The Panavia Tornado was designed as a multi-role combat aircraft to meet the needs of Germany Italy and the United Kingdom. Since the prototype flew in 1974, nearly 1000 Tornados have been produced in a number of variants serving as a fighter-bomber, a fighter and in the reconnaissance and electronic suppression roles. Deployed operationally in numerous theatres throughout the world, the Tornado has proved to be exceptionally capable and flexible. From its early Cold War roles it adapted to the rigours of expeditionary warfare from The Gulf to Kosovo to Afghanistan. The early "dumb" bombs were replaced by laser-guided weapons and cruise missiles and in the air-to-air arena fitted with the AMRAAM and ASRAAM missiles.

In this book David Gledhill explores the range of capabilities and, having flown the Tornado F2 and F3 Air Defence Variant, offers an insight into life in the cockpit of the Tornado. Lavishly illustrated, Darren Wilmin's superb photographs capture the essence of the machine both from the ground and in the air. This unique collection including some of David Gledhill's own air-to-air pictures of the Tornado F2 and F3 will appeal to everyone with an interest in this iconic aircraft.

"Tornado In Pictures _ The Multi Role Legend" - ISBN 978-1781554630 (print) published by Fonthill Media.

The process to deliver a modern combat aircraft from concept to introduction to service is often measured in decades. Described as a weapon system, modern designs such as the Eurofighter Typhoon are intricate jigsaws with a fusion of new techniques and sometimes unproven, emerging technologies. By the time the new weapons system reaches the front line it will have been tested by the manufacturer, evaluated by test pilots and assessed by service pilots. There have been examples of success but some spectacular failures with projects cancelled late in development. This book will investigate why and takes you from the original requirement through the complex testing and evaluation process showing recent examples of the path to declaring a new combat aircraft operational on the front line. It will look at how today's test organisations have matured to meet the task and investigate the pressures they face. It will also look at real-life examples of systems testing. David Gledhill and David Lewis, both experienced test evaluators, will uncover the reasons why some aircraft serve on the front line for years before becoming truly effective in their role.

Operational Test - Honing the Edge - ISBN 978-1781555712 (print) published by Fonthill Media.

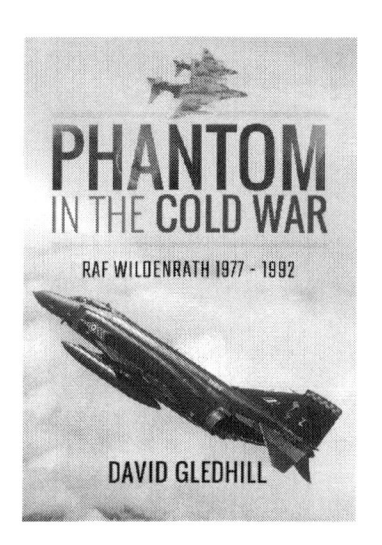

The McDonnell Douglas F4 Phantom was a true multi-role combat aircraft. Introduced into the RAF in 1968, it was employed in ground attack, air reconnaissance and air defence roles. Later, with the arrival of the Jaguar in the early 1970s, it changed over to air defence. In its heyday, it served as Britain s principal Cold War fighter; there were seven UK-based squadrons plus the Operational Conversion Unit, two Germany-based squadrons and a further Squadron deployed to the Falkland Islands. Phantom in the Cold War focuses predominantly on the aircraft s role as an air defence fighter, exploring the ways in which it provided the British contribution to the Second Allied Tactical Air Force at RAF Wildenrath, the home of Nos. 19 and 92 Squadrons during the Cold War. As with his previous books, the author, who flew the Phantom operationally, recounts the thrills, challenges and consequences of operating this sometimes temperamental jet at extreme low-level over the West German countryside, preparing for a war which everyone hoped would never happen.

Phantom in the Cold War: RAF Wildenrath 1977 - 1992 - ISBN 978-1526704085 published by Pen and Sword.

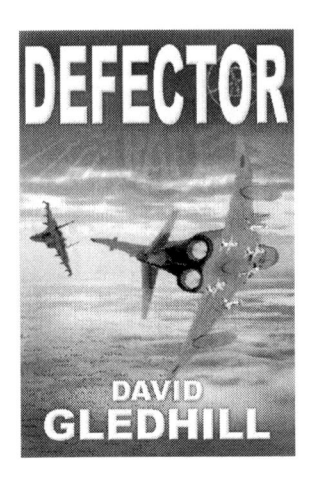

Colonel Yuri Andrenev, a respected test pilot is trusted to evaluate the latest Soviet fighter, the Sukhoi Su27 "Flanker", from a secret test facility near Moscow. Surely he is above suspicion? With thoughts of defection in his mind, and flying close to the Inner German Border, could he be tempted to make a daring escape across the most heavily defended airspace in the world? A flight test against a Mig fighter begins a sequence of events that forces his hand and after an unexpected air-to-air encounter he crosses the border with the help of British Phantom crews. How will Western Intelligence use this unexpected windfall? Are Soviet efforts to recover the advanced fighter as devious as they seem or could more sinister motives be in play? Defector is a pacy thriller which reflects the intrigue of The Cold War. It takes you into the cockpit of the Phantom fighter jet with the realism that can only come from an author who has flown operationally in the NATO Central Region.

"Defector" - ISBN 978-1-49356-759-1 (print) and ASIN B00EUYEUDK (e book) and Audiobook ASIN B00WB21MW0, published by DeeGee Media.

Combat veteran Major Pablo Carmendez holds a grudge against his former adversaries. Diverting his armed Skyhawk fighter-bomber from a firepower demonstration he flies eastwards towards the Falkland Islands intent on revenge. What is his target and will he survive the defences alerted of his intentions? Crucially, will his plan wreck delicate negotiations between Britain and Argentina designed to mend strained relations? Are Government officials charged with protecting the islanders' interests worthy of that trust or are more sinister motives in play? Maverick is an aviation thriller set in the remote outpost in the South Atlantic Ocean that takes you into the cockpits of the Phantom fighters based on the Islands where you will experience the thrills of air combat as the conspiracy unfolds.

"Maverick" - ISBN 978-1507801895 (print) and ASIN B00S9UL430 (e book) published by DeeGee Media.

When a hostage is snatched from the streets of Beirut by Hezbollah terrorists it sets in train a series of events from the UK to the Middle East that end in the corridors of power. A combined air operation is mounted from a base in Cyprus to release the agent from his enforced captivity. Phantom and Buccaneer crews help a special forces team to mount a daring raid, the like of which has not been attempted since Operation Jericho during World War 2. With Syrian forces ranged against them and Israeli and American friends seemingly bent on thwarting them, the outcome is by no means certain. As in his other novels David Gledhill takes you into the cockpit in this fast paced Cold War tale of intrigue and deception.

"Deception" - ISBN 978-1508762096 (print) and ASIN B00V8JTE40 (e book) published by DeeGee Media.

With tensions rising in post-war Europe, the Soviet Union closed the air corridors to Berlin, the former German capital, in a bid to starve the population into submission. The western allies responded by mounting the largest air supply operation the world had ever seen which would become known as the "Berlin Airlift".

Step forward into the 1980s with the Cold War at its height. A NATO reinforcement exercise held at a British airbase in West Germany, brings British, American and French fighter crews together to practice the air corridor policing mission. When a Pembroke transport aircraft engaged in a covert reconnaissance mission is intercepted by a Mig fighter and forced to land in East Germany, events escalate. Will the crew become a pawn in the relentless confrontation as the Soviets increase the rhetoric? Have western military plans been compromised by the unexpected aggression?

Provocation is a fast moving thriller that replays the tensions of the Cold War and its dark undertones. As with his other novels, David Gledhill takes you into the cockpit of the Phantom fighter jet to experience the action first hand.

"Provocation" ISBN 978-1515382584 (print) and ASIN B014GUHGKG (e book) and Audiobook ASIN B018EPFG06, published by DeeGee Media.

Flying the Jaguar bomber in a Cold War West Germany, Nick Gleason is, perhaps, at the peak of his career but he is a loner struggling with his conscience and he begins to question the morality of his role. If war in Europe breaks out, he would be tasked to deliver a thermo-nuclear weapon to a target in the East.

Two British fighter aircraft, one a Phantom, the second a Jaguar piloted by Gleason, converge at low level over the Osnabruck Ridge on the North German Plain. One is armed with a practice nuclear bomb, the other simply conducting a routine training exercise but their flight paths are destined to cross. Events have been far from routine as the crews are drawn towards the encounter that threatens to jeopardise their very existence. Was a mid-air collision inevitable from the outset or could the, seemingly, inexorable chain of events have been broken? Was destruction predestined? The countdown to impact is underway.

"Impact" ISBN: 978-1541371552 (print), ASIN B01N5GUIR8 (e book) and Audiobook ASIN B01MTAXJT8, published by DeeGee Media.

Visit my website and sign up for updates on my books: http://deegee-media.webnode.com/

Printed in Great Britain
by Amazon